Reso
the m
GUIL
and CHUCK HOGAN

THE STRAIN TRILOGY

"The first hundred pages of *The Strain* is a sustained exercise in terror that held this reader in spellbound delight, because del Toro and Hogan write with crisp authenticity about both the fantastical (vampires) and the completely real (New York City, with all its odd nooks and crannies). What began in *The Strain* comes to a sublimely satisfying conclusion in *The Night Eternal.*"
Stephen King

"Utterly engrossing, high-level entertainment . . . Most readers will find themselves turning pages with the momentum of an engaged movie viewer, with their own normal reality imperiled."
San Francisco Chronicle

"Spine-tingling suspense mixed with gritty vampire horror."
Seattle Post-Intelligencer

"A monstrous vision."
Chicago Sun-Times

"A visceral page-turner . . . The action moves swiftly and the violence is satisfyingly gruesome."
Baltimore Sun

"Glorious, violent mayhem . . . Insanely entertaining . . . Wildly imaginative."

Albuquerque Journal

"A fast-paced mix of gruesome horror and straightforward investigative crime fiction."

Philadelphia Inquirer

"At a time when brooding, sexy vampires are so ubiquitous in popular culture . . . [del Toro and Hogan] finally have given the creatures back some of their nasty, vicious, delicious bite."

Los Angeles Times

"This combination of classic folk tale and modern biological nightmare will have you shivering in the night . . ."

Louisville Courier-Journal

"Apocalyptic action . . . Part *The Andromeda Strain*, part *Night of the Living Dead*." Salon.com

"[Del Toro's] distinctive creatures and otherwordly parables use the realms of fantasy to explore fundamental human issues such as love, alienation, weakness, and, of course, fear.... [He is] a master of monsters." *USA Today*

"Guillermo del Toro and Chuck Hogan are not interested in chaste adolescent vampires or sexy rock-star vampires or vampires who drink artificial blood. The vampires in *The Strain* are just plain evil."

New York Times

"A cross between *The Hot Zone* and *'Salem's Lot.*"

Entertainment Weekly

"One of the most thrilling works of vampire fiction to hit the market in quite some time."

MTV.com

"A terrifying masterwork."

Denver Examiner

"[A] fast-paced, high-concept outing . . . A tale that blends genre thrills with eccentric detours into folklore and mordant comedy . . . The epitome of established, mass-culture storytelling . . . Diverting and never less than expertly crafted."

The Guardian

"Who among the fans of *Mimic, The Devil's Backbone,* or *Pan's Labyrinth* wouldn't want to see what this gifted film director can do with a vampire novel? . . . Can that fantastic visual imagination make the leap to the page? The answer is . . . yes . . . A fairy tale for adults . . . Good enough to make us break that vow to swear off vampire stories."

Newsweek

"Enthralling . . . gripping and vivid enough to spur a few nightmares."

Associated Press

"Guillermo del Toro and Chuck Hogan have crafted a deliciously creepy story that will literally make the hairs on your neck stand up."

Nelson DeMille

By Guillermo del Toro and Chuck Hogan

THE NIGHT ETERNAL
THE FALL
THE STRAIN

Also by Chuck Hogan

DEVILS IN EXILE
THE KILLING MOON
PRINCE OF THIEVES
THE BLOOD ARTISTS
THE STANDOFF

GUILLERMO
DEL TORO
CHUCK
HOGAN

THE NIGHT ETERNAL

Book III of The Strain Trilogy

HARPER

An Imprint of HarperCollins*Publishers*

This is a work of fiction. Names, characters, places, and incidents are products of the author's imagination or are used fictitiously and are not to be construed as real. Any resemblance to actual events, locales, organizations, or persons, living or dead, is entirely coincidental.

HARPER

An Imprint of HarperCollins*Publishers*
10 East 53rd Street
New York, New York 10022-5299

ISBN 978-0-06-213059-4

First Harper mass market international printing: June 2012
First William Morrow hardcover printing: November 2011

Printed in the United States of America

Visit Harper paperbacks on the World Wide Web at
www.harpercollins.com

10 9 8 7 6 5 4 3 2 1

THE NIGHT ETERNAL

To my parents.

Now I know how hard a job you had . . .

—GDT

For Charlotte, eternally.

—CH

THE NIGHT ETERNAL

RAIN OF ASHES

Extract from the Diary of Ephraim Goodweather

On the second day of darkness they rounded them up. The best and the brightest: all those in power, the wealthy, the influential.

Lawmakers and CEOs, tycoons and intellectuals, rebels and figures of great popular esteem. None were turned; all were slain, destroyed. Their execution was swift, public, and brutal.

Save for a few experts from each discipline, all leaders were eliminated. Out they marched, the damned, from the River House, the Dakota, the Beresford, and their ilk. They were all apprehended and herded into major metropolitan gathering places worldwide, such as the National Mall in Washington, DC, Nanjing Road in Shanghai, Moscow's Red Square, Cape Town Stadium, and Central Park in New York City.

There, in a horrific pageant of carnage, they were disposed of.

It was said that over one thousand strigoi *rampaged down Lexington and raided every building surrounding Gramercy Park. Offerings of money or favor fell on deaf ears. Soft, manicured hands implored and begged. Their bodies twitched—hanging from lampposts all along Madison Avenue. In Times Square, twenty-foot-high funeral pyres burned tanned, pampered flesh. Smelling much like barbecue, the elite of Manhattan illuminated the empty streets, closed shops—***EVERYTHING MUST GO***—and silent LED megascreens.*

The Master had apparently calculated the right number, the exact balance, of vampires needed to establish dominance without overburdening the blood supply; its approach was methodological and indeed mathematical. The elderly and infirm were also collected and eliminated. It was a purge and a putsch. Roughly one-third of the human population was exterminated over that seventy-two-hour period, which had since become known as, collectively, "Night Zero."

The hordes took control of the streets. Riot police, SWAT, the U.S. Army—the tide of monsters overtook them all. Those who submitted, those who surrendered themselves, remained as guards and keepers.

The Master's plan was a resounding success. In brutally Darwinian fashion, the Master had selected the survivors for compliance and malleability. Its growing strength was nothing short of terrifying. With the Ancients destroyed, its control over the horde—and through them, the world—had broadened and become ever more sophisticated. The strigoi *no longer roamed the streets like raving zombies, raiding and feeding at will. Their movements were coordinated. Like bees in a hive or ants in a hill, they apparently each had clearly defined roles and responsibilities. They were the Master's eyes on the street.*

In the beginning daylight was entirely gone. A few seconds of faint sunlight could be glimpsed when the sun was at its zenith, but other than that, the darkness was unremitting. Now, two years later, the sun filtered through the poisoned atmosphere for only two hours each day, but the pale light it gave was nothing like the sunlight that had once warmed Earth.

The strigoi *were everywhere, like spiders or ants, making sure that those left alive were truly fitting back into a routine . . .*

And yet the most shocking thing of all was . . . how little life had truly changed. The Master capitalized on the societal chaos of the first few months. Deprivation—of food, clean water, sanitation, law enforcement—terrorized the populace, so much so that, once basic infrastructure was restored, once a program of food rations was implemented and the rebuilt electrical grid chased off the darkness of the long nights, they responded with gratitude and obedience. Cattle need the recompense of order and routine—the unambiguous structure of power—to surrender.

In fewer than two weeks, most systems were

restored. Water, power . . . cable television was reintroduced, broadcasting all reruns now, without commercials. Sports, news, everything a repeat. Nothing new was produced. And . . . people liked it.

Rapid transit was a priority in the new world, because personal automobiles were extremely rare. Cars were potential bombs and as such had no place in the new police state. Cars were impounded and crushed. All vehicles on the street belonged to public services: police, fire department, sanitation—they were all operational, manned by complying humans.

Airplanes had suffered the same fate. The only active fleet was controlled by Stoneheart, the multinational corporation whose grip on food distribution, power, and military industries the Master had exploited in its takeover of the planet, and it consisted of roughly 7 percent of the planes that once crossed the world's skies.

Silver was outlawed and became trade currency, highly desirable and exchangeable for coupons or food points. The right amount of it could even buy you, or a loved one, a way out of the farms.

The farms were the only entirely different thing in this new world. That and the fact that there was no more educational system. No more schooling, no more reading, no more thinking.

The pens and slaughterhouses were manned twenty-four hours a day, seven days a week. Trained wardens and cattle drivers supplied the strigoi *with the nutrients needed. The new class system was quickly established. A system of biological castes: the* strigoi *favored B positive. Any blood type would do, but B positive either provided extra benefits—like different grades of milk—or held its taste and quality better outside the body and was better for packaging and storing. Non-B's were the workers, the farmers, the true grunts. B positives were the Kobe—the prime cut of beef. They were pampered, given benefits and nutrients. They even got double the exposure at the UV camps, to make sure their vitamin D took root. Their daily routine, their hormonal balance, and ultimately their reproduction were systematically regulated to keep up with the demand.*

And so it was. People went to work, watched TV, ate their meals, and went to bed. But in the dark and in the silence they wept and stirred, knowing all too well that those they knew, those next to them—even the ones sharing the very bed they were lying on—could suddenly be gone, devoured by the concrete structure of the closest farm. And they bit their lips and cried, for there was no choice but to submit. There was always someone else (parents, siblings, children) who depended on them. Always someone else who gave them the license to be afraid, the blessing of cowardice.

Who would have dreamed that we would be looking back with great nostalgia at the tumultuous nineties and early noughts. The times of turmoil and political pettiness and financial fraud that preceded the collapse of the world order . . . it was a golden era by comparison. All that we were became lost—all social form and order in the way our fathers and forefathers understood it. We became a flock. We became cattle.

Those of us who are still alive but have not joined the system . . . we have become the anomaly . . . We are the vermin. Scavengers. Hunted.

With no way to fight back . . .

Kelton Street, Woodside, Queens

A scream pealed in the distance, and Dr. Ephraim Goodweather startled awake. He thrashed on the sofa, flipping onto his back and sitting up, and—in one fluid, violent motion—gripped the worn leather sword handle jutting out of the pack on the floor at his side and slashed the air with a blade of singing silver.

His battle cry, hoarse and garbled, a fugitive from his nightmares, stopped short. His blade quivered, unmet.

He was alone.

Kelly's house. Her sofa. Familiar things.

His ex-wife's living room. The scream was a far-off siren, converted into a human shriek by his sleeping mind.

He had been dreaming again. Of fire and

shapes—indefinable but vaguely humanoid—made of blinding light. A flashpoint. He was in the dream and these shapes wrestled with him right before the light consumed it all. He always awoke agitated and exhausted, as if he had physically grappled with an opponent. The dream came out of nowhere. He could be having the most domestic kind of reverie—a picnic, a traffic jam, a day at the office—and then the light would grow and consume it all, and the silvery figures emerged.

He blindly groped for his weapon bag—a modified baseball gear bag, looted many months before off the high rack of a ransacked Modell's on Flatbush Avenue.

He was in Queens. Okay. *Okay.* Everything coming back to him now—accompanied by the first pangs of a jaw-clenching hangover. He had blacked out again. Another dangerous binge. He returned the sword to his weapons bag, then rolled back, holding his head in his hands like a cracked crystal sphere he had delicately picked up off the floor. His hair felt wiry and strange, his head throbbing.

Hell on earth. Right. Land of the damned.

Reality was an ornery bitch. He had awoken to a nightmare. He was still alive—and still human—which wasn't much, but it was the best he could expect.

Just another day in hell.

The last thing he remembered from sleep, the fragment of the dream that clung to his consciousness like sticky afterbirth, was an image of

Zack bathed in searing silver light. It was out of his shape that the flashpoint had occurred this time.

"Dad—" Zack said, and his eyes locked with Eph's—and then the light consumed it all.

The remembrance of it raised chills. Why couldn't he find some respite from this hell in his dreams? Wasn't that the way it was supposed to work? To balance out a horrible existence with dreams of flight and escape? What he wouldn't have given for a reverie of pure sentimentality, a spoonful of sugar for his mind.

Eph and Kelly fresh out of college, ambling hand-in-hand through a flea market, looking for cheap furniture and knickknacks for their first apartment . . .

Zack as a toddler, stomping fat-footed around the house, a little boss in diapers . . .

Eph and Kelly and Zack at the dinner table, sitting with hands folded before full plates, waiting for Z to plow through his obsessively thorough saying of grace . . .

Instead, Eph's dreams were like badly recorded snuff films. Familiar faces from his past—enemies, acquaintances, and friends alike—being stalked and taken while he watched, unable to reach them, to help them, or even to turn away.

He sat up, steadying himself and rising, one hand on the back of the sofa. He left the living area and walked to the window overlooking the backyard. LaGuardia Airport was not far away. The sight of an airplane, the distant sound of a jet engine, was cause for wonder now. No lights circled the sky. He remembered September 11, 2001, and how the emptiness of the sky had seemed so surreal back then, and what a strange relief it was when the planes returned a week later. Now there was no relief. No getting back to normal.

Eph wondered what time it was. Sometime o'clock in the morning, he figured, judging by his own failing circadian rhythm. It was summer—at least according to the old calendar—and so the sun should have been high and hot in the sky.

Instead, darkness prevailed. The natural order of night and day had been shattered, presumably forever. The sun was obliterated by a murky veil of ash floating in the sky. The new atmosphere was comprised of the detritus of nuclear explosions and volcanic eruptions distributed around the globe, a ball of blue-green candy wrapped inside a crust of poisonous chocolate. It had cured into a thick, insulating cowl, sealing in darkness and cold and sealing out the sun.

Perennial nightfall. The planet turned into a pale, rotting netherworld of rime and torment.

The perfect ecology for vampires.

According to the last live news reports, long since censored but traded like porn on Internet boards, these post-cataclysm conditions were much the same around the world. Eyewitness accounts of the darkening sky, of black rain, of ominous clouds knitting together and never breaking apart. Given the planet's rotation and wind patterns, the poles—the frozen north and south—were theoretically the only locations on Earth still receiving regular seasonal sunlight . . . though nobody knew this for certain.

The residual radiation hazard from the nuclear explosions and the plant meltdowns had been intense at first, catastrophically so at the various ground zeros. Eph and the others had spent nearly two months belowground, in a train tunnel beneath the Hudson River, and so were spared the short-term fallout. Extreme meteorological conditions and atmospheric winds spread the damage over large areas, which may have aided in dispersing the radioactivity; the fallout was expelled by the hard rainstorms created by the violent changes to the ecosystem, further diffusing the radiation. Fallout decays exponentially, and in the short term, areas without direct-impact exposure became safe for travel and decontamination within approximately six weeks.

The long-term effects were yet to come. Questions as to human fertility, genetic mutations, and increased carcinogenesis would not be answered for some time. But these very real concerns were overshadowed by the current situation: two years following the nuclear disasters and the vampiric takeover of the world, all fears were immediate.

The pealing siren went quiet. These warning systems, meant to repel human intruders and attract assistance, still went off from time to time—though much less frequently than in the early months, when the alarms wailed constantly, persistently, like the agonal screams of a dying race. Another vestige of civilization fading away.

In the absence of the alarm, Eph listened for intruders. Through windows, rising from dank cellars, descending from dusty attics—vampires entered through any opening, and nowhere was safe. Even the few hours of sunlight each day—a dim, dusky light, haven taken on a sickly amber hue—still offered many hazards. Daylight was human curfew time. The best time for Eph and the others to move—safe from direct confrontation by *strigoi*—was also one of the most dangerous, due to surveillance and the prying eyes of human sympathizers looking to improve their lot.

Eph leaned his forehead against the window. The coolness of the glass was a pleasant sensation against his warm skin and the throbbing inside his skull.

Knowing was the worst part. Awareness of insanity does not make one any less insane. Awareness of drowning does not make one any less of a drowning person—it only adds the burden of panic. Fear of the future, and the memory of a better, brighter past, were as much a source of Eph's suffering as the vampire plague itself.

He needed food, he needed protein. Nothing in this house; he had cleaned it out of food—and alcohol—many months ago. Even found a secret stash of Butterfingers in Matt's closet.

He backed off from the window, turning to face the room and the kitchen area beyond. He tried to remember how he got here and why. He saw slash marks in the wall where, using a kitchen knife, he had released his ex-wife's boyfriend, decapitating the recently turned creature. That was back in the early days of slaying, when killing vampires was nearly as frightening as the notion of being turned by one. Even when the vampire in question had been his ex-wife's boyfriend, a man poised to assume Eph's place as the most important male figure in Zack's life.

But that gag reflex of human morality was long gone now. This was a changed world, and Dr. Ephraim Goodweather, once a prominent epidemiologist with the Centers for Disease Control and Prevention, was a changed man. The virus of vampirism had colonized the human race. The plague had routed civilization in a coup d'état of astonishing virulence and violence. Insurgents—the willful, the powerful, and the strong—had all largely been destroyed or turned, leaving the meek, the defeated, and the fearful to do the Master's bidding.

Eph returned to his weapon bag. From a narrow, zippered pocket meant for batting gloves or sweatbands, he pulled out his creased Moleskine notebook. These days he remembered nothing without writing it down in his tattered diary. Everything went in there, from the transcendental to the banal. Everything must be recorded. This was his compulsion. His diary was essentially a long letter to his son, Zack. Leaving a record of his search for his only boy. Noting his observations and theories involving the vampire menace. And, as a scientist, simply recording data and phenomena.

At the same time, it was also a helpful exercise for retaining some semblance of sanity.

His handwriting had grown so cramped over the past two years, he could barely read his own entries. He recorded the date each day, because it was the only reliable method of tracking time without a proper calendar. Not that it mattered much—except for today.

He scribbled down the date, and then his heart pushed a double beat. Of course. That was it. Why he was back here yet again.

Today was Zack's thirteenth birthday.

You may not live beyond this point warned the sign affixed to the upstairs door, written in Magic Marker, illustrated with gravestones and skeletons and crosses. It was drawn in a younger hand, done when Zack was seven or eight. Zack's bedroom had been left essentially unchanged since the last time he'd occupied it, the same as the bedrooms of missing kids everywhere, a symbol of the stopping of time in the hearts of their parents.

Eph kept returning to the bedroom like a diver returning again and again to a sunken shipwreck. A secret museum; a world preserved exactly as it had once been. A window directly into the past.

Eph sat on the bed, feeling the mattress's familiar give, hearing its reassuring creak. He had been through everything in this room, everything his boy used to touch in the life he used to lead. He curated this room now; he knew every toy, every figurine, every coin and shoestring, every T-shirt and book. He rejected the notion that he was wallowing. People don't attend church or synagogue or mosque to wallow; they attend regularly as a gesture of faith. Zack's bedroom was a temple now. Here, and here alone, Eph felt a sense of peace and an affirmation of inner resolve.

Zack was still alive.

This was not speculation. This was not blind hope.

Eph knew that Zack was still alive and that his boy had not yet been turned.

In past times—the way the world used to work—the parent of a missing child had resources to turn to. They had the comfort of the police investigative process, and the knowledge that hundreds, if not thousands, of people identified and sympathized with their plight and were actively assisting in the search.

This abduction had occurred in a world without police, without human law. And Eph knew the identity of the being that had abducted Zack. The creature that was once his mother—yes. She committed the abduction. But her action was compelled by a larger entity.

The king vampire, the Master.

But Eph did not know why Zack had been taken. To hurt Eph, of course. And to satisfy his undead mother's drive to revisit her "Dear Ones," the beings she had loved in life. The insidious epidemiology of the virus spread in a vampiric perversion of human love. Turning them into fellow *strigoi* locked them to you forever, to an existence beyond the trials and tribulations of being human, devolving into only primal needs such as feeding, spreading, survival.

That was why Kelly (the thing that was once Kelly) had become so psychically fixated on their boy, and how, despite Eph's best efforts, she had been able to spirit him away.

And it was precisely this same syndrome, this same obsessive passion for turning those closest to them, that confirmed to Eph that Zack had not been turned. For if the Master or Kelly had drunk the boy, then Zack would surely have returned for Eph as a vampire. Eph's dread of this very occurrence—of having to face his undead son—had haunted him for two years now, at times sending him into a downward spiral of despair.

But why? Why hadn't the Master turned Zack? What was it holding him for? As a potential marker to be played against Eph and the resistance effort he was part of? Or for some other more sinister reason that Eph could not—dared not—fathom?

Eph shuddered at the dilemma this would present to him. Where his son was concerned, he was vulnerable. Eph's weakness was equal to his strength: he could not let go of his boy.

Where was Zack at that very moment? Was he being held somewhere? Being tormented as his father's proxy? Thoughts like these clawed at Eph's mind.

It was not knowing that unsettled him the most. The others—Fet, Nora, Gus—were able to commit fully to the resistance, all their energy and their focus, precisely because they had no hostages in this war.

Visiting this room usually helped Eph feel less alone in this accursed world. But today it had the opposite effect. He had never felt so acutely alone as he felt right here, at this very moment.

Eph thought again about Matt, his ex-wife's boyfriend—the one he had slain downstairs—and how he used to obsess over that man's growing influence on Zack's upbringing. Now he had to think—daily, hourly—about what sort of hell his boy must be living in, under the rule of this actual monster . . .

Overcome, feeling nauseous and sweaty, Eph dug out his diary and scratched down the same question that appeared throughout the notebook, like a koan:

Where is Zack?

As was his habit, he flipped back through the most recent entries. He spied a note about Nora and tried to make out his penmanship.

"Morgue." "Rendezvous." "Move at sunlight."

Eph squinted, trying to remember—as a sense of anxiety spread through him.

He was supposed to meet Nora and Mrs. Martinez at the old Office of the Chief Medical Examiner. In Manhattan. Today.

Shit.

Eph grabbed his bag with a clank of the silver blades, throwing the straps over his back, sword handles behind his shoulders like leather-wrapped antennae. He looked around quickly on his way out, spying an old Transformers toy next to the CD player on Zack's bureau. Sideswipe, if Eph remembered correctly from reading Zack's books outlining the Autobots' specs. A birthday present from Eph to Zack, just a few years before. One of Sideswipe's legs dangled, snapped from overuse. Eph manipulated the arms, remembering the way Zack used to effortlessly "transform" the toy from car to robot and back again like a Rubik's Cube grand master.

"Happy birthday, Z," whispered Eph before stuffing the busted toy into his weapons bag and heading for the door.

Woodside

THE FORMER KELLY Goodweather arrived outside her former residence on Kelton Street just minutes after Eph's departure. She had been tracking the human—her Dear One—since picking up his bloodbeat some fifteen hours before. But when the sky had brightened for the meridiem—the two to three hours of dull yet hazardous sunlight that filtered through the thick cloud cover each planetary rotation—she'd had to retire underground, losing time. Now she was close.

Two black-eyed feelers accompanied her—children blinded by the solar occlusion that coincided with the Master's arrival in New York City, who were subsequently turned by the Master itself and now gifted with the enhanced perception of second sight—small and fast, skittering along the sidewalk and over abandoned cars like hungry spiders, seeing nothing and sensing everything.

Normally, Kelly's innate attraction to her Dear One would have been sufficient for her to track and locate her ex-husband. But Eph's signal was weakened and distorted by the effects of ethanol, stimulants, and sedatives on his nervous and circulatory systems. Intoxication confused the synapses in a human brain, slowing its transfer rate and serving to cloak its signal, like interference over a radio channel.

The Master had taken a peculiar interest in Ephraim Goodweather, specifically in monitoring his movement throughout the city. That was why the feelers—formerly a brother and sister, now nearly identical, having shed their hair, genitals, and other human gender markers—had been sent by the Master to assist Kelly in her pursuit. Here, they began racing back and forth along the short fence in front of the house, waiting for Kelly to catch up to them.

She opened the gate and entered the property, walking once around the house, wary of traps. Once satisfied, she rammed the heel of her hand through a double windowpane, shattering glass as she reached up and unfastened the lock, raising the sash.

The feelers leaped inside, Kelly following, lifting one bare, dirty leg through, then bending and easily contorting her body to enter the three-foot-square opening. The feelers climbed all over the sofa, indicating it like trained police canines. Kelly stood very still for a long moment, opening her senses to the interior of the dwelling. She confirmed that they were alone and thus too late. But she sensed Eph's recent presence. Maybe there was more to be learned.

The feelers scooted across the floor to a north-facing window, touching the glass as though absorbing a recent, lingering sensation—then at once scrambled up the stairs. Kelly followed them, allowing them to scent and indicate. When she came upon them they were leaping around a bedroom, their psychic senses agitated by the urgency of Eph's recent occupation, like animals driven wild by some overwhelming but little-understood impulse.

Kelly stood in the center of the room, arms at her sides. The heat of her vampiric body, her blazing metabolism, instantly raised the temperature of the cool room a few degrees. Unlike Eph, Kelly suffered no form of human nostalgia. She felt no affinity for her former domicile, no pangs of regret or loss as she stood in her son's room. She no longer felt any connection to this place, just as she no longer felt any connection to her pitiable human past. The butterfly does not look back upon its caterpillar self, either fondly or wistfully; it simply flies on.

A hum entered her being, a presence inside her head and a quickening throughout her body. The Master, looking through her. Seeing with her eyes. Observing their near miss.

A moment of great honor and privilege . . .

Then, just as suddenly, the humming presence was gone. Kelly felt no reproach from the Master for having fallen short of capturing Eph. She felt only useful. Of all the others that served it, throughout this world, Kelly had two things the Master greatly valued. The first was a direct link to Ephraim Goodweather.

The second was Zachary.

Still, Kelly felt the ache of wanting—of needing—to turn her dear son. The urge had subsided but never vanished. She felt it all the time, an incomplete part of herself, an emptiness. It went against her vampire nature. But she bore this agony for one reason only: because the Master demanded it. Its immaculate will alone held Kelly's longing at bay. And so the boy remained human. Remained undelivered, unfinished. There was indeed a purpose to the Master's demand. In that, she trusted without any uncertainty. For the motive had not been revealed to her, because it was not for her to know yet.

For now it was quite enough to see the boy sitting at the Master's side.

The feelers leaped around her as Kelly descended the staircase. She crossed to the raised window and exited through it as she had entered, almost without breaking stride. The rains had started again, fat, black 'drops pelting her hot scalp and shoulders, disappearing in wisps of steam. Standing out on the center yellow line of the street, she sensed Eph's trail anew, his bloodbeat growing stronger as he became more sober.

With the feelers racing back and forth, she strode through the falling rain, leaving a faint trail of steam in her wake. She neared a rapid-transit station and felt her psychic link to him beginning to fade. This was due to the growing distance between them. He had boarded a subway train.

No disappointment clouded her thoughts. Kelly would continue to pursue Eph until they were reunited once and for all. She communicated her report back to the Master before following the feelers into the station.

Eph was returning to Manhattan.

The *Farrell*

THE HORSE CHARGED. In its wake was a plume of thick black smoke and orange flame.

The horse was on fire.

Fully consumed, the proud beast galloped with an urgency born not of pain but of desire. At night, visible from a mile away, the horse without rider or saddle raced through the flat, barren countryside, toward the village. Toward the watcher.

Fet stood transfixed by the sight. Knowing it was coming for him. He anticipated it. Expected it.

Entering the outskirts of the village, bearing down on him with the velocity of a flaming arrow, the galloping horse spoke—naturally, in a dream, it spoke—saying, *I live.*

Fet howled as the flaming horse overtook him—and he awoke.

He was on his side, lying on a fold-down bed

in the crew bunk beneath the foredeck of a rocking ship. The vessel pitched and swayed, and he pitched and swayed with it, the possessions around him netted and tied down tight. The other beds were folded up to the wall. He was the only one currently bunking.

The dream—always essentially the same—had haunted him since his youth. The flaming horse with burning hooves racing at him out of the dark night, awakening him just before impact. The fear he felt upon waking was deep and rich, a child's fear.

He reached for his pack beneath the bunk. The bag was damp—everything on the ship was damp—but its top knot was tight, its contents secure.

The ship was the *Farrell,* a large fishing boat used for smuggling marijuana, which, yes, was still a profitable black-market business. This was the final leg of a return trip from Iceland. Fet had hired the boat for the price of a dozen small arms and plenty of ammunition to keep them running pot for years to come. The sea was one of the few areas left on the planet that was essentially beyond the vampires' reach. Illicit drugs had become incredibly scarce under the new prohibition, the trade confined to homegrown and home-brewed narcotics such as marijuana and pockets of methamphetamine. They operated a smaller sideline business smuggling moonshine—and, on this trip, a few cases of fine Icelandic and Russian vodka.

Fet's mission to Iceland was twofold. His first

order of business was to travel to the University of Reykjavik. In the weeks and months following the vampire cataclysm, while still holed up inside the train tunnel beneath the Hudson River, waiting for the surface air to become habitable once again, Fet constantly paged through the book Professor Abraham Setrakian had died for, the book the Holocaust survivor–turned–vampire hunter had entrusted explicitly and exclusively to Fet's possession.

It was the *Occido Lumen,* loosely translated as "The Fallen Light." Four hundred eighty-nine folios, handwritten on parchment, with twenty illuminated pages, bound in leather and faced with plates of pure vampire-repelling silver. The *Lumen* was an account of the rise of the *strigoi,* based upon a collection of ancient clay tablets dating back to Mesopotamian times, discovered inside a cave in the Zagros Mountains in 1508. Written in Sumerian and extremely fragile, the tablets survived over a century until they fell into the hands of a French rabbi who was committed to deciphering them—more than two centuries before Sumerian was widely translated—in secret. The rabbi eventually presented his illuminated manuscript to King Louis XIV as a gift—and was immediately imprisoned for his effort.

The original tablets were pulverized upon royal order and the manuscript believed destroyed or lost. The king's mistress, a dabbler in the occult, retrieved the *Lumen* from a palace vault in 1671, and from there it changed hands many times in obscurity, acquiring its reputation as a cursed text. The *Lumen* resurfaced briefly in 1823 and again in 1911, each time coinciding with mysterious outbreaks of disease, before disappearing again. The text was offered for auction at Sotheby's in Manhattan no fewer than ten days following the Master's arrival and the start of the vampire plague—and was won, after great effort, by Setrakian with the backing of the Ancients and their accumulated wealth.

Setrakian, the university professor who shunned normal society following the turning of his beloved wife, becoming obsessed with hunting and destroying the virus-bred *strigoi,* had considered the *Lumen* the authoritative text on the conspiracy of vampires that had plagued the earth for most of the history of mankind. Publicly, his station in life had fallen to that of a lowly pawnbroker in an economically depressed section of Manhattan; yet in the bowels of his shop he had maintained an armory of vampire-fighting weapons and a library of ancient accounts and manuals regarding the dread race, accumulated from all corners of the globe throughout decades of pursuit. But such was his desire to reveal the secrets contained within the *Occido Lumen* that he ultimately gave his life so that it would fall into Fet's hands.

It had occurred to Fet, during those long, dark nights in the tunnel beneath the Hudson River, that the *Lumen* had to have been offered up for auction by someone. Someone had possessed the cursed book—but who? Fet thought that perhaps the seller had some further knowledge of its power and its contents. In the time since they surfaced, Fet had been diligently going through the tome with a Latin dictionary, doing the tedious work of translating the lexicon as best he could. On an excursion inside the vacated Sotheby's building on the Upper East Side, Fet discovered that the University of Reykjavik was to be the anonymous beneficiary of the proceeds from the sale of the extraordinarily rare book. With Nora he weighed the pros and cons of undertaking this journey, and together they decided that this lengthy voyage to Iceland was their only chance of uncovering who had actually put the book up for auction.

However, the university, as he discovered upon arrival, was a warren of vampires. Fet had hoped that Iceland might have gone the way of the United Kingdom, which had reacted swiftly to the plague, blowing up the Chunnel and hunting down *strigoi* after the initial outbreak. The islands remained nearly vampire-free, and their people, though completely isolated from the rest of the infected globe, remained human.

Fet had waited until daylight to search the ransacked administrative offices in hopes of tracing the book's provenance. He learned that the university trust itself had offered the book for auction, not a scholar employed there or a specific benefactor, as Fet had hoped. As the campus itself was deserted, this was a long way to travel to find a dead end. But it was not a total waste. For on a shelf in the Egyptology department, Fet had found a most curious text: an old, leather-bound book, printed in French in 1920. On its cover were the words *Sadum et Amurah*. The very last words that Setrakian had asked Fet to remember.

He took the text with him. Even though he spoke not a single word of French.

The second part of his mission proved to be much more productive. At some point early on in his association with these pot smugglers, after learning how wide their reach was, Fet challenged them to connect him with a nuclear weapon. This request was not as far-fetched as one might think. In the Soviet Union especially, where the *strigoi* enjoyed total control, many so-called suitcase nukes had been purloined by ex-KGB officers and were rumored to be available—in less-than-mint condition—on the black markets of Eastern Europe. The Master's drive to purge the world of these weapons—in order that they could not be used to destroy its site of origin, as the Master had itself destroyed the six Ancients—proved to Fet and the others that the Master was indeed vulnerable. Much like the Ancients, the Master's site of origin, the very key to its destruction, was encrypted within the pages of the *Lumen*. Fet offered the right price and had the silver to back it up.

This crew of smugglers put out feelers among their maritime compatriots, with the promise of a silver bounty. Fet was skeptical when the smugglers told him they had a surprise for him, but the desperate will believe in almost anything. They rendezvoused on a small volcanic island south of Iceland with a Ukrainian crew of seven aboard a junked-out yacht with six different outboard engines off the stern. The captain of the crew was young, in his midtwenties, and essentially one-handed, his left arm withered and ending in an unsightly claw.

The device was not a suitcase at all. It resembled a small keg or trash can wrapped in a black tarpaulin and netting, with buckled green straps around its sides and over its lid. Roughly three feet tall by two feet wide. Fet tried lifting it gently. It weighed over one hundred pounds.

"You sure this works?" he asked.

The captain scratched his copper beard with his good hand. He spoke broken English with a Russian accent. "I am told it does. Only one way to find out. It misses one part."

"One part is missing?" said Fet. "Let me guess. Plutonium. U-233."

"No. Fuel is in the core. One-kiloton capability. It misses the detonator." He pointed to a thatch of wires on the top and shrugged. "Everything else good."

The explosive force of a one-kiloton nuke equaled one thousand tons of TNT. A half-mile shockwave of steel-bending destruction. "I'd love to know how you came across this," said Fet.

"I'd like to know what you want it for," said the captain. "Best if we all keep our secrets."

"Fair enough."

The captain had another crewman help Fet load the bomb onto the smugglers' boat. Fet opened the hold beneath the steel floor where the cache of silver lay. The *strigoi* were bent on collecting every piece of silver in the same manner as they were collecting and disarming nukes. As such, the value of this vampire-killing substance rose exponentially.

Once the deal was consummated, including a side transaction between crews of bottles of vodka for pouches of rolling tobacco, drinks were poured into shot glasses.

"You Ukraine?" the captain asked Fet after downing the firewater.

Fet nodded. "You can tell?"

"Look like people from my village, before it disappear."

"Disappear?" said Fet.

The young captain nodded. "Chernobyl," he explained, raising his shriveled arm.

Fet now looked at the nuke, bungee-corded to the wall. No glow, no *tick-tick-tick*. A drone weapon awaiting activation. Had he bartered for a barrel full of junk? Fet did not think so. He trusted the Ukrainian smuggler to vet his own suppliers, and also the fact that he had to continue doing business with the pot smugglers.

Fet was excited, even confident. This was like holding a loaded gun, only without a trigger. All he needed was a detonator.

Fet had seen, with his own eyes, a crew of vampires excavating sites around a geologically active area of hot springs outside Reykjavik, known as Black Pool. This proved that the Master did not know the exact location of its own site of origin—not the Master's birthplace, but the earthen site where it had first arisen in vampiric form.

The secret to its location was contained in the *Occido Lumen*. All Fet had to do was what he as of yet had failed to accomplish: decode the work and discover the location of the site of origin himself. Were the *Lumen* more like a straightforward manual for exterminating vampires, Fet would have been able to follow its instructions—but instead, the *Lumen* was full of wild imagery, strange allegories, and dubious pronouncements. It charted a backward path throughout the course of human history, steered not by the hand of fate but by the supernatural grip of the Ancients. The text confounded him, as it did the others. Fet lacked faith in his own scholarship. Here, he missed most the old professor's reassuring wealth of knowledge. Without him, the *Lumen* was as useful to them as the nuclear device was without a detonator.

Still, this was progress. Fet's restless enthusiasm brought him topside. He gripped the rail and looked out over the turbulent ocean. A harsh, briny mist but no heavy rain tonight. The changed atmosphere made boating more dangerous, the marine weather more unpredictable. Their boat was moving through a swarm of jellyfish, a species that had taken over much of the open seas, feeding on fish eggs and blocking what little daily sun reached the ocean—at times in floating patches several miles wide, coating the surface of the water like pudding skin.

They were passing within ten miles of the coast of New Bedford, Massachusetts, which put Fet in mind of one of the more interesting accounts contained in Setrakian's work papers, the pages he had compiled to leave behind alongside the *Lumen*. In them, the old professor related an account of the Winthrop Fleet of 1630, which made the Atlantic voyage ten years after the *Mayflower,* transporting a second wave of Pilgrims to the New World. One of the fleet's ships, the *Hopewell,* had transported three pieces of unidentified cargo contained in crates of handsome and ornately carved wood. Upon landing in Salem, Massachusetts, and resettling in Boston (due to its abundance of freshwater) thereafter, conditions among the Pilgrims turned brutal. Two hundred settlers were lost in the first year, their deaths attributed to illness rather than the true cause: they had been prey for the Ancients, after having unwittingly conveyed the *strigoi* to the New World.

Setrakian's death had left a great void in Fet. He dearly missed the wise man's counsel as well as his company, but most acutely he missed his intellect. The old man's demise wasn't merely a death but—and this was not an overstatement—a critical blow to the future of humankind. At great risk to himself, he had delivered into their hands this sacred book, the *Occido Lumen*—though not the means to decipher it. Fet had also made himself a student of the pages and leather-bound notebooks containing the deep, hermetic ruminations of the old man, but sometimes filed away side by side with small domestic observations, grocery lists, financial calculations.

He cracked open the French book and, not surprisingly, couldn't make heads or tails of it either. However, some beautiful engravings proved quite illuminating: in a full-page illustration, Fet saw the image of an old man and his wife, fleeing a city, burning in a holy flash of fire—the wife turning to dust. Even he knew that tale . . . "Lot . . . ," he said. A few pages before he saw another illustration: the old man shielding two painfully beautiful winged creatures—archangels sent by the Lord. Quickly Fet slammed the book shut and looked at the cover. *Sadum et Amurah.*

"Sodom and Gomorrah . . . ," he said. "Sadum and Amurah are Sodom and Gomorrah . . ." And suddenly he felt fluent in French. He remembered an illustration in the *Lumen,* almost identical to the one in the French book. Not in style or sophistication but in content. Lot shielding the archangels from the men seeking congress with them.

The clues were there, but Fet was mostly unable to put any of this to good use. Even his hands, coarse and big as baseball mitts, seemed entirely unsuited for handling the *Lumen.* Why had Setrakian chosen him over Eph to guard the book? Eph was smarter, no doubt, much better-read. Hell, he probably spoke fucking French. But Setrakian knew that Fet would die before allowing the book to fall into the Master's hands. Setrakian knew Fet well. And loved him well—with the patience and the care of an old father. Firm but compassionate, Setrakian never made Fet feel too slow or uninformed; quite to the contrary, he explained every matter with great care and patience and made Fet feel included. He made him belong.

The emotional void in Fet's life had been filled by a most unsuspected source. When Eph grew increasingly erratic and obsessive, beginning in the earliest days inside the train tunnel but magnifying once they surfaced, Nora had come to lean more on Fet, to confide in him and to give and to seek comfort. Over time, Fet had learned how to respond. He had come to admire Nora's tenacity in the face of such overwhelming despair; so many others had succumbed to either hopelessness or insanity, or else, like Eph, had allowed their despair to change them. Nora Martinez evidently saw something in Fet—maybe the same thing the old professor had seen in him—a primal nobility, more akin to a beast of burden than a man, and something Fet himself had been unaware of until recently. And if this quality that he possessed—steadfastness, determination, ruthlessness, whatever it was—made him somehow more attractive to her under these extreme circumstances, then he was the better for it.

Out of respect for Eph, he had resisted this entanglement, denying his own feelings as well as Nora's. But their mutual attraction was more evident now. On the last day before his departure, Fet had rested his leg against Nora's. A casual gesture by any measure, except for someone like Fet. He was a large man but incredibly conscious of his personal space, neither seeking nor allowing any violation of it. He kept his distance, ultimately uncomfortable with most human contact—but Nora's knee was pressed against his, and his heart was racing. Racing with hope as the notion dawned on him: *She's holding. She is not moving away . . .*

She had asked him to be careful, to take care of himself, and in her eyes were tears. Genuine tears as she saw him leave.

No one had ever cried for Fet before.

Manhattan

EPH RODE THE 7 express inbound, clinging fast to the exterior of the subway train. He gripped the rear left corner of the last car, his right boot perched on the rear step, fingertips dug into the window frames, rocking with the motion of the train over the elevated track. The wind and the black rain whipped at the tails of his charcoal-gray raincoat, his hooded face turned in toward the shoulder straps of his weapon pack.

It used to be that the vampires had to ride on the outside of the trains, shuttling around the underground of Manhattan in order to avoid discovery. Through the window, whose dented frame he had pried his fingers under, he saw humans sitting and rocking with the motion of the train. The distant stares, the expressionless faces: a perfectly orderly scene. He did not look for long, for if there were any *strigoi* riding, their heat-registering night vision would have spotted him, resulting in a very unpleasant welcoming party at the next stop. Eph was still a fugitive, his likeness hanging in post offices and police stations throughout the city, the news stories concerning his successful assassination of Eldritch Palmer—cleverly edited from his unsuccessful attempt—still replayed on television every week or so, keeping his name and face foremost in the minds of the watchful citizenry.

Riding the trains required skills that Eph had developed through time and necessity. The tunnels were invariably wet—smelling of burned ozone and old grease—and Eph's ragged, smeared clothes acted as perfect camouflage, both visual and olfactory. Hooking up to the rear of the train—that required timing and precision. But Eph had it down. As a kid in San Francisco, he had routinely used the back of streetcars to hitch a ride to school. And you had to board them just in time. Too early and you would be discovered. Too late and you would be dragged and take a bad tumble.

And in the subway, he had taken some tumbles—usually due to drink. Once, as the train took a curve under Tremont Avenue, he had lost his footing as he calculated his landing jump and trailed on the back of the train, legs hopping frantically, bouncing against the tracks until he rolled on his side, cracking two ribs and dislocating his right shoulder—the bone popping softly as it hit the steel rails on the other side of the line. He barely avoided being hit by an oncoming train. Seeking refuge in a maintenance alcove saturated in human urine and old newspapers, he had popped the shoulder back in—but it bothered him every other night. If he rolled on it in his sleep he would wake up in agony.

But now, through practice, he had learned to seek the footholds and the crevices in the rear structure of the train cars. He knew every train, every car—and he had even fashioned two short grappling hooks to grab on to the loose steel panels in a matter of seconds. They were hammered out of the good silver set at the Goodweather household and, now and then, served as a short-range weapon with the *strigoi.*

The hooks were attached to wooden handles, made from the legs of a mahogany table Kelly's mother had given them as a wedding present. If she only knew . . . She had never liked Eph—not good enough for her Kelly—and now she would like him even less.

Eph turned his head, shaking off some of the wetness in order to look out through the black rain to the city blocks on either side of the concrete viaduct high above Queens Boulevard. Some blocks remained ravaged, razed by fires during the takeover, or else looted and long since emptied. Patches of the city appeared as though they had been destroyed in a war—and, indeed, they had.

Others were lit by artificial light, city zones rebuilt by humans overseen by the Stoneheart Foundation, at the direction of the Master: light was critical for work in a world that was dark for as many as twenty-two hours each calendar day. Power grids all across the globe had collapsed following initial electromagnetic pulses that were the result of multiple nuclear detonations. Voltage overruns had burned out electrical conductors, plunging much of the world into vampire-friendly darkness. People very quickly came to the realization—terrifying and brutal in its impact—that a creature race of superior strength had seized control of the planet and that man had been supplanted at the top of the food chain by beings whose own biological needs demanded a diet of human blood. Panic and despair swept the continents. Infected armies fell silent. In the time of consolidation following Night Zero, as the new, poisonous atmosphere continued to roil and cure overhead, so did the vampires establish a new order.

The subway train slowed as it approached Queensboro Plaza. Eph lifted his foot from the rear step, hanging from the blind side of the car so as not to be seen from the platform. The heavy, constant rain was good for one thing only: obscuring him from the vampires' watchful, blood-red eyes.

He heard the doors slide open, people shuffling in and out. The automated track announcements droned from overhead speakers. The doors closed and the train began moving again. Eph regripped the window frame with his sore fingers and watched the dim platform recede from his vision, sliding away down the line like the world of the past, shrinking, fading, swallowed up by the polluted rain and the night.

* * *

The subway train soon dipped underground, out of the driving rain. After two more stops, it entered the Steinway Tunnel, beneath the East River. It was modern conveniences such as this—the amazing ability to travel beneath a swift river—that contributed to the human race's undoing. Vampires, forbidden by nature from crossing a body of moving water under their own power, were able to circumvent such obstacles by the use of tunnels, long-distance aircraft, and other rapid-transit alternatives.

The train slowed, approaching Grand Central Station—and just in time. Eph readjusted his grip on the subway car's exterior, fighting fatigue, tenaciously holding on to his homemade hooks. He was malnourished, as thin now as he had been as a freshman in high school. He had grown accustomed to the persistent, gnawing emptiness in the pit of his belly; he knew that protein and vitamin deficiencies affected not only his bones and muscles but also his mind.

Eph hopped off before it came to a full stop, stumbling to the rock bed between the tracks. He rolled on his left shoulder, landing like an expert. He flexed his fingers, unlocking the arthritis-like paralysis of his knuckles, putting away the hooks. The train's rear light shrank up ahead, and he heard the grating of steel wheels braking against steel rails, a metallic shriek his ears never got used to.

He turned and hobbled off the other way, deeper into the tunnel. He had traveled this route enough times that he did not need his night scope to reach the next platform. The third rail was not a concern, covered with wood casing, in fact making for a convenient step up onto the abandoned platform.

Construction materials remained on the tile floor, a renovation interrupted at its earliest stage: scaffolding, a stack of pipe sections, bales of tubing wrapped in plastic. Eph pushed back his wet hood and reached into his pack for his night-vision scope, strapping it over his head, the lens fitting in front of his right eye. Satisfied that nothing had been disturbed since his last visit, he moved toward the unmarked door.

At its pre-vampire peak, half a million people daily crossed the polished Tennessee marble of the Grand Concourse floor somewhere above him. Eph could not risk entering the main terminal—the half-acre concourse afforded few places to hide—but he had been up on the catwalks on the roof. There, he had looked at the monuments to a lost age: landmark skyscrapers such as the MetLife Building and the Chrysler Building, dark and silent against the night. He had climbed above the two-story-high air-conditioning units on the terminal roof, standing on the pediment facing Forty-second Street and Park Avenue, among colossal statues of the Roman gods Minerva, Hercules, and Mercury above the great clock of Tiffany glass. On the central section of the roof, he had looked down more than a hundred feet to the cathedral-like Grand Concourse. That was as close as he had gotten.

Eph eased open the door, his scope seeing into the total darkness beyond. He climbed two long flights of stairs, then went through another unlocked door into a long corridor. Thick steam pipes ran the length of it, still functioning, groaning with heat. By the time he reached the next door, he was dripping with sweat.

He slid a small silver knife from his backpack, needing to be careful here. The cement-walled emergency exit was no place to get cornered. Black-tinged groundwater had seeped into the floor, pollution from the sky having become a permanent part of the ecosystem. This section of the underground was once regularly patrolled by maintenance workers, rooting out the homeless, the curious, the vandals. Then the *strigoi* briefly assumed control of the underworld of the city, hiding, feeding, spreading. Now that the Master had reconfigured the planet's atmosphere in order to free vampires from the threat of the sun's virus-killing ultraviolet rays, they had risen from this labyrinthine netherworld and claimed the surface for themselves.

The last door was plastered with a white-and-red sign: EMERGENCY EXIT ONLY—ALARM WILL SOUND. Eph returned his blade and his night-vision scope to his backpack, then pushed the pressure bar, the alarm wires having been snipped long ago.

A foul breeze from the stringy black rain exhaled into his face. He pulled up his damp hood and started walking east on Forty-fifth Street. He watched his feet splashing on the sidewalk, walking as he was with his head down. Many of the wrecked or abandoned cars from the initial days remained shoved to the curbs, making most of the streets one-way paths for work vans or supply trucks operated by the vampires and the Stoneheart humans. Eph's eyes remained low but vigilantly searched either side of the street. He had learned never to look around conspicuously; the city had too many windows, too many pairs of vampire eyes. If you looked suspicious, you were suspicious. Eph went out of his way to avoid any interaction with *strigoi*. On the streets, as everywhere, humans were second-class citizens, subject to search or any kind of abuse. A sort of creature apartheid existed. Eph could not risk exposure.

He hurried over to First Avenue, to the Office of the Chief Medical Examiner, quickly ducking down the ramp reserved for ambulances and hearses. He squeezed behind stretchers and a rolling wardrobe they had set there in order to obscure the basement entrance, and entered the unlocked door to the city morgue.

Inside, he stood a few moments in the dim silence, listening. This room, with its stainless steel autopsy tables and numerous sinks, was where the first group of passengers from doomed Regis Air Flight 753 had been brought two years before. Where Eph had first examined the needle-like breach in the necks of the seemingly dead passengers, exposing a puncture wound that extended to the common carotid artery—which they would soon discover had been caused by the vampires' stingers. Where he had also first been shown the strange antemortem augmentation of the vestibular folds around the vocal cords, later determined to be the preliminary stage of the development of the creatures' fleshy stingers. And where he had first witnessed the transformation of the victims' blood from healthy red to oily white.

Also, just outside on the sidewalk was where Eph and Nora first encountered the elderly pawnbroker Abraham Setrakian. Everything Eph knew about the vampire breed—from the killing properties of silver and ultraviolet light, to the existence of the Ancients and their role in the shaping of human civilization since the earliest times, to the rogue Ancient known as the Master whose journey to the New World aboard Flight 753 marked the beginning of the end—he had learned from this tenacious old man.

The building had remained uninhabited since the takeover. The morgue was not part of the infrastructure of a city administered by vampires, because death was no longer the necessary end point of human existence. As such, the end-of-life rituals of mourning and corpse preparation and burial were no longer needed and rarely observed.

For Eph, this building was his unofficial base of operations. He started up the stairs to the upper floors, ready to hear it from Nora: how his despair over Zack's absence was interfering with their resistance work. Dr. Nora Martinez had been Eph's number two in the Canary Project at the CDC. In the midst of all the stress and chaos of the rise of the vampires, their long-simmering relationship had gone from professional to personal. Eph had attempted to deliver Nora and Zack to safety, out of the city, back when the trains were still running beneath Penn Station. But Eph's worst fears were realized when Kelly, drawn to her Dear One, led a swarm of *strigoi* into the tunnels beneath the Hudson River, derailing the train and laying waste to the rest of the passengers—and Kelly attacked Nora and spirited his son away.

Zack's capture—for which Eph in no way held Nora accountable—had nonetheless driven a wedge between them, just as it had driven a wedge between Eph and everything. Eph felt disconnected from himself. He felt fractured and fragmented and knew that this was all he had to offer Nora now.

Nora had her own concerns: chiefly her mother, Mariela Martinez, her mind crippled by Alzheimer's disease. The OCME building was large enough that Nora's mother could roam the upper floors, strapped into her wheelchair, creeping down the hallway by the grip socks on her feet, conversing with people no longer present or alive. A wretched existence, but, in reality, not so far removed from that of the rest of the surviving human race. Perhaps better: Mrs. Martinez's mind had taken refuge in the past and thus could avoid the horror of the present.

The first sign Eph found that something was amiss was the overturned wheelchair, lying on its side near the door off the fourth-floor stairway, strap belts lying on the floor. Then the ammonia scent hit him, the telltale odor of vampire presence. Eph drew his sword, his pace quickening down the corridor, a sick feeling rising from his gut. The medical examiner's building had limited electricity, but Eph could not use lamps or light fixtures that would be visible from the street, so he proceeded down the dim corridor in a defensive crouch, mindful of doors and corners and other potential hiding places.

He passed a fallen partition. A ransacked cubicle. An overturned chair. "Nora!" he called. An incautious act, but if there were still any *strigoi* present, he wanted to draw them out now.

On the floor in a corner office, he discovered Nora's travel backpack. It had been ripped open, her clothes and personal items flung around the room. Her Luma lamp sat in the corner, plugged into its charger. Her clothes were one thing, but Eph knew that Nora would never go anywhere without her UV lamp, unless she had no choice. He did not see her weapon pack anywhere.

He picked up the handheld lamp, switching on the black light. It revealed swirling bursts of bright color on the carpet and against the side of the desk: vampire excrement stains.

Strigoi had marauded here; that was obvious. Eph tried to remain focused and calm. He thought he was alone, at least on this floor: no vampires, which was good, but no Nora, or her mother, which was devastating.

Had there been a fight? He tried to read the room, its swirling stains and overturned chair. He didn't think so. He roamed the hall looking for more evidence of violence beyond property damage but found none. Combat would have been her last resort, and had she made a stand here, the building would certainly be under the control of vampires now. This, to Eph's eye, looked more akin to a house raid.

While examining the desk, he found Nora's weapon bag stowed beneath it, her sword still inside. So evidently she had been surprised. If there was no battle—no silver-to-vampire contact—then her chances of meeting a violent end decreased exponentially. The *strigoi* weren't interested in victims. They were intent on filling their camps.

Had she been captured? It was a possibility, but Eph knew Nora, and she would never go without a battle—and he just didn't see any evidence of that. Unless they had captured her mother first. Nora might have acquiesced then out of fear for Mrs. Martinez's safety.

If so, it was unlikely that Nora would have been turned. The *strigoi*, under the Master's command, were reluctant to add to their ranks: drinking a human's blood and infecting them with the vampiric viral strain only created another vampire to feed. No, it was more likely that Nora would have been transported to a detention camp outside the city. From there, she could be assigned work or further disciplined. Not much was known about the camps; some of those who went in never reemerged. Mrs. Martinez, having lived well beyond her productivity years, would meet a more certain end.

Eph looked around, becoming frantic, trying to figure out what to do. This appeared to be a random incident—but was it? At times, Eph had to keep his distance from the others and carefully monitor his comings and goings from the OCME, because of Kelly's tireless pursuit of him. His discovery could lead the Master right to the heart of their resistance. Had something gone wrong? Was Fet compromised as well? Had the Master somehow gotten onto their entire cell?

Eph went to the laptop computer on the desk, opening it. It was still powered on, and he struck the space bar to wake up the screen. Workstation computers in the ME's building were hardwired to a still-functioning network server. The Internet was heavily damaged in spots and generally unreliable. One was more likely to receive an error message than a page load. Unrecognized and unauthorized Internet protocol addresses were particularly susceptible to worms and viruses, and many computers in the building had become either locked up due to hard-drive-damaging malware or slowed to an unusable crawl by corrupted operating systems. Mobile phone technology was no longer in existence, either for telecommunication or for Internet access. Why allow the human underclass access to a communications network capable of spanning the globe—something the vampires possessed telepathically?

Eph and the others operated under the assumption that all Internet activity was vampire-monitored. The page he was now looking at—that

Nora had apparently abandoned suddenly, without time to shut down the hard drive—was some sort of personal message exchange, a two-party chat conducted in shorthand.

"NMart" was obviously Nora Martinez. Her partner in conversation, "VFet," was Vasiliy Fet, the former New York City exterminator. Fet had joined their fight early, by way of an invasion of rats prompted by the arrival of the *strigoi*. He had proven himself invaluable to the cause, for both his vermin-killing techniques and his knowledge of the city, in particular the boroughs' subterranean passageways. He had become as much of a disciple of the late Setrakian as Eph was, coming into his own as a New World vampire hunter. Currently, he was on a freighter somewhere on the Atlantic Ocean, returning from Iceland on a very important errand.

This thread, full of Fet's grammatical idiosyncrasies, had started the day before, and it was mainly about Eph. He read words he was never meant to see:

NMart: E not here—missed rendezvous. You were right. I shouldn't have relied on him. Now all I can do is wait . . .

VFet: Don't wait there. Keep moving. Return to Roosvlt.

NMart: Can't—my mother is worse. Will try to stay another day at most. TRULY cannot take this anymore. He's dangerous. He's becoming a risk to us all. Just a matter of time before bitch-vamp

Kelly catches up with him or he leads her back here.

VFet: I hear you. But w need him. Most keep hm close.

NMart: He goes out on his own. Doesn't care about anything else.

VFet: He's 2 important. 2 them. 2 the M. 2 us.

NMart: I know it . . . it's just that I can't trust him anymore. I don't even know who he is . . .

VFet: We all just have to keep him from sinking all to the deep end. You especially. Keep him afloat. He dsn't know where the book is. That's our double blind. He can't hurt us that way.

NMart: He's at K's house again. I know it. Raiding it for memories of Z. Like stealing from a dream.

And then:

NMart: You know I miss you. How much longer?

VFet: Returning now. Missing you too.

Eph shrugged off his weapon pack, resheathing his sword, and dropped down into the office chair.

He stared at the most recent exchange, reading it again and again, hearing Nora's voice, then Fet's Brooklyn accent.

Missing you too.

He felt weightless, reading it—as though the force of gravity had been removed from his body. And yet, here he sat, still.

He should have felt more anger. More righteous fury. Betrayal. A jealous frenzy.

And he did feel all these things. But not deeply. Not acutely. They were there, and he acknowledged them, but it amounted to . . . more of the same. His malaise was so overwhelming that no other flavor, no matter how sour, could change his emotional palate.

How had this happened? At times, over these past two years, Eph had consciously kept his distance from Nora. He had done so to protect her, to protect them all . . . or so he said to himself, justifying plain abandonment.

Still—he couldn't understand it. He reread the other part. So he was a "risk." He was "dangerous." Unreliable. They seemed to think that they were carrying him. Part of him felt relief. Relief for Nora—*Good for her*—but most of him just throbbed with mounting rage. What was this? Was he jealous just because he couldn't hold her anymore? God knew he was not exactly minding the store; was he angry because someone else had found his forgotten toy and now he wanted it back? He knew himself so little . . . Kelly's mother used to tell him he was always ten minutes too late to all the major milestones of his life. Late for Zack's birth, late for the wedding, late to save his marriage from falling apart. God knew he was late to save Zack or save the world, and now—now this . . .

Nora? With Fet?

She was gone. Why didn't he do something before? Strangely, amid the pain and the sense of loss he also felt relief. He didn't need to worry anymore—he didn't need to compensate for his shortcomings, explain his absence, mollify Nora. But as that tenuous wave of relief was about to kick in, he turned around and caught himself in a mirror.

He looked older. Much older than he should have. And dirty, almost like a hobo. His hair was plastered against his sweaty forehead and his clothes were layered with months of grime. His eyes were sunk and his cheeks jutted out, pulling the taut, thin skin surrounding them. *No wonder,* he thought. *No wonder.*

He pulled himself back out of the chair in a daze. He walked down four flights of stairs and out of the medical examiner's building through the pissing black rain to nearby Bellevue Hospital. He climbed in through a broken window and walked the dark and deserted halls, following signs for the emergency room. Bellevue's ER was once a Level 1 trauma center, meaning it had housed a full range of specialists providing access to the best facilities.

As well as the best drugs.

He arrived at the nurses' station and found the drug cabinet door torn off. The locked refrigerator had also been pried open and ransacked. No

Percs, no Vikes, no Demerol. He pocketed some oxycodone and antianxiety meds in blister packs—self-diagnosing and self-medicating—tossing empty cartons over his shoulder. He popped two white oxys and dry-swallowed them—then froze.

He had been moving so quickly and making so much noise that he had not heard the bare feet approaching. Out of the corner of his eye, he saw movement from across the nurses' station and stood.

Two *strigoi*, staring at him. Fully formed vampires, hairless and pale, unclothed. He saw the thickened arteries bulging through their necks, running down over their clavicles into their chests like throbbing tree roots. One had once been a male human (larger body) and the other had been a female (breasts shriveled and pale).

The other distinguishing trait of these matured vampires was their loose, floppy wattle. Disgusting, stretched-out flesh that hung like a turkey neck, pale red when in need of nourishment, flushing crimson after feeding. The wattles of these *strigoi* hung pale and scrotumlike, swaying with a turn of their heads. A sign of rank, and the mark of an experienced hunter.

Were these the same two that had accosted Nora and her mother or otherwise rousted them from the OCME? There was no way to confirm it, but something told Eph this was the case—which, if true, meant that Nora might have gotten away clean after all.

He saw what he thought was a glimmer of recognition in their otherwise blank, red eyes. Normally there was no spark or hint of a brain at work behind a vampire's gaze—but Eph had seen this look before and knew that he had been recognized and identified. Their surrogate eyes had communicated their find to the Master, whose presence came flooding into their brains with the force of possession. The horde would be there in a matter of minutes.

"Doctor Goodweather . . . ," both the creatures said at the same time, their voices chirping in eerie synchrony. Their bodies rose like twin marionettes controlled by the same invisible string. The Master.

Eph observed, both fascinated and repulsed, how their blank stare gave way to the intelligence, the poise of the superior creature—undulating, snapping to attention, like a leather glove snapping into shape as the hand fills it with form and intention.

The pale, elongated faces of the creatures morphed as the will of the Master overtook the flaccid mouths and the vacant eyes . . .

"You look . . . quite tired . . . ," the twin marionettes said, their bodies moving in unison. *"I think you should rest . . . don't you think? Join us. Give in. I will procure for you. Anything you want . . ."*

The monster was right: he was tired—oh, so very, very tired—and yes, he would've liked to give in. *Can I?* he thought. *Please? Give in?*

His eyes brimmed with tears and he felt his knees give—just a little—like a man about to sit down. *"The people you love—the ones you miss—they live in my embrace . . . ,"* the twin messengers said, their message worded so carefully. So inviting, so ambiguous . . .

Eph's hands trembled as he reached back over each shoulder, gripping the worn leather handles of his two long swords. He drew them out straight so as not to slice his weapon pack. Maybe it was the opioid kicking in, but something clicked deep inside his brain, something that made him associate these two monstrosities, female and male, with Nora and Fet. His lover and his trusted friend, now conspiring against him. It was as though they themselves had come upon Eph here, rummaging through the drug cabinet like a junkie, witnessing him at his lowest moment—for which they were directly responsible.

"No," he said, renouncing the Master with a broken whimper, his voice breaking even in that single syllable. And rather than push his emotions aside, Eph brought them to the fore, molded them into rage.

"As you wish," the Master said. *"I will see you again . . . soon . . ."*

And then, the will gave way to the hunters. Snorting, huffing, the beasts came back, leaving behind the poised, erect stance and landing on all fours, ready to circle their prey. Eph did not give the vampires a chance to flank him. He rushed straight at the male first, both swords at the ready. The vamp leaped away from him at the last moment—they were agile and fast—but not before Eph's sword tip caught it across the side of its torso. The slash was deep enough to make the vampire land off-balance, the wound leaking white blood. *Strigoi* rarely felt any bodily pain, but they felt it when the weapon was silver. The creature twisted and gripped its side.

In that moment of hesitation and inattention, Eph spun and brought his other sword across at shoulder height. One slice removed the head from the neck and shoulders, severing it just beneath the jaw. The vampire's arms went up in a reflex of self-protection before its trunk and limbs collapsed.

Eph turned again just as the female was in the air. It had vaulted the counter, springing at him with its twin taloned middle fingers poised to cut at his face—but Eph was just able to deflect its arms with his own as the vampire flew past, landing hard against the wall, slumping to the floor. Eph lost both his swords in the process. His hands were so weak. *Oh, yes, yes, please—I want to give up.*

The *strigoi* quickly sprang onto all fours, facing Eph from a crouch. Its eyes bore into him, surrogates of the Master, the evil presence that had taken everything from him. Eph's rage flared anew. He swiftly produced his grappling hooks and braced for impact. The vampire charged and Eph went for it—the vampire wattle dangling beneath its chin made for a perfect target. He had done this move hundreds of times—like a worker in a fish plant scaling a big tuna. One hook connected with the throat behind the wattle, sinking quickly and jamming behind the cartilaginous tube that housed the larynx and launched the stinger. Pulling down on it—hard—he blocked the stinger and forced the creature to genuflect with a piglike squeal. The other hook connected to the eye socket, and Eph's thumb jammed under the jaw, locking the mouth shut. One summer, a long, long time ago, his father had shown him that move when catching snakes on a small river up north. *"Clamp the jaw,"* he had said, *"lock the mouth—so they can't bite."* Not many snakes were poisonous but a lot of them had a nasty bite and enough bacteria in their mouth to cause a lot of pain. Turned out that Eph—city boy Eph—was good at catching snakes. A natural. He had even been able to show off one good day, catching a snake in the driveway at home when Zack was still a child. He felt superior—a hero. But that was a long time ago. A zillion years BC.

Now Eph, weak and infirm, was hooking up a powerful, undead creature so hot to the touch, all angry energy and thirst. He was not knee-deep in a cool California stream or climbing out of his minivan to catch a city snake. He was in real danger. He could feel his muscles give. His strength was fading. *Yes . . . yes—I would like to give in . . .*

And his weakness made him angry. And he thought of everything he had lost—Kelly, Nora, Zack, the world—and he yanked hard, with a primal scream, ripping the trachial tube and snapping the tense cartilage. The jaw snapped and dislocated under his grimy thumb at the very same time. A surge of blood and worms sprang forth and Eph danced backward, avoiding them studiously, weaving like a boxer out of the reach of his opponent.

The vampire sprang to its feet, sliding along the wall, howling, wattle and neck torn and flapping, gushing. Eph feigned a strike, the vamp retreating a few steps, wheezing and wailing, an awkward, wet little sound—almost like a duck call. He feinted again, and the vamp didn't buy it at all this time. Eph had it lulled into a rhythm when the vamp stiffened, then ran off.

If Eph could ever put together a list of rules of engagement, near the top would have been *Never follow a fleeing vampire.* Nothing good could come from it. There was no strategic advantage to running down a *strigoi.* Its clairvoyant alert had already gone out. The vampires had developed coordinated attack strategies over the past two years. Running was either a stalling tactic or an outright ruse.

And yet, Eph, in his anger, did what he knew not to do. He picked up his swords and pursued it, down the hallway to a door marked STAIRS. Anger and a weird desire for proxy revenge made him hit the door and run up two flights. The female then left the stairwell, and Eph followed it out, the vampire loping down the corridor, Eph chasing after it with a long sword in each hand. The vamp turned right and then left, entering another stairwell, racing up one flight.

As Eph tired, common sense returned. He saw the female at the far end of the corridor and sensed that it had slowed, that it was waiting for him, making sure that Eph could see it rounding the corner.

He stopped. It couldn't be a trap. He had just

shown up in the hospital; there was no time. So the only other reason for the vampire to lead him on what amounted to a wild goose chase was . . .

Eph walked into the nearest patient room, crossing to the windows. The glass was streaked with oily black rain, the city below obscured by ripples of dirty water washing down the glass. Eph strained to see the streets, his forehead against the glass.

He saw dark forms, identifiable as bodies, racing out onto the sidewalks from facing buildings, flooding the street below. More and more, from around corners and out of doors, like firemen answering a six-alarm call, moving to the hospital entrance.

Eph backed away. The psychic call had indeed gone out. One of the architects of the human resistance, Dr. Ephraim Goodweather, was trapped inside Bellevue Hospital.

Twenty-eighth Street Subway

NORA STOOD AT the corner of Park and Twenty-eighth, rain rapping on the hood of her slicker. She knew she needed to keep moving, but she also needed to know she was not being followed. Otherwise, escaping into the subway system would instead be like walking into a trap.

Vampires had eyes all over the city. She had to appear like any other human on her way to work or home. The problem with that was her mother.

"I told you to call the landlord!" said her

mother, pulling back her hood to feel the rain on her face.

"Mama," said Nora, pushing the hood back over her head.

"Fix this broken shower!"

"Shhh! Quiet!"

Nora had to keep moving. Hard as it was for her mother, walking kept her quiet. Nora gripped her around her lower back, holding her close as she stepped to the curb, just as an army truck approached the intersection. Nora stepped back again, head lowered, watching the vehicle pass. The truck was driven by a *strigoi*. Nora held her mother tightly, stopping her from wandering into the street.

"When I see that landlord, he's going to be sorry he crossed us."

Thank goodness for the rain. Because rain meant raincoats, and raincoats meant hoods. The old and infirm had been rounded up long ago. The unproductive had no place in the new society. Nora would never take a risk such as this—venturing out in public with her mother—were there any other choice.

"Mama, can we play the quiet game again?"

"I'm tired of all that. This goddamn leaky ceiling."

"Who can be quietest the longest? Me or you?"

Nora started her across the street. Ahead, hanging from the pole that supported the street sign and the traffic signal, hung a dead body. Exhibition corpses were commonplace, especially along Park Avenue. A squirrel on the dead man's slumped shoulder was battling two pigeons for rights to the corpse's cheeks.

Nora would have steered her mother away from the sight, but her mother didn't even look up. They turned and started down the slick stairs into the subway station, the steps oily from the filthy rain. Once underground, Nora's mother again tried to remove her hood, which Nora quickly replaced, scolding her.

The turnstiles were gone. One old MetroCard machine remained for no reason. But the IF YOU SEE SOMETHING, SAY SOMETHING signs remained. Nora caught a break: the only two vampires were at the other end of the entrance, not even looking her way. She walked her mother down to the uptown platform, hoping a 4, 5, or 6 train would arrive quickly. She was holding down her mother's arms and trying to make the embrace appear natural.

Commuters stood around them as they had in the old days. Some read books. A few listened to music on portable music players. All that was missing were the phones and the newspapers.

On one of the poles people leaned against was an old police flyer featuring Eph's face: a copy of his old work ID photograph. Nora closed her eyes, cursing him silently. It was he whom they had been waiting for at the morgue. Nora didn't like it there, not because she was squeamish—she was anything but—but because it was too open. Gus—the former gangbanger who, following a life-changing encounter with Setrakian, had become a trusted comrade in arms—had carved out space for himself underground. Fet had Roosevelt Island—where she was headed now.

Typical Eph. A genius, and a good man, but always a few minutes behind. Always rushing to catch up at the end.

Because of him she had stayed there that extra day. Out of misplaced loyalty—and, yes, maybe guilt—she wanted to connect with him, to check up on him, to make sure he was okay. The *strigoi* had entered the morgue at street level; Nora had been typing into one of the computers when she heard the glass break. She had just enough time to find her mother, asleep in her wheelchair. Nora could have killed the vampires, but doing so would have given away her position, and the location of Eph's hideout, to the Master. And unlike Eph, she was too considerate to risk betraying their alliance.

Betraying it to the Master, that is. She had already betrayed Eph with Fet. Betrayed him within their alliance. Which she felt particularly guilty about, but again, Eph was always a few minutes late. This proved it. She had been so patient with him—too patient, especially with his drinking—and now she was living fully for herself.

And her mother. She felt the old woman pulling at her grip and opened her eyes.

"There's a hair in my face," said her mother, trying to swipe it away.

Nora examined her quickly. Nothing. But she pretended to see a single strand and released her mother's arm momentarily to pluck it away. "Got it," she said. "All set now."

But she could tell from her mother's fidgeting that her ploy had not worked. Her mother tried blowing at it. "Tickles. Let me go!"

Nora felt a head or two turn. She released her mother's arm. The old woman brushed at her face, then tried to remove her hood.

Nora forced it back on over her head, but not before a shock of unkempt silver-gray was briefly visible.

She heard someone gasp near her. Nora fought the urge to look, trying to remain as inconspicuous as possible. She heard whispering, or else imagined she did.

She leaned toward the yellow line, hoping to see train headlights.

"There he is!" shouted her mother. "Rodrigo! I see you. Don't pretend!"

She was yelling the name of their landlord from when Nora was a child. A rail-thin man, Nora recalled, with a great mop of black hair and hips so narrow he carried his tool belt rather than wore it. The man she was calling to now—dark-haired, but no double for the Rodrigo of thirty years ago—looked over attentively.

Nora turned her mother away, trying to shush her. But her mother twisted back around, her hood slipping back from her face as she tried to call to the phantom landlord.

"Mama," implored Nora. "Please. Look at me. Silence."

"He's always there to flirt with me, but when there is work to be done . . ."

Nora wanted to clamp her hand over her

mother's mouth. She fixed the hood and walked her away down the platform, only drawing more attention in the process. "Mama, *please.* We will be discovered."

"Lazy bastard, he is!"

Even if her mother was mistaken for a drunk, there would be trouble. Alcohol was prohibited, both because it affected the blood and because it promoted antisocial behavior.

Nora turned, thinking about fleeing the station—and saw headlights brightening the tunnel. "Mama, our train. Shhhh. Here we go."

It pulled in. Nora waited at the first car. A few passengers disembarked before Nora rushed her mother inside, finding a pair of seats together. The 6 train would get them to Fifty-ninth Street in a matter of minutes. She fixed her mother's hood back on her head and waited for the doors to close.

Nora noticed that no one else sat near them. She looked down the length of the car in time to see the other entering passengers look quickly away. Then she looked out onto the platform and saw a young couple out standing with two Transit Authority cops—humans—pointing at the first subway car. Pointing at Nora.

Close the doors, she pled silently.

And they did. With the same random efficiency the New York transit system had always exhibited, the doors slid shut. Nora waited for the familiar lurch, looking forward to getting back over to vampire-free Roosevelt Island and waiting there for Fet's return.

But the car did not start forward. She waited for it, one eye on her fellow passengers at the other end of the car, the other on the transit cops walking toward the car. Behind them now were the two vampires, red eyes fixed on Nora. Behind them stood the concerned couple who had pointed out Nora and her mother.

The couple had thought they were doing the right thing, following the new laws. Or perhaps they were spiteful; everyone else had to abandon their elders to the master race.

The doors opened and the human transit cops boarded first. Even if she could murder two of her own kind and release the two *strigoi* and escape from the underground station, she would have to do so alone. There was no way she could do so without sacrificing her mother, either to capture or to death.

One of the cops reached over and pulled back Nora's mother's hood, revealing her head. "Ladies," he said, "you have to come with us." When Nora did not stand right away, he placed his hand on her shoulder and squeezed tightly. "Now."

Bellevue Hospital

EPH BACKED AWAY from the window and the vampires converging on Bellevue Hospital on the streets below. He had screwed up . . . Dread burned at the pit of his stomach. It was all lost.

His first instinct was to keep rising, to buy time

by heading to the roof—but that was an obvious dead end. The only advantage to being on the roof was that he could throw himself off of it, were the choice death or vampire afterlife.

Going straight down meant fighting his way through them. That would be like running into a swarm of killer bees: he was almost certain to get stung at least once, and once was all it took.

So, running was not an option. Nor was making a suicidal final stand. But he had spent enough time in hospitals to consider this his home turf. The advantage was his; he just had to find it.

He hurried past the patient elevators, then stopped, doubling back, stopping before the gas control panel. An emergency shutoff for the entire floor. He cracked open the plastic shield and made sure the cutoff was open, then stabbed at the fixture until he heard a pronounced hiss.

He ran to the stairwell, charging up one flight, racing to that floor's gas control panel, and repeating the same damage. Then right back into the stairs—and this time he could hear the bloodsuckers charging up the lower flights. No outcry, because they had no voice. Only the slapping of dead, bare feet as they climbed.

He risked one more floor, making quick work of the access panel there. He pressed the nearby elevator button but did not wait for the car, instead running off in search of the service elevators, the ones the orderlies used to transport supply carts and bedridden patients. He located the bank of elevators and pressed the button, waiting for one to board.

The adrenaline of survival and the chase put a charge into his blood that was as sweet as any artificial stimulant he could find. This, he realized, was the high he sought from pharmaceuticals. Over the course of so many life-or-death battles, he had messed up his pleasure receptors. Too many highs and too many lows.

The elevator door opened and he pressed "B" for basement. Signs admonished him on the importance of patient confidentiality and clean hands. A child smiled at him from a grimy poster. Sucking on a lollipop and giving him a wink and a thumbs-up. EVERYTHING IS GOING TO BE A-OKAY said the printed moron. On the poster were timetables and dates for a pediatrics fair taking place a million years ago. Eph returned one sword to the bag on his back, watching the floor numbers go down. The elevator jerked once, and the car darkened and stopped between floors—stuck. A nightmare scenario, but then moments later it lurched and continued downward. Like everything else that depended on regular upkeep, these mechanical conveyances were not to be trusted—that is, if you had a choice.

The door dinged and opened finally, Eph exiting into the service wing of the hospital basement. Stretchers with bare mattresses were bunched up against the wall like supermarket carts awaiting customers. A giant canvas laundry cart sat beneath the open end of a wall chute.

In the corner, on a handful of long-handled dollies, stood a dozen or so green-painted oxygen tanks. Eph worked as fast as his fatigued body allowed, hustling the tanks into each of the three elevators, four tanks to a car. He pulled off their metal nose caps and used them to hammer at the feed nozzles until he heard the reassuring hiss of escaping gas. He pressed the buttons for the top floor, and all three doors closed.

He pulled a half-full can of charcoal lighter fluid from inside his pack. His box of all-weather matches was somewhere inside his coat pocket. With trembling hands, he tipped over the canvas laundry cart, emptying the crusty linen in front of the three elevators, then squeezed the lighter fluid can with wicked glee, pissing flammable liquid all over the heap of cotton. He struck a pair of matches and dropped them onto the pile, which ignited with a hot *whumph*. Eph pressed the call button for all three elevator cars—operated individually from the service basement—and then ran like hell, trying to find a way out.

Near a barred exit door, he saw a large control panel of colored pipes. He freed a fire ax from its glass cabinet—it felt so heavy, so big. Repeatedly, he chopped at the gaskets of all three feeds, using more the ax's weight than his own fading strength, until gas came whistling out. He pushed through the door and found himself in the spitting rain, standing in a muddy sitting area of park benches and cracked walkways overlooking Franklin D. Roosevelt Drive and the rain-swept East River. And for some reason all he could think of was a line from an old movie, *Young Frankenstein—"It could be worse. It could be raining."* He chuckled. He had seen that movie with Zack. For weeks they had quoted punch lines from it to each other. *"There wolf . . . there castle."*

He was behind the hospital. No time to run for the street. He instead rushed across the small park, needing to put as much space between him and the building as possible.

As he reached the far edge, he saw more vamps coming up the high wall from Roosevelt Drive. More assassins dispatched by the Master, their high-metabolism bodies steaming in the rain.

Eph ran at them, waiting for the building behind him to explode and collapse at any moment. He kicked back the first few, forcing them off the wall down to the parkway below—where they landed on their hands and feet, righting themselves immediately, like unkillables in a video game. Eph ran along the top edge of the wall, toward the NYU Medical Center buildings, trying to get away from Bellevue. Before him, a long-taloned vamp hand gripped the top of the wall, a bald, red-eyed face appearing. Eph dropped to his knee, jabbing the end of his sword blade into the vamp's open mouth, the point reaching the back of its hot throat. But he did not run it through, did not destroy it. The silver blade burned it, keeping its jaw from unhinging and unleashing its stinger.

The vampire could not move. Its red-rimmed eyes glared at Eph in confusion and pain.

Eph said, "Do you see me?"

The vamp's eyes showed no reaction. Eph was addressing not it but the Master, watching through this creature.

"Do you see this?"

He turned the sword, forcing the vamp's perspective toward Bellevue. Other creatures were scaling the wall, and some were already running out of the hospital, alerted to Eph's escape. He had only moments. He feared that his sabotage had failed, that the leaking gas had instead found a safe way out of the hospital building.

Eph got back in the vamp's face as though it were the Master's itself.

"Give me back my son!"

He had just finished the last word as the building erupted behind him, throwing Eph forward, his sword piercing the back of the vampire's throat and exiting its neck. Eph tumbled off the wall, gripping the handle of his sword, the blade sliding out of the vampire's face as together they twisted and fell.

Eph landed on the roof of an abandoned car, one of many lining the inside lane of the roadway. The vampire slammed into the road next to him.

Eph's hip took the brunt of the impact. Over the ringing in his ears, Eph heard a high whistling scream and looked up into the black rain. He watched something like a missile shoot out from high above, arc overhead, and splash down into the river. One of the oxygen tanks.

Mortar-heavy bricks thumped down onto the road. Shards of glass fell like jewels in the rain, shattering on the road. Eph covered his head with his coat as he slid down off the dented roof, ignoring the pain in his side.

Only as he stood up did he notice two shards of glass, lodged firmly in his calf. He yanked them out. Blood poured from the wounds. He heard a wet, excited squeal . . .

A few yards away, the vamp lay on its back, dazed, white blood gurgling from the perforation in the back of its neck—but still excited and hungry. Eph's blood was its call for dinner.

Eph got in its face, gripping its broken, dislodged chin, and saw its red eyes focus on him, then on the silver point of his blade.

"I want my son, you motherfucker!" yelled Eph.

He then released the *strigoi* with a vicious chop to the throat, severing its head and its communication with the Master.

Limping, bleeding, he got up again. *"Zack . . . ,"* he murmured. *"Where are you . . . ?"*

Then he started his long journey back home.

Central Park

BELVEDERE CASTLE, SET on the northern end of the Lake in Central Park along the Seventy-ninth Street Transverse Road, was a high Victorian Gothic and Romanesque "folly" constructed in 1869 by Jacob Wray Mould and Calvert Vaux, the original designers of the park. All Zachary Goodweather knew was that it looked spooky and cool, and that was what had always drawn him to it: this medieval (to his mind) castle in the center of the park in the center of the city. As a child, he used to make up tales about the castle, how it was in fact a giant fortress constructed by tiny trolls for the original architect of the city, a dark lord named Belvedere who dwelled in catacombs deep beneath the castle rock, haunting the dark citadel by night as he tended to his creatures throughout the park.

This was back when Zack still had to resort to fantasy for tales of the supernatural and the grotesque. When he needed to daydream in order to escape from the boredom of the modern world.

Now his daydreams were real. His fantasies were attainable. His wishes were requests, his desires realized.

He stood inside the open doorway to the castle, a young man now, watching black rain pummel the park. It slapped the overflowing Turtle Pond, once an algae-rich pool of shimmering green, now a muddy black hole. The sky above was ominously overcast, which was to say, normal. No blue in the sky meant no blue in the water. For two hours a day, some ambient light seeped through the tumultuous cloud cover, enough so that visibility improved to a point where he could see the rooftops of the city around him and the Dagobah-like swamp that the park had become. The solar-powered park lamps could not soak up enough juice in that time to illuminate the twenty-two hours of darkness, their light fading soon after the vampires returned from their retreat beneath ground and into the shadows.

Zack had grown—and grown strong—in this past year; his voice had started changing a few months ago, his jawline becoming defined and his torso elongating seemingly overnight. His strong legs carried him up, climbing the near staircase, a skinny iron spiral leading to the Henry Luce Nature Observatory on the second floor. Along the walls and beneath glass tables remained displays of animal skeletons, bird feathers, and papier-mâché birds set in plywood trees. Central Park had once been one of the richest bird-watching areas in the United States, but the climate change had ended that, probably forever. In the first weeks following the earthquakes and volcanic eruptions triggered by nuclear plant meltdowns and warhead detonations, the dark sky had hung thick with birds. Shrieks and calls all night. Mass bird deaths, winged corpses falling from the sky along with heavy black hail. As chaotic and desperate in the air as it was for humans on the ground. Now there were no longer any warmer southern skies to migrate to. For days, the ground had been literally covered with flapping, blackened wings. Rats feasted on the fallen voraciously. Agonized chirping and hooting punctuated the rhythm of the falling hail.

But now, the park was still and quiet when there was no rain, its lakes empty of waterfowl. A few grimy bones and feather strands melded in the mulch and the mud covering the soil and pavement. Ragged, mangy squirrels occasionally darted up trees, but their population in the park was way down. Zack looked out through one of the telescopes—he had jammed a quarter-sized stone into the pay slot so that the telescope operated without money—and his field of vision disappeared in the fog and the murky rain.

The castle had been home to a functioning meteorological station before the vampires came. Most of the equipment remained on the peaked tower roof, as well as inside the fenced compound south of the castle. New York City radio stations used to give the weather with, "The temperature in Central Park is . . . ," and the number they called was a reading taken from the turret observatory. It was July now, maybe August, what used to be known as the "dog days" of summer, and the highest temperature reading Zack had witnessed during one particularly balmy night was sixty-one degrees Fahrenheit, sixteen degrees Celsius.

August was Zack's birth month. There was a two-year-old calendar in the back office, and he wished that he had thought to keep track of the passing days more carefully. Was he thirteen years old yet? He felt that he was. He decided that yes, he was. Officially a teenager.

Zack could still—barely—remember the time his father had taken him to the Central Park Zoo one sunny afternoon. They had visited this very nature exhibit inside the castle, then ate Italian ices out on the stone wall overlooking the meteorological equipment. Zack remembered confiding in his father about how kids in school sometimes made wisecracks about his last name, Goodweather, saying that Zack was going to be a weatherman when he grew up.

"What are you going to be?" asked his dad.

"A zookeeper," Zack had answered. *"And probably a motocross racer."*

"Sounds good," said his dad, and they threw their empty paper cups into the recycling bin before moving on to an afternoon matinee. And, at the end of that day, after a perfect afternoon, father and son had vowed to repeat the excursion. But they never did. Like so many promises in the Zack-Eph story, this one went unfulfilled.

Remembering that was like recalling a dream now—if it had ever existed at all. His dad was long gone, dead along with Professor Setrakian and the rest. Once in a great while, he would hear an explosion somewhere in the city or see a thick plume of smoke or dust rising into the rain and wonder. There had to be some humans still resisting the inevitable. It made Zack think of the raccoons that pestered his family one Christmas vacation, raiding their garbage no matter what Dad did to secure it. This was like that, he supposed. A nuisance, but little more.

Zack left the musty exhibit and went back down the stairs. The Master had created a room for him that Zack had modeled on his old bedroom at home. Except that his old bedroom did not have a wall-sized video display screen taken from the Times Square ESPN Zone. Or a Pepsi machine, or entire store racks of comic books. Zack kicked a game controller he had left on the floor, dropping down into one of the luxe leather chairs from Yankee Stadium, the thousand-dollar seats behind home plate. Occasionally, kids were brought in for matches, or he played them online on a dedicated server, but Zack almost always won. Everybody else was out of practice. Domination could get boring, especially when there were no new games being produced.

At first, being at the castle was terrifying. He had heard all the stories about the Master. He kept waiting to be turned into a vampire, like his mom, but it never happened. Why? He had never been given a reason, nor had he asked for one. He was a guest there and, as the only human, almost like a celebrity. In the two years since Zack had become the Master's guest, no other nonvampire had been admitted to Belvedere Castle or anywhere near the premises. What had at first seemed like a kidnapping instead came to seem, gradually, over time, like selection. Like a calling. As though a special place had been reserved for him in this new world.

Over all others, Zack had been chosen. For what, he did not know. All he knew was that the being that had delivered him to this point of privilege was the absolute ruler of the new dominion. And, for some reason, he wanted Zack at his side.

The stories Zack had been told—of a fearsome giant, a ruthless killer, and evil incarnate—were obvious exaggerations. First of all, the Master was of average height for an adult. For an ancient being, it appeared almost youthful. Its black eyes were piercing, such that Zack could certainly see the potential for horror if someone fell into disfavor with it. But behind them—for one so fortunate to view them directly, as Zack had been—was a depth and a darkness that transcended humanity, a wisdom that reached back through time, an intelligence connected to a higher realm. The Master was a leader, commanding a vast clan of vampires throughout the city and the world, an army of beings answering its telepathic call from this castle throne in the swampy center of New York City.

The Master was a being possessed of actual magic. Diabolical magic, yes, but the only true magic Zack had ever witnessed. Good and evil were malleable terms now. The world had changed. Night was day. Down was the new up. Here, in the Master, was proof of a higher being. A superhuman. A divinity. His power was extraordinary.

Take Zack's asthma. The air quality in the new climate was extremely poor, due to stagnancy, elevated ozone readings, and the recirculation of particulate matter. With the thick cloud cover pressing down over everything like an unwashed blanket, weather patterns suffered, and ocean breezes did little to refresh the city's airflow. Mold grew and spores flew.

Yet, Zack was fine. Better than fine: his lungs were clear, and he breathed without wheezing or gasping. In fact, he hadn't had anything resembling an asthma attack in all the time he had been with the Master. It had been two years since he had used an inhaler, because he did not need one anymore.

His respiratory system was fully dependent upon one substance even more magically effective than albuterol or prednisone. A fine, white droplet of the Master's blood—administered orally, once weekly, from the Master's pricked finger onto Zack's waiting tongue—cleared Zack's lungs, allowing him to breathe free.

What had seemed weird and disgusting at first now came as a gift: the milky-white blood with its faint electrical charge and a taste of copper and hot camphor. Bitter medicine, but the effect was nothing short of miraculous. Any asthma sufferer would give just about anything never to feel the smothering panic of an asthma attack again.

This blood absorption did not make Zack a vampire. The Master prevented any of the blood worms from reaching Zack's tongue. The Master's only desire was to see Zack healthy and comfortable. And yet the true source of Zack's affinity and awe for the Master was not the power the Master exercised, but rather the power the Master conferred. Zack was evidently special in some way. He was different, exalted among humans. The Master had singled him out for attention. The Master had, for lack of a better term, befriended him.

Like the zoo. When Zack heard that the Master was going to close it down forever, he protested. The Master offered to spare it, to turn the entire zoo over to Zack, but on one condition: that Zack had to take care of it. Had to feed the animals and clean the cages, all by himself. Zack had jumped at the chance, and the Central Park Zoo became his. Just like that. (He was offered the carousel too, but carousels were for babies; he had helped them tear it down.) The Master could grant wishes like a genie.

Of course, Zack didn't realize how much work it was going to be, but he kept at it as best he could. The changed atmosphere claimed some of the animals quickly, including the red panda and most of the birds, making his job easier. Still, with no one to prod him along, he allowed the intervals between feeding times to grow and grow. It fascinated him how some of the animals turned on one another, both the mammals and the reptiles. The great snow leopard was Zack's favorite and the animal he feared most. So the leopard was fed most regularly: at first, thick slabs of fresh meat arriving by truck every other day. Then one day, a live goat. Zack led it into the cage and watched from behind a tree as the leopard stalked its prey. Then a sheep. Then a baby deer. But over time, the zoo fell deep into disrepair, the cages fouled with animal waste that Zack grew tired of cleaning. After many months he came to dread the zoo, and more and more he ignored his responsibilities. At night sometimes he heard the other animals cry out, but never the snow leopard.

After the better part of a year, Zack went to the Master and complained that the work was too much for him.

It will be abandoned, then. And the animals destroyed.

"I don't want them destroyed. I just . . . don't want to take care of them anymore. You could have any of your kind do it, and they would never complain."

You want me to keep it open just for your enjoyment only.

"Yes." Zack had asked for more extravagant things and always received them. "Why not?"

On one condition.

"Okay."

I have watched you with the leopard.

"You have?"

Watched you feed it animals to stalk and devour. Its agility and beauty attracts you. But its power frightens you.

"I guess."

I have also watched you allow other animals to starve.

Zack began to protest. "There are too many to take care of—"

I have watched you pit them against one another. It is natural enough, your curiosity. Watching how lesser species react under stress. Fascinating, isn't it? Watching them fight for survival . . .

Zack did not know if he should admit to this.

The animals are yours to do with what you wish. That includes the leopard. You control its habitat and its feeding schedule. You should not fear it.

"Well . . . I don't. Not really."

Then . . . why don't you kill it?

"What?"

Have you never thought about what it would be like, to kill such an animal?

"Kill it? Kill the leopard?"

You've grown bored with zoo-keeping because it is artificial, unnatural. Your instincts are correct, but your method is wrong. You want to own these primitive creatures. But they are not meant to be kept. Too much power. Too much pride. There is only one way to truly possess a wild animal. To make it your own.

"To kill it."

Prove yourself equal to this task, and I will reward you by seeing to it that your zoo remains open and the animals fed and cared for, while relieving you of your duties there.

"I . . . I can't."

Because it is beautiful or because you fear it?

"Just . . . because."

What is the one thing I have refused you? The one thing you asked for that I declined to allow?

"A loaded gun."

I will see to it that a rifle is maintained for your use within the confines of the zoo. The decision is yours . . . I want you to take a side . . .

So Zack went to the zoo the next day, just to hold the loaded weapon. He found it on an umbrella table inside the entrance, brand-new, small sized, with a satin walnut stock and a recoil pad, and a scope on top. It only weighed about seven pounds. He carefully carried the weapon around his zoo, sighting various targets. He wanted to shoot but wasn't sure how many rounds it held. It was a bolt-action rifle, but he wasn't 100 percent certain he could reload it, even if he could get more ammunition. He aimed for a sign that said RESTROOMS and fingered the trigger, not really squeezing, and the weapon jumped in his hands. The rifle butt slammed into his shoulder, the recoil shoving him backward. The report was a loud crack. He gasped and saw a wisp of smoke coming out of the muzzle. He looked at the sign and saw a hole punched through one of the *O*'s.

Zack practiced his aim for the next several days, utilizing the exquisite, whimsical bronze animals in the Delacorte clock. The clock still played music every half hour. As the figures moved along their circular track, Zack aimed at a hippopotamus playing the violin. He missed his first two shots entirely, and the third one grazed the goat playing the pipes. Frustrated, Zack reloaded and waited for the next go-around, sitting on a nearby bench as the distant sirens lulled him into a nap. The bells woke him thirty minutes later. This time he aimed ahead of his target rather than trying to track with it as it moved. Three shots at the hippo, and he distinctly heard one sharp ricochet off the bronze figure. Two days later, the goat had lost the tip of one of its two pipes, and the penguin had lost part of a drumstick. Zack was able to hit the figures now with speed and accuracy. He felt ready.

The leopard habitat consisted of a waterfall and a birch and bamboo forest, all contained within a high tent of stainless steel woven mesh. The terrain inside was steep, with tunnel-like tubes carved into the slope, leading to the windowed viewing area.

The snow leopard stood on a rock and looked at Zack, associating the boy's appearance with feeding time. The black rain had soiled her coat, but the animal still possessed a regal air. At four feet in length, she could leap forty or fifty feet if motivated, as when going after prey.

She stepped off the rock, prowling in a circle. The rifle report had antagonized her. Why did the Master want Zack to kill it? What purpose would it serve? It seemed like a sacrifice, as though Zack were being asked to execute the bravest animal in order that the others might survive.

He was shocked when the leopard came bounding toward the steel mesh separating them, baring her teeth. She was hungry and disappointed that she did not smell any food, as well as alarmed by the rifle shot—though that was not at all what it seemed like to Zack. He jumped back before reasserting himself, pointing the rifle at the snow leopard, answering her low, intimidating growl. She walked in a tight circle, never taking her eyes off him. She was voracious, and Zack realized that she would go through meal after meal and that, if the food ever ran out, she would feast on the hand that fed her without a moment's justification. She would take if she needed to take. She would attack.

The Master was right. He was afraid of the leopard, and rightly so. But which one was the keeper and which one the kept? Didn't she have Zack working for her, feeding her regularly over these many months? He was her pet as much as she was his. And suddenly, with the rifle in his hand, that arrangement didn't feel right.

He hated her arrogance, her will. He walked around the enclosure, the snow leopard following him on the other side of the mesh. Zack entered the ZOO EMPLOYEES ONLY feeding area, looking out through the small window over the door through which he dropped the leopard's meat or released livestock. Zack's deep breathing seemed to fill the entire room. He ducked through the top-hinged door, which slammed shut behind him.

He had never been inside the leopard's pen before. He looked up at the high tent overhead. A number of different-sized bones were scattered over the ground before him, remnants of past meals.

He had a grand fantasy of striding out into the small wood and tracking the cat, looking her in her eyes before deciding whether or not to pull the trigger. But the noise of the closing door was the equivalent of ringing the dinner bell, and at once the snow leopard came slinking around a boulder strategically set to shield the leopard's feeding from zoo visitors.

The leopard stopped short, surprised to see Zack inside there. For once there was no steel mesh between them. She lowered her head as though trying to understand this strange turn of events, and Zack saw that he had made a terrible mistake. He brought the rifle to his shoulder without aiming it and squeezed the trigger. Nothing happened. He pulled it again. Nothing.

He reached for the bolt handle and yanked it back and slid it forward. He squeezed the trigger, and the rifle jumped in his hands. He worked the bolt again, frantically, and squeezed the trigger, and the report was the only thing that reached his ringing ears. He worked the bolt again, and squeezed the trigger, and the rifle jumped. Another time, and the rifle clicked empty. Again, and still empty.

He realized only then that the snow leopard was lying on its side before him. He went to the animal, seeing the red bloodstains spreading over its coat. The animal's eyes were closed, its powerful limbs still.

Zack climbed up on the boulder and sat there with the empty rifle on his lap. Overcome with emotions, he shuddered and cried. He felt at once triumphant and lost. He looked out at the zoo from inside the pen. It had begun to rain.

Things began to change for Zack after that. His rifle only held four rounds, and for a while he returned to his zoo each day for target practice: more signs, benches, branches. He began to take more risks. He rode a dirt bike along the old jogging routes in the park, around and around the Great Lawn, riding the bike through the empty streets of Central Park, past the shriveled remains of hanging corpses or the ashes of funerary pyres. When he rode at night, he liked to turn the bike's headlight off. It was exciting, magical—an adventure. Protected by the Master, he felt no fear.

But what he did feel, still, was the presence of his mother. Their bond, which had felt strong even after her turning, had faded over time. The creature that had once been Kelly Goodweather now barely resembled the human woman who had been his mother. Her scalp was dirty, hairless, her lips thin and lacking even a hint of pink. The soft cartilage of her nose and ears had collapsed into mere vestigial lumps. Loose, ragged flesh hung from her neck, and an incipient, crimson wattle, undulating when she turned her head. Her chest was flat, her breasts shriveled, her arms and legs caked with a grime so thick the driving rain could not wash it away. Her eyes were orbs of black floating on beds of dark red, essentially lifeless . . . except for sometimes, rarely, perhaps only in Zack's imagination now, when he saw what he thought might be a glimmer of recognition reflective of the mother she once was. It wasn't so much an emotion or expression, but rather the way a certain shadow fell across her face, in a manner more obscuring of her vampire nature than revealing of her former human self. Fleeting moments, growing more rare with time—but they were enough. More psychologically than physically, his mother remained on the periphery of his new life.

Bored, Zack pulled the plunger on his vending machine, and a Milky Way bar dropped to the bottom drawer. He ate it as he went back up to the first floor, then outside, looking for some trouble to get into. As though on cue, Zack's mother came scrabbling up the craggy rock face that was the castle's foundation. She did so with feline agility, scaling the wet schist seemingly without exertion, her bare feet and talon-aided hands moving from purchase to purchase as though she had ascended that very path one thousand times before. At the top, she vaulted easily onto the walkway, two spiderlike feelers following behind her, loping back and forth on all fours.

As she neared Zack, standing in the doorway just out of the rain, he saw that her neck wattle was flush, engorged and red even through the accumulated dirt and filth. It meant that she had recently fed.

"Had a nice dinner out, Mom?" he asked, revolted. The scarecrow that had once been his mother stared at him with empty eyes. Every time he saw her, he felt the exact same contradictory impulses: repulsion and love. She followed him around for hours at a time, occasionally keeping her distance like a watchful wolf. He had, once, been moved to caress her head and afterward had cried silently.

She entered the castle without a glance at Zack's face. Her wet footprints and the muck tracked in by the feelers' hands and feet added to the grunge coating the stone floor. Zack looked at her and, for a fleeting moment—though distorted by vampiric mutation—saw his mother's face emerge. But, just as immediately, the illusion was broken, the memory soiled by this ever-present monster that he could not help but love. Everybody else he ever had in his life was gone. This was all Zack had left: a broken doll to keep him company.

Zack felt a warmth fill the breezy castle, as though left by a being in swift motion. The Master had returned, a slight murmur entering Zack's head. He watched his mother ascend the stairs to the upper floors and followed her, wanting to see what the commotion was about.

The Master

The Master had once understood the voice of God. It once held it within itself, and in a way, it retained a pale imitation of that state of grace. It was, after all, a being of one mind and many eyes, seeing all at once, processing it all, experiencing the many voices of its subjects. And like God's, the Master's voice was a concert of flow and contradiction—it carried the breeze and the hurricane, the lull and the thunder, rising and fading with dusk and dawn . . .

But the scale of God's voice encompassed it all—not earth, not the continents, but the *whole* world. And the Master could only witness it but no longer could make sense of it as it was able to once upon a time in the origin of it all.

This is, it thought, for the millionth time, *what it is to fall from grace . . .*

And yet, there the Master stood: monitoring the planet through the observations of its brood. Multiple sources of input, one central intelligence. The Master's mind casting a net of surveillance over the globe. Squeezing planet Earth in a fist of a thousand fingers.

Goodweather had just released seventeen serfs in the explosion of the hospital building. Seventeen lost, their number soon to be replaced; the arithmetic of infection was of paramount importance to the Master.

The feelers remained out searching the surrounding blocks for the fugitive doctor, seeking his psychic scent. Thus far, nothing. The Master's ultimate victory was assured, the great chess match all but over, except that its opponent obstinately refused to concede defeat—leaving to the Master the drudgery of chasing the last remaining piece around the board.

That final piece was not, in fact, Goodweather, but instead the *Occido Lumen*, the lone extant edition of the cursed text. In detailing the mysterious origin of the Master and the Ancients, the book also contained an indication for bringing about the Master's demise—the location of its site of origin—if one knew where to look.

Fortunately, the current possessors of the book were illiterate cattle. The tome had been stolen at auction by the old professor Abraham Setrakian, at that time the lone human on earth with the knowledge necessary to decrypt the tome and its arcane secrets. However, the old professor had little time to review the *Lumen* before his death. And in the brief time the Master and Setrakian were linked through possession—in those precious moments between the old professor's turning and his destruction—the Master learned, through their shared intelligence, every bit of knowledge the professor had gleaned from the silver-bound volume.

Everything—and yet it was not enough. The location of the Master's origin—the fabled "Black Site"—was still unknown to Setrakian at the time of his turning. This was frustrating, but it also proved that his loyal band of sympathizers did not know the location either. Setrakian's knowledge of folklore and the history of the dark clans was unsurpassed among humans and, like a snuffed flame, had died with him.

The Master was confident that even with the cursed book in hand, Setrakian's followers could not decode the book's mystery. But the Master needed the coordinates itself, in order to guarantee its safety for eternity. Only a fool leaves anything of importance to chance.

In that moment of possession, of unique psychological intimacy with Setrakian, the Master had also learned the identities of Setrakian's co-conspirators. The Ukrainian, Vasiliy Fet. Nora Martinez and Augustin Elizalde.

But none was more compelling to the Master than the one whose identity the Master had already known: Dr. Ephraïm Goodweather. What the Master had not known, and what came as a surprise, was that Setrakian considered Goodweather the strongest link among them. Even given Goodweather's obvious vulnerabilities—his temperament, and the loss of his former wife and his son—Setrakian believed him to be absolutely incorruptible.

The Master was not a being prone to surprise. Existing for centuries tended to dull revelations, but this one nagged at the Master. How could it be? Reluctantly, the Master admitted to having a high opinion of Setrakian's judgment—for a human. As with the *Lumen*, the Master's interest in Goodweather had begun as a mere distraction.

The distraction had become a pursuit.

The pursuit was now an obsession. All humans

broke at the end. Sometimes it took mere minutes, sometimes days, sometimes decades, but the Master always won at the end. This was endurance chess. His time frame was much broader than theirs, his mind far more trained—and void of delusions or hopes.

This was what had led the Master to Goodweather's progeny. This was the original reason the Master had not turned the boy. The reason the Master assuaged the discomfort in the boy's lungs with a drop or so of its precious blood every week—which also had the effect of enabling the Master to peer into the boy's warm and pliable mind.

The boy had responded to the Master's power. And the Master used this, engaging the boy mentally. Subverting his naïve ideas about divinity. After a period of fear and disgust, the boy, with assistance from the Master, had come to feel admiration and respect. His cloying emotions for his father had shrunk like an irradiated tumor. The boy's young mind was an agreeable lump of dough, one the Master continued to knead.

Preparing it. To rise.

The Master normally met such subjects at the end of the corruption process. Here, the Master had the unusual opportunity to participate in the corruption of the son and surrogate of the allegedly incorruptible. The Master was able to experience this downfall directly through the boy, thanks to the bond of the blood feeding. The Master had felt the boy's conflict when facing the snow leopard, felt his fear, felt his joy.

Never had the Master wanted to keep anyone alive before; never had he wanted them to remain human. The Master had already decided: this was the next body to inhabit. With that in mind, the Master was essentially preparing young Zachary. It had learned never to take a body younger than age thirteen. Physically, the advantages included boundless energy, fresh joints, and supple muscles, requiring little maintenance. But the disadvantages were still those of taking a weaker body, structurally fragile and with limited strength. So, even though the Master no longer required extraordinary size and strength—as it did with Sardu, the giant body inside which it had traveled to New York, the host the Master had to shed after it was poisoned by Setrakian—it also did not require extraordinary physical appeal and seductiveness, as with Bolivar. It would wait . . . What the Master sought for the future was convenience.

The Master had been able to view itself through Zachary's own eyes, which had been most illuminating. Bolivar's body had served the Master ably, and it was interesting to note the boy's response to his arresting appearance. He was, after all, a magnetic presence. A performer. A star. That, combined with the Master's dark talents, proved irresistible to the young man.

And the same could be said in reverse. The Master found itself telling Zachary things, not out of rank affection but in the manner of an older self to a younger self. A dialogue like that was a rarity in its prolonged existence. After all, it had consorted for centuries with some of the most hardened and ruthless souls. Sided with them, molded them to its will. In a contest of brutality, he knew no equal.

But Zack's energy was pure, his essence quite similar to his father's. A perfect pool to study and taint. All this contributed to the Master's curiosity about young Goodweather. The Master had, over the centuries, perfected the technique of reading humans, not only in nonverbal communication—known as a "tell"—but even in their omissions. A behaviorist can anticipate or detect a lie by the concert of micro-gestures that telegraphs it. The Master could anticipate a lie two beats before it even happened. Not that it cared, morally, one way or another. But to detect the truth or lie in a covenant was vital for it. It meant access or lack of it—cooperation or danger. Humans were insects to the Master and it an entomologist living among them. This discipline had lost all fascination for the Master thousands of years ago—until now. The more Zachary Goodweather tried to hide things, the more the Master was able to draw out of him—without the young man even knowing he was telling the Master everything it needed to know. And through the young Goodweather, the Master was amassing information about Ephraim. A curious name. Second son of Joseph and a woman once visited by an angel: Asenath. Ephraim, known only for his progeny—lost in the Bible, without identity or purpose. The Master smiled.

So the search continued on two fronts: for the

Lumen, containing the secret of the Black Site in its silver-bound pages, and for Ephraim Goodweather.

It occurred to the Master, many times, that he might claim both prizes at the same time.

The Master was convinced the Black Site was near at hand. All the clues indicated this was so—the very clues that had led it here. The prophecy that had forced it to cross the ocean. And yet, in an abundance of caution, its slaves continued their excavations in far-flung parts of the world to see if they could find it elsewhere.

The Black Cliffs of Negril. The Black Hills mountain range in South Dakota. The oil fields at Pointe-Noire, on the western coast of the Republic of the Congo.

In the meantime, the Master had nearly achieved complete worldwide nuclear disarmament. Having taken immediate control of the military forces of the world through the directed spread of vampirism among infantry and command officers, it now had access to much of the world's stockpiles. Rounding up and dismantling rogue nations' weaponry, as well as so-called loose nukes, would take some more time, but the end was close.

The Master looked at every corner of its Earth farm and was pleased.

The Master reached for Setrakian's wolf-headed staff, the one the vampire hunter had carried. The walking stick had once belonged to Sardu and had been refitted to include a silver blade when twisted open. It was nothing more than a trophy now, a symbol of the Master's victory. The token amount of silver in its silver handle did not bother the Master, though it took great care not to touch the ornamental wolf's head.

The Master carried it into the castle turret, the highest point in the park, and stepped outside into the oily rain. Beyond the spindly upper branches of the denuded treetops, through the thick haze of fog and pollution-heavy air, stood the dirty gray buildings, the East Side and the West Side. In the glowing register of his heat-sensitive vision, thousands upon thousands of empty windows stared down like the cold, dead eyes of fallen witnesses. The dark sky roiled above, voiding filth on the defeated city.

Below the Master, forming an arc around the base of the raised rock foundation, stood the guardians of the castle, twenty deep. Beyond them, in answer to the Master's psychic call, a sea of vampires had assembled on the fifty-five-acre Great Lawn, each staring up with black-moon eyes.

No cheer. No salute. No exultation. A still and quiet congregation; a silent army, awaiting its orders.

Kelly Goodweather appeared at the Master's side, and, next to her, the Goodweather boy. Kelly Goodweather had been summoned; the boy had wandered over out of pure curiosity.

The Master's command went out to every vampire's mind.

Goodweather.

There was no answer to the Master's call. The

only response would be action. In due time, he would kill Goodweather—first his soul, and then his body. Unbearable suffering would be endured.

He would make sure of that.

Roosevelt Island

PRIOR TO ITS late-twentieth-century reinvention as a planned community, Roosevelt Island was home to the city's penitentiary, its lunatic asylum, and its smallpox hospital, and was previously known as Welfare Island.

Roosevelt Island had always been a home for New York City's castaways. Fet was that now.

He had decided that he would rather live in isolation on this narrow, two-mile-long island in the middle of the East River than reside in the vampire-ruin city or its infested boroughs. He could not bear to live inside an occupied New York. Apparently, the river-phobic *strigoi* could find no use for this small satellite island of Manhattan, and so, soon after the takeover, they cleared the island of all residents and set it afire. The cables to the tram at Fifty-ninth Street had been cut and the Roosevelt Island Bridge destroyed at its terminus in Queens. The F line subway still ran through the island beneath the river, but the Roosevelt Island Station stop had been permanently walled up.

But Fet knew a different way in from the underwater tunnel up to the geographic center of the island. An access tunnel built to service the island community's unusual pneumatic tube system of refuse collection and disposal. The vast majority of the island, including its once-towering apartment buildings offering magnificent Manhattan views, was in ruins. But Fet had found a few mostly undamaged belowground units in the luxury apartment complex constructed around the Octagon, formerly the main building of the old lunatic asylum. There, well concealed among the destruction, he had sealed off the burned top floors and joined four bottom-floor units. The water and electricity pipes under the river had not been disturbed, so once the borough grids were repaired Fet had power and potable water.

Under cover of daylight, the smugglers dropped off Fet and the Russian nuke at the northern end of the island. He retrieved a wheeled hardware-store pallet cart he kept stashed in a hospital utility shed near the rocky shoreline and towed the weapon and his rucksack and a small Styrofoam cooler through the rain to his hideout.

He was excited to see Nora and even feeling a bit giddy. Return journeys will do that. Also, she was the only one who knew he was meeting with the Russians, and so he arrived with his great prize in tow like a boy with a school trophy. His sense of accomplishment was amplified by the excitement and enthusiasm he knew she would show him.

However, when he arrived at the charred door that led inside to his concealed subterranean chamber, he found it open a few inches. This was not a mistake Dr. Nora Martinez would ever make. Fet quickly removed his sword from his bag. He had to tow the cart inside in order to get it out of the rain. He left it in the fire-damaged hallway and walked down the partially melted flight of stairs.

He entered his unlocked door. His hideaway did not require much security, because it was so well hidden and because, other than the rare maritime smuggler risking a journey along the Manhattan interior, almost no one else ever set foot on the island anymore.

The spare kitchen was unoccupied. Fet lived largely on snack food pilfered and stockpiled after the first few months of the siege, crackers and granola bars and Little Debbie cakes and Twinkies that were now reaching or, in some cases, already surpassing their "sell by" dates. Contrary to popular belief, they *did* become inedible. He had tried his hand at fishing, but the sooty river water was so rife with blight he was worried that no flame could get hot enough to safely cook out the pollution.

He moved through the bedroom after a quick check of the closets. The mattress on the floor had been just fine with him until the prospect of Nora perhaps staying overnight made him hunt for a proper bed frame. The spare bathroom, where Fet kept the rat-hunting equipment he had salvaged from his old storefront shop in the Flatlands, a few instruments from his former vocation that he had been unable to part with, was otherwise empty.

Fet ducked through the hole he had sledge-hammered open, into the next unit, which he used as a study. The room was stocked with bookshelves and stacked cartons of Setrakian's library and writings, centered around a leather sofa under a low-hanging reading lamp.

At about two o'clock in the circularly arranged room stood a hooded figure, well over six feet tall, strongly built. His face receded into the black cotton hood, but the eyes were apparent, piercing and red. In his pale hands was a notebook filled with Setrakian's fine handwriting.

He was a *strigoi*. But he was clothed. He wore pants and boots in addition to the hooded sweatshirt.

He eyed the rest of the room, thinking ambush.

I am alone.

The *strigoi* put his voice directly into Fet's head. Fet looked again at the notebook in his hands. This was a sanctuary to Fet. This vampire had invaded it. He could easily have destroyed it. The loss would have been catastrophic.

"Where is Nora?" Fet asked, and then moved on the *strigoi*, unsheathing his sword as fast as a man of Fet's size can move. But the vampire at once eluded him and pushed him down to the ground. Fet roared in anger and tried to wrestle his opponent, but no matter what he did, the *strigoi* would retaliate with a block and a crippling move, immobilizing Fet—hurting him just enough.

I have been here alone. Do you, by chance, remember who I am, Mr. Fet?

Fet did, vaguely. He remembered that this one

had once held an iron spike at his neck, inside an old apartment high above Central Park.

"You were one of those hunters. The Ancients' personal bodyguards."

Correct.

"But you didn't vaporize with the rest."

Obviously not.

"Q something."

Quinlan.

Fet freed his right arm and tried to connect with the creature's cheek but the wrist was clamped and twisted in the blink of an eye. This time it hurt. A lot.

Now, I can dislocate this arm or I can break it. Your choice. But think about it. If I wanted you dead, you would be by now. Over the centuries I have served many masters, fought many wars. I have served emperors and queens and mercenaries. I have killed thousands of your kind and hundreds of rogue vampires. All I need from you is a moment. I need you to listen. If you attack me again, I will kill you instantly. Do we understand each other?

Fet nodded. Mr. Quinlan released him.

"You didn't die with the Ancients. Then you must be one of the Master's breed . . ."

Yes. And no.

"Uh-huh. That's convenient. Mind me asking how you got here?"

Your friend Gus. The Ancients had me recruit him for sun hunting.

"I remember. Too little, too late, as it turned out."

Fet remained guarded. This didn't add up. The

Master's wily ways made him paranoid, but it was precisely this paranoia that had kept Fet alive and unturned over the past two years.

I am interested in viewing the Occido Lumen. *Gus told me that you might be able to point me in the right direction.*

"Fuck you," said Fet. "You'll have to go through me to get it."

Mr. Quinlan appeared to smile.

We seek the same goal. And I have a little more of an edge when it comes to deciphering the book and Setrakian's notes.

The *strigoi* had closed Setrakian's notebook—one that Fet had reread many times. "Good reading?"

Indeed. And impressively accurate. Professor Setrakian was as learned as he was cunning.

"He was the real deal, all right."

He and I almost met once before. About twenty miles north of Kotka, in Finland. He had somehow tracked me there. At the time I was wary of his intentions, as you might imagine. In retrospect, he would have made for an interesting dinner companion.

"As opposed to a meal himself," said Fet. He thought that perhaps a quick test was in order. He pointed at the text in Q's hands. "Ozryel, right? Is that the name of the Master?" he said. Fet had brought along with him on his voyage some copied pages of the *Lumen* to study whenever possible—including an image Setrakian had first focused on upon opening the *Lumen*. The archangel whom Setrakian referred to as Ozryel. The old professor had lined up this illuminated page with the alchemical symbol of three crescent moons combined to form a rudimentary biohazard sign, in such a way that the twinned images achieved a kind of geometric symmetry. "The old man called Ozy 'the angel of death.' "

It's "Ozy" now, is it?

"Sorry, yeah. Nickname. So—it was Ozy who became the Master?"

Partially correct.

"Partially?"

Fet had lowered his sword by now and leaned on it like a cane, the silver point making another notch in the floor.

"See, Setrakian would have had one thousand questions for you. Me, I don't even know where to start."

You already started.

"I guess I did. Shit, where were you two years ago?"

I've had work to do. Preparations.

"Preparations for what?"

Ashes.

"Right," Fet said. "Something about the Ancients, collecting their remains. There were three Old World Ancients."

You know more than you think you do.

"But still not enough. See, I just returned from a journey myself. Trying to track down the provenance of the *Lumen*. A dead end . . . but something else broke my way. Something that could be big."

Fet thought of the nuke, which made him remember his excitement at returning home, which made him remember Nora. He moved to a laptop computer, waking it from a weeklong sleep. He checked the encrypted message board. No postings from Nora since two days ago.

"I have to go," he told Mr. Quinlan. "I have many questions, but there might be something wrong, and I have to go meet someone. I don't suppose there's any chance you'll wait here for me?"

None. I must have access to the Lumen. *Like the sky, it is written in a language beyond your comprehension. If you produce it for me . . . next time we meet I can promise you a plan of action . . .*

Fet felt an overwhelming urge to hurry, a sudden sense of dread. "I'll have to talk to the others first. This is not a decision I can make alone."

Mr. Quinlan remained still in the half-light.

You may find me through Gus. Just know there is precious little time. If ever a situation called for decisive action, this is it.

INTERLUDE I

MR. QUINLAN'S STORY

THE YEAR 40 AD, THE LAST FULL YEAR OF THE REIGN of Gaius Caligula, emperor of Rome, was marked by extraordinary displays of hubris, cruelty, and insanity. The emperor began appearing in public dressed as a god, and various public documents of the time refer to him as "Jupiter." He had the heads removed from statues of gods and replaced with images of his own head. He forced senators to worship him as a physical living god. One of these Roman senators was his horse, Incitatus.

The imperial palace on the Palatine was extended to annex a temple erected for Caligula's worship. Among the emperor's court was a former slave, a pale, dark-haired boy of fifteen years, summoned by the new sun god at the behest of a soothsayer who was never again seen. The slave was renamed Thrax by the emperor.

Legend held that Thrax had been discovered in an abandoned village in the savage hinterlands of the far East: the frozen regions, inhabited only by the most Barbaric tribes. His reputation was that of a being of great brutality and cunning despite his innocent, fragile appearance. Some claimed he was gifted with the power of prophecy, and Caligula was instantly enthralled by him. Thrax was only seen at night, usually seated at Caligula's side, where he exerted great influence for one so young—or else alone in the temple under the light of the moon, his pale skin glowing like alabaster. Thrax spoke several Barbaric tongues, and quickly learned Latin and science—his voracious desire for knowledge surpassed only by his appetite for cruelty. He quickly earned a sinister reputation in Rome, at a time when it was considered an achievement to distinguish oneself by cruelty alone. He advised Caligula politically and dispensed or withdrew imperial favor with complete ease. Regardless, he encouraged the emperor's rise to divinity. They could be seen sitting side by side at the Circus Maximus, fervently supporting the Roman Green stables in the horse races. It was rumored, in fact, that it was Thrax who suggested they poison the rival stables after a loss of their team.

Caligula could not swim, and neither could Thrax, who inspired the emperor to erect his greatest folly: a temporary floating bridge, more than two miles long, using ships as pontoons, connecting the port city of Baiae to the port city of Puteoli. Thrax was not present when Caligula triumphantly rode Incitatus across the Bay of Baiae, attired in Alexander the Great's original breastplate—but it was said that the former slave later made many night crossings, always in a litter carried by four Nubian slaves, dressed in the finest garments, an unholy *sedia gestatoria* flanked by a dozen guards.

Habitually, once a week, seven handpicked female slaves were brought to Thrax in his gold and alabaster chamber beneath the temple. He demanded they be virgins, in perfect health, and no older than nineteen. Tiny swabs of their sweat would be used to select them during the course of the week. At nightfall on the seventh day, the ironwood door would be barred from within.

The first killing took place on a green marble pedestal at the center of the chamber, with sculptural relief depicting a mass of writhing, pleading bodies, raising their supplicant eyes and arms toward the heavens. Twin canals at the base redirected the flowing slave blood into gold cups encrusted with rubies and garnets.

Thrax emerged out of a passage, wearing only his *subligar*, and quietly ordered the slave to climb upon the pedestal. There he drank her in full view of the seven bronze mirrors hanging from the chamber walls, biting her fiercely as he punctured her throat with his stinger. The suction was so sudden, so swift, that one could actually see the veins collapsing beneath the slave's skin as the color drained from her flesh within seconds. Thrax's wiry arms restrained the slave's torso with great strength and expert control.

When the entertainment of the ensuing panic faded, a second slave was swiftly attacked, feasted on, and brutally killed. There followed a third and a fourth and so on, until one terrorized slave remained. Thrax savored the final kill the most. Satiating.

But one night late in winter, Thrax slowed before finishing the final slave, having detected an extra pulse in the slave's blood. He felt her belly through her tunic and found it firm and swollen. Confirming her pregnancy, Thrax brutally slapped her down, her blood trailing from his mouth. He went for a gold dagger, kept next to a cornucopia of fresh fruit. He sliced at her, going for the neck—only to have his expert blow deflected by her bare forearm, severing her outer muscles and missing the tendons by mere millimeters. Thrax lunged again but was stopped by the girl. Despite his speed and skill, he remained at a disadvantage due to his underdeveloped, adolescent body. So *weak* in spite of his time-honed technique.

The Master thereby resolved never again to occupy any vehicle younger than thirteen years of age. The slave girl wept and begged the Master to spare her life and that of her unborn child—all the while bleeding deliciously. She invoked the names of her gods. But her pleas meant nothing to the Master—except as part of the feeding process: the sizzling sound of bacon in the frying pan.

At that moment, palace guards came pounding at his door. Their orders were to never interrupt his weekly ceremony, but, because they knew his penchant for cruelty, the Master knew that their reason for disturbing him must be one of importance. Accordingly, the Master unbarred the door and admitted them to the gory scene. Months of palace duty had inured the guards to the sight of such desecration and perversion. They informed Thrax that Caligula had survived an assassination attempt and summoned him to the emperor's side.

The slave needed to be dispatched and her pregnancy terminated. The rules dictated as much. But the Master did not want to be cheated of his weekly sport, and so Thrax ordered that the doors be guarded until his return.

It turned out that the supposed assassination plot was simply a bout of imperial hysteria, resulting in the slaying of seven innocent orgy guests. Thrax returned to his chamber not much later to discover that while he was away assuaging the sun god, the centurions had cleared the palace grounds, including the temple, in order to quell the phantom coup. The pregnant slave—infected, wounded—was gone.

As dawn approached, Thrax persuaded Caligula to dispatch soldiers into all the surrounding cities to find the slave and return her to the temple. Despite a near-sacking of their own land, the soldiers failed to find her. When nightfall finally returned, Thrax went out in search of the slave, but his imprint upon her mind was weak due to her pregnancy. The Master was only a few hundred years old at the time and still apt to make mistakes.

This particular omission would dog the Master for centuries to come. For within the first month of the new year, Caligula was indeed assassinated, and his successor, Claudius, after a brief period of exile, came into power by procuring the support of the Praetorian guard—and the evil slave Thrax found himself purged and on the run.

The pregnant slave girl kept moving south, back to the land of her Dear Ones. She gave birth to a pale, nearly translucent baby boy, its skin the color of marble in moonlight. He was born in a cave amid an olive field near Sicily and in that dry land they hunted for years. The slave and the baby shared a weak psychic bond, and although they both survived on the blood of humans, the boy lacked the infecting pathogen necessary to turn his victims.

Rumors of a demon spread throughout the Mediterranean as the Born grew—and grew quickly. The half boy could sustain limited exposure to the sun without perishing. But otherwise, tainted by the curse of the Master, he possessed all of the vampiric attributes, with the exception of the enslaving link to his creator.

But if the Master was ever destroyed, so he would be too.

A decade later, as the Born was returning to his cave just before dawn, he sensed a presence. He saw, within the shadows of the cave, a deeper shadow still, stirring, watching him. Then he felt the voice of his mother waning within him—her signal extinguished. He knew instantly what had happened: whatever was in there had done away with his mother . . . and now awaited him. Without even seeing his enemy, the Born knew the intensity of its cruelty. The thing in the shadows knew no mercy. With absolutely no hesitation, the Born turned away and escaped toward his only refuge: the light of the morning sun.

The Born survived as best he could. He scavenged and hunted and occasionally robbed travelers in the Sicilian crossroads. Soon he was captured and brought to justice. He was indentured and trained as a gladiator. In exhibitions, the Born defeated every challenger, human or beast, and his unnatural talents and peculiar appearance drew the attention of the senate and the Roman military. On the eve of their ceremonial branding, an ambush by multiple rivals jealous of his success and attention resulted in multiple sword wounds, fatal blows that, miraculously, did not kill him. He healed quickly and was immediately withdrawn from the gladiator school, taken in by a senator, Faustus Sertorius, who had a passing familiarity with the dark arts and held a considerable collection of primitive artifacts. The senator recognized the gladiator as the fifth immortal to be birthed by human flesh and vampiric blood, and thus named him Quintus Sertorius.

The strange *peregrinus* was inducted into the army's *auxilia* at first but quickly rose through the ranks and joined the third legion. Under the banner of Pegasus, Quintus crossed the ocean to wage war in Africa against the fierce Berbers. He became proficient in handling the *pilum*, the

Roman elongated lance, and it is said that he could throw it with such force as to take down a horse in full gallop. He wielded a double-edged steel sword, a *gladius hispaniensis*, forged specially for him—void of any silver ornaments and with a bone grip made from a human femur.

Through the decades, Quintus took the victorious march from the temple of Bellona to the Porta Triumphalis many times and served through generations and various reigns, at the pleasure of every emperor. Rumors about his longevity added to his legend and he grew to be both feared and admired. In Brittania, he struck terror into the hearts and minds of the Pict army. Among the German Gamabrivii, he was known as the Shadow of Steele, and his mere presence kept the peace along the banks of the Euphrates.

Quintus was an imposing figure. His chiseled physique and preternaturally pale skin gave him the appearance of a living, breathing statue carved of the purest marble. Everything about him was martial and combative, and he carried himself with the greatest assurance. He put himself at the head of every charge, and he was the last to leave the battleground. For the first few years he kept trophies, but, as the slaughter became repetitive, and as these keepsakes began to clutter his domicile, he lost interest. He broke down the rules of combat to exactly fifty-two moves: techniques of balletic precision that brought down his adversaries in fewer than twenty seconds.

At every step of his career, Quintus felt the persecution of the Master, who had long since abandoned the fifteen-year-old slave Thrax's body as its host. There were thwarted ambushes, slave vampire attacks, and, only rarely, direct assaults by the Master in various guises. At first Quintus was confused by the nature of these attacks, but over time, he became curious about his progenitor. His Roman military training taught him to go on the offensive when threatened, and so he began tracking the Master, in a search for answers.

At the same time, the Born's exploits and his growing legend brought him to the attention of the Ancients, who approached him one night in the middle of battle. Through his contact with them, the Born learned the truth about his lineage and the background of the wayward Ancient they referred to as "the Young One." They showed him many things under the assumption that, once their secrets were revealed to him, the Born would naturally join them.

But Quintus refused. He turned his back on the dark order of vampire lords born of the same cataclysmic force as the Master. Quintus had spent all his life among humans, and he wanted to try to adapt to their kind. He wanted to explore that half of him. And, despite the threat the Master posed to him, he wished to live as an immortal among mortals, rather than—as he thought of himself then—a half-breed among purebreds.

Having been born out of omission rather than action, Quintus was unable to procreate in any way. He was unable to reproduce and could never truly claim a woman as his very own. Quintus lacked the pathogen that would have allowed him to spread the infection or subjugate any humans to his will.

At the end of his campaign days, Quintus found himself a legate and was given a fertile plot of land and even a family: a young Berber widow with olive skin, dark eyes, and a daughter of her own. In her, he found affection and intimacy and eventually love. The dark woman sang for him sweet songs in her native tongue and lulled him to sleep in the deep cellars of his home. During a time of relative peace, they kept house on the shore of southern Italy. Until one night when he was away, and the Master visited her.

Quintus came back to find his family turned and lying in wait, attacking him along with the Master. Quintus had to fight them all at once, releasing his savage wife and then her child. He barely survived the Master's onslaught. At the time, the vehicle chosen by the Master was the body of a fellow legionnaire, an ambitious, ruthless tribune named Tacitus. The short but sturdy and muscular body gave the Master ample margin in the fight. There were almost no legionnaires under five foot ten, but Tacitus had been admitted because he was strong as an ox. His arms and neck were thick and short and made of bulging strands of muscle. His mountainous shoulders and back gave him a slightly hunched aspect but now, as he towered over a beaten Quintus, Tacitus was as straight as a marble column. Quintus had, however, prepared for this occasion—both fearing it and hoping it would one day come. In a hidden fold of his belt, he hid a narrow silver blade—sheathed away from his skin but with a carved sandalwood handle that allowed him to retrieve it fast. He pulled it out and slashed Tacitus across the face, bisecting his eye and snapping his right cheekbone in two. The Master howled and covered its injured eye, out of which blood and vitreous humor poured forth. In a single bound, it jumped out of the house and into the darkened garden beyond.

When he recovered, Quintus felt a loneliness that would never leave him again. He swore revenge upon the creature that created him—even though such an act would mean his own demise as well.

Many years later, upon the advent of the Christian faith, Quintus returned to the Ancients, acknowledging who and what he was. He offered them his wealth, his influence, and his strength, and they welcomed him as one of their own. Quintus warned them of the Master's perfidy, and they acknowledged the threat but never lost confidence in their numerical advantage and the wisdom of their years.

Through the ensuing centuries Quintus continued his quest for vengeance.

But for the next seven centuries, Quintus—later Quinlan—never got closer to the Master than he did one night in Tortosa, in what is now known as Syria, when the Master called him "son."

My son, wars this long can only be won by yielding. Lead me to the Ancients. Help me destroy them and you may take your rightful place at my side. Be the prince that you truly are . . .

The Master and Quintus were standing at the edge of a rocky cliff overlooking a vast Roman necropolis. Quinlan knew that the Master had no escape. The nascent rays of daylight were already causing him to smoke and burn. The Master's words were unexpected and his voice, in Quinlan's head, an intrusion. Quinlan felt an intimacy that scared him. And for a moment—which he would live to regret for the rest of his life—he felt true belonging. This thing—having taken refuge in the tall, pale body of an ironworker—was his father. His true father. Quinlan lowered his weapon for an instant, and the Master rapidly crawled down the rocky cliff face, disappearing into a system of crypts and tunnels below.

Centuries later, a ship sailed from Plymouth, England, to Cape Cod in the newly discovered territory of America. The ship was carrying 130 passengers according to the official manifest, but within the cargo compartments several boxes containing earth could be found. The items listed within were earth and tulip bulbs; presumably their owner wanted to take advantage of the coastal climate. The reality was far darker. Three of the Ancients and their loyal ally Quinlan established themselves rather rapidly in the New World, under the auspices of a rich merchant: Kiliaen Van Zanden. The settlements in the New World were in fact little more than a collective banana republic whose mercantile ways were grown into the preeminent economic and military power on the planet in fewer than two centuries' time—all of which was essentially a front for the real business being conducted belowground and behind closed doors. All efforts were focused on the acquisition of the *Occido Lumen*, in hopes of answering what, at that time, was the only question remaining for Quinlan and the Ancients:

How could they destroy the Master?

Camp Liberty

Dr. Nora Martinez awoke to the shrill camp whistle. She lay in a canvas stretcher hanging from the ceiling, enveloping her like a sling. The only way out was to shimmy under her blanket, escaping through the end, feet first.

Standing, she sensed immediately that something wasn't right. She turned her head this way and that. It felt too light. Her free hand went immediately to her scalp.

Bare. Completely bald. This shocked her. Nora didn't have many vanities, but she'd been blessed with gorgeous hair, keeping it long even though—as an epidemiologist—it was an impractical choice for a professional. She gripped her scalp now as though fighting a searing migraine, feeling bare flesh where she never had before. Tears rolled down her cheeks and she suddenly felt smaller and—somehow, but truly—weakened. In shaving off her hair, they had also cut away a bit of her strength.

But her unsteadiness wasn't just the result of her bare scalp. She felt groggy, swaying for balance. After the confusing admittance process, and her attendant anxiety, Nora was amazed she had been able to sleep at all. In fact, she now remembered that she had been determined to remain awake, in order to learn as much as she could about the quarantine area before proceeding into the general population of the absurdly named Camp Liberty.

But this taste in her mouth now—as though she had been gagged with a fresh cotton sock—told Nora that she had been drugged. That bottle of drinking water she had been issued—they had doped it.

Anger rose inside her, some of it aimed at Eph. Unproductive. Instead, she focused on Fet, yearning for him. She was almost certain never to see either of those two men again. Not unless she could find some way out of this place.

The vampires who ran the camp—or perhaps their human co-conspirators, contract members of the Stoneheart Group—wisely enforced a quarantine for new entries. This type of encampment was tinder for an infectious disease event, one that had the potential to wipe out the camp population, their precious blood providers.

A woman entered the room through the canvas flaps that hung over the doorway. She wore a slate-gray jumpsuit, the same color and bland style as Nora's. Nora recognized her face, remembering her from yesterday. Terrifically thin, her skin a pale parchment wrinkled at the corners of her eyes and her mouth. Her dark hair was close-cropped, her scalp due for a shave. Yet the woman appeared upbeat, for some reason Nora could not fathom. Her function here was apparently that of a camp mother of sorts. Her name was Sally.

Nora asked her, as she had the day before, "Where is my mother?"

Sally's smile was all customer service, tolerant and disarming. "How did you sleep, Ms. Rodriguez?"

Nora had given a false name upon admission, as her association with Eph had certainly landed her name on every watch list. "I slept just fine," she said. "Thanks to the sedative mixed into my water. I asked you where my mother is."

"My assumption is that she has been transferred to Sunset, which is a sort of active retirement community associated with the camp. That is normal procedure."

"Where is it? I want to see her."

"It's a separate part of the camp. I suppose a visit is possible at some point, but not now."

"Show me. Where it is."

"I could show you the gate, but . . . I've never been inside myself."

"You're lying. Or else you really believe it. Which means you're lying to yourself."

Sally was just a functionary, a messenger. Nora understood that Sally was not intentionally trying to mislead her but simply repeating what she had been told. Perhaps she had no idea, nor capacity to suspect, that this "Sunset" might not exist exactly as advertised.

"Please listen to me," said Nora, growing frantic. "My mother is not well. She is sick, she is confused. She has Alzheimer's disease."

"I am sure she'll be well looked after—"

"She will be put down. Without a moment's hesitation. She's outlived her usefulness to these things. But she is sick, she is panicked, she needs to see a familiar face. Do you understand? I just want to see her. One last time."

This was a lie, of course. Nora wanted to bust the both of them out of there. But she had to find her mother first.

"You're human. How can you do this—how?"

Sally reached out to squeeze Nora's left arm reassuringly but mechanically. "She truly is in a better place, Ms. Rodriguez. The elderly have rations sufficient to support their health and aren't required to produce anything in return. I envy them, frankly."

"Do you really believe that?" said Nora, amazed.

"My father is there," said Sally.

Nora gripped her arm. "Don't you want to see him? Show me where."

Sally was entirely sympathetic—to the point where Nora wanted to slap her. "I know it is difficult, the separation. What you have to focus on now is taking good care of yourself."

"Was it you who drugged me?"

Sally's smile drained of conviviality, replaced by concern—perhaps concern for Nora's sanity, for her future potential as a productive camp member. "I have no access to medication."

"Do they drug you?"

Sally offered no opinion on Nora's response. "Quarantine is over," she said. "You're to be part of the general camp community now, and I'm to show you around, to help you get acclimated."

Sally led her out through a small, open-air buffer zone, along a walkway beneath a tarpaulin keeping them from being soaked by rainfall. Nora looked out at the sky: another starless night. Sally had papers for the human at the checkpoint, a man in his fifties wearing a white doctor's coat over his slate-gray jumpsuit. He looked over the forms, glanced at Nora with the eyes of a customs agent, then let them through.

Rain found them despite the overhead canopy, splashing at their legs and feet. Nora wore hospital-style foam sandals with spongy soles. Sally wore a comfortable, if damp, pair of Saucony sneakers.

The path of crushed stone fed into a wide circular walkway surrounding a high lookout post similar to a lifeguard's station. The rotary formed a hub of sorts, with four other paths extending from it. Warehouse-style buildings stood nearby, long and low, with what appeared to be factory-style buildings farther away. No signs marked the way, only arrows fashioned out of white stone embedded in the muddy ground. Low-wattage lights marked the paths, necessary for human navigation.

A handful of vampires stood around the rotary like sentinels, and on seeing them, Nora fought back a chill. They were completely exposed to the elements—bare, pale skin covered by no coat or clothes—and yet showed no discomfort, the black rain striking their bare heads and shoulders, streaming down their pellucid flesh. Arms hanging limply, the *strigoi* watched the humans come and go with grave indifference. They were policemen, guard dogs, and security cameras all in one.

"Security enforces routine so that everything runs in a very orderly manner," said Sally, picking up on Nora's fright and distress. "In fact, there are very few incidents."

"Of people resisting?"

"Of any disruptions," said Sally, surprised at Nora's assumption.

Being this close to them without any sharpened silver to protect herself made Nora's skin crawl. And they smelled it. Their stingers clicked softly against their palates as they sniffed the air, alerted by the scent of her adrenaline.

Sally nudged Nora's arm in order to get her moving. "We cannot linger here. It is not allowed."

Nora felt the sentinels' black and red eyes tracking them as Sally led her down a long offshoot path leading past the warehouselike buildings. Nora sized up the high fences that formed the camp walls: chain link laced with orange hurricane stripping, obscuring the view outside the camp. The tops of the fences were angled out at forty-five degrees, beyond her view, though at a few points she glimpsed tufts of barb wire sticking up like cowlicks. She would have to find another way out.

Beyond, she saw the bare tops of distant trees. She already knew she was out of the city. There were rumors of a large camp north of Manhattan and two smaller camps in Long Island and northern New Jersey. Nora had been transported there with a hood placed over her head, and she had been too anxious and concerned about her mother to think about estimating travel time.

Sally led Nora to a rolling wire gate standing twelve feet high and at least that length wide. It was locked and manned by two female guards standing inside a gatehouse, who nodded familiarly to Sally and worked together to unlatch it and push the gate open just wide enough to admit them.

Inside stood a large barracks house resembling a homey-looking medical building. Behind it, dozens of small mobile homes were arranged in rows like a neatly maintained trailer park.

They entered the barracks house, stepping inside a wide common area. The space resembled a cross between an upscale waiting room and the lounge of a college dormitory. An old episode of *Frasier* was playing, the laugh track ringing so falsely, like the mocking of carefree humans from the past.

In cushioned, pastel-colored chairs, a dozen women sat around in clean white jumpsuits, as opposed to Nora's and Sally's dull gray. Their bellies bulged noticeably, each woman in her second or third trimester of pregnancy. And something else: they were allowed to grow their hair, made thick and lustrous from the pregnancy hormones.

And then Nora saw the fruit. One of the women was snacking on a soft, juicy peach, its inside threaded with red veins. Saliva gushed inside Nora's mouth. The only fresh, not-canned fruit she had tasted in the past year or so were mushy apples from a dying tree in a Greenwich Village courtyard. She had trimmed out the spoiled spots with a multitool blade until the remaining fruit looked like it had already been eaten.

The expression on her face must have reflected her desire, for the pregnant woman, upon meeting Nora's eyes, looked away uncomfortably.

"What is this?" said Nora.

"The birthing barracks," said Sally. "This is where pregnant women convalesce and where their infants are ultimately delivered. The trailers outside are among the best and most private living quarters in the entire compound."

"Where did she get"—Nora lowered her voice—"the fruit?"

"Pregnant women also receive the best food rations. And they are excused from being bled for the length of their pregnancy and nursing."

Healthy babies. The vampires needed to replenish the race, and their blood supply.

Sally went on. "You are one of the lucky ones, the twenty percent of the population with B-positive blood type."

Nora knew her own blood type, of course.

B positives were the slaves that were more equal than the others. For that, their reward was camp internment, frequent bloodletting, and forced breeding.

"How could they bring a child into this world as it is now? Into this so-called camp? Into captivity?"

Sally looked either embarrassed for Nora or ashamed of her. "You may come to find that childbirth is one of the few things that makes life worth living here, Ms. Rodriguez. A few weeks of camp life and you might feel different. Who knows? You may even look forward to this." Sally pushed her gray sleeve back, revealing bull's-eye bruises that looked like terrible bee stings, purpling and browning her skin. "One pint every five days."

"Look, I don't mean to offend you personally, it's just that—"

"You know, I'm trying to help you here," she said. "You're young enough still. You have opportunities. You could conceive, deliver a baby. Make a life for yourself in this camp. Some of the rest of us . . . are not so fortunate."

Nora saw this from Sally's perspective for a moment. She understood that blood loss and malnutrition had weakened Sally and everyone else, sapping the fight from them. She understood the pull of despair, the cycle of hopelessness, that sense of circling the drain—and how the prospect of childbirth could be their only source of hope and pride.

Sally went on. "And someone like yourself

who finds this so distasteful, you might appreciate being segregated from the other kind for months at a time."

Nora made sure she'd heard that correctly. "Segregated? There are no vampires in the birthing area?" She looked around and realized it was true. "Why not?"

"I don't know. It is a strict rule. They are not allowed."

"A rule?" Nora struggled to make sense of this. "Is it pregnant women who have to be segregated from vampires, or vampires who have to be segregated from pregnant women?"

"I told you, I don't know."

A tone rang, akin to a doorbell, and the women set aside their fruit or their reading material and pushed themselves up from their chairs.

"What's this?" asked Nora.

Sally had straightened up a bit as well. "The camp director. I strongly suggest you be on your best behavior."

On the contrary, she looked for a place to run to, a door, an escape. But it was too late. A contingent of camp officials arrived, humans, bureaucrats, dressed in casual business wear, not jumpsuits. They entered the central walkway, eyeing the inmates with barely concealed distaste. Their visit seemed to Nora to be an inspection, and a spot one at that.

Trailing them were two huge vampires, arms and necks still bearing tattoos from their human days. Once convicts, Nora surmised, now upper-level guards in this blood factory. Both carried dripping black umbrellas, which Nora thought strange—vampires caring about the rain—until the last man entered behind them, evidently the camp director. He wore a resplendent, mudless, blindingly white suit. Freshly laundered, as clean an article of clothing as Nora had seen in months. The tattooed vampires were this camp commandant's personal security detail.

He was old, sporting a trim, white mustache and a pointed beard, which gave him the mien of a grandfatherly Satan—the sight of which nearly choked her. She saw medals on the breast of the white suit, fit for a navy admiral.

Nora stared in disbelief. Such a bald, stunned stare that it immediately drew his attention, too late for her to turn away.

She saw the look of recognition on his face, and a sick feeling spread throughout her body like a sudden fever.

He stopped, his eyes widening in similar disbelief, then turned on his heel, walking toward her. The tattooed vampires trailed him, the old man approaching her with his hands clasped behind his back—his disbelief spreading into a sly smile.

He was Dr. Everett Barnes, the onetime director of the Centers for Disease Control and Prevention. Nora's former boss, who, now nearly two years after the fall of the government, still insisted on wearing the uniform symbolic of the Centers' origin as a branch of the U.S. Navy.

"Dr. Martinez," he said in his soft Southern drawl. "Nora . . . Why, this is a most welcome surprise."

ZACK COUGHED AND gagged as the camphor scent burned the back of his throat and overwhelmed his palate. His breathing returned, his heartbeat slowed down, and he looked up at the Master—standing before him in the form of the rock star Gabriel Bolivar—and smiled.

At night, the beasts of the zoo became very active, their instincts kicking in for a hunt that would never come behind those bars. In consequence, the night was full of noise. Monkeys howled and big cats roared. Humans now tended the cages and cleaned the streets as a reward for Zack's hunting skills.

The boy had become quite deft at shooting and the Master rewarded each kill with a new privilege. Zack was curious about girls. Women, really. The Master saw to it that he was brought some. Not to talk. Zack wanted to watch them. Mostly from a place where they couldn't see him looking. He wasn't inordinately shy or scared. If anything, he was crafty and he didn't want to be seen. He didn't want to touch them. Not yet. But he looked at them—much as he had watched the leopard in the cage.

In all his years on this earth, the Master had rarely experienced something like this: the chance to groom the body he was to occupy with such care, such attention. For hundreds of years, even under the patronage of the powerful, the Master had been in hiding, feeding and living in the shadows, avoiding its enemies and held back by the truce with the Ancients. But now the world was new, and the Master had a human pet.

The boy was bright and his soul was entirely permeable. The Master was an expert at manipulation. It knew how to push the buttons of greed, desire, vengeance—and at present, its body was quite regal. Bolivar was indeed a rock star and so, by extension, was the Master now.

If the Master suggested Zack was smart, the boy would instantly turn smarter: he would be stimulated into giving the Master his very best. Consequently, if the Master suggested the boy was cruel and cunning, the boy adopted these characteristics to please it. So, through the months and the many nights of conversation and interaction, the Master was training the boy, grooming the darkness that was already in his heart. And the Master felt something it hadn't felt in centuries: it felt admired.

Was this what it felt like—being a human father—and was being a father always such a monstrous endeavor? Molding the soul of your beloved ones in your image, in your shadow?

The end was near. The decisive times. The Master felt it in the rhythm of the universe, in the small signs and portents, in the cadence of the voice of God. The Master was to inhabit one more body for all time and its reign on Earth would endure. After all, who could stop the Master with the thousand eyes and the thousand mouths? The Master who now governed the armies and the slaves and who held the world in fear?

It could manifest its will instantly in the body of a lieutenant in Dubai or in France simply by thought. It could order the extermination of thousands and no one would know because the media existed no more. Who would try that? Who would succeed?

And then, the Master would look into the boy's eyes and at the boy's face and in them see traces of his enemy. The one enemy who, no matter how insignificant he was, would never give up.

Goodweather.

The attacks Goodweather and his group perpetrated on the Master's installation amounted to very little—vandalism at most. But their actions were murmured about—spoken of in the farms and the factories and aggrandized with every repetition. They were becoming some sort of symbol. And the Master knew the importance of symbols. On Night Zero, it had made a point to have many buildings burn in every city that he overtook. It wanted the ashes and molten metal to remain on the ground, checkering the city maps with symbols of its power. Reminders of its will.

There were other dissidents—drug dealers, smugglers, looters—but they were anarchic vectors that never intersected with the Master's plan, and so the Master cared little for their transgressions. But Goodweather was different. He and his group were remnants of Setrakian's presence on Earth, and as such their very existence was an affront to the Master's power.

But the Master held hostage the very thing that would lure Goodweather to him.

The Master smiled at the boy. And the boy smiled back.

Office of the Chief Medical Examiner, Manhattan

AFTER THE BELLEVUE Hospital explosion, Eph had worked his way north up along East River Drive, using the abandoned cars and trucks for cover. He jogged as fast as he could with his sore hip and wounded leg, moving the wrong way down an entrance ramp, back toward Thirtieth Street. He knew he had pursuers, probably including some of the juvenile feelers, the freakish, blind psychic trackers who moved on all fours. He dug out his night-vision scope and hurried back to the Office of the Chief Medical Examiner, thinking that the last place the vampires would look would be a building they had recently infiltrated and cleared.

His ears continued to ring from the concussive blast. A few car alarms honked and blared, and freshly broken glass lay in the street, high windows shattered by the force of the explosion. As he came to the corner of Thirtieth and First, he noticed chunks of bricks and mortar in the road, part of a building façade had failed, raining debris into the street. As he got closer, through the green light of his scope, he noticed a pair of legs sticking out from behind two old traffic safety barrels.

Bare legs, bare feet. A vampire lying facedown off the sidewalk.

Eph slowed, circling the barrels. He saw the vampire laid out among chunks of brick and concrete. White, worm-infested blood lay in a small pool beneath its downturned face. It wasn't released: subcutaneous worms continued to ripple beneath its flesh, meaning its blood was still circulating. Evidently, this wounded creature was unconscious, or its undead equivalent.

Eph looked for the largest chunk of brick and concrete. He lifted it over his head to finish the job . . . until a sense of gruesome curiosity came over him. He used his boot to roll the *strigoi* onto its back, the creature lying flat and still. It must have heard the rumbling of the loose bricks and looked skyward, because its face was bashed in.

The chunk of bricks grew heavy in his hands, and he lowered it, tossing it aside, letting it crash against the sidewalk just a foot away from the creature's head. No reaction.

The medical examiner's building was right across the street. A great risk—but if the creature was indeed blind, as it appeared, then it could not feed the Master its vision. And if it was also brain-damaged . . . then it could not communicate with the Master at all, and its current location could not be traced.

Eph moved quickly, before he could talk himself out of it. He got his hands beneath the creature's armpits, careful of the sticky mass of blood, and rescue-dragged him off the curb, across the street, and around to the ramp leading to the basement morgue.

Inside, he nudged over a step stool to help

him load the vampire onto an autopsy table. He worked quickly, binding the creature's wrists beneath the table with rubber tubing, then similarly affixing its ankles to the table legs.

Eph looked at the *strigoi* laid out upon the examining table. Yes, he was indeed about to do this. He pulled a pathologist's full-length smock from the closet, pulling on twin pairs of latex gloves. He taped the wrists to his sleeves and his leg cuffs to the tops of his boots, creating a seal. In a cabinet over one of the sinks, he found a clear plastic splash guard and fit it over his face. Then he wheeled over a tray and arranged upon it a dozen different stainless steel implements, all of them cutting tools.

As he was looking at the vampire, it roused into consciousness, stirring at first, rolling its head this way and that. It sensed the bindings and began to struggle against them, bucking its waist up and down off the table. Eph used another length of tubing around its waist and beneath the table, and then another across its neck, knotting it tightly underneath.

From behind the creature's head, Eph used a probe to tempt its stinger, allowing for the possibility that it still might be functioning even within its smashed face. He saw the vampire's throat buck and heard a clicking in its jaw as it tried to activate its stinging mechanism. But the mandible had been damaged internally. His only concern therefore was the blood worms, for which he kept his Luma lamp close at hand.

He drew the scalpel across the being's throat,

opening it around the tube ligature, peeling back the folds. Eph was most careful here, watching the throat column jerk, the jaw attempt to de-hinge. The fleshy protuberance that was the stinger remained retracted and limp. Eph seized its narrow tip with a clamp and pulled, the stinger extending generously. The creature tried to retake control of it, the muscle at the base twitching.

For his own safety, Eph reached for his small silver blade and amputated the appendage.

The being tensed as though shot through with pain and defecated a small amount of discharge, the smell of ripe ammonia stinging Eph's nose. White blood spilled out around the throat incision, the caustic fluid seeping onto the stretched rubber tube.

Eph carried the writhing organ to the counter, where he lay it next to a digital scale. He examined it under the light of a magnifying lens, and as it twitched like a severed lizard's tail, he noted the tiny double tip at the end. Eph bisected the organ lengthwise, then peeled back the pink flesh, exposing dilated bifurcated canals. He already knew that one canal introduced, along with the virus-infected parasitic worm, a narcotizing agent and a salivary blend of anticoagulants when a vampire stung its victim. The other canal siphoned the blood meal. The vampire did not suck the blood out of its human victim but instead relied on physics to do the extraction, the second stinger canal forming a vacuum-like connection through which arterial blood was drawn up as easily as water crawls up the stem of a plant.

The vampire could speed the capillary action if necessary by working the base of its stinger like a piston. Amazing that this complex biological system arose out of radical endogenous growth.

Human blood is more than 95 percent water. The rest is proteins, sugars, and minerals, but no fat. Tiny bloodsuckers such as mosquitoes, ticks, and other arthropods could survive on blood meals just fine. As efficient as the vampires' transmuted bodies were, as large sanguivores they had to consume a steady blood diet in order to avoid starvation. And because human blood was mostly water, they expressed waste frequently, including while feeding.

Eph left the flayed stinger upon the counter, returning to the creature. The acidic white vampire blood had eaten through the tubing across its neck, but the vampire's thrashing had subsided. Eph opened up the creature's chest, cutting down from sternum to waist in a classic Y. Through the calcified bone of the rib cage, he saw that the interior of the chest had mutated into quadrants, or chambers. He had long ago surmised that the entire digestive tract was transformed by the vampiric disease syndrome, but never, until now, had he viewed the chest cavity in its mature form.

The scientist in him found it truly extraordinary.

The human survivor in him found it absolutely repellent.

He stopped cutting when he heard footsteps on the floor above him. Hard steps—shoes—but some creatures occasionally still wore them, as quality footwear lasted longer than most other articles of clothing. He looked at the vampire's smashed face and dented head and hoped he hadn't underestimated the power of the Master's reach, unwittingly inviting a fight.

Eph took up his long sword and lamp. He stepped back into a recess near the door to the walk-in cooler, giving him a good view of the stairs. No point in hiding; vamps could hear the beating of a human heart, circulating the red blood they craved.

The footsteps descended slowly—until the last few steps, which they ran down and kicked open the door. Eph saw a flash of silver, a long blade like his own, and knew immediately who it was—and relaxed.

Fet saw Eph standing against the wall and narrowed his eyes in that way he did. The exterminator wore wool trousers and a deep-blue anorak, the buckled leather strap of his bag slung across his chest. He pulled his hood back, further revealing his grizzled face, and sheathed his blade.

"Vasiliy?" said Eph. "What the fuck are you doing here?"

Fet saw Eph's pathology smock and gloved hands, then turned toward the still-animate *strigoi* eviscerated upon the table.

"What the hell are *you* doing here?" Fet asked, lowering his sword. "I just arrived today . . ."

Eph stepped away from the wall and returned his own sword to the pack on the floor. "I am examining this vampire."

Fet came forward to the table, looking at the creature's crushed face. "Did you do that?"

"No. Not directly. He was struck by a chunk of falling concrete, caused by a hospital I blew up."

Fet looked at Eph. "I heard it. That was you?"

"They had me cornered. Almost."

Eph felt relief as soon as he saw Vasiliy—but he also felt a bolt of anger tensing his body. He stood there, frozen. Not knowing what to do. Should he embrace the ratcatcher? Or beat the shit out of him?

Fet turned back to the *strigoi* on the table, wincing at the sight. "And so you decided to bring him down here. To play with him."

"I saw an opportunity to answer some outstanding questions about our tormentors' biological system."

Fet said, "Looks more like torture to me."

"Well, that is the difference between an exterminator and a scientist."

"Maybe," said Fet, circling the table so that he faced Eph across it. "Or maybe you can't tell the difference. Maybe, since you can't hurt the Master, you grabbed this thing in its place. You do realize this creature won't tell you where your boy is."

Eph didn't like it when they threw Zack back at him like that. Eph had a stake in this battle that none of the others understood. "In studying its biology, I am looking for weaknesses in the design. Something we can exploit."

Fet said, standing across the vampire's opened body from Eph, "We know what they are. Forces of nature who invade us and exploit our bodies. Who feed off us. They are no mystery to us anymore."

The creature moaned softly and stirred on the table. Its hips thrust forward and its chest heaved as though humping an invisible partner.

"Jesus, Eph. Destroy this fucking thing." Fet backed away from the table. "Where's Nora?"

He had tried to make it sound casual and failed.

Eph took a deep breath. "I think something's happened to her."

"What do you mean 'something'? Talk."

"When I got back here, she was gone. Her mother, too."

"Gone where?"

"I think they got rousted from here and left. I haven't heard from her since. If you haven't either, then something's happened."

Fet stared, stunned. "And you figured the best thing to do was stay here and dissect a fucking vamp?"

"To stay here and wait for one of you two to get in touch with me, yes."

Fet scowled at Eph's attitude. He felt like slapping the guy—slapping him and telling him what a waste of time he was. Eph had it all and Fet had nothing, and yet Eph repeatedly squandered or overlooked his good fortune. He would have liked to slap the guy a couple of times alright. But instead he sighed heavily and said, "Take me through this."

Eph walked him upstairs, showed him the overturned chair and Nora's abandoned lamp, clothes, and weapons bag. He watched Fet's eyes, saw them burning. Given Fet's and Nora's deception, Eph had thought it might feel good to see Fet suffer—but it didn't. Nothing about this felt good. "It's bad," said Eph.

"Bad," said Fet, turning toward the windows looking out at the city. "That's all you got?"

"What do you want to do?"

"You say that as though we even have a choice. We have to go get her."

"Ah. Simple."

"Yes! Simple! You wouldn't want us to go after you?"

"I wouldn't expect it."

"Really?" said Fet, turning to him. "I guess we have fundamentally different ideas about loyalty."

"Yes, I guess we do," said Eph with enough edge on his words to make them stick.

Fet didn't respond, but he didn't back down either. "So you think she was grabbed. But not turned."

"Not here. But how can we know for sure? Unlike Zack, she has no Dear One to go after. Right?"

Another jab. Eph couldn't help himself. The computer containing their intimate correspondence was right there on the desk.

Fet understood now that Eph at least suspected something. Maybe he was daring Eph to come right out and make an open accusation, but Eph would not give him the satisfaction. So, instead of answering Eph's insinuations, Fet countered as usual, attacking Eph's vulnerable spot. "I assume you were at Kelly's house again instead of here to meet Nora at the appointed time? This obsession with your son has warped you, Eph. Yes, he needs you. But we need you too. *She* needs you. This isn't just about you and your son. Others are relying on you."

"And what about you?" said Eph. "Your obsession with Setrakian. That's what your trip to Iceland was. Doing what you think he would have done. Did you figure out all the secrets in the *Lumen*? No? I thought not. You could have been here as well, but you chose to follow in the old man's shoes, his self-appointed disciple."

"I took a chance. We have to get lucky sometime." Fet stopped himself, throwing up his hands. "But—forget all that. Focus on Nora. She's our only problem right now."

Eph said, "Best-case scenario, she's in a heavily guarded blood camp. If we guess right on which one, then all we have to do is get ourselves inside, find her, and get back out again. I can think of easier ways to commit suicide."

Fet began packing up Nora's things. "We need her. Pure and simple. We can't afford to lose anyone. We need all hands on deck if we're gonna have any chance of digging ourselves out of this mess."

"Fet. We've seen two years of this. The Master's system has taken root. We are lost."

"Wrong—just because I might have struck out on the *Lumen* doesn't mean I came back empty-handed."

Eph tried to figure out that one. "Food?"

"That too," said Fet.

Eph was not in the mood for a guessing game. Besides, at the mention of real food, his mouth had begun to water, his belly twisting into a fist. "Where?"

"In a cooler, stashed nearby. You can help me carry it."

"Carry it where?"

"Uptown," said Fet. "We need to go get Gus."

Staatsburg, New York

NORA RODE IN the backseat of a town car, speeding through rainy rural New York. The upholstery was dark and clean, but the floor mats were filthy from foot mud. Nora sat all the way over on the right, curled up in the corner, not knowing what was to come next.

She did not know where she was being taken. After her shocking encounter with her former boss Everett Barnes, Nora was led by two hulking vampires to a building with a room full of curtainless showers. The vampires remained near the only door, standing together. She could have made a stand there and refused but felt it was best to go along and see what was to come, perhaps a better chance to escape.

So she disrobed and showered. Self-consciously at first, but when she looked back at the big vampires, their eyes were focused on the far wall with their trademark distant stare, lacking any interest in the human form.

The cool spray—she could not get it hot—felt alien against her bare scalp. Her skin was prickled by needles of cold water, and the runoff spilled unimpeded down the back of her neck and naked back. The water felt good. Nora grabbed a half bar of soap sitting in a recessed tile niche. She lathered her hands and head and bare stomach and found relief in the ritual. She washed her shoulders and neck, pausing to smell the soap right against her nose—rose and lilac—a relic from the past. Someone, somewhere had made this bar of soap. Along with thousands of others, and packaged and shipped it in a normal day with traffic jams and school drops and hurried lunches. Someone had thought the bar of soap with rose and lilac scent would sell well and designed it—its shape and scent and color—to attract the attention of housewives and mothers on the crowded shelves of a Kmart or a Walmart. And now that bar of soap was here—in a processing plant. An archaeological artifact that smelled of roses and lilacs and of times gone by.

A new gray jumper was folded on a bench in the middle of the room, with a pair of white cotton panties set on top. She dressed and was led back through the quarantine station to the front gates. Above her, on an arch of rusting iron, dripped the word LIBERTY. The town car arrived, as did another one behind it. Nora got in the back of the first car; no one entered the second car.

A glasslike partition of hard plastic separated the driver from her passenger. She was a human in her early twenties, dressed in a man's chauffeur suit and cap. Her hair was shaved tight below the back of her cap brim, leading Nora to assume that she was bald, and therefore perhaps a camp resident herself. And yet the pinkness of her flesh on the back of her neck and the healthy color of her hands made Nora doubt that she was a regular bleeder.

Nora turned again, obsessing over the tail car as she had done since pulling away from the camp. She couldn't be sure, through the glare of its headlights in the dark rain, but something about the driver's posture made her think it was a vamp. A backup car, maybe, in case she tried to escape. Her own doors were completely stripped of their inside panels and armrests, with the lock and window controls removed.

She expected a long ride, but little more than two or three miles away from the camp the town car pulled off the road through an open driveway gate. Rising out of the foggy gloom at the end of a long, curling driveway was a house larger and grander than most any she had ever seen. It appeared out of the New York countryside like a European manor, with nearly every window lit warmly yellow, as though for a party.

The car stopped. The driver remained behind the wheel as a butler exited the door, holding two umbrellas, one open over his head. He pulled Nora's door open and shielded her from the dirty rain as she exited the vehicle and walked with him up slick marble steps. Inside, he disposed of the umbrellas and snapped a white towel off a nearby rack, dropping to one knee to attend to her muddied feet.

"This way, Dr. Martinez," he said. Nora followed him, her bare soles silent upon the cool floor down a wide hallway. Brightly lit rooms, floor vents pushing warm air, the pleasing odor of cleaning solution. It was all so civilized, so human. Which is to say, so dreamlike. The difference between the blood camp and this mansion was the difference between ash and satin.

The butler pulled open twin doors, revealing an opulent dining room featuring a long table with only two settings laid out, adjoining one corner. The dishes were gold-rimmed with fluted edges, a small coat of arms in the center. The glassware was crystal, but the silverware was stainless steel—not silver. It was apparently the only concession in the entire mansion to the reality of the vampire-run world.

Arranged on a brass platter kitty-corner between the twin settings were a bowl of gorgeous plums, a porcelain basket of assorted pastries, and two dishes of chocolate truffles and other confectionery treats. The plums called to her. She reached for the bowl before stopping herself, remembering the drugged water they had given her in the camp. She needed to resist temptation and, despite her hunger, make smart choices.

She did not sit, remaining standing on bare feet. Music played faintly elsewhere inside the house. There was a second door across the room, and she considered trying the knob. But she felt watched. She looked for cameras and saw none.

The second door opened. Barnes entered, again wearing his formal, all-white admiral's uniform. His skin beamed healthy and pink around his trim white Vandyke beard. Nora had almost forgotten how healthy a well-nourished human being could look.

"Well," he said, striding down the length of the table toward her. He kept one hand tucked in his pocket, aping a gentleman of the manor. "This is a much more amenable setting to reacquaint ourselves, isn't it? Camp life is so dreary. This place is my great escape." He swirled his hand at the room and the house beyond. "Too big for only me, of course. But with eminent domain, everything on the menu is priced the same, so why settle for less than the very best? It was once owned by a pornographer, I understand. Smut bought all this. So I don't feel all that bad." He smiled, the corners of his mouth pulling up the trimmed edges of his pointy beard, as he reached her end of the table. "You haven't eaten?" he said, looking at the food tray. He reached for a pastry drizzled with a sugary glaze. "I imagined you'd be famished." He looked at the pastry with pride. "I have these made for me. Every day in a bakery in Queens, just for me. I used to long for them as a kid—but I couldn't afford them . . . But now . . ."

Barnes took a bite of the pastry. He sat down at the head of the table and unfolded his napkin, smoothing it out on his knee.

Nora, once she knew the food was untainted, grabbed a plum and made quick work of it, devouring the fruit. She grabbed her own napkin to swipe at her juice-slicked chin, then reached for another.

"You bastard," she said with her mouth full.

Barnes smiled flatly, expecting better from her. "Wow, Nora—straight to the point . . . 'Realist' is more like it. You want 'opportunist'? That I might accept. Maybe. But this is a new world now. Those who accept this fact and acclimate themselves to it are much better off."

"How noble. A sympathizer with these . . . these monsters."

"On the contrary, I would say that sympathy is one trait that I lack."

"A profiteer, then."

He considered that, playing at polite conversation, finishing off his pastry and licking each of his fingertips. "Maybe."

"How about 'traitor'? Or—'motherfucker'?"

Barnes slammed his hand against the table. "Enough," he said, waving off the word as one would a pesky fly. "You're clinging to self-righteousness because that is all you have left! But look at me! Look at all that I have got . . ."

Nora didn't take her eyes from him. "They killed all the real leaders in the first weeks. The opinion makers, the powerful. Leaving room for someone like you to float to the top. That can't feel so good either. Being the floater in the flush."

Barnes smiled, pretending her opinion of him did not matter. "I am trying to be civilized. I am trying to help you. So sit . . . Eat . . . Converse . . ."

Nora pulled the other chair back from the table, in order to give herself some distance from him.

"Allow me," he said. Dull knife in hand, Barnes began preparing a croissant for her, swiping in butter and raspberry preserves. "You are using wartime terms such as 'traitor' and 'profiteer.' The war, if there ever was one, is over. A few humans such as yourself haven't accepted this new reality yet, but that is your delusion. Now—does this mean we all have to be slaves? Is that the only choice? I don't think so. There is room in the middle, even room near the top. For those few with exceptional skills and the perspicacity to apply them." He set the croissant on her plate.

"I had forgotten how slippery you were," she said. "And how ambitious."

He smiled as though she had offered him a compliment. "Well—camp living can be a fulfilled existence. Not only living for oneself but for others. This basic human biological function—the creation of blood—is an enormous resource to their kind. Do you think that leaves us with no leverage? If one plays things right, that is. If one can demonstrate to them that one has real value."

"As a jailer."

"Again—so reductive. Yours is the language of losers, Nora. I believe that the camp exists neither to punish nor oppress. It is simply a facility, constructed for mass production and maximum efficiency. My opinion—though I consider it a simple fact—is that people quickly come to appreciate living a life with clearly defined expectations. With simple, understandable rules for survival. If you provide, you will be provided for.

There is real comfort in that. The human population has decreased by almost a third worldwide. A lot is the doing of the Master, but people kill each other pursuing simple things . . . like the food you have before you. So I assure you, camp life, once you give yourself over to it fully, is remarkably stress-free."

Nora ignored the croissant prepared by his hands, pouring some lemon water from a pitcher into her glass instead. "I think the scariest thing is that you actually do believe this."

"The notion that we humans were somehow more than mere animals, mere creatures set upon this earth—that we were instead chosen to be here—is what got us into trouble. Made us settled, made us complacent. Privileged. When I think about the fairy tales we used to tell ourselves and each other about God . . ."

A servant opened the double doors, entering with a gold-foil-topped bottle balanced upon a brass tray.

"Ah," said Barnes, sliding his empty glass toward the servant. "The wine."

Nora watched the servant pour a bit into Barnes's glass. "What is all this about?" she asked.

"Priorat. Spanish. Palacios, L'Ermita, '04. You'll like it. Along with this fine house, I inherited a quite wonderful wine cellar."

"I mean all this. Me being brought here. Why? What do you want?"

"To offer you something. A great opportunity. One that could improve your lot in this new life considerably, and perhaps forever."

Nora watched him sample and okay the wine, allowing the servant to fill his glass. She said, "You need another driver? A dishwasher? A wine steward?"

Barnes smiled, with something shy behind the smile. He was looking at Nora's hands as though he wanted to take them in his own. "You know, Nora, I have always admired your beauty. And . . . to be quite candid, I always thought Ephraim didn't deserve a woman such as you . . ."

Nora opened her mouth to speak. No sound came out, only breath, emptying her lungs with a silent exhalation.

"Of course, back then, in an office environment, a government setting, it would have been . . . unprofessional to make any sort of advance on a subordinate. Termed harassment or some such. Remember those ridiculous and unnatural rules? How fussy civilization got toward the end? Now we have a much more natural order of things. He who wants and can . . . conquers and takes."

Nora swallowed finally and found her voice. "Are you saying what I think you are saying, Everett?"

He blushed a little, as though lacking the conviction of his boorishness. "There aren't many people left from my previous life. Or yours. Mightn't it be nice every once in a while to reminisce? That could be very pleasant, I think—to share experiences we had together. Work anecdotes . . . dates and places. Remembering the way things used to be? We have so much in common—our professional backgrounds, our work experience. You could even practice medicine at the camp, if you wish. I seem to recall you have a background in social work. You could tend to the ill, ready them to return to productivity. Or even pursue more serious work, if you desire. You know, I have much influence."

Nora kept her voice at an even pitch. "And in return?"

"In return? Luxury. Comfort. You would reside here, with me—on a trial basis, at first. Neither of us would want to commit to a bad situation. Over time, I think the arrangement would come together nicely. I am sorry that I didn't find you before they shaved your lovely hair. But we have wigs—"

He reached for her bare scalp, but Nora straightened fast, pulling back.

"Is this how your driver got her job?" she said.

Barnes slowly drew back his hand; his face showed regret. Not for himself, but for Nora, as though she had rudely crossed a line that could not be uncrossed.

"Well," he said, "you seemed to fall in with Goodweather, who was your boss at the time, quite easily."

She was less offended than incredulous. "So that's it," she said. "You didn't like that. You were my boss's boss. You thought you were the one who should . . . First-night rights, is that it?"

"I am merely reminding you that this is apparently not your first time around this particular block." He sat back, crossing his legs and arms, in the manner of a debater with supreme confidence in his side of the argument. "This is not an unusual situation for you to find yourself in."

"Wow," said Nora. "You really are the imbecilic bigot I always thought you would be . . ."

Barnes smiled, unfazed. "I think your choice is an easy one. Life in the camp or—potentially, if you play your cards right—life here. It is a choice no sane person would deliberate over very long."

Nora felt herself smiling in disbelief, her face twisted uncomfortably. "You dirty fuck," she said. "You are worse than a vampire, you know that? It's not need for you, just opportunity. A power trip. Real rape would be too messy for you. You'd rather tie me up with 'luxuries.' You want me grateful and compliant. Appreciative for your exploitation of me. You're a monster. I can see why you fit so well into their plans. But there are not enough plums in this house, or on this ruined planet, that would make me—"

"Perhaps a few days in a harsher environment will change your mind." Barnes's eyes had hardened while she was dressing him down. Now suddenly he appeared even more interested in her, as though feeding off this power disparity. "And if you do indeed choose to remain there, isolated and in the dark—which is of course your right—let me remind you of what you have to look forward to. Your blood type happens to be B positive, which, for whatever reason—taste? some vitamin-like benefit?—is most desirable to the vampire class. This means that you will be bred. Since you have entered the camp without a mate, one will be selected for you. He will also be B positive, in order to increase the chances for birthing more B-positive offspring. Someone such as myself. That can easily be arranged. Then, for the rest of your fertility life cycle, you will be either pregnant or nursing. Which has its advantages, as you may have seen. Better housing, better rations, two fruit and vegetable servings per day. Of course, if you should have any trouble conceiving, then after a reasonable amount of time, allowing for numerous attempts using a variety of fertility drugs, you will be relegated to camp labor and five-day bloodletting. After a while, if I may be completely candid, you will die." Barnes wore a tight smile on his face. "In addition, having taken the liberty of reviewing your intake forms, 'Ms. Rodriguez,' I believe you were admitted to the camp with your mother."

Nora felt the skin on the back of her neck—where she once had hair—tingling.

"You were apprehended on the subway while trying to hide her. I wonder where you two were going."

"Where is she?" said Nora.

"Still alive, in fact. But, as you might know, due to her age and obvious infirmity, she is scheduled to be bled and then permanently retired."

These words clouded Nora's vision.

"Now," said Barnes, unfolding his arms in order to select a white-chocolate truffle, "it is entirely possible she could be spared. Perhaps . . . this is just coming to me now, but perhaps even brought here, in a sort of semi-retirement. Given her own room, possibly a nurse. She could be well cared for."

Nora's hands trembled.

"So . . . you wanna fuck me *and* you wanna play house?"

Barnes bit into his treat, delighted to find sweet cream inside. "You know, this could have gone much more congenially. I tried the soft sell. I am a gentleman, Nora."

"You are a son of a bitch. That's what you are."

"Ha." He nodded in enjoyment. "Your Spanish temper, right? Feisty. Good."

"You goddamn monster."

"You said that, yes. Now, there is one more thing that I want you to consider. You should know that what I should have done the instant I saw you there in the detention house was identify you and turn you over to the Master. The Master would be only too pleased to learn more about Dr. Goodweather and the rest of your band of rebels. Such as their current whereabouts and the extent of their resources. Even simply where you and your mother were headed on that Manhattan subway car—or where you were coming from." Barnes smiled and nodded. "The Master would be extremely motivated to learn such information. I can say in total confidence that I believe the Master would enjoy your company even more than I would. And it would use your mother to get to you. No question about that. If you go back to the camp without me you will eventually be discovered. I can assure you of that, too." Barnes stood, smoothing out the creases in his admiral's uniform, brushing away the crumbs. "So—now you understand that you have a third option as well. A date with the Master, with eternity as a vampire."

Nora's gaze blurred into the middle distance. She felt lethargic, almost dizzy. She believed that this was something like what it must feel like to be bled.

"But you have a decision to mull over," said Barnes. "I won't keep you any longer. I know you want to get right back to the camp—to your mother, while she is still alive." He went to the double doors, pushing them open out into the grand hallway. "Do think it over, and let me know what you decide. Time is running out . . ."

Unseen by him, Nora pocketed one of the butter knives at the table.

Beneath Columbia University

COLUMBIA UNIVERSITY HAD been, Gus knew, a big-shot school. Lots of old buildings, crazy expensive tuition, mucho security and cameras. He used to see some of the students out trying to mix with the neighborhood, some for community-minded reasons, which he never understood, and others for more illicit reasons, which he understood very well. But as for the university itself, the derelict Morningside Heights campus and all of its facilities, there was nothing much worth his time.

Now it was Gus's base, his headquarters and his home. The Mexican gangbanger would never be made to leave his turf; indeed, he would blow it all up before allowing that to happen. As his sabotage and hunting activities dwindled in number and became more regimented, Gus started to look for a permanent base. He really needed it. It was hard to be efficient in this mad new world. Sticking it to the man became a 24/7 occupation, and one that was less and less rewarding every time. Police and fire departments, medical services, traffic surveillance—everything had been co-opted. When searching his old Harlem haunts for a place to coop, he'd connected with two of his La Mugre gangbangers and fellow saboteurs, Bruno Ramos and Joaquin Soto.

Bruno was fat—no other way to say it—fed mostly with Cheetos and beer. Joaquin was tight and lean. Groomed, tattooed, and full of 'tude. They were both brothers to Gus and they would die for him. Born ready.

Joaquin had done jail time with Gus. They'd done cell time together. Sixteen months for Gus. They'd watched each other's back and Joaquin had done solitary for a good stretch after elbowing the teeth out of a guard, a big black guy named Raoul—what a fucked-up name for someone with no teeth: Raoul. After the vampires' arrival—what some called the Fall—Gus had reconnected with Joaquin during the looting of an electronics store. Joaquin and Bruno helped him carry a big plasma TV and a box of video games.

Together they had taken the university and found it to be only slightly infested. Windows and doors were boarded and sealed with steel plates, the interiors razed and desecrated with ammonia waste. The students had all fled early, trying to evacuate the city and get back home. Joaquin guessed they never got very far.

What they found, in prowling around the deserted buildings, was a system of tunnels below the foundation. A book in the display case at the admissions office tipped Joaquin off to the fact that the campus had originally been erected on the grounds of a nineteenth-century insane asylum. The university architects had leveled all the existing hospital buildings except one and then built upon the existing foundations. Many of the linking tunnels were used for utilities, steam pipes generating scalding condensation, miles of electric wiring. Over time, a number of these passages had been boarded up or otherwise sealed in order to prevent injury to thrill-seeking students and urban spelunkers.

Together they had explored and claimed for themselves much of this underground network linking almost all of Columbia's seventy-one campus buildings located between Broadway and Amsterdam on New York's Upper West Side. Some more remote sections remained unexplored, simply because there wasn't enough time in the day or night for hunting vampires, sowing chaos throughout Manhattan, and clearing musty tunnels.

Gus had carved out his own digs, concentrated in one quadrant of the campus's main plaza. His domain started beneath the only remaining building original to the asylum, Buell

Hall; ran beneath the Low Memorial Library and Kent Hall; and terminated at Philosophy Hall, the building outside of which was a bronze statue of a naked dude just sitting there, thinking.

The tunnels made for a cool crib, a real villain's lair. The failure of the steam system meant he could access areas rarely visited in at least a century—the coarse black fibers sticking out of cracks in the underground walls were actual horsehairs used to strengthen the plaster mix—which had led him into a dank subbasement of iron-barred cells.

The loony bin. Where they caged up the maddest of the mad. No skeletons in chains or anything like that, though they had found scratches in the stonemasonry, like the jagged clawing of fingernails, and it didn't take much imagination to hear ghostly echoes of the hideous, soul-baring screams from centuries past.

This was where he kept her. His *madre*. In an eight-by-six cage made of iron bars running ceiling to floor, forming a semicircle creating a corner cell. Gus's mother's hands were manacled behind her back with a pair of thick wrist cuffs he had found under a table in a nearby chamber, for which there was no key. A full-face black motorcycle helmet covered her head, much of the finish chipped away from her repeated headlong ramming against the bars during the first few months of her captivity. Gus had superglued the neck curtain of the helmet to her flesh. This was the only way he could fully contain her vampire stinger, for his own safety. It also covered the growing turkey wattle, the sight of which sickened him. He had removed the clear plastic face plate and replaced it with a padlocked iron flat, sprayed black and hinged at the sides. He had baffled the ear molds inside the helmet with thick cotton wadding.

She could therefore neither see nor hear anything, and yet, whenever Gus entered the chamber, the helmet turned and tracked him. Her head turned, eerily attuned to his walk, following him across the room. She gurgled and squealed as she stood in the center of the rounded corner cell, unclothed, her worn vampire body grimy from the asylum's century-old dust. Gus had once attempted to clothe her through the bars, using cloaks, coats, then blankets, but they all fell away. She had no need for clothes and no concept of modesty. The soles of her feet had developed a pad of calluses, as thick as the treads on a pair of tennis sneakers. Insects and lice wandered freely over her body and her legs were stained, tanned by repeated defecation. Chaps of brown skin were delineated around her veiny, pale thighs and calves.

Months ago, after the fight inside the Hudson River train tunnel, once the air had cleared, Gus had separated from the others. Part of it was his nature, but part of it was his mother. He knew that she would soon find him—her Dear One—and he prepared for her arrival. When she did, Gus got the drop on her, bagging her head and hog-tying her. She fought him with ridiculous vampire strength, but Gus managed to jam the helmet on her, caging her head and trapping her stinger. Then he manacled her wrists and dragged her by the neck of the helmet to this dungeon. Her new home.

Gus reached in through the bars, sliding up her faceplate. Her dead black pupils, rimmed with scarlet, stared out at him, mad, soulless, but full of hunger. Every time he raised the iron shield, he could feel her desire to unleash her stinger, and sometimes, if she tried repeatedly, thick curtains of lubricant oozed out of any fissure in the seal.

In the course of their domestic life, Bruno, Joaquin, and Gus had formed a great, imperfect family together. Bruno was always ebullient and for some reason, he had the gift of cracking up both Gus and Joaquin. They shared every duty in the household but only Gus was allowed direct contact with his mother. He washed her, head to toe, every week and kept her cell as clean and dry as he humanly could.

The dented helmet gave her a machinelike appearance, like a banged-up robot or android. Bruno remembered a bad old movie he saw on TV late one night called *Robot Monster*. In the film, the titular creature had a steel helmet screwed atop a brutish apelike body. This is how he saw the Elizaldes: *Gustavo vs. the Robot Monster.*

Gus pulled a small pocketknife from his jacket and unfolded the silver blade. His mother's eyes watched him carefully—like a caged animal's. He pushed back his left sleeve, then extended both arms through the iron bars, holding them above her helmeted head as her dead eyes tracked the silver blade. Gus pressed the sharpened point against his left forearm, cutting, leaving a thin incision of less than half an inch in length. Rich, red blood spilled from the wound. Gus angled his arm so that the blood ran down to his wrist, dripping into the open helmet.

He watched his mother's eyes as her mouth and stinger worked unseen inside the helmet, ingesting the blood meal.

She got maybe a shot glass's worth of him before he pulled his arms back outside the cage. Gus retreated to a small table he kept across the room, ripping a square of paper towel from a thick brown roll and applying direct pressure to the wound, then sealing the cut with liquid bandage squeezed from an almost-empty tube. He pulled a baby wipe from a pop-up box and cleaned off the bloodstain on his arm. The length of his left forearm was scored with similar knife scratches, adding to his already impressive display of body art. In feeding her, he kept tracing and retracing the same pattern, opening and reopening the same old wounds, carving the word *"MADRE"* into his flesh.

"I found you some music, Mama," he said, producing a handful of battered and burned CDs. "Some of your favorites: Los Panchos, Los Tres Ases, Javier Solis . . ."

Gus looked at her standing inside the cage, feasting on her son's blood, and tried to remember the woman who raised him. The single mother with a sometime husband and occasional boyfriends. She did her best for him, which was different from always doing the right thing. But it was the best she knew how to do. She had lost the custody battle, her versus the street. The barrio had raised him. It was the street behavior he emulated, rather than that of his *madre*. So many things he regretted now but could not change. He chose to remember their younger days. Her caressing him—treating his wounds after a neighborhood fight. And, even in her angriest moments, the kindness and love in her eyes.

All gone now. All disappeared.

Gus had disrespected her in life. So why did he now revere her in undeath? He did not know the answer. He did not understand the forces that drove him. All he knew was that visiting with her in this state—feeding her—charged him up like a battery. Made him crazy for revenge.

He placed one of the CDs in a luxurious stereo system he had pillaged from a car full of corpses. He had jimmied a few speakers of different brands and managed to get a good sound out of it. Javier Solis started singing *"No te doy la libertad"* (I will not give you freedom), an angry and melancholic bolero that proved eerily appropriate for the occasion.

"Do you like it, *Madre*?" he said, knowing all too well that this was just another monologue between them. "You remember it?"

Gus returned to the cage wall. He reached inside to close the faceplate, sealing her back in the darkness, when he saw something change in her eyes. Something came into them.

He had seen this before. He knew what it meant.

The voice, not his mother's, boomed deep inside his head.

I can taste you, boy, said the Master. *I taste your blood and your yearning. I taste your weakness. I know who you are in league with. My bastard son.* The eyes remained focused on him, with a hint of a spark behind them, like that tiny red light on a camera that tells you it is passively recording.

Gus tried to clear his mind. He tried to think nothing. Yelling at the creature through his mother brought him nothing. That much he had learned. Resist. The way old man Setrakian would have advised him. Gus was training himself to withstand the dark intelligence of the Master.

Yes, the old professor. He had plans for you. If only he could see you here. Feeding your madre *in the same manner he used to feed the infested heart of his long-lost wife. He failed, Gus. As you will fail.*

Gus focused the pain in his head on the image of his mother as she once was. His mind's eye stared at this image in an attempt to block out everything else.

Bring me the others, Augustin Elizalde. Your reward will be great. Your survival will be assured. Live like a king, not as a rat. Or else . . . no mercy. However much you beg for a second chance, I will no longer hear you. Your time is growing short . . .

"This is my house," said Gus, aloud but quietly. "*My mind,* demon. You are not welcome here."

What if I gave her back? Her will is stored in me along with the millions of voices. But I can find it for you, invoke it for you. I can give you your mother back . . .

And then, Gus's mother's eyes became almost human. They softened and became wet and full of pain.

"Hijito," she said. "My son. Why am I here? Why am I like this . . . ? What are you doing to me?"

It hit him all at once, her nakedness, the madness, the guilt, the horror.

"No!!" he screamed, and reached in through the bars with a trembling hand, sliding the faceplate shut at once. Immediately, once it was closed, Gus felt released, as though by an invisible hand. And in the helmet, the laughter of the Master exploded. Gus covered his ears but the voice continued resounding in his head until, like an echo, it faded away.

The Master had attempted to engage him long enough to get a fix on Gus's location, so it could send in his army of vampires to wipe him out.

It was just a trick. *Not my mother. Just a trick.* Never deal with the devil—that much he knew. *Live like a king.* Right. The king of a ruined world. The king of nothing. But down here, he was alive. An agent of chaos. *Caca grande.* The shit in the Master's soup.

Gus's reverie was interrupted by footfalls in the tunnels. He went to the door and saw artificial light coming around the corner.

Fet came first, Goodweather behind him. Gus had seen Fet a month or two before, but the doctor he had not seen in quite some time. Goodweather looked the worst he'd ever seen him.

They had never seen Gus's mother before, never even knew he had her here. Fet saw her first, moving to the bars. Gus's mother's helmet tracked him. Gus explained the situation to them—how he had it all under control, how she was not a threat to him, his homies, or the mission.

"Holy Christ," said the big exterminator. "Since when?"

"Long time now," answered Gus. "I just don't like to talk about it."

Fet moved laterally, watching her helmet follow him. "She can't see though?"

"No."

"The helmet works? Blocking out the Master?"

Gus nodded. "I think so. Plus, she doesn't even know where she is . . . it's a triangulation thing. They need sight and sound and something inside the brain to home in on you. I keep one fully blocked all the time—her ears. Faceplate blocks her sight. It's her vampire brain and her sense of smell spotting you now."

"What are you feeding her?" asked Fet.

Gus shrugged. The answer was obvious.

Goodweather spoke up then. "Why? Why do you keep her?"

Gus looked at him. "I guess that's still none of your fucking business, doctor . . ."

"She's gone. That thing in there—that's not your mother."

"You really think I don't know that?"

Goodweather said, "There's no reason to keep her otherwise. You need to release her. Now."

"I don't need to do anything. This is my decision. My *madre*."

"Not anymore she isn't. My son, if I find that he has been turned, I will release him. I will cut him down myself, without a moment's hesitation."

"Well, this ain't your son. Or any of your business."

Gus couldn't see Goodweather's eyes clearly in the dim room. Last time they had met, Gus could tell that he had been hyped on speed. The good doctor was self-medicating then, and he thought now, too.

Gus turned away from him, back to Fet, cutting Goodweather out of the conversation. "How was your vacation, *hombre*?"

"Ah. Funny. Very relaxing. No, it was a wild goose chase, but with an interesting ending. How's the street battle?"

"I'm taking it to them as best I can. Keeping the pressure up. Program Anarchy, you know? Agent Sabotage, reporting for duty, every damn night. Burned down four vamp lairs last week. Blew up a building the week before. Never knew what hit 'em. Guerilla warfare and dirty fucking tricks. Fight the power, *manito*."

"We need it. Any time something explodes in the city, or a thick plume of smoke or dust rises up into the rain, it has to register with people that there are still some in the city who are fighting back. And it's another thing for the vampires to have to explain away." Fet motioned to Goodweather. "Eph brought down an entire hospital building a day ago. Detonated oxygen tanks."

Gus turned to him. "What were you looking for in the hospital?" he asked, letting the doc know that he knew his dirty little secret. Fet was a fighter, a killer like Gus. Goodweather was something more complicated, and simplicity was what they needed now. Gus didn't trust him. Turning back to Fet, he said, "You remember El Angel de Plata?"

"Of course," said Fet. "The old wrestler."

"The Silver Angel." Gus kissed his thumb and saluted the wrestler's memory with a fist. "So—call me the Silver Ninja. Got moves that would make your head spin so hard, all your hair would fall out. Two other homeboys with me, we're on a tear like you wouldn't believe."

"Silver Ninja. I like it."

"Vampire assassin. I'm legendary. And I ain't gonna rest until I got all their heads on spikes running the length of Broadway."

"They're still hanging corpses from street signs. They would love to have yours."

"And yours. They think they're badass, but I'm ten times as dangerous as any bloodsucker. *Viva las ratas!* Long live the rats!"

Fet smiled and shook Gus's hand. "I wish we had a dozen more like you."

Gus waved that off. "You get a dozen of me, we'd end up killing off each other."

Gus led them back out of the tunnels to the basement of Buell Hall, where Fet and Goodweather had left the Coleman cooler. He then led them back underground to Low Memorial Library, then up through its administrative offices to the roof. A cool, dark afternoon-night with no rain, only an ominously black cloud of fog rolling in off the Hudson.

Fet popped open the top of the cooler, revealing two magnificent headless tunas sloshing around in what was left of the ice from the ship's hold.

"Hungry?" asked Fet.

Eating it raw was the obvious thing to do, but Goodweather laid down some medical science on them, insisting that they cook the fish because of the climate changes altering the ocean's ecosystem; no one knew what kind of lethal bacteria were lurking in raw fish.

Gus knew where to get a decent-sized camping grill from the catering department and Fet helped him carry it up to the roof. Goodweather was sent to break off old car antennas for skewers. They built their fire on the Hudson side between two large roof fans, blocking the flame light from the street and obscuring it from most rooftops.

The fish blackened up nice. Crisp-skinned and warm pink on the inside. A few bites in, Gus immediately felt better. He was so hungry all the time, he was unable to see how malnutrition ran him down both mentally and physically. The protein feast recharged him. Already he was looking forward to heading out on another daylight raid.

"So," said Gus, with the pleasure of warm food on his tongue, "what is the occasion of this feast?"

"We need your help," said Fet. He told Gus what they knew about Nora, Fet's manner turning grave, intense. "She's got to be in the nearest blood camp, the one north of the city. We want to get her out."

Gus checked Goodweather, who was supposed to be her boyfriend. Goodweather looked back at him, but strangely without the same fire that Fet had. "Tall order."

"The tallest. We have to move as soon as possible. If they find out who she is, that she knows us . . . it will be bad for her and worse for us."

"I'm all for combat, don't get me wrong. But I try to be strategic, too, these days. My job is not only staying alive but dying human. We all know the risks. Is it worth going in to get her? And I'm just asking, homes."

Fet nodded, looking at the flames licking at the skewered fish. "I get your point. At this stage, it's like, what are we doing this for? Are we trying to save the world? World's already gone. If the vampires disappeared tomorrow, what would we do? Rebuild? How? For whom?" He shrugged, looking to Goodweather for support. "Maybe someday. Until this sky clears, it'd be a fight for survival no matter who runs this planet." Fet paused to wipe some tuna off the whiskers around his lips. "I could give you a lot of reasons. But, bottom line, I'm just tired of losing people. We're gonna do this with or without you."

Gus waved his hand. "Never said anything about doing it without me. Just wanted to get your thinking on it. I like the doc. My boys are due back soon; we can arm up then." Gus picked off another hot chunk of tuna. "Always wanted to fuck up a farm. All I needed was a good reason."

Fet was flush with gratitude. "You save some of this food for your guys, energize them."

"Beats squirrel meat. Let's put this fire out. I have something to show you."

Gus wrapped the rest of the fish in paper to save for his *hombres*, then doused the flames with the melted ice. He led them down through the building and across the vacant campus to Buell Hall, into the basement. In a small side room, Gus had wired a stationary bicycle to a handful of battery chargers. A desk held a variety of devices scavenged from the university audiovisual department, including late-model digital cameras with long lenses, a media drive, and some small, portable high-def monitors—all the stuff they just didn't make anymore.

"Some of my boys been recording our raids and recon. Good propaganda value, if we can get it out there some way. Also been doing some recon work. You know about the castle in Central Park?"

"Of course," said Fet. "The Master's nest. Surrounded by an army of vamps."

Goodweather was intrigued now, moving to the seven-inch monitor as Gus fed it a waiting battery pack and wired in a camera.

The screen came to life, soupy green and black.

"Night-vision lens. Found a couple dozen in collector's boxes of a shooter video game. They fit on the end of a telephoto. Not a perfect match—and the quality is basically shit, I know. But keep watching."

Fet and Goodweather bent forward to better view the small screen. After a few moments of deep concentration, the ghostly dark figures in the image started to come together for them.

"The castle, right?" said Gus, outlining it with his finger. "Stone foundation, the lake. Over here, your army of vamps."

Fet asked, "Where'd you take this from?"

"Roof of the Museum of Natural History. Close as I could get. Had it on a tripod like a sniper."

The image of the castle parapet trembled mightily, the zoom setting maxed out.

"There we go," said Gus. "See it?"

As the image stabilized again, a figure emerged onto the high ledge of the parapet. The army below turned their heads toward it in a mass gesture of complete allegiance.

"Holy shit," said Fet. "Is that the Master?"

"It's smaller," said Goodweather. "Or is the perspective out of whack?"

"It's the Master," said Fet. "Look at the drones below, how they turn their heads toward him at once. Like flowers bending toward the sun."

Eph said, "It changed. Jumped bodies."

"It must have," said Fet, bursting pride evident in his voice. "The professor did hurt it after all. He had to have. I knew it. Wounded it so that it *had* to take on a new form." Fet straightened. "I wonder how he did it."

Gus watched Goodweather concentrating hard on the muddy, trembling image of the new Master moving. "It's Bolivar," said Goodweather.

"What's that?" asked Gus.

"Not what. Who. Gabriel Bolivar."

"Bolivar?" said Gus, searching his memory. "The singer?"

"That's him," said Goodweather.

"Are you sure?" said Fet, knowing exactly who Goodweather was referring to. "It's so dark, how can you tell?"

"The way he moves. Something about him. I'm telling you—he is the Master."

Fet looked closely. "You're right. Why him? Maybe the Master had no time to choose. Maybe the old man hit it so hard, it had to change immediately."

As Goodweather stared at the image, another vague form joined the Master out on the high parapet. Goodweather seemed to freeze, then tremble as though suffering a chill.

"It's Kelly," he said.

Goodweather said this with authority, without any trace of doubt.

Fet pulled back a bit, having more trouble with the image than Goodweather. But Gus could tell that he too was convinced. "Jesus."

Goodweather steadied himself with a hand on the table. His vampire wife was serving at the side of the Master.

And then a third figure emerged. Smaller, skinnier than the other two. Reading darker on the night-vision scale.

"See that there?" said Gus. "We got a human being living among the vampires. Not just the vampires—the Master. Want to guess?"

Fet stiffened. That was Gus's first sign that

something was wrong. Then Fet turned to look at Goodweather.

Goodweather let go of the table. His legs gave out and he slumped back into a sitting position on the floor. His eyes were still locked on the soupy image, his stomach burning, suddenly flushed with acid. His lower lip trembled, and tears welled up in his eyes.

"That's my son."

International Space Station

TAKE IT DOWN.

Astronaut Thalia Charles didn't even turn her head anymore. When the voice came now, she just accepted it. She almost—yes, she could admit this—welcomed it. As alone as she was—indeed, she was one of the most alone human beings in the history of human beings—she was not alone with her thoughts.

She was isolated aboard the International Space Station, the massive research facility disabled and tumbling through Earth's orbit. Its solar-powered thrusters firing sporadically, the man-made satellite continued to drift in an elliptical trajectory some two hundred miles above its home planet, passing from day into night roughly every three hours.

For nearly two calendar years now—racking up eight orbital days for every one calendar day—she had existed in this state of quarantined suspension. Zero gravity and zero exercise had taken a great toll on her wasting body. Most of her muscle was gone, her tendons atrophied. Her spine, arms, and legs had bent in odd, disturbing angles and most of her fingers were useless hooks, curled upon themselves. Her food rations—mainly freeze-dried borscht brought up on the last Russian transport before the cataclysm—had dwindled to almost nothing, but on the other hand her body required little nutrition. Her skin was brittle, and flakes of it floated about the cabin like dandelion snow. Much of her hair was gone, which was also for the best, as it only got in the way in zero gravity.

She had all but disintegrated, both in body and in mind.

The Russian commander had died just three weeks after the ISS began to malfunction. Massive nuclear explosions on Earth excited the atmosphere, leading to multiple impacts with orbiting space junk. They had taken shelter inside their emergency escape capsule, the *Soyuz* spacecraft, following procedure in the absence of any communiqué from Houston. Commander Demidov volunteered to don a space suit and venture bravely out into the main facility in an attempt to repair the oxygen tank leaks—and succeeded in restoring and rerouting one of them into the *Soyuz,* before apparently suffering a massive heart attack. His success allowed Thalia and the French engineer to survive much longer than anticipated, as well as redistribute one-third of their rations of food and water.

But the result had been as much a curse as a blessing.

Then, within a few months, Maigny, the engineer, began showing signs of dementia. As they watched the planet disappear behind a black, octopus-ink-like cloud of polluted atmosphere, he rapidly lost faith and began speaking in strange voices. Thalia fought to maintain her own sanity in part by attempting to restore his and believed she was making real progress, until she caught a reflection of him making bizarre faces when he thought she could not see him. That night, as she pretended to sleep, spinning slowly inside the tight cabin space with her eyes half-closed, she watched in gravity-free horror as Maigny quietly unpacked the survival kit located between two of the three seats. He removed the three-barreled pistol from inside, more like a shotgun than a simple handgun. Some years ago, a Russian space capsule had, upon reentry and descent, crash-landed in the Siberian wilderness. It was hours before they were located, during which time the cosmonauts had to fight off wolves with little more than stones and tree branches. Since that episode, the specially made oversized gun—complete with a machete inside its detachable buttstock—had been included as standard mission equipment inside the "*Soyuz* Portable Survival Kit."

She watched him feel up the barrel of the weapon, exploring the trigger with his finger. He removed the machete and spun it in the air, watching the blade go around and around and catching a glint of the distant sun. She felt the blade pass near her and saw, like the glint of the sun, a hint of pleasure in his eyes.

She knew then what she would have to do in order to save herself. She continued to pursue her amateur therapy so as not to alert Maigny to her concern, all the while preparing for the inevitable. She did not like to think of it, even now.

Occasionally, depending on the rotation of the ISS, his corpse floated into view through the door to the station, like a macabre Jehovah's Witness making a house call.

Again—one fewer person to consume food rations. One fewer set of lungs.

And more time endured trapped alone inside this incapacitated space can.

Take it down.

"Don't tempt me," she muttered. The voice was male, indistinct. Familiar, but she could not place it.

Not her husband. Not her late father. But somebody she knew . . .

She did feel something, a presence with her inside the *Soyuz*. Didn't she? Or was it only a desire for companionship? A want, a need? What person's voice was she using to fill up this blank space in her life?

She looked out through the windows as the ISS again crossed into sunlight.

As she stared out the window at the dawning sun, she saw colors come into the sky. She called it "the sky," but it was not the sky up there; nor was it "night." It was the universe and it wasn't "black" either; it was absent of light. It was void. The purest nothingness. Except . . .

There it was again: colors. A spray of red and a

burst of orange, just outside her peripheral vision. Something like the bright explosions one sees in one's tightly shut eyes.

She tried this, shutting her eyes, pressing her lids with her dry, cracked thumbs. Again, an absence of light. The void of the inside of her head. A fountain of undulating colors and stars came into the nothingness—and then she opened her eyes again.

Blue brightened and disappeared in the distance. Then, in another area, a spray of green. And violet!

Signs. Even if they were purely fictions created in her mind, they were signs. Of something.

Take it down, dearie.

"Dearie?" Nobody ever called her "dearie." Never her husband, not any of her teachers, nor the astronaut program administrators, nor her parents or grandparents.

Still, she didn't question the voice's identity too strongly. She was happy for the company. She was happy for the counsel.

"Why?" she asked.

No answer. The voice never answered on request. And yet she kept expecting that someday it would.

"How?" she asked.

No answer again, but as she drifted through the bell-shaped cabin, her boot caught on the survival kit between the seats.

"Really?" she said, addressing the kit itself as though it were the source of the voice.

She hadn't touched the thing since she had last

used it. She pulled it out now, opening the kit, the combination lock unclasped. (Had she left it that way?) She lifted out the TP-82, the long-barreled handgun. The machete was gone; she had tossed it out with Maigny. She raised the weapon to eye level, as though aiming it at the window . . . and then released it, watching it twist and float before her like a word or an idea hanging in the air.

She inventoried the rest of the kit. Twenty rifle rounds. Twenty flares. Ten shotgun shells.

"Tell me why," she said, wiping away a rogue teardrop, watching the speck of moisture sail away. "After all this time—why now?"

She held still, her body barely rotating. She was certain an answer was going to come. A reason. An explanation.

Because it's time . . .

The flaming light burst past her window with such silent alacrity that she choked on her own breath. She began to hyperventilate, grabbing the seat back and propelling herself to the window to watch the tail of the comet burn away into Earth's atmosphere, snuffing itself out before reaching the tumorous lower atmosphere.

She whipped around, again feeling a presence. Something not human.

"Was that . . . ?" she started to ask, but could not complete the question.

Because obviously, it was.

A sign.

When she was a girl, a falling star streaking across the sky made her want to become an astronaut. That was the story she told whenever called upon to visit schools or do interviews in the months leading up to launch, and yet it was entirely true: her fate had been written across the sky in her youth.

Take it down.

Again, her breath got caught in her throat. The voice—at once she recognized it. Her dog at home in Connecticut, a Newfoundland named Ralphie. This was the voice she heard in her head whenever she would talk to him, when she would rough up his coat and engage him and he would nuzzle against her leg.

Want to go out?

Yes indeed I do I do.

Want a treat?

Do I! Do I!

Who's a good boy?

I am I am I am.

I'll miss you lots while I'm in space.

I'll miss you back, dearie.

This was the voice with her now. The same one she had projected onto her Ralphie. Her and not her, the voice of companionship and trust and affection.

"Really?" she asked again.

Thalia thought about what it would be like, moving through the cabins, blowing out the thrusters until she breached the hull. This great scientific facility of conjoined capsules listing and plummeting from its orbit, catching fire as it entered the upper atmosphere, streaking downward like a flaming burr and penetrating the poisonous crust of the troposphere.

And then certainty filled her like an emotion. And even if she were merely insane, at least she could move without doubt now, without question. And—at the very, very least—she would not be going out like Maigny, hallucinating and foaming at the mouth.

The shotgun shells loaded in manually from the breech side.

She would scuttle the hull to let the airlessness in and then go down with the ship. In a way she had always suspected this was to be her destiny. This was a decision formed of beauty. Born of a falling star, Thalia Charles was about to become a falling star herself.

Camp Liberty

NORA LOOKED AT the shank.

She had been working on it all night long. She was exhausted but proud. The irony of a butter-knife shank was not lost on her. Such a dainty piece of cutlery, now sharpened into a jagged point and edge. Still a few more hours to go—she could sharpen it to perfection.

She had muffled the sound of the grinding—against a corner piece in the concrete—by covering it with her lumpy bed pillow. Her mother was asleep a few feet away. She didn't wake up. Their reunion would be brief. The afternoon before, perhaps an hour after she had returned from seeing Barnes, they had been handed a processing order. In it was a request for Nora's mother to leave the recreation courtyard at dawn.

Feeding time.

How would they "process" her? She didn't know. But she would not allow it. She would call for Barnes, give in, get close to him, and then kill him. She would either save her mother or get him. If her hands were going to be empty they would be stained with his blood.

Her mother murmured something in her sleep and then lapsed back into the deep but gentle snoring that Nora knew so well. As a child Nora had been lulled to sleep by that sound and the rhythmic up-and-down of her chest. Her mother was, back then, a formidable woman. A force of nature. She worked, indefatigable, and raised Nora properly—always vigilant of her, always able to provide an education and a degree and the clothes and luxuries that go with them. Nora got a graduation dress and the expensive textbooks and not once had her mother complained.

But there was that one night right before Christmas, when Nora had been awakened by a soft sobbing. She was fourteen and had been particularly nasty about getting a *quinceañera* dress on her upcoming birthday . . .

She quietly climbed down the steps and stood at the kitchen door. Her mother was sitting alone, a half glass of milk by her side—reading glasses and bills all over the table.

Nora was paralyzed by this sight. Sort of like sneaking up on God crying. She was about to step in and ask her what was wrong when her mother's sobbing became louder—a roar. She suffocated the noise by grotesquely covering her mouth with both hands, while her eyes exploded in tears. This terrified Nora. Made the blood freeze in her veins. They never spoke about the incident, but Nora had been imprinted with that image of pain. She changed. Perhaps forever. She took better care of her mother and of herself and always worked harder than anyone else.

As dementia settled in, Nora's mother started to complain. About everything and all the time. Her resentments and anger, accumulated through the years and quieted by civility, came forth in torrents of incoherent nagging. And Nora took it all. She would never abandon her mother.

Three hours before dawn, Nora's mother opened her eyes. And for a fleeting moment she was lucid. It happened now and then but less often than before. In a way, Nora thought, her mother, like the *strigoi,* was supplanted by another will and it was quite eerie whenever she snapped out of the trancelike disease and looked at Nora. At Nora as she was, right here, right now.

"Nora? Where are we?" she said.

"Shh, Mama. We are okay. Go back to sleep."

"Are we in a hospital? Am I sick?" she asked, agitated.

"No, Mama. It's all right. Everything is fine." Nora's mother held her daughter's hand firmly and lay back down in her cot. She caressed her shaved head.

"What happened? Who did this to you?" she asked, mortified.

Nora kissed her mother's hand. "Nobody, Mom. It will grow back. You'll see."

Nora's mother looked at her with great lucidity, and after a long pause she asked, "Are we going to die?"

And Nora didn't know what to say. She began to sob, and her mother hushed her now and hugged her and kissed her softly on the head. "Don't cry, my dear. Don't cry."

She then held her head and looked her daughter straight in the eye and said, "Looking back on one's life, you see that love was the answer to everything. I love you, Nora. I always will. And that we will have forever."

They fell asleep together and Nora lost track of the time. She woke up and saw that the sky was clearing.

What now? They were trapped. Away from Fet, away from Eph. With no way out. Except the butter knife.

She took a final look at the shank. She would go to Barnes and use it and then . . . then maybe she would turn it on herself.

Suddenly it didn't look sharp enough. She worked on the edge and the tip until dawn.

Sewage Processing Plant

THE STANFORD SEWAGE Processing Plant lay beneath a hexagonal red brick building on La Salle Street between Amsterdam and Broadway. Built in 1906, the plant was meant to keep up with the area's demands and growth for at least a century. During its first decade, the plant processed thirty million gallons of raw sewage a day. But the influx of people delivered by two consecutive world wars soon made that rate insufficient. The neighbors also complained about shortness of breath, eye infections, and a general sulfurous smell emanating from the building 24/7. The plant shut down partially in 1947 and completely five years after that.

The inside of it was immense, even majestic. There was a nobility to industrial turn-of-the-century architecture that has since been lost. Twin wrought-iron staircases led to the catwalks above, and the cast-iron structures that filtered and processed the raw sewage had barely been vandalized over the years. Faded graffiti and a three-feet-deep deposit of silt, dry leaves, dog poop, and dead pigeons were the only signs of abandonment. A year before, Gus Elizalde had stumbled onto it and had cleaned one of the reservoirs by hand, turning it into his own personal armory.

The only access was through a tunnel, and only by using a massive iron valve locked with a heavy stainless steel chain.

Gus wanted to show off his weapons cache, so they could load up for the raid on the blood camp. Eph had stayed behind—needing some alone time after finally seeing his son, via video, after two long years, standing alongside the Master and his vampire mother. Fet had renewed understanding for Eph's unique plight, the toll the vampire strain had taken on his life, and Fet sympathized completely. But still, on their way to the improvised armory, Fet discreetly complained about Eph, about how his focus was slipping. He complained in only practical terms, without malice, without rancor. Maybe with just a touch of jealousy, since Goodweather's presence still could get in the way of him and Nora.

"I don't like him," said Gus. "Never did. Guy bitches about what he doesn't have, loses sight of what he does have, and is never happy. He's what you call a—what's that word?"

"Pessimist?" said Fet.

"Asshole," said Gus.

"He's gone through a lot," said Fet.

"Oh, really. Oh, I'm so fucking sorry. I always wanted my mother to stand naked in a cell with a fucking helmet glued to her fucking *cabeza*."

Fet almost smiled. Gus was ultimately right. No man should ever have to go through what Eph was going through. But still, Fet needed him functional and battle-ready. Their corps was shrinking, and getting everyone's best effort was critical.

"He's never fucking happy. His wife nags him too much? Bam!! She is gone!! Now, boo-hoo-boo, if only I could get her back . . . Bam!! She's undead, boo-hoo-boo, poor me, my wife is a fucking vampire . . . Bam!! They take his son. Boo-hoo-fucking-boo, if only I could have him back . . . It never fucking ends with him. Who you love or who you protect is all there is, man. Fucked-up as it may be. If my mother looks like the ugliest porno Power Ranger, I don't care, man. That's what I have. I have my mama. See? I don't give up," said Gus. "And I don't give a fuck. When I go, I wanna go fighting those fuckers. Maybe because I'm a fire sign."

"You're a what?" said Fet.

"Gemini," said Gus. "In the zodiac. A fire sign."

"Gemini is an air sign, Gus," said Fet.

"Whatever. I still don't give a fuck," said Gus. Then after a long pause, he added, "If we still had the old man here, we'd be on top by now."

"I believe that," said Fet.

Gus slowed in the darkened underground tunnel and started to unlock the padlock.

"So, about Nora," he said. "Have you . . . ?"

"No—no," said Fet, blushing. "I . . . no."

Gus smiled in the dark. "She doesn't even know, huh?"

"She knows," said Fet. "At least—I think she does. But we haven't done much about it."

"You will, big boy," said Gus as he opened the access valve to the armory. *"Bienvenido a Casa Elizalde!"* he said, extending his arms and showing a wide array of automatic weapons and swords and ammo of all calibers.

Fet patted him on the back while nodding. He eyed a box of hand grenades. "Where the fuck did you get these?"

"Pfft. A boy needs his toys, man. And the bigger, the better."

Fet said, "Any specific uses in mind?"

"Too many. I'm saving 'em for something special. Why, you got any ideas?"

Fet said, "How about detonating a nuclear bomb?"

Gus laughed harshly. "That actually sounds like fun."

"I'm glad you think so. Because I didn't come back from Iceland completely empty-handed."

Fet told Gus about the Russian bomb he had bought with silver.

"No mames?" Gus said. "You have a nuclear bomb?"

"But no detonator. That's where I was hoping you could help me out."

"You're serious?" Gus asked. He hadn't moved past the previous exchange. "A nuclear bomb?"

Fet nodded modestly.

"Much respect, Fet," said Gus. "*Much* respect. Let's take out the island. Like—right fucking now!"

"Whatever we do with it . . . we get one shot. We need to be sure."

"I know who can get us the detonator, man. The only asshole that is still capable of getting anything dirty, anything crooked on the whole East Coast. Alfonso Creem."

"How would you go about contacting him? Crossing to Jersey is like going into East Germany."

"I have my ways," said Gus. "You just leave it to Gusto. How you think I got the fucking grenades?"

Fet went silent, pensive, and then looked back at Gus.

"Would you trust Quinlan? With the book?"

"The old man's book? The Silver whatever?"

Fet nodded. "Would you share it with him?"

"I don't know, man," said Gus. "I mean, sure—it's just a book."

"The Master wants the book for a reason. Setrakian sacrificed his life for it. Whatever is inside must be real. Your friend Quinlan thinks as much . . ."

"What about you?" asked Gus.

"Me?" Fet said. "I have the book—but I can't do much with it myself. You know that saying 'He's so dumb, he couldn't find a prayer in the Bible'? Well, I can't find much. There's some trick to it, maybe. We should be so close."

"I've seen him, man—Quinlan. Shit, I've recorded that motherfucker cleaning a nest in a New York minute. Two, three dozen vampires."

Gus smiled, cherishing his memories. Fet liked Gus even more when he smiled.

"In jail you learn that there are two kinds of guys in this world—and I don't care if they're human or bloodsuckers—there's the ones that take it and the ones that hand it out. And this guy, man—this guy gives it out like fucking candy . . . He wants the hunt, man. He wants the hunt. And he's maybe the one other orphan out here who hates the Master as much as we do."

Fet nodded. In his heart the matter was resolved.

Quinlan would get the book. And Fet would get some answers.

Extract from the Diary of Ephraim Goodweather

Most midlife crises are not this bad. In the past, it used to be that people would watch their youth fade, their marriage break, or their careers grow stagnant. Those were the breaks, usually eased by a new car, a dab of Just for Men, or a big Mont Blanc pen, depending on your budget. But what I have lost cannot be compensated for. My heart races every time I think of it, every time I sense it. It is over. Or it will be over soon enough. Whatever I had, I have squandered—and what I hoped for will never be. Things around me have taken their permanent, horrible final form. All the promise in my life—youngest graduate in my class, the big move east, meeting the perfect girl—all that is gone. The evenings of cold pizza and a movie. Of feeling like a giant in my son's eyes . . .

When I was a kid, there was this guy on TV called Mr. Rogers, and he used to sing: "You can never go down / can never go down / can never go down the drain." What a fucking lie.

Once, I might have gathered my past in order to present it as a CV or a list of accomplishments, but now . . . now it seems like an inventory of trivialities, of things that could have been but are not. As a young man I felt the world and my place in it was all part of a plan. That success, whatever that is, was something to be gained simply by focusing on my work—on being good at "What I did." As a workaholic father, I felt that the day-to-day grind was a way to provide, to see us through while life took its final shape. And now . . . now that the world around me has become an unbearable place, and all I have is the nausea of wrong turns taken and things lost. Now I know this is the real me. The permanent me. The solidified disappointment of that young man's life—the subtraction of all those achievements of youth—the minus of a plus that was never tallied. This is me: weak, infirm, fading. Not giving up, because I never do . . . but living without faith in myself or my circumstance.

My heart flutters at the notion of never finding Zack—at the idea that he is gone forever. This I cannot accept. I will not accept.

Not thinking straight. But I will find him, I know I will. I have seen him in my dreams. His eyes looking at me, making of me that giant once again, calling me by the truest name a man can ever aspire to: "Dad."

I have seen a light surrounding us. Purging us. Absolving me—of the booze and the pills and the blind spots of my heart. I have seen this light. I long for it again in a world this dark.

Beneath Columbia University

Eph wandered away through the subterranean tunnels of the former insane asylum beneath the former Columbia University. All he wanted to do was walk. Seeing Zack atop Belvedere Castle with Kelly and the Master had shaken Eph to the core. Of all the fates he had dreaded for his son—Zack murdered or starving in a locked cage somewhere—standing at the Master's side had never occurred to him.

Was it the demon Kelly who had drawn their son into the fold? Or was it the Master who wanted Zack with him, and if so, why?

Perhaps the Master had threatened Kelly, and Zack had no choice but to play along. Eph wanted to cling to this hypothesis. Because the idea that the boy would freely align himself with the Master was unimaginable. The corruption of one's child is a parent's worst fear. Eph needed to believe in Zack as a little lost boy, not a wayward son.

But his fear wouldn't let him slip into this fantasy. Eph had walked away from the video screen feeling like a ghost.

He dug into his coat pocket, finding two white Vicodin tablets. They glowed in his palm, made brilliant by the light of his battery-powered headlamp. He thrust them into his mouth, dry-swallowing them. One of them lodged at the base of his esophagus, and he had to jump up and down a few times in order to force it down.

He is mine.

Eph looked up fast. Kelly's voice—muffled and distant, but distinctly hers. He turned around twice but found himself quite alone in the underground passage.

He has always been mine.

Eph drew his sword a few inches out of its sheath. He started forward, toward a short flight of stairs heading down. The voice was in his head, but some sixth sense was showing him the way.

He sits at the right hand of the Father.

Eph running now, furious, the light from his headlamp shaking, turning down another dim corridor, turning into . . .

The dungeon room. Gus's caged mother.

Eph swept the room. It was otherwise empty. Slowly he turned to the helmeted vampire standing still in the center of its cage. Gus's vampire mother stood very still, Eph's light casting a grid shadow onto her body.

Kelly's voice said, *Zack believes you are dead.*

Eph drew his sword fully from its sheath. "Shut up," he said.

He is starting to forget. The old world and all its ways. It's gone now, a dream of youth.

"Quiet!" Eph said.

He is attentive to the Master. He is respectful. He is learning.

Eph thrust his sword in between two bars. Gus's mother flinched, repelled by the presence of silver, her pendulous breasts swinging in the half light. "Learning what?" said Eph. "Answer me!"

Kelly's voice did not.

"You're brainwashing him," said Eph. The boy was in isolation, mentally vulnerable. "Are you brainwashing him?"

We are parenting him.

Eph winced as though cut by her words. "No. No . . . what can you know about that? What can you know about love—about being a father or being a son . . . ?"

We are the fertile blood. We have birthed many sons . . . Join us.

"No."

It is the only way you will be reunited with him.

Eph's arm lowered a bit. "Fuck you. I will kill you—"

Join us and be with him forever.

Eph froze there a moment, paralyzed by despair. She wanted something from him. The Master wanted something. He made himself pull back. Deny them. Stop talking. Walk away.

Shut the fuck up—! he thought, his rage louder than his voice. He held tightly to his silver blade at his side. He ran back out of the room and into the passageways, Kelly's voice staying in his head.

Come to us.

He turned a corner, thrusting open a rusty door.

Come to Zack.

He kept running. With each step, he grew angrier, becoming enraged.

You know you want to.

And then her laughter. Not her human laugh, high and light and infectious, but a taunting laugh, meant to provoke him. Meant to turn him back.

But on he ran. And the laughter melted away, fading with distance.

Eph went on blindly, his sword blade clanging into the legs of discarded chairs and scraping against the floor. The Vikes had kicked in, and he was swimming a bit, his body numb but not his head. In walking away, he had turned a corner in his own mind. Now more than ever he wanted to free Nora from the blood camp. To deliver her from the clutches of the vampires. He wanted to show the Master—show it that even in a fucked-up time such as this, it could be done: a human could be saved. That Zack was not lost to Eph, and that the Master's hold on him was not as secure as it might think.

Eph stopped to catch his breath. His headlamp was dimming, and he tapped it, the light flickering. He needed to figure out where he was and surface, or else be lost in this dark labyrinth. He was anxious to let the others know that he was ready to go to the camp and fight.

He turned the next corner, and at the end of the long, dark corridor, Eph saw a figure. Something about its stance—low-armed, knees lightly flexed—said "vampire."

Eph's sword came up. He went a few steps forward, hoping to light the creature better.

It remained still. The narrow corridor walls drifted a bit in Eph's vision, wobbling thanks to the Vikes. Maybe he was seeing things—seeing what he wanted to see. He had wanted a fight.

Convinced now that it was a figment of his imagination, Eph grew more emboldened, approaching the ghost.

"Come here," he said, his rage at Kelly and the Master still brimming. "Come and get it."

The creature stood its ground, allowing Eph a better look. A sweatshirt hood formed a triangular cotton point over its head, shadowing its face and obscuring its eyes. Boots and jeans. One arm hung low at its side, the other hand just hidden behind its back.

Eph strode toward the figure with angry determination, like that of a man crossing a room to slam a door shut. The figure never moved. Eph planted his back leg and delivered a two-handed baseball swing aimed at the neck.

To Eph's surprise, his sword clanged and his arms kicked back, the handle almost springing loose from his grip. A burst of sparks briefly lit the corridor.

It took Eph a moment to realize that the vampire had parried his blow with a length of steel.

Eph regripped his sword with his stinging palms and rattled knuckles and reared back to swing again. The vampire wielded his steel bar one-handedly, easily deflecting the attack. A sudden boot thrust into Eph's chest sent him sprawling, tripping over his own feet as he collapsed to the floor.

Eph stared up at the shadowy figure. Entirely real, but . . . also different. Not one of the semi-intelligent drones he was used to facing. This vamp had a stillness, a self-composure, that set him apart from the seething masses.

Eph scrambled back up onto his feet. The challenge stoked the fire burning inside him. He didn't know what this vampire was, and he didn't care. "Come on!" he shouted, beckoning the vamp. Again, the creature did not move. Eph evened out his blade, showing the vamp the sharp silver point. He feigned a stab, spinning quickly, one of his best moves, slashing with enough force to cut the creature in two. But the vamp foresaw the move, raising his steel to parry, and Eph countered again, dodging, coming back around the other way and going straight for its neck.

The vamp was ready for him. Its hand grabbed Eph's forearm, closing on it like a hot clamp. It twisted Eph's arm with such force that Eph had to arch backward to keep his elbow and shoulder from snapping under pressure. Eph howled in pain, unable to keep his grip on the sword. It popped from his hand and clattered to the floor. With his free hand, Eph went to his belt for his hip dagger, slashing at the vampire's face.

Surprised, the thing shoved Eph to the floor, reeling back.

Eph crawled away, his elbow burning with pain. Two more figures came running from his end of the hallway, two humans. Fet and Gus.

Just in time. Eph turned toward the outnumbered vamp, expecting it to hiss and charge.

Instead, the creature reached down to the floor, lifting Eph's sword by its leather-wrapped handle. It turned the silver-bladed weapon this way and that, as though judging its weight and construction.

Eph had never seen a vampire willingly get that close to silver before—much less take a weapon into its hands.

Fet had drawn his sword, but Gus stopped him with a hand, walking past Eph without offering to help him up. The vampire tossed Eph's sword to Gus, casually, grip first. Gus caught it easily and lowered the blade.

"Of all the things you taught me," said Gus, "you left out the part about making these great fucking entrances."

The vampire's response was telepathic and exclusive to Gus. It pushed back its black hood, revealing a perfectly bald and earless head, preternaturally smooth, almost in the way that thieves appear with nylons stretched over their faces.

Except for its eyes. They glowed fiercely red, like those of a rat.

Eph stood up, rubbing his elbow. This thing was obviously *strigoi,* and yet Gus stood near it. Stood *with* it.

Fet, his hand still on his own sword grip, said, "You again."

"What the hell is this?" said Eph, apparently the last one to this party.

Gus tossed Eph's sword back at him, harder than was necessary. "You should remember Mr. Quinlan," said Gus. "The Ancients' top hunter. And currently the baddest man in the whole damn town." Gus then turned back to Mr. Quinlan. "A friend of ours got herself thrown into a blood camp. We want her back."

Mr. Quinlan regarded Eph with eyes informed by centuries of existence. His voice, when it entered Eph's mind, was a smooth, measured baritone.

Dr. Goodweather, I presume.

Eph locked eyes with him. Barely nodded. Mr. Quinlan looked at Fet:

I'm here in the hopes that we can reach an arrangement.

Low Memorial Library, Columbia University

INSIDE THE COLUMBIA University library, in a research room off the cavernous rotunda—once, and still, the largest all-granite dome in the country—Mr. Quinlan sat at a reading table across from Fet.

"You help us break into the camp—you get to read the book," said Fet. "There is no further negotiation . . ."

I will do that. But you know that you will be vastly outnumbered by both strigoi *and human guards?*

"We know," said Fet. "Will you help us in? That's the price."

I will.

The burly exterminator unzipped a hidden pocket in his backpack and pulled out a large bundle of rags.

You had it on you? asked the Born, incredulous.

"Can't think of a safer place," said Fet, smiling. "Hidden in plain sight. You want the book, you go through me."

A daunting task, to be sure.

Fet shrugged. "Daunting enough." He unwrapped a volume lying within the rags. "The *Lumen*," said Fet.

Quinlan felt a wave of cold travel up his neck. A rare sensation in one so old. He studied the book as Fet turned to face him. The cover was ragged leather and fabric.

"I pulled off the silver cover. Ruined the spine a little bit, but too bad. It looks humble and unimportant, doesn't it?"

Where's the silver cover?

"I have it socked away. Easy to retrieve."

Quinlan looked at him. *You're full of surprises, aren't you, exterminator?*

Felt shrugged off the compliment.

The old man chose well, Mr. Fet. Your heart is uncomplicated. It knows what it knows and acts accordingly. Greater wisdom is hard to find.

The Born sat with his black cotton hood sloughed off his immaculately smooth, white head. Before him, open to one of the illuminated pages, lay the *Occido Lumen*. Because its silver edging was repellent to his vampiric nature, he carefully turned the pages using the eraser top of a pencil. Now, at once, he touched the interior of the page with his fingertip, almost in the way a blind man would search a loved one's face.

This document was holy. It contained the creation and history of the world's vampire race, and as such included several references to Borns. Imagine a human allowed access to a book outlining human creation and answers to most if not all of life's mysteries. Mr. Quinlan's deeply red eyes scanned the pages with intense interest.

The reading is slow. The language is dense.

Fet said, "You're telling me."

Also, there is much that is hidden. In images and in the watermarks. They appear much clearer to my eyes than yours—but this is going to require some time.

"Which is exactly what we do not have. How much time will it take?"

The Born's eyes continued scanning back and forth.

Impossible to say.

Fet was aware that his anxiety was a distraction to Mr. Quinlan.

"We are loading the weapons. You have an

hour or so—then you'll come with us. We are getting Nora back . . ."

Fet turned around and walked away. Three steps later, the *Lumen*, the Master, and the apocalypse evaporated. There was only Nora in his mind.

Mr. Quinlan returned his attention to the pages of the *Lumen* and started to read.

INTERLUDE II

OCCIDO LUMEN:

THE MASTER'S TALE

THERE WAS A THIRD.

Each of the holy books, the Torah, the Bible, and the Koran, tells the tale of the destruction of Sodom and Gomorrah. So, in a way, does the *Lumen*.

In Genesis 18, three archangels appear before Abraham in human form. Two are said to proceed from there to the doomed cities of the plain, where they reside with Lot, enjoy a feast, and are later surrounded by the men of Sodom, whom they blind before destroying their city.

The third archangel is deliberately omitted. Hidden. Lost.

This is his story.

Five cities shared the vast, lush plain of the

Yarden River, near what is today the Dead Sea. And out of all of these Sodom was the proudest, the most beautiful. It rose from its fertile surroundings as a landmark, a monument to wealth and prosperity.

Irrigated by a complex canal system, it had grown randomly through the centuries, radiating outward from the waterways and ending up in a shape that vaguely resembled a dove in flight. Its ten-acre contours crystallized in that form when the surrounding walls were erected around 2024 BC. The walls were over forty feet tall and six feet thick, constructed of baked mud brick and plastered in gypsum to make them shine brightly in the sun. Within them, mud-brick buildings were built so close together as to be almost on top of one another, the tallest of which was a temple erected to honor the Canaanite god Moloch. The population of Sodom fluctuated around two thousand. Fruits, spices, and grains were abundant, driving the city's prosperity. The glass and gilded bronze tiles of a dozen palaces were visible at once, glinting in the dying sunlight.

Such wealth was guarded by the enormous gates that gave entrance into the city. Six irregular stones of enormous size and heft created a monumental archway with gates fashioned from iron and hardwoods impervious to fire or battering rams.

It was at these gates that Lot, son of Haran, nephew of Abram, was when the three creatures of light arrived.

Pale they were, and radiant and remote. Part

of the essence of God and, as such, void of any blemish. From each of their backs, four long appendages emerged, suffused with feathery light, easily confused with luminous wings. The four jutting limbs fused in the back of the creatures and flapped softly with their every step, as naturally as one would compensate for forward movement by swaying one's arms. With each step they acquired form and mass, until they stood there, naked and somewhat lost. Their skin was radiant like the purest alabaster and their beauty was a painful reminder of Lot's mortal imperfection.

They were sent there to punish the pride, decadence, and brutality that had bred within the prosperous walls of the city. Gabriel, Michael, and Ozryel were God's emissaries—His most trusted, most cherished creations and His most ruthless soldiers.

And among them it was Ozryel who held His greatest favor. He was intent upon visiting the town square that night, where they had been instructed to go—but Lot beseeched them to stay with him at his residence instead. Gabriel and Michael agreed, and so Ozryel, the third, who was most interested in the wicked ways of these cities, was made to acquiesce to his brothers' wishes. Of the three, it was Ozryel who held the voice of God within himself, the power of destruction that would erase the two sinful cities from the earth. He was, as it is told in every tale, God's favorite: His most protected, His most beautiful creation.

Lot had been blessed aplenty, with land and

cattle and a pious wife. So the feast at his home was abundant and varied. And the three archangels feasted as men, and Lot's two virginal daughters washed their feet. These physical sensations were new to all three of the angels, but for Ozryel the sensations were overwhelming, achieving a profundity that escaped the other two. This represented Ozryel's first experience of individuality, of apartness from the energy of the deity. God is an energy, rather than an anthropomorphic being, and God's language is biology. Red blood cells, the principle of magnetic attraction, neurological synapse: each is a miracle, and in each is the presence and flow of God. When Lot's wife cut herself while preparing the herbs and oil for the bath, Ozryel beheld her blood with great curiosity; the smell of it excited him. Tempted him. And its color was precious, lush . . . like liquid rubies glinting in the candlelight. The woman—who had protested the men's presence from the start—recoiled when she discovered the archangel staring at her wound, enraptured.

Ozryel had come to earth many times. He had been there when Adam died at the age of nine hundred thirty and he had been there when the men who laughed at Noah drowned in the raging dark waters of the Flood. But he had always traversed this plane in spirit form, his essence still connected to the Lord, never having been made flesh.

So Ozryel had never before experienced hunger. Never before experienced pain. And now a flood of sensations besieged him. Having now felt the crust of the earth beneath his feet . . . felt the cold night air caress his arms . . . tasted food grown of the land and carved from its lower mammals, what he thought he would be able to appreciate at a remove, with the detachment of a tourist, he instead found drawing him closer to humankind, closer to the land itself. Closer to this breed of animal. Cool water cascading over his feet. Digested food breaking down inside his mouth, his throat. The physical experiences became addictive, and Ozryel's curiosity got the best of him.

When the men of the city converged upon Lot's house, having heard that he was harboring mysterious strangers, Ozryel was enthralled by their shouts. The men, brandishing torches and weapons, demanded to be shown the visitors, so that they might know them. So aroused were they by the rumored beauty of these travelers, they desired to possess them sexually. The brute carnality of the mob fascinated Ozryel, reminded him of his own hunger, and when Lot went to bargain with them—offering his virginal daughters instead, only to be refused—Ozryel used his power to slip outside of the house, unseen.

He shadowed the crowd, briefly. He kept a few feet away, hidden in an alley, feeling the delirious energy of the mass movement—an energy so unlike God's. Yet they were filled with the same beauty and glory that were gifts of the divine. These undulating sacs of flesh—their faces never at rest—raved as one, seeking communion with the unknown in the most animalistic manner possible. Their lust was so pure—and so intoxicating.

Much has been made of the vices in Sodom and Gomorrah but little could be seen as Ozryel walked the streets of that city, lit by a complex system of bronze oil lamps and paved in raw alabaster. Gold and silver door frames adorned the porticos of every door within its three concentric plazas.

A gold portico announced wares of the flesh and a silver one announced darker pleasures. Those who crossed the silver doorways would seek cruel or violent sensations. It was this very cruelty that God could not forgive. Not the abundance and not the abandon but the rank sadism the citizens of Sodom and Gomorrah would show to travelers and slaves. Inhospitable cities they were, and uncaring. Slaves and captured enemies were bought from caravans to please the patrons of the silver porticos.

And, whether by design or by accident, it was a silver threshold Ozryel crossed. His hostess was a stocky woman of light olive skin. Unrefined, ungroomed—the wife of a slave driver and interested only in commerce. But that night, when the hostess looked up from her post at the vestibule of the pleasure house, she saw the most beautiful, benevolent human-appearing creature standing before her by the golden light of the burning oil. The archangels were perfect, sexless vessels. No hair on their bodies or faces and immaculate, opalescent skin and pearlescent eyes. Their gums were as pale as the ivory of their teeth and the grace of their elongated limbs came from perfect proportions. They had no trace of genitalia: a biological detail that would be echoed obliquely in the horror that would spawn.

Such was the beauty—the benign magnificence—of Ozryel that the woman felt like weeping and asking for forgiveness. But years at the trade gave her the fortitude to peddle her services. As Ozryel witnessed the refined violence within the walls of the establishment, the archangel sensed his primal grace wane—abandoning him as desire arose—and even though he did not know exactly what he was looking for, he found it.

On impulse, Ozryel gripped the hostess's neck, walking her back against a low stone wall, watching the woman's expression change into fear. Ozryel felt the strong yet delicate tendons around the woman's throat, then kissed them, licked them, tasting her salty rancid sweat. And then, on an impulse, he bit, deep and hard, and tore open her flesh, plucking her arteries like harp strings with his teeth—*ping-ping*—and savagely drinking of the blood essence that poured forth. Ozryel slayed this woman, not as an offering to his almighty Lord but simply in order to know Him. *To know. To possess. To dominate and conquer.*

And the taste of the blood, and the death of the burly woman, and the fluidity of the exchange of power, was sheer ecstasy. To consume the blood, made of the essence and glory of the divine—and, in doing so, disrupting the flow that was the presence of God—put Ozryel into a frenzy.

He wanted more. Why had God denied him, His favorite, *this*? The ambrosia hidden in these imperfect creatures.

It was said that wine fermented from the worst berries tasted sweetest.

But now Ozryel wondered: what about wine from the richest berries of all?

Left with the limp body at his feet, the spilled blood shining silvery in the high light of the moon, Ozryel was left with one thought only:

Do angels have blood?

Low Memorial Library, Columbia University

Mr. Quinlan closed the pages of the *Lumen* and looked up to meet Fet and Gus, fully armed and ready to go. Much was left to learn about the Master's origins, but already his head was swimming with the information that the book held. He jotted down a few notes, circled a few transcriptions, and rose. Fet took the book and wrapped it up again, put it in his backpack, and then handed it to Mr. Quinlan.

"I will not take it with us," he said to Mr. Quinlan. "And if we don't make it, you should be the one to know where the book is hidden. If they catch us and they try to get it out of us . . . well, even if you bleed, you cannot talk about what you don't know . . . right?"

Mr. Quinlan nodded gently, accepting the honor.

"Glad to get rid of it, actually . . ."

If you say so.

"I say so. Now—if we don't make it . . . ," Fet said. "You have the most necessary tool. Finish the fight. Kill the Master."

New Jersey

ALFONSO CREEM SAT in a plush, eggshell-white La-Z-Boy recliner, his untied Pumas up on the leg rest, a hard rubber chew toy in his hand. Ambassador and Skill, his two wolf-dog hybrids, lay on the dining room floor, leashed to the broad wooden legs of the heavy table, their silvery eyes watching the red-and-white-striped ball.

Creem squeezed the toy and the dogs growled. For some reason, this amused him and thus he repeated the process over and over again.

Royal, Creem's first lieutenant—of the battle-worn Jersey Sapphires—sat on the bottom step of the staircase, spitting coffee into a mug. Nicotine, ganja, and the like were getting harder and harder to find, so Royal had jerry-rigged a delivery system for the only reliably available new-world vice: caffeine. He would tear off a small section of coffee filter, form a pouch for sprinkling ground coffee inside, then tuck it up against his gum like chaw. It was bitter, but it kept him fired up.

Malvo sat by the front window, keeping an eye on the street, watching for truck convoys. The

Sapphires had resorted to hijacking in order to keep themselves alive. The bloodsuckers varied their routes, but Creem himself had witnessed a food shipment go by a few days ago and figured they were due.

Feeding himself and his crew was Creem's first priority. It was no surprise that starvation was bad for morale. Feeding Ambassador and Skill was Creem's second priority. The wolf-hounds' keen noses and innate survival skills had more than once alerted the Sapphires to an impending night attack from the bloodsuckers. Feeding their women came third. The women were nothing very special, a few desperate strays they had picked up along the way—but they were women and they were warm and alive. "Alive" was very sexy these days. Food kept them quiet, grateful, and close, and that was good for his crew. Besides, Creem didn't go for sickly-looking, skinny women. He liked his plump.

For months now, he had been mixing it up with bloodsuckers on his old turf, just fighting to stay alive and free. It was impossible for a human to gain a foothold in this new blood economy. Cash and property meant nothing; even gold was worthless. Silver was the only black-market item worth trafficking in, besides food. The Stoneheart humans had been confiscating all the silver they could get their dirty hands on, sealing it up inside unused bank vaults. Silver was a threat to the bloodsuckers, though first you had to fashion it into a weapon, and there weren't many silversmiths around these days.

So food was the new currency. (Water was still plentiful, so long as you boiled it and filtered it.) Stoneheart Industries, after transforming their meatpacking slaughterhouses into blood camps, had left in place their basic food-transportation apparatus. The bloodsuckers, by seizing the entire organization, now controlled the spigot. Food was farmed by the humans who slaved in the camps. They supplemented the brief, two-to-three-hour window of pale sunlight each day with massive indoor ultraviolet lamp farms: glowing greenhouses for fruits and vegetables; vast warehouses for chicken, pigs, and cattle. The UV lamps were fatal for bloodsuckers, and so they were the sole human-only areas of the camps.

All this Creem had learned from hijacked Stoneheart truck drivers.

Outside the camp, food could be obtained with ration cards earned through work. You had to be a documented worker to get a ration card: you had to do the bloodsuckers' bidding in order to eat. You had to obey.

The bloodsuckers were essentially psychic cops. Jersey was a police state, with every stinger watching everything, reporting automatically, so that you never knew you had been fingered until it was too late. The suckers just worked, fed, and, for those few sunny hours each day, lay in their dirt. In general, these drones were disciplined, and—like the slave humans—ate what and when they were told: usually these packs of blood that came from the camps. Though Creem had seen a few go off the reservation. You could walk the streets at night among the bloodsuckers if you looked like you were working, but humans were expected to defer to them like the second-class citizens they were. But that just wasn't Creem's style. Not in Jersey, no sir.

He heard a little bell and collapsed the recliner, pushing himself to his feet. The bell meant a message had arrived from New York. From Gus.

Atop Gus's hideaway, the Mexican had fashioned a small coop for pigeons and some chickens. From the chickens, every once in a while he got a fresh egg packed with protein, fat, vitamins, and minerals—as valuable as a pearl from an oyster. From the pigeons, he got a way to connect to the world outside Manhattan. Safe, uncompromised, and undetected by the bloodsuckers. Some days Gus used the pigeons to set a delivery from Creem: weapons, ammo, a little porn. Creem could get almost anything for the right price.

Today was one such day. The pigeon—Harry, "the New Jersey Express," as Gus called him—had landed in a little perch by the window and was pecking at the bell, knowing that Creem would give him some food.

Creem unfastened the elastic band from its leg and removed the small plastic capsule and took out the thin roll of paper. Harry cooed softly.

"Cool it, you little shit," said Creem as he unsealed a small Tupperware container of precious corn feed and spilled some into a cup for the pigeon's reward, popping some into his own mouth before recapping it.

Creem read Gus's request. "A detonator?" He snickered. "You gotta be fucking shitting me . . ."

Malvo made a *snick-snick* noise with his tongue against his teeth. "Scout car coming," he said.

The wolf-hounds sprang up, but Creem waved at them to keep quiet. He undid their leashes from the table leg, pulling back sharply on the chain chokers to keep them silent and at his heels. "Signal the others."

Royal led the way to the attached garage. Creem was still a huge presence, despite having lost sixty pounds. His short, powerful arms were still too broad to cross over his nearly square midsection. While at home, he sported all his silver, his knuckle bling and his tooth-capping grille. Creem was into silver back when it was just shiny shit, before it became the mark of a warrior and an outlaw.

Creem watched the others slide into the Tahoe with their weapons. The transports usually traveled in a three-vehicle military convoy, bloodsuckers in the lead and the rear, with the bread truck driven by humans in the middle. Creem wanted to see some grains this time: cereal, rolls, butter loaves. Carbohydrates filled them up and lasted for days, sometimes weeks. Protein was a rare gift, and meat even rarer, but difficult to keep fresh. Peanut butter was the organic kind with oil on top—because no foods were processed anymore, ever—which Creem couldn't stand, but both Royal and the wolf-hounds loved it.

The vamps showed no fear of the wolf-hounds, but the human drivers sure did. They saw the silver glint in their lupine-canine eyes and routinely shit themselves. Creem had trained the animals only as well as he cared to train them, meaning that they always heeded him, the one who fed them. But they were not creatures meant to be domesticated or tamed, which was why Creem identified with them and kept them close at his side.

Ambassador strained at his choker; Skill's paw nails scratched at the garage floor. They knew what was coming. They were about to earn their meal. In that, they were even more motivated than the rest of the Sapphires, because for a wolf-hound, the economy had never changed. Food, food, food.

The garage door went up. Creem heard the trucks rumbling around the corner, nice and loud because there was no other traffic noise to compete with. This would be a typical jam-up. They had, idling between two houses across the street, a tow truck ready to smash the lead vehicle. Backup cars would cut off the bloodsuckers in the rear, bottlenecking the convoy in this residential street.

Keeping their cars running was another of Creem's priorities. He had guys good at that. Gasoline was at a premium, as were car batteries. The Sapphires used two garages in Jersey for chopping up food trucks for parts and fuel.

The lead truck rounded the corner fast. Creem picked up on an extra vehicle in the convoy, a fourth, but this didn't trouble him too much. Right on time, the tow truck came screeching out from across the street, tearing across the muddy front yard and bumping off the curb—ramming the rear quarter of the lead truck, putting it into a backspin hard enough that it was facing the wrong way when it came to rest. Support cars closed in fast, bumper-locking the rear truck. The middle vehicles in the convoy braked hard, veering off to the curb. Two soft-sided transports—maybe a double haul.

Royal drove the Tahoe straight at the food truck, stopping just inches from its grille. Creem released Ambassador and Skill, who went racing over the muddy yard toward the scene. Royal and Malvo jumped out, each bearing a long silver sword and a silver knife. They went right at the bloodsuckers emptying out of the lead vehicle. Royal was especially vicious. He had bolted silver spikes to the toes of his boots. The hijacking looked to be over in less than one minute.

The first thing Creem noticed that was wrong was the food truck. The human operators remained inside the cab, rather than jumping out and running. Ambassador leaped up at the driver's-side door, his choppers snapping at the closed window, the man inside looking down into the wolf-hound's angry mouth and bared teeth.

Then the soft canvas sides of the twin army trucks were pulled up like curtains. Instead of food, some twenty or thirty bloodsucker vampires came tearing out, their fury, speed, and intensity matching the wolf-hounds'. Malvo slashed off three of them hard before one got up in his face, knocking him back. Malvo twisted and fell—and they were on him.

Royal backed off, retreating like a kid with a sand pail in his hand facing an incoming tidal wave. He bumped up against his own vehicle, delaying his escape.

Creem could not see what was happening in the rear . . . but he heard the screams. And if there was one thing he had learned, it was that . . .

Vampires don't scream.

Creem ran—as much as a man of his size can run—toward his boy Royal, who was backed up against the front of the Tahoe by a gang of six bloodsuckers. Royal was all but done for, but Creem could not let him go out like that. Creem carried a .44 Magnum on his hip, and the rounds weren't made of silver, but he liked the weapon anyway. He drew it and capped off two vampires' heads, *blam, blam,* the white, acid-like vamp blood spraying into Royal's face, blinding him.

Creem saw, beyond Royal, Skill with its fangs clamped on the elbow of one of the marauding bloodsuckers. The sucker, oblivious to pain, slashed at Skill's furry throat with the hardened nail of its talonlike middle finger, opening up the wolf-hound's neck in a mess of silver-gray fur and rich, red blood.

Creem blasted the bloodsucker, opening up two holes in its throat. The sucker went down right next to the whimpering Skill in a mess of carnage.

Another pair of bloodsuckers had fallen upon Ambassador, their vampire strength overpowering the fierce animal. Creem fired away, taking chunks of head and shoulder and arm, but the silverless bullets failed to stop the suckers from ripping apart the wolf-hound.

What the gunfire did achieve was that it attracted attention to Creem. Royal was gone already, two suckers with their stingers in his neck, feeding on him right there in the middle of the street. The humans remained locked inside the cab of the decoy truck, watching, their eyes wide, with not horror but excitement. Creem got off two rounds in their direction and heard glass breaking but could not slow to see if he had hit them.

He squeezed himself through the open driver's door of the Tahoe, his bulk pushed up against the steering wheel. He threw the vehicle in reverse, the engine still running, and chewed up some yard mud as he backed away. He slammed on the brakes, tearing up more yard, then twisted the wheel to the left. Two bloodsuckers leaped into his way, and Creem hit the gas hard, the Tahoe bursting forward and running them down, its tires grinding them into the sidewalk. Creem fishtailed into the road, gunning the engine but forgetting that it had been a while since he'd operated an automobile.

He skidded sideways, grinding up against the opposite curb, blowing one of the tires off its rim. He swung the other way, overcorrecting. Creem stomped the pedal flat to the floor, got a burst of speed out of the Tahoe—and then the engine sputtered and quit.

Creem checked the dashboard panel. The gas gauge glowed "E." His crew had poured in just enough fuel for the job. The getaway van, the one with the half-full tank, was in the rear.

Creem threw open his door. He grabbed the frame and pulled himself from the vehicle, seeing the bloodsuckers running toward him. Dirty-pale, barefoot, naked, bloodthirsty. Creem reloaded his .44 from the only other clip on his belt, blasting holes in the bastards, who, as in nightmares, kept coming. When the gun clicked empty, Creem threw it aside and went at the suckers with his silver-covered fists, his bling punches packing extra force and pain. He yanked off one of his chains and started strangling a bloodsucker with it, swinging the creature's body around to block the other ghouls' clutching, battering hands.

But he was weak from malnutrition, and, big as he was, he tired easily. They overtook him, but rather than go right at his throat, they locked his big arms in their own and with preternatural strength dragged the sweat-drenched gang leader off the street. They hauled him up two steps into a looted convenience store, bracing him there in a seated position on the floor. Gassed, Creem unleashed a string of curses until heavy breathing dizzied him, and he started to black out. As the store spun in his vision, he wondered what the hell they were waiting for. He wanted them to choke on his blood. He had no worries about being turned into a vampire; that was one of the distinct advantages to having a mouth full of repellent silver.

Two humans stepped inside, Stoneheart employees in neat black suits like the undertakers they were. Creem thought they had arrived to strip him of his silver, and he rallied, fighting with all he had left. The bloodsuckers kneeled into his arms, twisting them in pain. But the Stonehearts merely watched over him as he slumped on the floor, gasping for air.

Then the atmosphere inside the store changed. The only way to describe it is the way things get so still outside right before a storm. Creem's hair stood up on the back of his neck. Something was about to happen. This was like the moment when two hands go rushing toward each other, the instant before the clap.

A humming entered Creem's brain like the rumble of a dentist's drill, only without the vibration. Like the roar of an approaching helicopter without the wind. Like the droning chant of a thousand monks—only without the song.

The bloodsuckers stiffened up like soldiers awaiting inspection. The two Stonehearts stepped to the side, against an empty aisle rack. The suckers on either side of Creem relinquished their grip on him, pulling away, leaving him sitting alone in the middle of the dirty linoleum . . .

. . . as a dark figure entered the store.

Camp Liberty

THE TRANSPORT JEEP was a repurposed military vehicle with an expanded cargo bed and no roof. Mr. Quinlan drove at breakneck speed through the lashing rain and inky darkness; his vampire vision required no headlights. Eph and the others bumped along in the back, getting soaked as they hurtled blindly through the night. Eph closed his eyes against the rain and the rocking, feeling like a small boat caught in a typhoon, battered but determined to ride it out.

They stopped finally, and Eph lifted his head and looked up at the immense gate, dark against the dark sky. No light was necessary. Mr. Quinlan cut the Jeep's engine, and there were no sounds or voices, other than the rain and the mechanical rumble of a distant generator somewhere inside.

The camp was enormous and all around it a featureless concrete wall was being erected. At least twenty feet high, it had crews working on it day and night, raising rebar, pouring concrete by stadium quartz lights. It would be ready very soon, but for the time being, a gate constructed of chain link backed by wooden planks gave access to the camp.

For some reason, Eph had imagined he would hear children crying, adults screaming, or some other form of audible anguish, being near so much human suffering. The darkly quiet exterior of the camp spoke to an oppressive efficiency that was almost as shocking.

No doubt they were being watched by unseen *strigoi*. Mr. Quinlan's body registered bright and hot in the vampires' heat-sensitive vision, with the five other beings in the back of the Jeep reading as cooler humans.

Mr. Quinlan lifted a baseball equipment bag from the passenger seat and lay it across his shoulder as he exited the Jeep. Eph stood dutifully, his wrists, waist, and ankles bound by nylon rope. The five of them were knotted together with only a few feet of slack between them, like members of a chain gang. Eph was in the middle, Gus in front of him, Fet in back. First and last were Bruno and Joaquin. One by one they hopped down from the back of the vehicle, landing in the mud.

Eph could smell the *strigoi,* their feverlike earthiness and their ammoniac waste. Mr. Quinlan walked alongside Eph, accompanying his prisoners into the camp.

Eph felt as though he were walking into the mouth of the whale and feared being swallowed. He knew going in that the odds were no better than even that he would ever emerge from this slaughterhouse again.

Communication was handled wordlessly. Mr. Quinlan was not exactly on the other vampires' wavelength, telepathically, but the existence of his psychic signal was enough to pass first inspection. Physically, he appeared less gaunt than the rank-and-file vampires, his pale flesh more lily-petal smooth than dead and plastic, his eyes a brighter red with an independent spark. They shuffled down a narrow canvas tunnel beneath a roof constructed of chicken fencing. Eph looked up through the wire into the falling rain and the sheer blackness of the starless sky.

They arrived at a quarantine station. A few battery-powered work lamps illuminated the room, as this area was manned by humans. With the low-wattage light casting shadows against the walls, and the relentless rain outside, and the palpable sense of being surrounded by hundreds of malevolent beings, the quarantine station resembled a scared little tent in the middle of a vast jungle.

The staff's heads were all shaved. Their eyes were dry and tired-looking, and they wore slate-gray prison-grade jumpsuits and perforated rubber clogs.

The five were asked to provide their names, and each man lied. Eph signed a scribble next to his pseudonym with a dull pencil. Mr. Quinlan stood in the background, before a canvas wall thumping with rain, while four *strigoi* stood golemlike, one pair of sentries at either flap door.

Mr. Quinlan's story was that he had captured five outliers squatting in a cellar beneath a Korean market on 129th Street. A blow to the head, suffered in the act of subduing his cargo, explained his glitchy telepathy—whereas, in fact, Quinlan was actively blocking the vampires from accessing his true thoughts. He had shed his oversized pack, laying it down on the damp canvas floor near his boots.

The humans first tried to untie the binding knots, in hopes of preserving the rope for reuse. But the wet nylon would not budge and had to be cut. Under the watchful eyes of the vampire guards, Eph remained standing with his eyes down, rubbing his raw wrists. It was impossible for him to look a vampire in the eye without showing hatred. Also, he was concerned about being recognized by the *strigoi* hive mind.

He was aware of a disturbance brewing inside the tent. The quiet was awkward, the sentries directing their attention at Mr. Quinlan. The *strigoi* had picked up on something different about him.

Fet noticed this too, because he suddenly started talking, trying to direct attention away from Quinlan. "When do we eat?" he asked.

The human with the clipboard looked up from his note-taking. "Whenever they feed you."

"Hope it's not too rich," he said. "I don't do well with rich foods."

They stopped what they were doing, staring at Fet as though he were insane. The lead man said, "I wouldn't worry about it."

"Good," said Fet.

One of the *strigoi* noticed that Mr. Quinlan's pack remained on the floor in the corner of the room. The vampire reached for the long, heavy bag.

Fet stiffened near Eph. One of the human personnel grasped Eph's chin, using a penlight to examine the interior of his mouth. The man had bags beneath his eyes the color of black tea. Eph said, "Were you a doctor?"

"Sort of," said the man, looking at Eph's teeth.

"How 'sort of'?"

"Well, I was a veterinarian," he said.

Eph closed his mouth. The man flicked the light beam in and out of Eph's eyes, intrigued by what he saw.

"You've been taking some medication?" asked the vet.

Eph didn't like the vet's tone. "Sort of," he answered.

"You're in pretty bad shape. Kinda tainted," said the vet. Eph saw the vampire drawing the zipper back on the pack. The nylon shell was lined with lead from the X-ray aprons of a midtown dentist's office. Once the *strigoi* felt the disruptive properties of the silver blades, he dropped the pack as though scalded.

Mr. Quinlan rushed for the pack. Eph pushed the veterinarian, knocking the man all the way across the tent. Mr. Quinlan shoved past the *strigoi* and pulled a sword quickly from the pack, turning, holding it out. The vampires were at first too stunned to move as the surprise presence of silver, in the form of a weapon, held them back. Mr. Quinlan advanced slowly in order to give Fet, Gus, and the others time to grab their weapons. Eph felt a hell of a lot better once he got a sword into his hands. The weapon Mr. Quinlan brandished was actually Eph's blade, but there was no time to quibble.

The vampires did not react as humans would. None of them ran out the door to escape or warn others. The alarm went out psychically. Their attack, after the initial shock, came swiftly.

Mr. Quinlan cut one down with a blow to the neck. Gus rushed forward, meeting a charging vampire and running his blade straight through its throat. Decapitation was difficult in close quarters because the broad slashing required to sever the neck risked wounding others, and the blood spray was caustic, laden with infectious worm parasites. Close-quarters combat with *strigoi* was always a last resort, and so the five of them fought their way out of the quarantine intake room as quickly as possible.

Eph, the last to arm himself, was set upon not by vampires but by humans. The veterinarian and one other. He was so startled, he reacted to the attack as though they were *strigoi* and stabbed the vet through the base of his neck. Red arterial spray spritzed the wooden supporting pole in the center of the room as both Eph and the veterinarian stared at each other with wide eyes. "What the hell are you doing!" yelled Eph. The veterinarian sank to his knees, and the second man turned his attention to his wounded friend.

Eph backed away slowly from the dying man, pulled on his shoulder by one of the others. He was shaken; *he had killed a man.*

They stepped out of the tent, emerging into the open air inside the camp. The rain had slowed to a misty drizzle. A canvas-roofed path lay before them, but the night prevented Eph from taking in the camp as a whole. No *strigoi* yet, but they knew that the alarm had gone out. It took their eyes a few moments to adjust to the darkness—out of which the vampires came running.

The five of them fanned out in an arc, taking on all comers. Here there was room to swing the blade freely, to plant one's rear foot and drive the sword with enough force to lift the head from the shoulders. Eph hacked hard, moving and slashing and checking constantly behind him.

In this way, they repelled the initial wave.

They continued ahead, though without any intelligence as to the organization of the camp. They looked for some indication of where the general population was located. Another pair of vampires came at them from the left, and Mr. Quinlan, protecting his flank, cut them down, then led the others in that general direction.

Ahead, silhouetted against the darkness, was a tall, narrow structure: a lookout post in the center of a stone circle. More vampires came running at top speed and the five men tightened up, moving as a unit, five silver blades cutting together almost as one wide one.

They needed to kill fast. The *strigoi* had been known to sacrifice one or more of their number in an attempt at improving their chances of capturing and turning a human aggressor. Their strategy was such that one or three or even ten vampires were worth sacrificing for the elimination of one human slayer.

Eph curled back behind the others, taking the rear, walking backward as they formed a moving oval, a ring of silver to hold the swarming vampires at bay. His eyes becoming more acclimated to the dark, Eph perceived other *strigoi* slowing in the distance, congregating, holding back. Tracking without attacking. Planning some more coordinated assault.

"They're massing," he told the others. "I think we're being pushed this way."

He heard the wet cut of a sword, then Fet's voice. "A building up ahead. Our only hope is to go zone by zone."

We broke out into the camp too early, said Mr. Quinlan.

The sky as yet was showing no sign of brightening. Everything hinged upon that unreliable window of sunlight. The trick now was to last inside enemy territory until the uncertain dawn.

Gus swore and cut down another creature. "Stay tight," said Fet.

Eph continued his slow walk backward. He could just make out the faces of the first line of vampires pursuing them, staring intently. Staring—it seemed—at him.

Was it just his imagination? Eph slowed, then stopped altogether, allowing the others to progress a few yards without him.

The pursuing vampires stopped as well.

"Ah, shit," said Eph.

They had recognized him. The equivalent of an all-points bulletin on the vampire psychic network was a hit. The hive was alerted to his presence, which meant only one thing.

The Master knew that Eph was there. Watching this through its drones.

"Hey!" said Fet, doubling back to Eph. "What the hell are you doing stopping . . . ?" He saw the *strigoi,* maybe two dozen of them, staring. "Jesus. What are they, starstruck?"

Awaiting orders.

"Christ, let's just—"

The camp whistle went off—jolting them—a shrill steam scream followed by four more in quick succession. Then silence again.

Eph understood the alarm's purpose: to alert

not just the vampires but also the humans. A call to take shelter, perhaps.

Fet looked to the nearest building. He again checked the sky for light. "If you can lead them away from here, from us—we can get in and out of this place that much more quickly."

Eph had no desire to be a bouncing red chew toy for this pack of bloodsuckers, but he saw the logic in Fet's plan. "Just do me a favor," he said. "Make it fast."

Fet called back, "Gus! Stay with Eph."

"No way," said Gus. "I'm going in. Bruno, get with him."

Eph smiled at Gus's obvious distaste for him. He caught Mr. Quinlan's arm and pulled him back, trading the sword he carried for his own.

I will take care of the human guards, Mr. Quinlan said, and disappeared in a flash.

Eph regripped the familiar leather handle, then waited for Bruno to come up at his side. "You okay with this?"

"Better than okay," said Bruno, out of breath but smiling wide, like a kid. His super-white teeth looked great against his light-brown skin.

Eph lowered his sword, jogging off to the left and away from the structure. The vamps hesitated a moment before following. Eph and Bruno rounded the corner of a long, shedlike outbuilding, all dark. Beyond it, light shone from inside a window.

Lights meant humans.

"This way!" said Eph, breaking into a run. Bruno kept pace, panting. Eph looked back and, sure enough, the vampires were charging around the corner after them. Eph ran toward the light, seeing a vampire standing near the door to the building.

He was a big male, backlit by the faint window light. On his large chest and the sides of his trunk-like neck, Eph saw fading tattoo ink, turned green by the white blood and multiple stretch marks.

At once, like a traumatic memory forcing its way back into his consciousness, the Master's voice was inside Eph's head.

What are you here for, Goodweather?

Eph stopped and pointed his sword at the big vamp. Bruno spun around next to him, keeping an eye on the drones behind them.

What is it you came here to get?

Bruno roared next to Eph, hacking down two charging vampires. Eph turned, momentarily distracted, seeing the others bunched up just a few yards away—respecting the silver—and then, realizing he had allowed himself to become distracted, turned back fast with his sword up.

The tip of his sword caught the charging vampire in the right breast, entering skin and muscle but not running him through. Eph withdrew quickly and stabbed at the vampire's throat, just as the thing's jaw was beginning to drop, baring its stinger. The tattooed vampire shivered and dropped to the ground.

"Fuckers!" yelled Bruno.

They were all coming now. Eph wheeled and readied his sword. But there were just too many, and all moving at once. He started backpedaling—

You are here searching for someone, Goodweather.

—and felt stones beneath his feet as he neared the building. Bruno kept hacking and slaying as Eph backed up three steps, feeling for the door handle, opening the latch, the door giving way.

You are mine now, Goodweather.

The voice boomed, disorienting him. Eph pulled on Bruno's shoulder, motioning to the gangbanger to follow him inside. They ran past makeshift cages on either side of the narrow walkway, containing humans in various stages of distress. A madhouse of sorts. The people howled at Eph and Bruno as they hurried through.

Dead end, Goodweather.

Eph shook his head hard, trying to chase the Master's voice from his mind. Its presence was addling, like the voice of madness itself. Add to that the people clawing at the cages as he passed, and Eph was caught in a cyclone of confusion and terror.

The first of the pursuing vampires entered the other end. Eph tried one door, leading to an office of sorts, with a dentist-style chair whose headrest, and the floor beneath it, was crusted with dry, red human blood. Another door led outside, Eph jumping down three steps. More vampires awaited him, having gone around the building rather than through it, and Eph swung and chopped, turning just in time to catch one female leaping at him from the roof.

Why did you come here, Goodweather?

Eph leaped back from the slain female. He and Bruno backed away, side by side, heading toward an unlit, windowless structure set against the high perimeter fence. Perhaps the vampires' quarters? The camp *strigoi*'s nest?

Eph and Bruno angled themselves, only to find that the fence turned sharply and ended at another unlit structure.

Dead end. I told you.

Eph stood up to the vampires coming toward them in the dark.

"Undead end," Eph muttered. "You bastard."

Bruno glanced over at him. "Bastard? You the one who ran us into this trap!"

Once I catch you and turn you, I will know all your secrets.

That turned Eph cold. "Here they come," he said to Bruno—and got ready for them.

Nora had arrived at Barnes's office inside the administrative building ready to agree to anything, including giving herself to Barnes, in order to save her mother and get close to him. She despised her former boss even more than the vampire oppressors. His immorality sickened her—but the fact that he believed she was weak enough to simply bend to his will made her nauseous.

Killing him would show him that. If his fantasy was her submission, her plan was to drive the shank into his heart. Death by butter knife: how fitting!

She would do it as he lay in bed or in the middle of his dinner patter, so hideously civilized. He was more evil than the *strigoi*: his corruption was not a disease, was not something inflicted *upon* him. His corruption was opportunistic. A choice.

Worst of all was his perception of her as a potential victim. He had fatally misread Nora, and all that was left was for her to show him the error of his ways. In steel.

He made her wait out in the hallway, where there was no chair or bathroom, for three hours. Twice he left his office, resplendent in his crisp, white admiral's uniform, strolling past Nora carrying some papers but never acknowledging her, passing without a word, disappearing behind another door. And so she waited, stewing, even when the single camp whistle signaled the rations call, one hand across her grumbling stomach—her mind squarely focused on her mother and murder.

Finally, Barnes's assistant—a young female with clean, shoulder-length auburn hair, wearing a laundered gray jumpsuit—opened the door, admitting Nora without a word. The assistant remained in the doorway as Nora passed through. Perfumed skin and minty breath. Nora returned the assistant's look of disapproval, imagining just how the woman had secured such a plum position in Barnes's world.

The assistant sat behind her desk, leaving Nora to try the next door, which was locked. Nora turned and retreated to one of the two hard folding chairs against the wall facing the assistant. The assistant made busy noises in an effort to ignore Nora while simultaneously asserting her superiority. Her telephone buzzed and she lifted the receiver, answering it quietly. The room, save for the unfinished wooden walls and the laptop computer, resembled a low-tech 1940s-era office: corded telephone, a pen and paper set, blotter. On the near corner of the desk, just off the blotter, sat a thick chocolate brownie on a small paper plate. The assistant hung up after a few whispered words and noticed Nora staring at the treat. She reached for the plate, taking just a nibble of the dessert cake, a few stray crumbs sprinkling down into her lap.

Nora heard a click in the doorknob, followed by Barnes's voice.

"Come in!"

The assistant moved her treat to the other side of her desk, out of Nora's reach, before waving her through. Nora again walked to the door and turned the knob, which, this time, gave way.

Barnes was standing behind his desk, stuffing files into an open attaché case, preparing to leave for the day. "Good morning, Carly. Is the car ready?"

"Yes, sir, Dr. Barnes," sang the assistant. "They just called up from the gate."

"Call down and make sure the heat is on in the back."

"Yes, sir."

"Nora?" said Barnes, still stuffing, not looking up. His demeanor was much changed from their previous encounter at his palatial home. "You have something you wish to discuss with me?"

"You win."

"I win? Wonderful. Now tell me, what is it I have won?"

"Your way. With me."

He hesitated just a moment before closing the case, snapping the clasps. He looked at her and nodded slightly to himself, as though having trouble remembering his original offer. "Very good," he said, then went rooting in a drawer for some other nearly forgotten thing.

Nora waited. "So?" she said.

"So," he said.

"Now what?"

"Now I am in a very great rush. But I will let you know."

"I thought . . . I'm not going back to your house now?"

"Soon. Another time. Busy day and all."

"But—I'm ready now."

"Yes. I thought you would grow a bit more eager. Camp life doesn't agree with you? No, I didn't think so." He took up the handle of his case. "I'll soon call for you."

Nora understood: he was making her wait on purpose. Prolonging her agony as payback for not immediately falling into bed with him that day at his house. A dirty old man on a power trip.

"And please note for future reference that I am not a man to be kept waiting. I trust that is clear to you now. Carly?"

The assistant appeared in the open doorway. "Yes, Dr. Barnes?"

"Carly, I can't find the ledger. Maybe you can search around and bring it by the house later."

"Yes, Dr. Barnes."

"Say, around nine thirty?"

Nora saw in assistant Carly's face not the satisfied swagger she was anticipating but instead a hint of distaste.

They stepped out into the anteroom, whispering. Ridiculous, as if Nora were Barnes's wife.

Nora took the opportunity to rush to Barnes's desk, searching it for anything that might help her cause, any bit of information she was not supposed to see. But he had taken most everything with him. Sliding out the center drawer, she saw a computer-generated map of the camp with each zone color-coded. Beyond the birthing area she had already visited, and in the same general direction as where she understood the "retirement" section of camp was established, was a zone named "Letting." This zone contained a shaded area labeled "Sunshine." Nora tried to rip up the map in order to take it with her, but it was glued to the bottom of the drawer. She scanned it again, quickly memorizing it, then shut the drawer just as Barnes returned.

Nora worked hard to mask the fury in her face, to regard him with a smile. "What about my mother? You promised me—"

"And if indeed you hold up your end of the bargain, I shall of course hold up mine. Scout's honor."

It was clear he wanted her to beg, which was something she simply could not bring herself to do.

"I want to know that she is safe."

Barnes nodded, grinning a little. "You want to

make demands, is what you want. I alone dictate the timing of this and everything else that occurs inside the walls of this camp."

Nora nodded, but her mind was elsewhere now, her wrist already wriggling behind her back, pushing the shank forward.

"If your mother is to be processed, she will be. You have no say in the matter. They probably picked her up already and she is on her way to be cleaned up. Your life, however, is still a bargaining chip. Hope you cash it in."

Now she had the shank in her hand. She gripped it.

"Is that understood?" he said.

"Understood," she said through gritted teeth.

"You will need to come with a much more agreeable attitude when I do call for you, so please be ready. And smile."

She wanted to fucking kill him where he stood.

From the outer office, his assistant's panicked voice broke the mood. "Sir?"

Barnes stepped away before Nora could act, returning to the anteroom alone.

Nora heard the footsteps charging up the stairs. Slapping at the floor: bare feet.

Vampire feet.

A team of four large-framed, once-male vampires burst into the office. These undead goons wore tribal prison-style tattoos on their sagging flesh. The assistant gasped and backed away into her corner as the four went right after Barnes.

"What is it?" he said.

They told him, telepathically—and fast. Barnes

barely had time to react before they grabbed his arms and practically picked him up, running him out the door and away down the hall. Then the camp whistle started shrieking.

Shouting outside. Something was happening. Nora heard and felt the vibration of doors slamming downstairs.

The assistant remained in the corner, behind her desk, the phone to her ear. Nora heard hard footsteps charging up the stairs. Boots equaled humans. The assistant cowered while Nora moved to the door—just in time to see Fet rushing inside.

Nora was struck speechless. He carried his sword but no other weapons. His face was wild with the look of the hunt. A grateful, open-mouthed smile appeared on her face.

Fet glanced at Nora and then at the assistant in the corner, then turned to leave. He was back out the door and almost out of sight around the corner before he stopped, straightened, and looked back.

"Nora?" he said.

Her baldness. Her jumpsuit. He hadn't recognized her at first.

"V," she said.

He gripped her, and she clawed at his back, burying her face in his smelly, unwashed shoulder. He pulled her off him for a second look, at once exulting in his great luck in finding her and trying to make sense of her shaved head.

"It's you," he said, touching her scalp. Then he looked over the rest of her. "You . . ."

"And you," she said, tears springing from the corners of her eyes. *Not Eph, again. Not Eph. You.*

He embraced her again. More bodies followed behind him. Gus and another Mexican. Gus slowed when he saw Fet hugging a bald camp member. It was a long moment before he said, "Dr. Martinez?"

"It's me, Gus. Is it really you?"

"*A guevo!* You better believe it," he said.

"What is this building?" asked Fet. "Administration or something? What are you doing here?"

For a moment, she couldn't remember. "Barnes!" she said. "From the CDC. He runs the camp—runs all the camps!"

"Where the hell is he?"

"Four big vampires just came and got him. His own security force. He went that way."

Fet stepped out into the empty hall. "This way?"

"He has a car out by the gate." Nora stepped into the hallway. "Is Eph with you?"

A pang of jealousy. "He's outside holding them off. I'd go after this guy Barnes for you, but we have to get back to Eph."

"And my mother." Nora gripped Fet's shirt. "My mother. I'm not leaving without her."

"Your mother?" said Fet. "She's still here?"

"I think so." She held Fet's face. "I can't believe you're here. For me."

He could've kissed her. He could have. Amid the chaos and the turmoil and the danger—he could've. The world had vanished around them. It was her—only her in front of him.

"For you?" said Gus. "Hell, we like this killing shit. Right, Fet?" His grin undercut his words. "We gotta get back to my homeboy Bruno."

Nora followed them out the door, then abruptly stopped. She turned back to Carly, the assistant, still standing behind her desk in the far corner of the anteroom, the telephone in her hand hanging low at her side. Nora rushed back toward her, Carly's eyes widening with fright. Nora reached across her desk, grabbing the rest of the brownie off its paper plate. She took a big bite and threw the rest at the wall next to the assistant's head.

But in her moment of triumph, Nora felt only pity for the young woman. And the brownie didn't taste anywhere near as good as Nora thought it would.

Out in the open yard, Eph hacked and swung, clearing as much space around himself as possible. Six feet was the outside limit for vampire stingers; the combined length of his arm and his sword gave him about that distance. So he kept slashing, carving out a six-foot-wide radius of silver.

But Bruno did not share Eph's strategy. He instead took on each individual threat as it appeared, and, because he was a brutally efficient killer, he had gotten away with it thus far. But he was also tiring. He went after a pair of vampires threatening from his blind side, but it was a ruse. When he took the bait, the *strigoi* separated him from Eph, filling in the gap between them. Eph tried to slice his way back over to Bruno, but the vampires stuck to their strategy: separate and destroy.

Eph felt the building at his back. His circle of silver became a semicircle, his sword like a burning torch keeping the darkness of vampirism at bay. A few of them dropped to all fours, trying to dart underneath his reach and pull him down by the legs, but he managed to strike at them, and strike hard, the mud at his feet turning white. But as the bodies piled up, Eph's radius of safety continued to contract.

He heard Bruno grunt, then howl. Bruno was backed up against the high perimeter fence. Eph watched him slice off a stinger with his sword, but too late. Bruno had been stung. Just a moment of contact, of penetration, but the damage had been done: the worm implanted, the vampire pathogen entering his bloodstream. But Bruno had not been drained of blood, and he continued to battle, in fact with renewed vigor. He fought on, knowing that, even if he were to survive this onslaught, he was doomed. Dozens of worms wriggled under the skin of his face and neck.

The other *strigoi* around Eph, psychically apprised of this success, sensed victory and surged toward Eph with abandon. A few came off Bruno to shove the encroaching vampires from behind, further shrinking Eph's zone of safety. Elbows tucked at his sides, he swung and cut at their wild faces, their swaying crimson wattles and open mouths. A stinger shot out at him, striking the wall near his ear with an arrow-like thump.

He sliced it down, but there were more. Eph tried to keep up a wall of silver, his arms and shoulders screaming in pain. All it took was for one stinger to get through. He felt the force of the vampire mob closing in on him. Mr. Quinlan landed in the middle of the fight and joined instantly. He made a difference but they all knew they were just holding back the tide. Eph was about to be overrun.

It would be over soon.

A flare of light opened in the sky above them. Eph believed it was in fact a flare or some other pyrotechnic device sent up by the vampires as an alert signal or even a deliberate distraction. One moment of inattention and Eph was done for.

But the flare light kept shining, intensifying, expanding overhead. It was moving, higher than he realized.

Most important, the vampire attack slowed. Their bodies stiffened as their openmouthed heads turned toward the dark sky.

Eph could not believe his good fortune. He readied his sword to cut a swath through the *strigoi* in a last-gasp gambit to kill his way to safety . . .

But even he couldn't resist. The sky-fire was too seductive. He too had to risk a peek at the polluted sky.

Across the black sackcloth of planet-smothering ash, a fierce flame was falling, cutting like the blaze from an acetylene torch. It burned through the darkness like a comet, a head of pure flame leading a narrowing tail. A searing teardrop of red-orange fire unzipping the false night.

It could only have been a satellite—or something even bigger—plummeting from the outer orbit, reentering Earth's atmosphere like a fiery cannonball launched from the defeated sun.

The vampires backed away. With their red eyes locked on the streak of flame, they stumbled over one another with a rare lack of coordination. This was fear, thought Eph—or something like it. The sign in the sky reached their elemental selves, and they possessed no mechanism to express this terror other than a squealing noise and a clumsy retreat.

Even Mr. Quinlan retreated a bit. Overwhelmed by the light and the spectacle.

As the falling satellite burned bright in the sky, it parted the dense ash cloud and a brutal shaft of daylight penetrated the air like the finger of God, burning it all, falling over a three-mile radius that included the outer edges of the farm.

As the vampires burned and squealed, Fet and Gus and Joaquin met them coming the other way. The three of them ran into the panicked mob, cutting down the outliers before their attack triggered a full-blown riot, the vampires running off in every direction.

For a moment, the majestic column of light revealed the camp around them. The high wall, the dour buildings, the mucky ground. Plain verging on ugly, but only menacing in its ordinariness. This was like the back lot behind the showroom or the dirty restaurant kitchen: the place without artifice, where the real work gets done.

Eph watched the streak burn across the sky

with increasing intensity, its head flaming thicker and brighter until it finally consumed itself and the angry trail of fire thinned to a wisp of flame—and then nothing.

Behind it, the much anticipated daylight had finally begun brightening the sky, as though heralded by that timely streak of flame. The pale outline of the sun was barely visible behind the ash cloud, a few of its rays filtering down through seams and weaknesses in the pollution cocoon. It was barely enough light for early dawn in the former world—but it was enough. Enough to drive the fleeing creatures underground for an hour or two.

Eph saw a camp prisoner following Fet and Gus, and despite her bald head and shapeless jumpsuit, he instantly recognized her as Nora. A jarring mix of emotions struck him. It seemed as though years instead of weeks had passed since they'd last met. But right now there were more pressing issues.

Mr. Quinlan retreated into the shadows. His tolerance to UV had been tested to its limit.

I will meet you . . . back at Columbia . . . I wish you all good luck.

With that, he bolted up the walls and out of the camp, effortlessly. In the blink of an eye, he was gone.

Gus noticed Bruno gripping his neck and went to him. *"Qué pasó, vato?"*

"Fucker's in me," said Bruno. The gangbanger grimaced, wetting his dry lips, then spitting onto the ground. His posture was open and strange, as though he could feel the worms already crawling inside him. "I'm damned, homes."

The others all went silent. Gus, in his shock, reached for Bruno's face, examining his throat. Then he pulled him into a hard hug. "Bruno," he said.

"Fucking savages," said Bruno. "Lucky fucking shot."

"Goddamn it!" yelled Gus, pulling away from him. He didn't know what to do. No one did. Gus stepped away and launched a ferocious howl.

Joaquin went toward Bruno with tears in his eyes. "This place," he said, jabbing the point of his sword into the ground. "This is fucking hell on earth." Then he raised his sword toward the sky, bellowing, *"I am gonna slay every last one of these bloodsuckers in your name!"*

Gus came back fast. He pointed at Eph. "You made it okay, though. Huh? How's that? You were supposed to stay together. What happened to my boy?"

Fet stepped between them. "It's not his fault."

"How you know that?" said Gus, hurt burning in his eyes. "You was with me!" Gus spun around, went back to Bruno. "Tell me it was this motherfucker's fault, Bruno, I'll kill him right here, right now. Tell me!"

But Bruno, if he even heard Gus, didn't answer. He was examining his hands and arms, as though looking for the worms infesting him.

Fet said, "It's the vampires who are to blame, Gus. Stay focused."

"Oh, I'm focused," said Gus. He moved toward

Fet threateningly, but Fet let him come up on him, knowing he had to vent his despair. "Like a laser fucking beam. I'm the Silver Ninja." Gus pointed at Eph. "I'm focused."

Eph started to defend himself but held his tongue, realizing that Gus wasn't interested in what really happened. Anger was the only way the young gangbanger could express his pain.

Fet turned to Eph. "What was that thing in the sky?"

Eph shrugged. "I don't know. I was done for, like Bruno. They were on me—it was over. And then that thing streaked across the sky. Something falling to earth. Spooked the *strigoi*. Extraordinary dumb luck."

"That wasn't luck," said Nora. "That was something else."

Eph stared, thrown off by Nora's bald appearance. "Something else like what?"

"You can deny it," said Nora, "or maybe you don't want to know. Maybe you don't even care. But that didn't just *happen,* Ephraim. That happened to *you*. To *us*." She eyed Fet and clarified. "To all of us . . ."

Eph was confused. A thing burning up in the atmosphere happened because of them?

"Let's get you out of here," he said. "And Bruno. Before anyone else gets hurt."

"No way," said Gus. "I'm tearing this place down. I want to find the fucker who did my boy."

"No," said Nora, stepping forward, the smallest among them. "We're going to get my mother first."

Eph was stunned. "But, Nora . . . you don't really think she's still here, do you?"

"She is still alive. And you of all people are not going to believe who told me this."

Nora told Eph about Everett Barnes. Eph was mystified at first, wondering why she would joke about something like that. Then he was flat-out flabbergasted. "Everett Barnes, in charge of a blood camp?"

"In charge of all the blood camps," said Nora.

Eph resisted it a moment more, only to see how right it was. The worst thing about this news was how much sense it made. "That son of a bitch."

"She's here," said Nora. "He said she was. And I think I know where."

"Okay," said Eph, exhausted and wondering how far he could push this delicate matter. "But you remember what Barnes tried to do to us before."

"That doesn't matter."

"Nora." Eph did not want to spend any more time than was necessary inside this death trap. "Don't you think Barnes would have told you anything—"

"We need to go get her," Nora said, half turning away from him.

Fet came to her defense. "We have sun-time," he said. "Before the cloud of ashes closes again. We're going to look."

Eph looked at the big exterminator, then back at Nora. They were making decisions together. Eph was outvoted.

"Fine," said Eph. "Let's make it quick."

* * *

With the sky glow allowing a bit of light into the world—like a dimmer slowly rotated from the lowest to the second-to-lowest setting—the camp appeared as a dingy, military-style outpost and prison. The high fence ringing the perimeter was topped with tangles of concertina wire. Most of the buildings were cheaply constructed and caked with grime from the polluted rain—with the notable exception of the administration building, on the side of which was displayed the old Stoneheart corporate symbol: a black orb bisected laterally by a steel-blue ray, like an eye blinking shut.

Nora quickly led them under the canvas-covered path running deeper into the camp, passing other interior gates and buildings.

"The birthing area," she told them, pointing out the high gate. "They isolate pregnant women. Wall them off from the vampires."

"Maybe superstition?"

Nora said, "It looked more like quarantine to me. I don't know. What would happen to an unborn fetus if the mother were turned?"

Fet said, "I don't know. Never thought about that."

"They have," said Nora. "Seems like they've taken careful precautions against it ever happening."

They continued past the front gate, along the interior wall. Eph kept checking behind them. "Where are all the humans?" he asked.

"The pregnant women live in trailers back there. The bleeders live in barracks to the west. It's like a concentration camp. I think they will process my mother in that area farther ahead."

She pointed at two dark buildings beyond the birthing zone, neither of which looked promising. They hurried farther along to the entrance to a large warehouse. Guard stations set up outside were empty at the moment.

"Is this it?" asked Fet.

Nora looked around, trying to get her bearings. "I saw a map . . . I don't know. This isn't what I envisioned."

Fet checked the guard stations first. Inside was a bank of small-screen monitors, all dark. No on/off switches, no chairs.

"Vamps guard this place," said Fet. "To keep humans out—or in?"

The entrance was not locked. The first room inside, which would have been the office or reception area, was stocked with rakes, shovels, hoes, hose trolleys, tillers, and wheelbarrows. The floor was dirt.

They heard grunts and squeals coming from inside. A nauseating shudder rippled through Eph, as he at first thought they were human noises. But no.

"Animals," said Nora, moving to the door.

The vast warehouse was a humming brightness. Three stories tall, and twice the size of a football field or a soccer pitch, it was essentially an indoor farmstead and impossible to take in all at once. Suspended from the rafters high above were great lamps, with more lighting rigs erected over large garden plots and an orchard. The heat inside the warehouse was extreme but mitigated by a manufactured breeze that circulated via large vent fans.

Pigs congregated in a muddy enclosure outside an unroofed sty. A high-screened henhouse sat opposite, near what sounded like a cowshed and a sheep shelter. The smell of manure carried on the ventilating breeze.

Eph had to shield his eyes at first, with the lights pouring down from above, all but eliminating any surface shadows. They started down along one of the lanes, following a perforated irrigation pipe set on two-foot-high legs.

"Food factory," said Fet. He pointed out cameras on the buildings. "People work it. Vamps keep an eye on them." He squinted up into the lights. "Maybe there's UV lights mixed in with the regular lamps up there, mimicking the range of light offered by the sun."

Nora said, "Humans need light too."

"Vamps can't come inside. So people are left alone in here to tend the flock and harvest produce."

Eph said, "I doubt they are left alone."

Gus made a hissing noise to get their attention. "Rafters," he said.

Eph looked up. He turned around, taking in a three-hundred-sixty-degree view until he saw the figure moving along a catwalk maybe two-thirds of the way up the long wall.

It was a man, wearing a long, drab, duster-style coat and a wide-brimmed rain hat. He was moving as fast as he could along the narrow, railed walkway.

"Stoneheart," said Fet. Eldritch Palmer's league of fellow travelers, who since his demise had transferred their allegiance to the Master when the Master assumed control of Palmer's corporation's vast industrial infrastructure. *Strigoi* sympathizers and—in terms of the new food-and-shelter-based economy—profiteers.

"Hey!" yelled Fet. The man did not respond but only lowered his head and moved more quickly.

Eph ran his eyes along the walkway to the corner. Mounted on a wide, triangular platform—both an observation post and a sniper's perch—was the long barrel of a machine gun, tipped toward the ceiling, awaiting an operator.

"Get low!" said Fet, and they scattered, Gus and Bruno running back toward the entrance, Fet grabbing Nora and running her to the corner of the henhouse, Eph hustling toward the sheep shelter, Joaquin heading for the gardens.

Eph ducked and ran along the fence, this bottleneck being the very thing he had feared. He wasn't going to perish by human hands, though. That much he had decided long ago. They were open targets down here in the serene, brightly lit interior farmstead—but Eph could do something about that.

The sheep were agitated, bleating too loudly for Eph to hear anything else. He glanced back at the corner and saw Gus and Bruno racing toward a ladder to the side. The Stoneheart reached the perch and was fooling with the mounted repeater, turning the muzzle end down toward the ground. He lashed out first at Gus, strafing the ground behind him until he lost the angle. Gus and Bruno started up the left-side wall, but the ladder did not run directly beneath; the Stoneheart might have another chance at them before they reached the catwalk.

Eph threw off the wire loops holding the sheep inside their shelter. The gate door banged open and they went bleating into the enclosure. Eph found the hinged section of fence and vaulted over it, working the outside catch. He grabbed the fence and raised his feet just in time, riding it open in order to avoid being trampled by the escaping sheep.

He heard gunfire but didn't look back, running to the cowshed and doing the same, throwing up the rolling door and turning the herd loose. These were not fat Holsteins but rather cows in the dictionary definition of the term only: thin, loose-hided, walleyed, and fast. They went every which way, a number of them galumphing into the orchard and knocking into the weak-trunked apple trees.

Eph went around the dairy, looking for the others. He saw Joaquin far right, behind one of the garden lamps with a tool in his hand, using it to aim the hot lamp up at the corner shooter. A genius idea, it worked perfectly, distracting the Stoneheart so that Gus and Bruno could charge up the exposed section of ladder. Joaquin dove for cover as the Stoneheart ripped at the lamp, exploding the bulb in a shower of sparks.

Fet was up and running, using one wayward heifer as a partial shield as he broke for a ladder on the near wall, to the right of the shooter's perch. Eph edged around the corner of the dairy, thinking about making a run for the wall himself, when the dirt started popping before his feet. He bolted backward just as the rounds chewed the wooden corner where his head had been.

The ladder shivered under his weight as Fet climbed hand-over-hand toward the catwalk. The Stoneheart was swung all the way around, trying to angle his fire at Gus and Bruno, but they were low on the walkway, his rounds clanking off the intervening iron slats. Someone below turned another lamp on the Stoneheart, and Fet could see the man's face locked in a grimace, as though he knew he was going to lose. Who were these people who would willingly do the vampires' bidding?

Inhuman, he thought.

And that thought powered Fet up the last few rungs. The Stoneheart was still unaware of his blind-side approach but could turn at any time. Imagining the long barrel of the gun swinging his way made him run faster, drawing his sword from his pack.

Inhuman motherfuckers.

The Stoneheart heard or felt Fet's pounding boots. He swung around, wide-eyed, firing the gun before he had completed the sweep, but too late. Fet was too close. He ran his sword through the Stoneheart's belly, then pulled it back.

Bewildered, the man slumped to his knees, appearing as shocked by Fet's betrayal of the new vampiric order as Fet was by the Stoneheart's betrayal of his own kind. Out of this offended expression vomited bile and blood, bursting onto the barrel of the smoking weapon.

The man's agonal suffering was wholly unlike any vampire's. Fet was not used to killing fellow humans. The silver sword was well suited for vampire killing but completely inefficient for dispatching humans.

Bruno came charging from the other catwalk, seizing the man before Fet could react, grabbing him up and dumping him over the low edge of the perch. The Stoneheart twisted in the air, trailing gore, landing headfirst.

Gus grabbed the trigger end of the hot weapon. He swung it around, surveilling the artificial farmstead below them. He tipped it up, aiming it at the multitude of lights beaming down on the farm like cooking lamps.

Fet heard yelling and recognized Nora's voice, finding her below, waving her arms and pointing at the gun as sheep trotted past.

Fet grabbed the tops of Gus's arms, just below his shoulders. Not restraining him, just getting his attention. "Don't," he said, referring to the lamps. "This food is for humans."

Gus winced. He wanted to light up the place. Instead, he pulled away from the bright lamps and fired straight out across the cavernous building, rounds punching holes in the far wall, ejected cartridges raining onto the perch.

Nora was the first one out of the indoor farm. She could feel the others pulling on her to leave; the pale light would fade from the sky soon. She grew more frantic with each step, until she was running.

The next building was surrounded by a fence covered with opaque black netting. She could see the building inside, an older structure, original to the former food-processing plant, not vast like the farmstead. A faceless, industrial-appearing building that fairly screamed "slaughterhouse."

"Is this it?" asked Fet.

Beyond it, Nora could see a turn in the perimeter fence. "Unless . . . unless they changed it from the map."

She clung to hope. This was obviously not the entrance to a retirement community or any sort of hospitable environment.

Fet stopped her. "Let me go in first," he said. "You wait here."

She watched him start away, the others closing around her like doubts in her mind. "No," she said at once, and caught up with him. Her breath was short, her words coming quietly. "I'm going too."

Fet rolled back the gate just wide enough for them to enter. The others followed to a side doorway apart from the main entrance, where the door was unlocked.

Inside, machinery hummed. A heavy odor permeated the air inside, difficult to place at first.

The metallic smell of old coins warmed in a sweaty fist. Human blood.

Nora shut down a little then. She knew what she was going to see even before she reached the first pens.

Inside rooms no larger than a handicapped restroom stall, high-backed wheelchairs were reclined beneath coiled plastic tubes dangling from longer feeder tubes overhead. Flushed clean, the tubes were meant to carry human blood into larger vessels suspended from tracks. The pens were empty now.

Farther ahead, they passed a refrigeration room where the product collected from this terrible blood drive was packed and stored. Forty-two days was the natural limit for viability, but as vampire sustenance—as pure food—maybe the window of time was shorter.

Nora imagined seniors being brought here, sitting slumped in the wheelchairs, tubes taking blood from their necks. She saw them with their eyes rolling back in their sockets, perhaps guided here by the Master's control of their older, fragile minds.

She grew more frantic and kept moving, knowing the truth but unable to accept it. She tried calling her mother's name, and the silence that answered was awful, leaving her own voice echoing in her ears, ringing with desperation.

They came to a wide room with walls tiled three-quarters of the way to the ceiling and multiple drains in the red-stained floor. An abattoir. Wrinkled bodies sagged on hooks, flayed skin lying like pelts piled upon the floor.

Nora gagged, but there was nothing in her stomach to come up. She gripped Fet's arm, and he helped her stay on her feet.

Barnes, she thought. That uniform-wearing butcher and liar. "I am going to kill him," she said.

Eph appeared at Fet's side. "We have to go."

Nora, her head buried in his chest, felt Fet nod.

Eph said, "They'll send helicopters. Police, with regular guns."

Fet wrapped Nora in his arm and walked her to the nearest door. Nora didn't want to see any more. She wanted to leave this camp for good.

Outside, the dying sky glowed a jaundiced yellow. Gus climbed into the cab of a backhoe parked across the dirt roadway, near the fence. He fooled with the controls, and the engine started.

Nora felt Fet stiffen, and she looked up. A dozen or so ghostlike humans in jumpsuits stood near, having wandered over from the barracks in violation of curfew. Drawn by the machine gun fire, no doubt, and curiosity over the cause of the alarms. Or perhaps these dozen had drawn the short straws.

Gus came down from the backhoe to yell at them, berating them for being so passive and cowardly. But Nora called on him to stop.

"They're not cowards," she said. "They're malnourished, they have low blood pressure, hypotension . . . We have to help them help themselves."

Fet left Nora to climb into the cab of the backhoe, trying out the controls.

"Gus," said Bruno. "I'm staying here."

"What?" said Gus.

"I'm staying here to fuck up this sick shit. Time for a little revenge. Show them they bit the wrong motherfucker."

Gus got it. Immediately, he understood. "You're one fucking badass hero, *hombre*."

"The baddest. Badder than you."

Gus smiled, the pride he felt for his friend choking him up. They gripped hands, pulling each other in for a tight bro-hug. Joaquin did the same.

"We'll never forget you, man," said Joaquin.

Bruno's face was set angry to hide his softer emotions. He looked back at the bloodletting building. "Neither will these fuckers. I guarantee it."

Fet had turned the backhoe around and now drove it forward, ramming straight into the high perimeter fence, the tractor's wide treads riding up and over it.

Police sirens were audible now. Many of them, growing closer.

Bruno went to Nora. "Lady?" he said. "I'm going to burn down this place. For you and for me. Know that."

Nora nodded, still inconsolable.

"Now go," said Bruno, turning and starting back into the slaughterhouse with his sword in hand. "All of you!" he yelled at the humans wearing camp jumpsuits, scaring them away. "I need every minute I got."

Eph offered Nora his hand, but Fet had returned for her, and she left under Fet's arm, moving past Eph—who, after a moment, followed them over the downed razor wire.

Bruno, raging with pain, felt the worms move inside of him. The enemy was inside his circulatory system, spreading throughout his organs and wriggling inside his brain. He worked quickly to transport the stand-alone UV lamps from the farmstead garden to the bloodletting factory, setting them inside the doors to delay the incursion of the vampires. Then he set about severing the tubes and dismantling the blood-collecting apparatus as though he were tearing apart his own infected arteries. He stabbed and sliced the refrigerated packs of blood, leaving the floor and his clothes awash in scarlet. It splattered everywhere, drenching him, but not before he made sure he wasted every last unit. Then he went about destroying the equipment itself, the vacuums and pumps.

The vampires trying to enter were getting fried by the UV light. Bruno tore down the carcasses and human pelts but did not know what else to do with them. He wished for gasoline and a source of flame. He started up the machinery and then hacked at the wiring, hoping to short-circuit the electrical system.

When the first policeman broke through, he found a wild-eyed, bloody-red Bruno trashing the place. Without any warning he fired upon

Bruno. Two rounds broke his collarbone and snapped his left shoulder, shattering it to pieces.

He heard more entering and climbed up a ladder alongside storage shelves, ascending to the highest point in the building. He hung one-handed over the approaching cops and vampires driven wild both by the destruction he had wrought and by the blood soaking his body, dripping to the floor. As vampires ran up the ladder, bounding toward him, Bruno arched his neck over the hungry creatures below, pressing his sword to his throat, and—*Fuck you!*—wasted the very last vessel of human blood remaining in the building.

New Jersey

THE MASTER LAY still within the loam-filled coffin—long ago handcrafted by the infidel Abraham Setrakian—loaded into the cargo hold of a blacked-out van. The van was part of a four-vehicle convoy crossing from New Jersey back into Manhattan.

The many eyes of the Master had seen the bright trace of the burning spaceship blazing across the dark sky, ripping open the night like God's own fingernail. And then the column of light and the unfortunate but not surprising return of the Born . . .

The timing of the brilliant streak in the sky coincided exactly with Ephraim Goodweather's moment of crisis. The fiery bolt had spared his life. The Master knew: there were no coincidences, only omens.

Which meant what? What did this incident portend? What was it about Goodweather that had provoked the agencies of nature to come to his rescue?

A challenge. A true and direct challenge—one that the Master welcomed. For victory is only as great as one's enemy.

That the unnatural comet burned the skies over New York confirmed the Master's intuition that the site of its origin, still unknown, was somewhere within that geographic region.

This knowledge engaged the Master. In a way, it echoed the comet that had announced the birthing site of another god walking the earth two thousand years ago.

Night was about to fall, the vampires about to rise. Their king reached out, readying them for battle, mobilizing them with its mind.

Every last one of them.

JACOB AND THE ANGEL

Saint Paul's Chapel, Columbia University

Acid rain had continued to fall abundantly and steadily, staining everything, soiling the city.

Atop the exterior domed structure on Saint Paul's Chapel, Mr. Quinlan observed as the column of daylight started to close and lightning detonated within the dark clouds. Sirens were audible now. Police cars were visible heading toward the camp. Human police would soon be there. He hoped Fet and the others could evacuate soon.

He found the small maintenance niche at the base of the dome. There he retrieved the book: the *Lumen*. He crawled deeper into the niche and found refuge in a structural alcove—away from the rain and the incipient daylight. It was a cramped place beneath the granite roof structure and Mr. Quinlan fit snugly. In a notebook he had jotted some observations, annotated some clues. Safe and dry, he carefully laid down the book.

And he began to read again.

INTERLUDE III

OCCIDO LUMEN:

SADUM AND AMURAH

THE ANGEL OF DEATH SANG WITH THE VOICE OF GOD as the cities were destroyed in a rain of sulfur and fire. God's face was revealed and His light burned it all in a flash.

The exquisite violence of the immolation was, however, nothing to Ozryel—not any longer. He yearned for more personal destruction. He longed to violate the order, and in doing so, achieve mastery over it.

As Lot's family fled, his wife turned back and gazed into God's face, ever changing, impossibly radiant. Brighter than the sun, it burned everything around her and turned her into a pillar of white, crystalline ashes.

The explosion transformed the sand within

a five-mile radius of the valley into pure glass. And over it the archangels walked on, their mission accomplished, ordered to return to the ether. Their time as men on earth was at an end.

Ozryel felt the warm smooth glass beneath his soles and felt the sun upon his face and felt an evil impulse rising within him. With the flimsiest of excuses, he lured Michael away from Gabriel, leading him up a rocky bluff, where he cajoled Michael into spreading his silver wings and feeling the heat of the sun upon them. Thus aroused, Ozryel could not control his impulses any longer and fell upon his brother with extraordinary strength, tearing open the archangel's throat and drinking his luminous, silvery blood.

The sensation was beyond belief. Transcendent perversion. Gabriel came upon him in the throes of violent ecstasy, Ozryel's brilliant wings open to their full expanse, and was appalled. The order was to return immediately, but Ozryel, still in the grip of mad lust, refused and tried to turn Gabriel away from God.

Let us be Him, here on earth. Let us become gods and walk among these men and let them worship us. Have you not tasted the power? Does it not command you?

But Gabriel held fast, summoning Raphael, who arrived in human form on an arrow of light. The beam paralyzed Ozryel, fixing him to the earth he so loved. He was held between two rivers. The very rivers that fed the canals in Sadum. God's vengeance was swift: the archangels were ordered to rend their brother to pieces and scatter his limbs around the material world.

Ozryel was torn asunder, into seven pieces, his legs, arms, and wings cast to distant corners of the earth, buried deep, until only his head and throat remained. As Ozryel's mind and mouth were most offensive to God, this seventh piece was flung far into the ocean, submerged many leagues deep. Buried in the darkest silt and blackest sand at the bottom. No one could ever touch the remains. No one could remove them. There they would stay until the day of judgment at the end of days when all life on earth would be called forth before the Creator.

But, through the ages, tendrils of blood seeped out of the interred pieces and gave birth to new entities. The Ancients. Silver, the closest substance to the blood they drank, would forever have an ill effect on them. The sun, the closest thing to God's face on earth, would always purge them and burn them away, and as in their very origin, they would remain trapped between moving bodies of water and could never cross them unassisted.

They would know no love and could breed only by taking life. Never giving it. And, should the pestilence of their blood ever spread without control, their demise would come from the famine of their kind.

Columbia University

Mr. Quinlan saw the different glyphs and the coordinates that signaled the location of the internments.

All the sites of origin.

Hastily, he wrote them down. They corresponded perfectly to the sites the Born had visited, gathering the dusty remains of the Ancients. Most of them had a nuclear plant built above them and had been sabotaged by the Stoneheart Group. The Master had of course prepared this coup very carefully.

But the seventh site, the most important of them all, appeared as a dark spot on the page. A negative form in the northeastern Atlantic Ocean. With it, two words in Latin: *Oscura. Aeterna.*

Another, odd shape was visible in the watermark.

A falling star.

The Master had sent helicopters. They had seen them from the windows of their cars on the slow drive south, back to Manhattan. They crossed the Harlem River from Marble Hill, staying off the parkways, abandoning their vehicles near Grant's Tomb and then making their way through the steady night rain like regular citizens, slipping onto the abandoned campus of Columbia University.

While the others went below to regroup, Gus crossed Low Plaza to Buell Hall and rode the service dumbwaiter to the roof. He had his coop up there, for the messenger pigeons.

His "Jersey Express" was back, squatting underneath the perch gutter Gus had fashioned.

"You're a good boy, Harry," said Gus as he unfurled the message, scrawled in red pen on a strip of notebook paper. Gus immediately recognized Creem's all-capitals handwriting, as well as his former rival's habit of crossing out his *O*'s like null signs.

HEY MEX.
BAD HERE—ALWAYS HUNGRY.
MIGHT CØØK BIRD WHEN IT FLY BACK.
GØT YR MESSAGE ABØUT DETØNATØR.
GØT IDEA 4 U. GIMME YR LØCATIØN

AND PUT ØUT SØME DAMN FØØD.
CREEM CØMIN 2 TØWN. SET MEET.

Gus ate the note and found the carpenter's pencil he stowed with the corn feed and shreds of paper. He wrote back to Creem, okaying the meet, giving him a surface address on the edge of campus. He didn't like Creem, and he didn't trust him, but the fat Colombian was running the black market in Jersey, and maybe, just maybe, he could come through for them.

Nora was exhausted but could not rest. She cried for long bouts. Shuddering, howling, her abs hurting from the intense sobbing.

And when silence finally came she kept running her palm over her bare head, her scalp tingling. In a way, she thought, her old life, her old self—the one that had been born that night in the kitchen, the one birthed out of tears—was now gone. Born to tears, died by tears.

She felt jittery, empty, alone . . . and yet somehow renewed. The nightmare of their current existence, of course, paled in comparison to imprisonment in the camp.

Fet sat at her side constantly, listened attentively. Joaquin sat near the door, leaning against the wall, resting a sore knee. Eph leaned against the far wall, his arms crossed, watching her try to make sense of what she had seen.

Nora thought that Eph had to suspect her feelings for Fet by now; this was clear from his posture and his location across the room from them. No one had spoken of it yet, but the truth hung over the room like a storm cloud.

All this energy and these overlapping emotions kept her talking fast. Nora was still most hung up on the pregnant campers in the birthing zone. Even more so than on her mother's death.

"They're mating women in there. Trying to produce B-positive offspring. And rewarding them with food, with comfort. And they . . . *they seem to have adjusted to it.* I don't know why that part of it haunts me so. Maybe I'm too hard on them. Maybe the survival instinct isn't this purely noble thing we make it out to be. Maybe it's more complicated than that. Sometimes surviving means compromise. *Big* compromise. Rebellion is hard enough when you're fighting for yourself. But once you have another life growing in your belly . . . or even a young child . . ." She looked at Eph. "I understand it better now, is what I'm trying to say. I know how torn you are."

Eph nodded once, accepting her apology.

"That said," said Nora, "I wish you had met me at the medical examiner's office when you were supposed to. My mother would still be here today."

"I was late," said Eph, "I admit that. I got hung up—"

"At your ex-wife's house. Don't deny it."

"I wasn't going to."

"But?"

"Just that you being found here wasn't my fault."

Nora turned toward him, surprised by the challenge. "How do you figure that?"

"I should have been there. Things would have been different had I been there on time. But I didn't lead the *strigoi* to you."

"No? Who did?"

"You did."

"I . . . ?" She could not believe what she was hearing.

"Computer use. The Internet. You were using it to message Fet."

There. It was out. Nora stiffened at first, a wave of guilt, but quickly shook it off. "Is that right?"

Fet rose to defend her. All six feet plus of him. "You shouldn't talk to her like that."

Eph did not back up. "Oh, I shouldn't—? I've been in that building for months with almost no problem. They're monitoring the Net. You know that."

"So I brought this on myself." Nora slipped her hand underneath Fet's. "My punishment was a just punishment—in your eyes."

Fet shuddered at the touch of her hand. And as her fingers wrapped around his thick digits, he felt as if he could cry. Eph saw the gesture—small under any other circumstances—as an eloquent public expression of the end of his and Nora's relationship.

"Nonsense," Eph said. "That's not what I meant."

"That is what you are implying."

"What I am implying—"

"You know what, Eph? It fits your pattern."

Fet squeezed her hand to slow her down, but she blew past that stop sign. "You're always showing up just after the fact. And by 'showing up,' I mean 'getting it.' You finally figured out how much you loved Kelly . . . *after* the breakup. You realized how important being an involved father was . . . *after* you weren't living with Zack anymore. Okay? And now . . . I think maybe you're going to start realizing how much you needed me. 'Cause you don't have me anymore." It shocked her to hear herself saying these things out loud, in front of the others—but there it was. "You're always just a little too late. You've spent half your life battling regrets. Making up for the past rather than getting it done in the present. I think the worst thing that ever happened to you was all your early success. The 'young genius' tag. You think if you work hard enough, you can fix the precious things you've broken—rather than being careful with them in the first place." She was slowing down now, feeling Fet pulling her back—but her tears were flowing, her voice hoarse and full of pain. "If there's one thing you should have learned since this terrible thing started, it's that nothing is guaranteed. Nothing. Especially other human beings . . ."

Eph remained still across the room. Pinned to the floor, actually. So still that Nora wasn't sure her words had gotten through to him. Until, after an appropriate amount of silence, when what Nora said appeared to be the last word, Eph stood off the wall and slowly walked out the door.

* * *

Eph walked the ancient corridor system, feeling numb. His feet made no impact upon the floor.

Twin impulses had torn at him in there. At first, he wanted to remind Nora how many times her mother had nearly gotten them captured or turned. How badly Mrs. Martinez's dementia had slowed all of them down over the past many months. Evidently, it didn't matter now that Nora had, numerous times, directly expressed her wish that her mother be taken from them. No. Everything that went wrong was Eph's fault.

Second, he was stunned to see how close she seemed to Fet now. If anything, her abduction and ultimate rescue had brought them closer together. Had strengthened their new bond. This twisted most sharply in his side, because he had seen saving Nora as a dry run for saving Zack, but all it had done was expose his deepest fear: that he might save Zack and still find him changed forever. Lost to Eph—forever.

Part of him said it was already much too late. That part of him was the depressive part, the part he tried to stave off constantly. The part he medicated with pills. He felt around for the pack on his back and unzipped the small compartment meant for keys or loose change. His last Vicodin. He placed it on his tongue and then held it there as he walked, waiting to work up enough saliva to swallow it.

Eph conjured up the video image of the Master overlooking its legion in Central Park, standing high upon Belvedere Castle with Kelly and Zack at its side. This green-tinted image haunted him, ate at him as he kept walking, only half-aware of his direction.

I knew you would return.

Kelly's voice and the words were like a shot of adrenaline, straight to his heart. Eph turned into a familiar-looking corridor and found the door, heavy wood and iron-hinged, not locked.

Inside the asylum chamber, in the center of the corner cage, stood the vampire that was once Gus's mother. The dented motorcycle helmet tilted ever so slightly, acknowledging Eph's entrance. Her arms remained bound behind her back.

Eph approached the cage door. The iron bars were spaced six inches apart. Vinyl-sleeved, braided steel-cable bicycle locks secured the door at the top, bottom, and through the old padlock clasp in the middle.

Eph waited for Kelly's voice. The creature stood still, its helmet steady—perhaps it was expecting its daily blood feed. He wanted to hear her. Eph grew frustrated and stepped back, looking around the room.

On the rear wall, hanging from a rusty nail, was a small ring containing a single, silver key.

He retrieved the key, bringing it to the cell door. No movement from the creature. He fit the key into the top lock and it opened. Then the bottom, and then the middle lock. Still no indication of awareness from the vampire that was Gus's mother. Eph unwound the cables from the iron bars and slowly pulled open the door.

The door scraped against its frame, but the

hinges were oiled. Eph pulled the door wide and stood in the opening.

The vampire did not move from her spot in the center of the cell.

You can never go down / can never go down . . .

Eph drew his sword and stepped inside. Closer now, he saw his dim reflection in the black-tinted face shield, his sword low at his side.

The creature's silence pulled him nearer to his reflection.

He waited. A vampiric hum in his head, but slight.

This thing was reading him.

You have lost another. Now you have no one. No one but me.

"I know who you are," Eph said.

Who am I?

"You have Kelly's voice. But these are the Master's words."

You came to me. You came to listen.

"I don't know why I came."

You came to hear your wife's voice again. It is as much a narcotic as those pills you take. You really need it. You really miss it. Don't you?

Eph did not ask how the Master knew about that. He only knew that he had to be on his guard at all times—even mentally.

You want to come home. To return home.

"Home? Meaning, to you? To the disembodied voice of my former wife? Never."

Now it is time to listen. Now is not the time to be obstinate. Now is the time to open your mind.

Eph said nothing.

I can give you back your boy. And I can give you back your wife. You can release her. Start anew with Zack by your side.

Eph held his breath in his mouth before exhaling, hoping to slow his rising heart rate. The Master knew how desperate Eph was for Zack's release and return, but it was important to Eph that he not *appear* desperate.

He is unturned, and will remain that way, a lesser being, as you wish.

And then, out of his mouth came the words he never thought he would utter: "What is it you want in return?"

The book. The Lumen. *And your partners. Including the Born.*

"The what?"

Mr. Quinlan, I think you call him.

Eph frowned. "I can't do that."

Certainly you can.

"I *won't* do that."

Certainly you will.

Eph closed his eyes and tried to clear his head, reopening them a moment later. "And if I refuse?"

I will proceed as planned. The transformation of your boy will happen immediately.

"Transformation?" Eph trembled, sickened, but fought to suppress his emotions. "What does that mean?"

Submit while you still have something with which to bargain. Give yourself to me in your son's stead. Get the book and bring it to me. I will take the information contained in the book . . . and the information contained in your mind. I will know all. You can even return the book. No one will know.

"You would give Zack to me?"

I will give him his freedom. The freedom to be a weak human, just like his father.

Eph tried to hold back. He knew better than to allow himself to be drawn into this conversation, to be lulled into an exchange with the monster. The Master continued to poke around his mind, looking for a way in.

"Your word means nothing."

You are correct, in that I have no moral code. There is nothing to compel me to uphold my end of the bargain. But you might consider the fact that I keep my word more often than not.

Eph stared at his reflection. He fought, relying on his own moral code. And yet . . . Eph was indeed tempted. A straight-up trade—his soul for Zack's—was one he would make in a minute. The thought of Zack falling prey to this monster—either as a vampire or as an acolyte—was so abhorrent, Eph would have agreed to nearly anything.

But the price was far greater than his own tarnished soul. It meant the souls of the others as well. And the fate, more or less, of the entire human race, in that Eph's capitulation would give the Master final and lasting stewardship of the planet.

Could he trade Zack for everything? Could his decision be the right one? One he wouldn't look back at with the greatest regret?

"Even if I were to consider this," said Eph, talking as much to his reflected self as he was to the Master, "there is one problem. I don't know the location of the book."

You see? They are keeping it from you. They don't trust you.

Eph saw that the Master was right. "I know they don't. Not anymore."

Because it would be safer for you to know where it was, as a fail-safe.

"There is a transcription—some notes I have seen. Good ones. I can deliver you a copy."

Yes. Very good. And I will deliver to you a copy of your boy. Would you like that? I require possession of the original. There is no substitute. You must find out its location from the exterminator.

Eph suppressed his alarm at the Master knowing about Fet. Did the Master get it from Eph's mind? Was he raiding Eph's knowledge as they spoke here?

No. Setrakian. The Master must have turned him before the old man destroyed himself. The Master had seized all of Setrakian's knowledge just as he now wanted to seize all of Eph's: through possession.

You have proven yourself quite resourceful, Goodweather. I am confident you can find the Lumen.

"I haven't agreed to anything yet."

Haven't you? I can tell you now that you will have some assistance in this endeavor. An ally. One among your inner circle. Not physically turned—no. Only sympathetically. A traitor.

Eph did not believe this. "Now I know that you are lying."

Do you? Tell me this. How would this lie profit me?

". . . By stirring up discontent."

There is already plenty of that.

Eph thought about it. It seemed true: he could find no advantage for the Master in lying.

There is one among you who will betray you all.

A turncoat? Had another one of them been co-opted? And then Eph realized that, in expressing it that way, he was already counting himself as having been co-opted as well.

"Who?"

This person will reveal themselves to you, in time.

If another had been compromised and chose to deal with the Master without Eph—then Eph could lose his last, best chance at saving his son.

Eph felt himself swaying. He felt this enormous tension in his mind. Fighting to keep the Master out, and fighting to keep his doubts in.

"I . . . would need a little time with Zack beforehand. Time to explain my actions. To justify them, and to know that he is fine, to tell him—"

No.

Eph waited for more. "What do you mean, no? The answer is yes. Make it part of the deal."

It is not part of any deal.

"Not part of any . . . ?" Eph saw his dismay in the faceplate reflection. "You don't understand. I can barely even consider doing what you have proposed here. But there is no way—no way in hell—that I go through with this unless I get a guaranteed opportunity to see my boy and know that he is fine."

And what you don't understand is that I have nei-

ther patience nor sympathy for your superfluous human emotions.

"No patience . . . ?" Eph pointed the tip of his silver sword at the helmet in angry disbelief. "Have you forgotten that I have something you want? Something you apparently very desperately need?"

Have you forgotten that I have your son?

Eph stepped backward as though shoved. "I can't believe what I am hearing. Look—this is simple. I'm inches away from saying yes. All I'm asking for is ten goddamned minutes . . ."

It is even simpler than that. The book for your boy.

Eph shook his head. "No. Five minutes—"

You forget your place, human. I have no respect for your emotional needs and will not make them part of the terms. You will give yourself to me, Goodweather. And you will thank me for the privilege. And every time I look at you for the rest of eternity here on this planet, I will regard your capitulation as representative of the character of your entire race of civilized animals.

Eph smiled, his crooked mouth like a weird gash across his face, so stunned was he by the creature's abject heartlessness. It reminded him of what he was up against—what they were all up against—in this cruel and unforgiving new world. And it astounded him how tone-deaf the Master was when it came to human beings.

In fact, it was this lack of comprehension—this utter inability to feel sympathy—that had caused the Master to underestimate them time and time again. A desperate human is a dangerous human, and this was one truth the Master could not divine.

"You would like my answer?" asked Eph.

I have your answer, Goodweather. All I require is your capitulation.

"Here is my answer."

Eph reared back and swung at the proxy vampire standing before him. The silver blade sliced low through the neck, lifting the helmeted head from the shoulders, and Eph no longer had to stare at the reflection of his traitorous self.

Minimal spray as the body sagged, the caustic white blood pooling on the ancient floor. The helmet clunked and clattered into the corner, rolling around wobblingly before settling on its side.

Eph had not struck at the Master so much as he had struck at his own shame and his anguish at this no-win situation. He had slain the mouthpiece of temptation in lieu of striking down the temptation itself—an act he knew to be utterly symbolic.

The temptation remained.

Footsteps approached from the hallway, and Eph backed away from the decapitated body, at once realizing the consequence of his actions.

Fet was first inside. Nora followed, stopping short. "Eph! What have you done . . . ?"

In isolation, his impetuous attack seemed just. Now the consequences came rushing at him, with new footsteps from the hall: Gus.

He did not see Eph at first. He was focused on the interior of the cell in which he kept his mother the vampire. He roared and pushed past the other two and saw the headless body collapsed on the floor, its hands still manacled behind its back, the helmet in the corner.

Gus let out a cry. He drew a knife from his backpack, then rushed at Eph faster than Fet could react. Eph raised his sword at the last moment, to parry Gus's attack—as a dark blur filled the space between them.

A starkly white hand gripped Gus's collar, holding him off. Another hand thrust against Eph's chest as the hooded being separated them with powerful strength.

Mr. Quinlan. Dressed in his black hoodie, radiating vampire heat.

Gus swore and kicked, fighting to get free, his boots a few inches from the ground. Tears of rage flowing freely from his eyes. "Quinlan, let me at this fuck!"

Slow.

Mr. Quinlan's rich baritone invaded Eph's head.

"Let me *go*!" Gus slashed with his knife, but it was little more than a bluff. As furious as Gus was, he still had the presence of mind to respect Mr. Quinlan.

Your mother is destroyed. It is done. And it is for the best. She was gone a long time ago and what was left—it was no good for you here.

"But that choice was mine—! What I did or not—my choice!"

Settle your differences as you wish. But—later. After the final battle.

Quinlan turned his piercing red eyes toward Gus, glowing hot within the dark shadow of his cotton hood. A royal red, richer than the hue of any natural object Gus had ever seen—even the freshest human blood. More red than the reddest autumn leaf and brighter and deeper than any plumage.

And yet, even as Quinlan was one-handedly lifting a man from the floor, these eyes were in repose. Gus would not like to see them turned on him in anger. At least for the moment, he held back his attack.

We can take the Master. But our time is short. We must do it—together.

Gus pointed past Mr. Quinlan, at Eph. "This junkie is worthless to us. He got the lady doctor caught, he cost me one of my men, and he is a fucking hazard and—worse than that—he's a curse. This shit is bad luck. The Master has his son and has adopted him and leashed him like a fucking pet."

It was Eph's turn to go after Gus. Mr. Quinlan's hand quickly came up against Eph's chest with the restraining force of a steel pole.

"So tell us," said Gus, not letting up. "Tell us what that motherfucker was whispering to you in here, just now. You and the Master having a heart-to-heart? I think the rest of us have a right to know."

Quinlan's hand rose and fell with Eph's deep breaths. Eph stared at Gus, feeling Nora's and Fet's eyes on him.

"Well?" said Gus. "Let's hear it!"

"It was Kelly," said Eph. "Her voice. Taunting me."

Gus sneered, spitting into Eph's face. "Weak-minded piece of shit."

Again a scuffle started. Fet and Mr. Quinlan were needed to keep the two men from tearing each other apart.

"He's so desperate for the past, he came here to be talked down to," said Gus. "Some dysfunctional family shit you got going." To Mr. Quinlan, Gus said, "I tell you, he brings nothing. Let me fucking kill him. Let me get rid of this dead weight."

As I said, you may settle this any way you desire. But, after.

It was apparent to all, even to Eph, that Mr. Quinlan was protecting him for some reason. That he was treating Eph differently than he might have treated the others—which meant that there was something different about Eph.

I need your help, gathering one final piece. All of us. Together. Now.

Mr. Quinlan released Gus, who surged toward Eph one last time, but with his knife down. "I have nothing left," he said, up in Eph's face like a snarling dog. "Nothing. I will kill you when this is all over."

The Cloisters

THE HELICOPTER'S ROTORS fought off wave after wave of stinging black rain. The dark clouds had unleashed a torrent of polluted precipitation, and yet, despite the darkness, the Stoneheart pilot wore aviator sunglasses. Barnes feared the man was flying blind and could only hope that they remained at a sufficient altitude over the Manhattan skyline.

Barnes swayed in the passenger compartment, hanging on to the seat belt straps crossing over his shoulders. The helicopter, chosen from among a number of models at the Bridgeport, Connecticut, Sikorsky plant, shook laterally as well as vertically. The rain seemed to be getting in under the rotor, slapping sideways against the windows as though Barnes were aboard a small boat in a storm at sea. Accordingly, his stomach lurched and its contents began to rise. He unclipped his helmet just in time to vomit into it.

The pilot pushed his joystick forward, and they began to descend. Into what, Barnes had no clue. Distant buildings were blurred through the wavy windshield, then treetops. Barnes assumed they were setting down in Central Park, near Belvedere Castle. But then a hostile gust of wind spun the helicopter's tail like a weather vane arrow, the pilot fighting the joystick for control, and Barnes glimpsed the turbulent Hudson River to his near right, just beyond the trees. It couldn't be the park.

They touched down roughly, first one skid, then the other. Barnes was just grateful to be back on solid ground, but now he had to walk out into a maelstrom. He pushed open the door, exiting into a blast of wet wind. Ducking under the still-spinning rotors and shielding his eyes, he saw, on a hilltop above, another Manhattan castle.

Barnes gripped his overcoat collar and hurried through the rain, up slick stone steps. He was out of breath by the time he reached the door. Two vampires stood there, sentries, unbowed by the pelting rain, yet half obscured by the steam emanating from their heated flesh. They did not acknowledge him, nor did they open the door.

The sign read, THE CLOISTERS, and Barnes recognized the name of a museum near the northern tip of Manhattan, administered by the Metropolitan Museum of Art. He pulled on the door and entered, waiting for it to close, listening for movement. If there was any, the pounding rain obscured it.

The Cloisters was constructed from the remnants of five medieval French abbeys and one Romanesque chapel. It was an ancient piece of southern France transported to the modern era, which in turn now resembled the Dark Ages. Barnes called out, "Hello?" but heard nothing in response.

He wandered through the Main Hall, still short of breath, his shoes soaked, his throat raw. He looked out at the garden cloisters, once planted to represent the horticulture of medieval times, which now, due to negligence and the oppressive vampiric climate, had degenerated into a muddy swamp. Barnes continued ahead, turning twice at the sound of his own dripping but apparently alone within the monastery walls.

He wandered past hanging tapestries, stained-glass windows begging for sunlight, and medieval frescoes. He passed the twelve Stations of the Cross, set in the ancient stone, stopping briefly at the strange crucifixion scene. Christ, nailed to the center cross, was flanked by the two thieves, their arms and legs broken, tied to smaller crosses. The carved inscription read PER SIGNU SANCTECRUCIS DEINIMICIS NOSTRIS LIBERA NOS DEUS NOSTER. Barnes's rudimentary Latin translated this as "Through the sign of the Holy Cross, from our enemies, deliver us, our God."

Barnes had many years ago turned his back on his given faith, but there was something about this ancient carving that spoke to an authenticity he believed was missing in modern organized religion. These devotional pieces were remnants of an age when religion was life and art.

He moved on to a smashed display case. Inside were two illuminated books, their vellum pages ruffled, the gold leaf flaking, the hand-detailed artwork filling the pages' lavish borders smudged with dirty fingerprints. He noticed one oversized oval that could only have been left by a vampire's large talonlike middle finger. The vampire had no need for or appreciation for hoary, human-illustrated books. The vampire had no need for or appreciation for anything produced by a human.

Barnes passed through open double doors underneath a giant Romanesque archway, into a large chapel with an immense barrel-vault ceiling and heavily fortified walls. A fresco dominated the apse over the altar at the northern end of the chamber: the Virgin and Child together, with winged figures poised at either side. Written over their heads were the archangel names Michael and Gabriel. The human kings below them were depicted as the smallest figures.

As he stood before the empty altar, Barnes felt the pressure change inside the cavernous room. A breath of air warmed the back of his neck like the sigh of a great furnace, and Barnes turned slowly.

At first glance, the cloaked figure standing behind him resembled a time-traveling monk arrived from a twelfth-century abbey. But only at first glance. This monk gripped a long, wolf-headed staff in its left hand, and the hand contained the telltale vampire-talon middle finger.

The Master's new face was just visible inside the dark folds of the cloak's hood. Behind the Master, near one of the side benches, was a female vampire in tatters. Barnes stared, recognizing her vaguely, trying to match the bald, red-eyed fiend to a younger, attractive, blue-eyed woman he once knew . . .

"Kelly Goodweather," said Barnes, so stunned he uttered her name out loud. Barnes, who had believed himself inured to any further new-world shocks, felt his breath go out a bit. She lurked behind the Master, a slinky, pantherlike presence.

Report.

Barnes nodded quickly, having anticipated this. He related the details of the rebels' break-in exactly the way he had practiced, perfunctorily, aiming to minimize the incursion. "They timed it to occur in the hour before the meridiem. And they had assistance from one who was not human, who escaped before the sun appeared."

The Born.

This surprised Barnes. He had heard some stories and had been directed to structure the camps with segregated quarters for pregnant women. But before this moment he had never been made aware that any actually existed. Barnes's mercenary mind saw immediately that this was good for him, in that it removed much of the blame for the disruption from him and his security procedures at Camp Liberty.

"Yes, so they had help entering. Once inside, they took the quarantine crew by surprise. They went on to do great damage to the letting facilities, as I reported. We are working hard to resume production and could be back up to twenty percent capacity within a week or ten days. We did claim one of theirs, as you know. He was turned but self-destroyed a few minutes after sundown. Oh, and I believe I have uncovered the true reason for their attack."

Dr. Nora Martinez.

Barnes swallowed. The Master knew so much.

"Yes, I had just recently discovered that she had been placed inside the camp."

Recently? I see . . . How recently?

"Moments before the upheaval, sir. In any event, I was actively engaged in trying to derive information from her pertaining to Dr. Goodweather's location and his resistance partners. I thought a less formal, more congenial exchange might be advantageous. As opposed to direct confrontation, which I believe would only have given her the opportunity to prove her fidelity to her friends. I hope you agree. Unfortunately, it was at that time that the marauders entered the main camp, and the alarm was given, and security arrived to evacuate me."

Barnes could not help but glance at the former Kelly Goodweather now and then, standing in the distance behind the Master, her arms hanging slack. So strange to be talking about her husband and yet see no reaction from her.

You located a member of their group and failed to inform me immediately?

"As I said, I barely had any time to react and . . . I . . . I was quite surprised, you understand, caught off guard. I thought I might get farther using a personal approach—she used to work for me, you realize. I had hoped I might be able to leverage my personal relationship with her to derive some helpful information before turning her over to you."

Barnes maintained a smile, even the fake confidence behind it, as he felt the Master's presence inside his mind, like a thief rummaging through an attic. Barnes was certain that human prevarication was a concern well beneath the vampire lord.

The head within the hood lifted a moment, and Barnes realized the Master was regarding the religious fresco.

You lie. And you are terrible at it. So—why don't

you try telling me the truth and see if you're any better at that?

Barnes shuddered and before he realized it, he had explained all the details of his clumsy attempts at seduction and his relationship to both Nora and Eph. The Master said nothing for a moment, then turned.

You killed her mother. They will seek you. For revenge. And I will keep you available for them . . . that will bring them to me. From this time forward, you may commit your attention fully to your assigned duty. The resistance is nearly at an end.

"It is?" Barnes quickly closed his mouth; he certainly had not meant to question or doubt. If the Master said it was so, then it was so. "Good, then. We have the other camps coming into production, and as I say, repairs on the letting facility at Camp Liberty are ongoing—"

Say no more. Your life is safe for now. But never lie to me again. Never hide from me again. You are neither brave nor smart. Efficient extraction and packaging of human blood is your mission. I recommend that you excel at it.

"I plan to. I mean—I will, sir. I am."

Central Park

ZACHARY GOODWEATHER WAITED until Belvedere Castle was quiet and still. He emerged from his room into the sickly sunlight of the meridiem. He walked to the edge of the stone plaza at the top of the rise and looked out at the vacant land below.

The vampire guards had retreated from the wan light into caves specially blasted into the schist that formed the foundation of the castle. Zachary returned inside the castle to retrieve his black parka before jogging down the walk into the park in violation of the human curfew.

The Master enjoyed watching the boy break rules, test boundaries. The Master never slumbered in the castle, deeming it too vulnerable to attack during the two-hour sun window. The Master preferred his hidden crypt at the Cloisters, buried in a cool bed of old soil. During the downtime of the daylight slumber, the Master had taken to seeing the surface world through Zachary's eyes, exploiting their bond formed by the Master's blood treatment of Zachary's asthma.

The boy unplugged his all-terrain Segway Personal Transporter and rode silently along the park path south to his zoo. At the entrance, he made three circles before opening the front gate, part of his developing obsessive-compulsive disorder. Inside, he rode to the locked case his rifle was kept in, producing the key he had stolen months before. He touched the key to his lips seven times and, properly reassured, undid the lock and pulled out the rifle. He checked the four-round load, double- and triple-checking it until his compulsion was satisfied, and then set off through the zoo with the weapon at his side.

His interest did not lie with the zoo anymore. He had created for himself a secret exit in the wall behind the Tropic Zone and now got off the Segway and emerged into the park, walking west. He stayed off the trails, preferring the tree cover as he walked past the skating rink and the old baseball fields, now mud fields, counting his steps in multiples of seventy-seven until he reached the far side of Central Park South.

He emerged from the trees, venturing out as far as the old Merchant's Gate entrance, remaining on the sidewalk behind the USS *Maine* monument. Columbus Circle stood before him, only half of the fountain shoots working, the rest clogged with sediment from the polluted rain. Beyond it, the high-rise towers stood like the smokestacks of a closed factory. Zachary sighted the figure of Columbus atop the fountain statue, blinking his eyes and smacking his lips in unison seven times before he was comfortable.

He saw movement across the wide traffic circle. People, humans, striding across the far sidewalk. Zachary could only make out their long coats and backpacks at that distance. Curfew breakers. Zachary ducked behind the monument at first, flushed with the danger of being discovered, then crept to the other edge of the monument base, peering around it.

The group of four people continued, unaware of him. Zachary sighted them with his weapon, blinking and lip-smacking, using what he had learned about shooting to gauge trajectory and distance. They were tightly grouped, and Zachary thought he had a clear shot, a good chance.

He wanted to fire. He wanted to open up on them.

And so he did, but purposefully pulled his aim

high at the last second before squeezing the trigger. A moment later the group stopped, looking his way. Zack remained low and still next to the monument base, certain he would blend in with the backdrop.

He fired three more times: *Crack! Crack! Crack!* He got one! One was down! Zack quickly reloaded.

The targets ran, turning down the avenue and out of Zack's view. He drew aim on a traffic light they had passed, just able to make out a sign indicating one of the old police security cameras posted there. He turned and ran back into the cover of the park trees, chased only by the sensation of his secret thrill.

This city in daylight was the domain of Zachary Goodweather! Let all trespassers be warned!

On the street, bleeding from the bullet wound—being dragged away—was Vasiliy Fet, the rat exterminator.

One Hour Earlier

THEY HAD DESCENDED into the subway at 116th Street a full hour before daylight, in order to give themselves plenty of time. Gus showed them where to wait, near a sidewalk grate through which they could hear the approach of a 1 train, minimizing the amount of time they would have to spend on the platform below.

Eph stood against the nearest building, his eyes closed, asleep on his feet in the pissing rain.

And even in those brief intervals he dreamed of light and fire.

Fet and Nora whispered occasionally, while Gus paced and said nothing. Joaquin declined to accompany them, needing to vent his frustration over Bruno's passing by continuing their program of sabotage. Gus had tried to dissuade him from going out into the city on a bad knee, but Joaquin's mind was set.

Eph was roused to consciousness by the subterranean shriek of the approaching train, and they bustled down the station steps like the other commuters rushing to get off the streets before the sunlight curfew. They boarded a silver-colored subway car and shook the rain from their coats. The doors closed and a quick glance up and down the length of the car told Eph that there were no vampires on board. He relaxed a bit, closing his eyes as the subway took them fifty-five blocks south beneath the city.

At Fifty-ninth Street and Columbus Circle, they disembarked, rising up the steps to the street. They ducked inside one of the large apartment buildings and found a place to wait behind the lobby, until the dark shroud of night lifted just enough, the sky becoming merely overcast.

When the streets were empty, they emerged into the faded glory of day. The orb of the sun was visible through the dark cloud cover like a flashlight pressed against a charcoal-gray blanket. Street-level windows of certain cafés and shops remained smashed since the initial days of panic and looting, while glass in the upper-story windows largely remained intact. They walked around the southern curve of the immense traffic circle, long since cleared of abandoned cars, the central fountain spewing black water out of every second or third nozzle. The city, during curfew, had a perpetual early-Sunday-morning feel to it, as though most of the residents were sleeping in, the day slow to start. In that sense, it gave Eph a feeling of hope that he tried to savor, even though he knew it to be false.

Then a sizzling sound creased the air overhead.

"What the . . . ?"

The loud crack followed, a gunshot report, sound traveling more slowly than the round itself. The delay said the shot had been fired from a distance, seemingly from somewhere inside the trees of Central Park.

"Shooter!" said Fet. They ran across Eighth Avenue, quickly but not panicked. Gunshots at daylight meant humans. There had been a lot more insanity in the months following the takeover. Humans driven crazy by the fall of their kind and the rise of the new order. Violent suicides. Mass murders. After those died out, Eph would still see people out during the meridiem especially, ranting, wandering the streets. Rarely would he see any people out during the curfew now. The crazies had been killed or otherwise dispatched, and the rest behaved.

Three more shots were fired, *crack, crack, crack*—

Two of the bullets hit a mailbox, but the third one hit Vasiliy Fet squarely in the left shoulder. It made him twirl, leaving behind a ribbon of blood. The bullet traveled clean through his body, tearing muscle and flesh but miraculously missing the lungs and the heart.

Eph and Nora grabbed Fet as he fell and, with the help of Mr. Quinlan, dragged him away.

Nora pulled Fet's hand back from his shoulder, quickly examining the wound. Not too much blood, no bone fragments.

Fet eased her back. "Let's keep moving. Too vulnerable here."

They cut down Fifty-sixth Street, heading for the F-line subway stop. No more gunfire, no one following them. They entered without encountering anyone, and the underground platform was empty. The F line ran north here, the track curving underneath the park as it headed east to Queens. They jumped down onto the rails, waiting again to make sure they were not followed.

It is only a little farther. Can you make it? It will be a better place to provide you with some medical attention.

Vasiliy nodded to Mr. Quinlan. "I've had it much worse." And he had. In the last two years he had been shot three times, twice in Europe and once while in the Upper East Side after curfew.

They walked the rails by night vision. The cars generally stopped running during the meridiem, the vampires shutting down, though the underground protection from the sun allowed them to move trains if necessary. So Eph remained alert and aware.

The tunnel ceiling was angled, rising to the right, the high cement wall serving as a mural for graffiti artists, the shorter wall to their left supporting pipes and a narrow ledge. A form awaited them at the curve ahead. Mr. Quinlan had gone ahead of them, getting underground well in advance of the sunrise.

Wait here, he told them, then jogged quickly back in the direction from which they came, checking for tails. He returned, apparently satisfied, and, without ceremony or prelude, opened a panel inside the frame of a locked access door. A lever inside released the door, which opened inward.

The short corridor inside was notable for its dryness. It led, through one left turn, to another door. But rather than open that door, Mr. Quinlan instead pried open a perfectly invisible hatch in the floor, revealing an angled flight of stairs.

Gus went down first. Eph was the second to last, Mr. Quinlan securing the hatch behind him. The stairs bottomed out into a narrow walkway constructed by different hands than any of the many subway tunnels Eph had seen over the past year of his fugitive existence.

You are safe accessing this complex in my company, but I strongly recommend that you do not attempt to return here on your own. Various safeguards have been in place for centuries, meant to keep anyone from the curious homeless to a vampire hit squad from entering. I have now deactivated the traps, but for the future, consider yourselves warned.

Eph looked around for evidence of booby traps but saw none. Then again, he had not seen the hatch door that led them here.

At the end of the walkway, the wall slid aside under Mr. Quinlan's pale hand. The room revealed was round and vast, at first glance resembling a circular train garage. But it was apparently a cross between a museum and a house of Congress. The sort of forum Socrates might have thrived in, had he been a vampire condemned to the underworld. Soupy green in Eph's night vision, the walls were in reality alabaster-white and preternaturally smooth, spaced by generous columns and rising to a high ceiling. The walls were empty, conspicuously so, as though the masterpieces that once hung there had long ago been taken down and stored away. Eph could not see all the way to the opposite end, so large was the room, the range of his night-vision goggles terminating in a cloud of darkness.

They rapidly tended to Fet's wound. In his backpack he always carried a small emergency kit. The bleeding had almost stopped, consistent with the bullet having missed any major arteries. Both Nora and Eph were able to clean the wound with Betadine and applied antibiotic cream, Telfa pads, and an absorbent layer on top. Fet moved his fingers and arm and, even in great pain, proved himself still able.

He took a look around. "What is this place?"

The Ancients constructed this chamber soon after their arrival in the New World, after they determined that New York City, and not Boston, would be the port city serving as the headquarters for the human economy. This was a safe, secure, and sanctified retreat in which they could meditate for long periods of time. Many great and lasting decisions about how best to shepherd your race were made in this room.

"So this was all a ruse," said Eph. "The illusion of freedom. They shaped the planet through us, pushing us toward developing fossil fuels, toward nuclear energy. The whole greenhouse gas thing. Whatever suited them. Preparing for the eventuality of their takeover, their move to the surface. This was going to happen regardless."

But not like this. You must understand, there are good shepherds, who care for their flock, and there are bad shepherds. There are ways in which the dignity of the livestock can be preserved.

"Even if it's all a lie."

All belief systems are elaborate fabrications, if logic is followed out to the end.

"Good Christ," muttered Eph under his breath—but the room was like a whispering chamber. Everyone heard him and looked his way. "A dictator is a dictator, benign or not. Whether it pets you or bleeds you."

Did you honestly believe you were absolutely free to begin with?

"I did," said Eph. "And even if it was all a fraud, I still prefer an economy based on metal-backed currency than one based on human blood."

Make no mistake, all currency is blood.

"I would rather live in a dream world of light than a real world of darkness."

Your perspective continues to be that of one who has lost something. But this has always been their world.

"*Was* always their world," said Fet, correcting the Born. "Turned out they were even bigger suckers than we were."

Mr. Quinlan was patient with Fet under the circumstances.

They were subverted from within. They were aware of the threat but believed they could contain it. It is easier to overlook dissension within your own ranks.

Mr. Quinlan briefly looked at Eph before moving on.

For the Master, it is best to consider the whole of recorded human history as a series of test runs. A set of experiments carried out over time, in preparation for the final masterstroke. The Master was there during the rise and fall of the Roman Empire. He learned from the French Revolution, the Napoleonic wars. He nested in the concentration camps. He lived among you like a deviant sociologist, learning everything he could from and about you, in order to engineer your collapse. Patterns over time. The Master learned to align himself with influential power brokers, such as Eldritch Palmer, and corrupt them. He devised a formula for the mathematics of power. The perfect balance of vampires, cattle, and wardens.

The others digested this. Fet said, "So your kind, the Ancients, has fallen. Our kind has also. The question is, what can we do about it?"

Mr. Quinlan crossed to an altar of sorts, a granite table upon which were set six circular wooden receptacles, each one not much bigger than a can of soda. Each receptacle glowed faintly in the lens of Eph's night-vision device, as though containing a source of light or heat.

These. We must carry these back with us. I have spent most of the past two years arranging passage and traveling to and from the Old World in order to collect the remains of all the Ancients. Here I have preserved them in white oak, in accordance with the lore.

Nora said, "You have been around the world? To Europe, the Far East?"

Mr. Quinlan nodded.

"Is it . . . is it the same there? All over?"

Essentially. The more developed the region, the better the existing infrastructure, the more efficient the transition.

Eph moved closer to the six wooden crematory urns. He said, "What are you preserving them for?"

The lore told me what to do. It did not tell me to what end.

Eph looked around to see if anyone else questioned this. "So you traveled all around the world sweeping up their ashes at great danger to yourself, and you had no interest in why or what for?"

Mr. Quinlan looked at Eph with those red eyes.

Until now.

Eph wanted to press him more on the explanation of the ashes but held his tongue. He did not know the extent of the vampire's psychic reach, and he was worried about being read and found to be questioning the entire endeavor. For he was still wrestling with the temptation of the Master's offer. Eph felt like a spy there, allowing Mr. Quinlan to reveal this secret location to him. Eph did not want to know any more than he already did. He was afraid that he was capable of betraying them all. Of trading them and the world for his boy and paying for the transaction with his soul. He grew sweaty and fidgety just thinking about it.

He looked at the others standing there inside the vast underground chamber. Had one among them been corrupted already, as the Master had claimed? Or was this another of the Master's lies, meant to soften Eph's own resistance? Eph studied each one in turn, as though his night-vision scope could reveal some identifiable trace of their treachery, like a malignant black stain spreading out from their chest.

Fet spoke up, addressing Mr. Quinlan. "So why did you bring us here?"

Now that I have retrieved the ashes and read the Lumen *I am ready to proceed. We have little time left to destroy the Master, but this lair allows us to keep an eye on him. Be close to his own hideout.*

"Wait a minute . . . ," said Fet, a curious tone in his voice. "Won't destroying the Master also destroy you?"

It is the only way.

"You want to die? Why?"

The simple and honest answer is that I am tired. Immortality lost its luster for me many centuries ago. In fact, it removes the luster from everything. Eternity is tedium. Time is an ocean, and I want to come ashore. The one bright spot I have left in this world—the one hope—is the potential destruction of my creator. It is revenge.

Mr. Quinlan spoke of what he knew. What he had learned in the *Lumen*. He spoke in plain terms and with as much clarity as was possible. He explained the origin of the Ancients and the myth of the sites of origin and the emphasis on finding the Black Site, the birth site of the Master.

The part that Gus clicked with most was the three archangels—Gabriel, Michael, and the forgotten third angel, Ozryel—dispatched to fulfill God's will in destroying the cities of Sodom and Gomorrah.

"God's hardasses," said Gus, identifying with the avenging angels. "But what do you think. Angels? Really? Gimme a fucking break, *hermano.*"

Fet shrugged. "I believe what Setrakian believed. And he believed in the book."

Gus agreed with him but couldn't let it go just yet. "If there is a God, or some something who can send angel assassins—then what the hell's He waiting for? What if it is all just stories?"

"Backed up by actions," said Fet. "The Master located each of the six buried segments of Ozryel's body—the origin sites of the Ancients—and destroyed them with the only force that could accomplish the task. A nuclear meltdown. The only Godlike energy on Earth, powerful enough to obliterate sacred ground."

With that, the Master not only wiped out its competition but made itself six times more powerful. We know it is still searching for its own site of origin, not to destroy it but to protect it.

"Great. So we just have to find the burial site," said Nora, "before the Master does, and build an itty-bitty nuclear reactor on it, then sabotage the thing. Is that it?"

Fet said, "Or detonate a nuclear bomb."

Nora laughed harshly. "That actually sounds like fun."

Nobody else laughed.

"Shit," Nora said. "You have a nuclear bomb."

"But no detonator," Fet said sheepishly, and looked to Gus. "We are trying to get a line on some sort of solution to that, right?"

Gus answered, lacking Fet's enthusiasm. "My man Creem, you remember him? Silver-blinged-up banger, built like a big, fat truck? I put him on it, and he says he's ready to deal. He's hooked into everything black market in Jersey. Thing is, he's still a drug dealer at heart. Can't trust a man with no code."

Fet said, "All of this is moot if we don't have a target to shoot at." He looked at Mr. Quinlan. "Right? And that's why you wanted to see the *Lumen*. You think you can learn something from it we couldn't?"

I trust you all saw the sky mark.

Mr. Quinlan paused and then locked eyes with Eph. And Eph felt as if the Born could read every secret in his soul.

Beyond the limits of circumstance and organization, there exists design. What it was that fell from the sky does not matter. It was an omen, prophesied ages ago and meant to signal the birth site. We are close. Think of it—the Master came here for that very reason. This is the right place and the right time. We will find it.

Gus said, "No disrespect, but I don't get it. I mean, if you all want to go read a book and think it has little clues for you on how to slay a fucking vampire, then go to it. Pull up a comfortable chair. But me? I think we figure out how to confront this king bloodsucker and blow its ass up. The old man showed us the way, but at the same time, this mystical mumbo jumbo has gotten us where we are—starving, hunted, living like rats." Gus was pacing, going a little stir-crazy in this ancient chamber. "I got the Master on video. Belvedere Castle. I say we get this bomb together and take care of business directly."

"My son is there," said Eph. "It's not just the Master."

"Do I look like I give a fuck about your brat?" said Gus. "I don't want you to get the wrong impression—'cause I don't give a fuck."

Fet said, "Cool down, everyone. If we blow this chance, it's over. Nobody would ever get close to the Master again."

Fet looked to Mr. Quinlan, whose silence and stillness communicated his agreement.

Gus frowned but didn't argue the point. He respected Fet, and more so, he respected Mr. Quinlan. "You say we can blow a hole in the ground and the Master disappears. I'm down with that, if it works. And if it doesn't? We just give up?"

He had a point. The others' silence confirmed it.

"Not me," said Gus. "No fucking way."

Eph felt the hairs go up on the back of his neck. He had an idea. He started talking before he could think himself out of it.

"There might be one way," he said.

"One way to what?" said Fet.

"To get close to the Master. Not by laying siege

to his castle. Without endangering Zack. What if instead we draw it to us?"

"What is this shit?" said Gus. "Suddenly you have a plan, *hombre*?" Gus smiled at the others. "This ought to be good."

Eph swallowed to keep his voice in check. "The Master is keyed in on me for some reason. It's got my son. What if I offer it something to trade?"

Fet said, "The *Lumen*."

"This is bullshit," said Gus. "What are you selling?"

Eph put out his hands and patted the air, asking for patience and consideration for what he was about to suggest. "Hear me out. First of all, we dummy up a fake book in its place. I say I stole it from you and want to exchange it. For Zack."

Nora said, "Isn't that pretty dangerous? What if something happens to Zack?"

"It's a huge risk, but I can't see getting him back by doing nothing. But if we destroy the Master . . . it's all over."

Gus wasn't buying it. Fet looked concerned, and Mr. Quinlan gave no indication of his opinion.

But Nora was nodding. "I think this could work."

Fet looked at her. "What? Maybe we should talk alone about this first."

"Let your lady speak," said Gus, never missing an opportunity to twist the knife in Eph's side. "Let's hear this."

Nora said, "I think Eph could lure him in. He's right—there is something about him, something the Master wants or fears. I keep going back to that light in the sky. Something's going on there."

Eph felt a burning sensation ride up from his back to his neck.

"It could work," said Nora. "Eph double-crossing us makes sense. Draw the Master out with Eph and the fake *Lumen*. Leave it vulnerable to ambush." She looked at Eph. "If you're sure you're up for such a thing."

"If we have no other choice," he said.

Nora went on. "It's crazy dangerous. Because if we blow it, and the Master gets you . . . then it's over. It would know everything you know—where we are, how to find us. We would be finished."

Eph remained still while the others mulled it over. The baritone voice spoke inside his head: *The Master is immeasurably more cunning than you are giving it credit for.*

"I don't doubt that the Master is devious," said Nora, turning to Mr. Quinlan. "But isn't this kind of an offer it cannot refuse?"

The Born's quietness signaled his acceptance, if not his full agreement.

Eph felt Mr. Quinlan's eyes on him. Eph was torn. He felt now that this gave him flexibility: he could potentially carry out this double-cross or stick to the plan if indeed it appeared it would succeed. But there was another question troubling him now.

He searched the face of his former lover, illuminated by night vision. He was looking for some sign of treachery. Was she the traitor? Had they gotten to her during her brief stay inside the blood camp?

Nonsense. They had killed her mother. Her duplicity would make no sense.

In the end, he prayed that they both possessed the integrity he hoped they'd always had.

"I want to do this," said Eph. "We proceed on both fronts simultaneously."

They all were aware that a dangerous first step had just been taken. Gus looked doubtful, but even he seemed willing to go along with it. The plan represented direct action, and, at the same time, he was eager to give Eph just enough rope to hang himself with.

The Born began encasing each wooden receptacle inside a protective plastic sleeve and setting them inside a leather sack.

"Wait," said Fet. "We're forgetting one very important thing."

Gus said, "What's that?"

"How the hell do we make this offer to the Master? How do we get in touch with it at all?"

Nora touched Fet on his unbandaged shoulder and said, "I know of just the way."

Spanish Harlem

SUPPLY TRUCKS ENTERING Manhattan from Queens traveled the cleared middle inbound lane on the Queensboro Bridge across the East River, turning either south on Second Avenue or north on Third.

Mr. Quinlan stood on the sidewalk outside the George Washington Houses between Ninety-seventh and Ninety-eighth, forty blocks north of the bridge. The Born vampire waited in the spitting rain with his hood covering his head, watching the occasional vehicle pass. Convoys were ignored. Also Stoneheart trucks or vehicles. Mr. Quinlan's first concern was alerting the Master in any way.

Fet and Eph stood in the shadows of a doorway in the first block of the houses. In the past forty-five minutes, they had seen one vehicle every ten minutes or so. Headlights raised their hopes; Mr. Quinlan's disinterest dashed them. And so they remained in the darkened doorway, safe from the rain but not from the new awkwardness that was their relationship.

Fet was running their audacious new plan through his head, trying to convince himself that it might work. Success seemed like an incredible long shot—but then again, it wasn't as though they had dozens of other prospects lined up and ready to go.

Kill the Master. They had tried once, by exposing the creature to the sun, and failed. When the dying Setrakian apparently poisoned its blood, using Fet's anticoagulant rodent poison, the Master had merely sloughed off its human host, assuming the form of another healthy being. The creature seemed invincible.

And yet, they had hurt it. Both times. No matter what the creature's original form was, it apparently needed to exist in possession of a human. And humans could be destroyed.

Fet said, "We can't miss this time. We'll never get a better chance."

Eph nodded, looking out into the street. Waiting for Mr. Quinlan's signal.

He seemed guarded. Maybe he was having second thoughts about the plan, or maybe it was something else. Eph's unreliability had caused a rift in their relationship—but the Nora situation had driven home a permanent wedge.

Fet's main concern now was that Eph's irritation with Fet not negatively impact their efforts.

"Nothing has happened," Fet said, "between Nora and me."

"I know," said Eph. "But *everything* has happened between her and me. It's over. And I know it. And there will be a time when you and I will talk about it and maybe even have a fistfight over it. But now it's not that time. This has to be our focus now. All personal feelings aside . . . Look, Fet, we are paired. It was you and me or Gus and me. I'd rather take you."

"Glad we're all on the same page again," said Fet.

Eph was about to respond when headlights appeared once more. This time, Mr. Quinlan moved into the street. The truck was too far away for any human to make out the operator, but Mr. Quinlan knew. He stood right in the truck's path, headlights brightening him.

One of the rules of the road was that any vampire could commandeer a vehicle operated by a human, in the same manner as a soldier or a cop could a civilian's in the old United

States. Mr. Quinlan raised his hand, his elongated middle finger evident, as were his red eyes. The truck stopped, and its driver, a Stoneheart member wearing a dark suit underneath a warm duster, opened the driver's-side door with the engine still running.

Mr. Quinlan approached the driver, obscured from Fet's view by the passenger side of the truck. Fet watched as the driver jerked suddenly inside the cab. Mr. Quinlan leaped up into the doorway. Through the rain-smeared windows, they appeared to be grappling.

"Go," said Fet, and he and Eph both ran out from their hiding spot, into the rain. They splashed off the curb and across to the driver's side of the truck. Fet almost ran up into Mr. Quinlan, pulling back only at the last moment when he saw that Mr. Quinlan wasn't the one struggling. Only the driver was.

Mr. Quinlan's stinger was engorged, jutting out from the base of his throat at his unhinged jaw, tapering to its tip, which was firmly inserted in the neck of the human driver.

Fet pulled back sharply. Eph came around and saw it too, and there was a moment of bonding between them, of shared disgust. Mr. Quinlan fed quickly, his eyes locked on those of the driver, the driver's face a mask of paralysis and shock.

For Fet, it served as a reminder of how easily Mr. Quinlan could turn on them—any of them—in an instant.

Fet did not look back until he was certain the feeding was over. He caught sight of Mr. Quinlan's retracted stinger, its narrow end lolling out of his mouth like the hairless tail of some animal he had otherwise swallowed. Flush with energy, Mr. Quinlan lifted the limp Stoneheart driver out of the truck and carried him, as easily as a bundle of clothes, off the street. Half in the shadows of the doorway, in a gesture of both mercy and convenience, Mr. Quinlan snapped the man's neck with a firm rotation.

Mr. Quinlan left the destroyed corpse in the doorway before rejoining them on the street. They needed to get moving before another vehicle happened along. Fet and Eph met him at the rear of the truck, where Fet opened the unlocked clasp, raising the sliding door.

A refrigerated truck. "Damn the luck," said Fet. They had a good hour's ride ahead of them, maybe two, and for Fet and Eph it was going to be a cold one, because they could not be seen riding in the front. "Not even any decent food," said Fet, climbing inside and rustling through the scraps of cardboard.

Mr. Quinlan pulled on the rubber strap that lowered the door, closing Fet and Eph in darkness. Fet made certain there were vents for airflow, and there were. They heard the driver's door close, and the truck slipped into gear, jerking them as the vehicle lurched forward.

Fet found an extra fleece sweatshirt from his pack, pulled it on, and buttoned his coat over it. He laid out some cardboard and set the soft part of his pack behind his head, trying to get comfortable. From the sound of it, Eph was doing the same. The rattling of the truck, both noise and vibration, precluded conversation, which was just as well.

Fet crossed his arms, trying to let go of his mind. He focused on Nora. He knew he would likely never have attracted a woman of her caliber under normal circumstances. Times of war bring men and women together, sometimes for necessity's sake, sometimes for convenience, but occasionally because of fate. Fet was confident that their attraction was a result of the latter. Wartime is also when people find themselves. Fet had discovered his best self here in this worst situation, whereas Eph, on the other hand, at times appeared to have lost himself completely.

Nora had wanted to come along with them, but Fet convinced her that she needed to remain behind with Gus, not only to conserve her energy but because he knew that she would not be able to stop herself from attacking Barnes if she saw him again, thereby threatening their plan. Besides, Gus needed assistance with his own important errand.

"What do you think?" she had asked Fet, rubbing her bald head in a quieter moment.

Fet missed her long hair, but there was something beautiful and spare about her unadorned face. He liked the fine slope of the back of her head, the graceful line moving across the nape of her neck to the beginning of her shoulders.

"You look reborn," he said.

She frowned. "Not freakish?"

"If anything, a little more delicate. More vulnerable."

Her eyebrows lifted in surprise. "You want me to be more vulnerable?"

"Well—only with me," he said frankly.

That made her smile, and him. Rare things, smiles. Rationed like food in these dark days.

"I like this plan," Fet said, "in that it represents possibility. But I'm also worried."

"About Eph," Nora said, understanding and agreeing with him. "This is make-or-break time. Either he falls apart, and we deal with that, or he rises to the occasion."

"I think he'll rise. He has to. He just has to."

Nora admired Fet's faith in Eph, even if she wasn't convinced.

"Once it starts growing back in," she said, feeling her cooling scalp again, "I'll have a butchy-looking crew cut for a while."

He shrugged, picturing her like that. "I can deal with it."

"Or maybe I'll shave it, keep it like this. I wear a hat most times anyway."

"All or nothing," said Fet. "That's you."

She found her knit cap, pulling it down tight over her scalp. "You wouldn't mind?"

The only thing Fet cared about was that she wanted his opinion. That he was a part of her plans.

Inside the cold, rumbling truck, Fet drifted off with his arms crossed tight as if he were holding on to her.

Staatsburg, New York

THE DOOR ROLLED open and Mr. Quinlan stood there, watching them get to their feet. Fet hopped down, his knees stiff and his legs cold, shuffling around to get his circulation up. Eph climbed down and stood there with his pack on his back like a hitchhiker with a long way still to go.

The truck was parked on the shoulder of a dirt road, or perhaps the edge of a long, private driveway, far enough in from the street to be obscured by the trunks of the bare trees. The rain had let up, and the ground was damp but not muddy. Mr. Quinlan abruptly jogged off without explanation. Fet wondered if they were meant to follow him but decided he had to warm up first.

Near him, Eph looked wide-awake. Almost eager. Fet wondered briefly if Eph's apparent zeal had some pharmaceutical source. But no, his eyes looked clear.

"You look ready," said Fet.

"I am," said Eph.

Mr. Quinlan returned moments later. An eerie sight, still: steam came thickly from his scalp and within his hoodie, but none came from his mouth.

A few gate guards, more at the doors. I see no way to prevent the Master from being alerted. But perhaps, in light of the plan, that is not an unfortunate thing.

"What do you think?" asked Fet. "Of the plan. Honestly. Do we even have a chance?"

Mr. Quinlan looked up through the leafless

branches to the black sky. *It is a gambit worth pursuing. Drawing out the Master is half the battle.*

"The other half is defeating it," said Fet. He eyed the Born vampire's face, still upturned, impossible to read. "What about you? What chance would you have against the Master?"

History has shown me to be unsuccessful. I have been unable to destroy the Master, and the Master has been unable to destroy me. The Master wants me dead, just as he wants Dr. Goodweather dead. This we have in common. Of course, any lure I put out there on my behalf would be transparent as a ploy.

"You can't be destroyed by man. But you could be destroyed by the Master. So maybe the monster is vulnerable to you."

All I can say with absolute certainty is that I have never before tried to kill it with a nuclear weapon.

Eph had fixed his night-vision scope on his head, anxious to get going. "I'm ready," he said. "Let's do this before I talk myself out of it."

Fet nodded, tightening up his straps, fixing his pack high on his back. They followed Mr. Quinlan through the trees, the Born vampire following some instinctual sense of direction. Fet could discern no path himself, but it was easy—too easy—to trust Mr. Quinlan. Fet did not believe he would ever be able to lower his guard around a vampire, Born or not.

He heard a whirring somewhere ahead of them. The tree density began to thin out, and they came to the edge of a clearing. The whirring noise was a generator—maybe two—powering the estate that Barnes apparently occupied. The house was massive, the grounds considerable. They were just right of the rear of the property, facing a wide horse fence ringing the backyard and, within that, a riding course.

The generators would mask much of the noise they might make, but the vampires' heat-registering night sight was all but impossible to evade. Mr. Quinlan's flat hand signal held Fet and Eph back as the Born vampire slipped through the trees, darting fluidly from trunk to trunk around the perimeter of the property. Fet quickly lost sight of him, and then, just as suddenly, Mr. Quinlan broke from the trees almost a quarter of the way around the wide clearing. He emerged striding quickly and confidently but not running. Nearby guards left their post at the side door, spotting Mr. Quinlan and going to meet him.

Fet knew a distraction when he saw one. "Now or never," he whispered to Eph.

They ducked out from the branches into the silvery darkness of the clearing. He did not dare to pull out his sword yet, for fear that the vampires could sense the nearness of silver. Mr. Quinlan was evidently communicating with the guards somehow, keeping their backs to Fet and Eph as they ran up over the soft, dead, gray grass.

The guards picked up on the threat behind them when Fet was twenty feet off. They turned and Fet drew his sword out of his backpack—held it with his good arm—but it was Mr. Quinlan who overpowered them, his strong arms a blur as they came around to choke and quickly crush the muscles and bones of the vampire guards' necks.

Fet, without hesitating, closed the gap and finished both creatures with his sword. Quinlan knew that the alarm had not been raised telepathically, but there was not a moment to lose.

Mr. Quinlan set off in search of other guards, Fet right on his tail, leaving Eph to head for the unsecured side door.

Barnes liked the second-floor sitting room the best. Book-lined walls, a tiled fireplace with a broad oak mantel, a comfortable chair, an amber-shaded floor lamp, and a side table upon which his brandy snifter was set like a perfect glass balloon.

He unfastened the top three buttons of his uniform shirt and took in the last of his third brandy Alexander. Fresh cream, such a luxury now, was the secret to the thick, sweet richness of this decadent concoction.

Barnes exhaled deeply before rising from his chair. He took a moment to steady himself, his hand on the plush arm. He was possessed by the spirits he had imbibed. Now the entire world was a delicate glass balloon, and Barnes floated around it on a gently swirling bed of brandy.

This house had once belonged to Bolivar, the rock star. His genteel country getaway. Eight figures, this manor had once been worth. Barnes vaguely recalled the media stink when Bolivar first purchased it from the old-money family that had fallen on hard times. The event was a bona fide curiosity because it had seemed so out of character for the goth showman. But that was how the world had become before it all went to hell: rock stars were scratch golfers, rappers played polo, and comedians collected modern art.

Barnes moved to the high shelves, weaving gently before Bolivar's collection of vintage erotica. Barnes selected a large, thin, handsomely bound edition of *The Pearl* and opened it upon a nearby reading stand. Ah, the Victorians. So much spanking. He next retrieved a hand-bound text, more of an illustrated scrapbook than a properly published book, consisting of early photographic prints glued onto thick paper pages. The prints retained some silver emulsion, which Barnes was careful to keep off his fingers. He was a traditionalist, partial to the early male-dominated arrangements and poses. He fancied the subservient female.

And then it was time for his fourth and final brandy. He reached for the house phone and dialed the kitchen. Which of his attractive domestics would be bringing him his notorious fourth brandy Alexander tonight? As master of the house, he had the means—and, when properly inebriated, the gumption—to make his fantasies come true.

The phone rang unanswered. Impertinence! Barnes frowned, then hung up and redialed, fearing he might have pressed the wrong button. As it rang a second time, he heard a loud thump somewhere in the house. Perhaps, he imagined, his request had been anticipated and its fulfillment was on its pretty way to him right now. He grinned a brandy smile and replaced the receiver in its old-fashioned cradle, making his way across the thick rug to the large door.

The wide hallway was empty. Barnes stepped out, his polished white shoes creaking just a bit.

Voices downstairs. Vague and muffled, reaching his ears as little more than echoes.

Not answering his phone call and making noise downstairs were clear enough grounds for Barnes to personally inspect the help and select who should bring him his brandy.

He put one shoe in front of the other along the center of the hallway, impressed at his ability to follow a straight line. At the head of the landing leading downstairs, he pressed the button to call for the elevator. It rose to him from the foyer, a gilded cage, and he opened the door and slid the gate aside and entered, closing it, pulling down on the handle. The cage descended, transporting him to the first floor like Zeus upon a cloud.

He emerged from the elevator, pausing to regard himself in a gilded mirror. The top half of his uniform shirt was flapped down, hidden medals hanging heavy. He licked his lips and fixed his hair to look more full upon his head, smoothing out his goatee and generally assuming a look of inebriated dignity before venturing into the kitchen.

The wide, L-shaped room was empty. A pan of cookies lay cooling on a rack on the long central island, a pair of red oven mitts next to them. In front of the liquor cabinet, a bottle of cognac and an unsealed pitcher of cream stood next to measuring cups and an open jar of nutmeg. The phone receiver hung on its wall-mounted cradle.

"Hello?" Barnes called.

First came a rattling sound, like a shelf being bumped.

Then two female voices at once: "In here."

Intrigued, Barnes continued along the center island to the corner. Rounding it, he saw five of his staff of female domestics—all well-fed, comely, and with full heads of hair—restrained to the end poles of a shelving unit of gourmet cooking tools with flexible zip ties.

His mind-set was such that his first impulse, upon seeing their wrists bound and their full, imploring eyes, was pleasure. His brandy-steeped mind processed the scene as an erogenous tableau.

Reality was slow to part the fog. It was a long, floundering moment before he realized that apparently someone had broken in and restrained his staff.

That someone was inside the house.

Barnes turned and ran. With the women calling after him, he slammed his hip into the island, the pain doubling him over as he groped his way along the counter to the doorway. He rushed out, moving blindly across the first-floor landing and around another corner, heading for the front entrance, his addled mind thinking, *Escape!* Then he saw, through the violet-tinged glass panes framing the double doors, a struggle outside, ending with one of his vampire guards being struck down by a dark, brute figure. A second figure closed in, slashing with a silver blade. Barnes backed away, stumbling over his own feet, watching more guards from other positions around the grounds moving to engage the raiding party.

He ran as best he could back to the landing. He panicked at the thought of becoming trapped inside the elevator cage and so mounted the curling staircase, pulling himself hand-over-hand along the broad banister. Adrenaline neutralized some of the alcohol in his blood.

The study. That was where the pistols were displayed. He threw himself down the long hallway toward the room—when a pair of hands grabbed him from the side, pulling him into the open doorway of the sitting room.

Barnes instinctively covered his head, expecting a beating. He fell sprawling, thrown into one of the chairs, where he remained, cowering in fear and bewilderment. He did not want to see the face of his attacker. Part of his hysterical fear came from a voice inside his head that most closely resembled that of his dearly departed mother, saying, *You're getting what you deserve.*

"Look at me."

The voice. That angry voice. Barnes relaxed his grip around his head. He knew the voice but could not place it. Something was off. The voice had become roughened over time, deeper.

Curiosity outstripped fear. Barnes removed his trembling arms from his head, raising his eyes.

Ephraim Goodweather. Or, more reflective of his personal appearance, Ephraim Goodweather's evil twin. This was not the man he used to know, the esteemed epidemiologist. Dark circles raccooned his fugitive eyes. Hunger had drained his face of all cheer and turned his cheeks into crags, as though all the meat had been boiled off the bone. Mealy whiskers clung to his gray skin but failed to fill out the hollows. He wore fingerless gloves, a filthy coat, and faded boots under wet cuffs, laced with wire rather than string. The black knit cap crowning his head reflected the darkness of the mind beneath. A sword handle rose from the pack on his back. He looked like a vengeful hobo.

"Everett," Eph said, his voice hoarse, possessed.

"Don't," said Barnes, terrified of him.

Eph picked up the snifter, its bottom still coated and chocolaty. He brought the mouth of the glass to his nose, drawing in the scent. "Nightcap, huh? Brandy Alexander? That's a fucking prom drink, Barnes." He placed the large glass in his former boss's hand. Then he did exactly what Barnes feared he would do: he closed his fist over Barnes's hand, crushing the glass between his ex-boss's fingers. Closing them over the multiple shards of glass, cutting his flesh and tendons and slicing to the bone.

Barnes howled and fell on his knees, bleeding and sobbing. He cringed. "Please," he said.

Eph said, "I want to stab you in the eye."

"Please."

"Step on your throat until you die. Then cremate you in that little tile hole in the wall."

"I was saving her . . . I wanted to deliver Nora from the camp."

"The way you delivered those pretty maids downstairs? Nora was right about you. Do you know what she would do to you if she were here?"

So she wasn't. Thank God. "She would be reasonable," Barnes said. "She would see what I had to offer to you. How I could be of service."

"Goddamn you," said Eph. "Goddamn your black soul."

Eph punched Barnes. His hits were calculated, brutal.

"No," whimpered Barnes. "No more . . . please . . ."

"So this is what absolute corruption looks like," said Eph. He hit Barnes a few times more. "Commandant Barnes! You're a goddamn piece of shit, sir—you know that? How could you turn on your own kind like this? You were a doctor—you were the fucking head of the CDC for Christ's sake. You have no compassion?"

"No, please." Barnes sat up a little, bleeding all over the floor, trying to ease this conversation into something productive and positive. But his PR skills were hampered by the growing inflammation of his mouth and the teeth that were missing. "This is a new world, Ephraim. Look what it's done to you."

"You let that admiral's uniform go right to your fucking head." Eph reached out and gripped Barnes's thinning thatch of hair, yanking his face upward, baring his throat. Barnes smelled the decay of Eph's body. "I should murder you right here," he said. "Right now." Eph drew out his sword and showed it to Barnes.

"You . . . you're not a murderer," gasped Barnes.

"Oh, but I am. I have become that. And unlike you, I don't do it by pushing a button or signing an order. I do it like this. Up close. Personal."

The silver blade touched Barnes's throat over his windpipe. Barnes arched his neck farther.

"But," said Eph, pulling the sword back a few inches, "luckily for you, you are still useful to me. I need you to do something for me, and you're going to do it. Nod yes."

Eph nodded Barnes's head for him.

"Good. Listen closely. There are people outside waiting for me. Do you understand? Are you sober enough to remember this, brandy Alexander boy?"

Barnes nodded, this time under his own power. Of course, at that moment he would have agreed to anything.

"My reason for coming here is to make you an offer. It will actually make you look good. I am here to tell you to go to the Master and tell it I have agreed to trade the *Occido Lumen* for my son. Prove to me you understand this."

"Double-crossing is something I understand, Eph," said Barnes.

"You can even be the hero of this story. You can tell him that I came here to murder you, but now I am double-crossing my own people by offering you this deal. You can tell him you convinced me to take his offer and volunteered to take it back to the Master."

"Do the others know about this . . . ?"

Emotions surged. Tears welled in Eph's eyes. "They believe I am with them, and I am . . . but this is about my boy."

Emotions swelled in Ephraim Goodweather's heart. He was dizzy, lost . . .

"All you need to do is tell the Master that I accept. That this is no bluff."

"You are going to deliver this book."

"For my son . . ."

"Yes—yes . . . of course. Perfectly understandable . . ."

Eph grabbed Barnes by the hair and punched again. Twice in the mouth. Another tooth cracked.

"I don't want your fucking sympathy, you monster. Just deliver my message. You got it? I am somehow going to get the real *Lumen* and get word to the Master, maybe through you again, when I am ready to deliver."

Eph's grip on Barnes's hair had relaxed. Barnes realized he was not to be killed or even harmed any further. "I . . . I heard that the Master had a boy with him . . . a human boy. But I didn't know why . . ."

Eph's eyes blazed. "His name is Zachary. He was kidnapped two years ago."

"By Kelly, your wife?" said Barnes. "I saw her. With the Master. She is . . . well, she is no longer herself. But I suppose none of us are."

Eph said, "Some of us even became vampires without ever getting stung by anything . . ." Eph's eyes grew glassy and damp. "You are a capitulator and a coward, and for me to join your ranks tears at my insides like a fatal disease, but I see no other way out, and I have to save my son. I have to." His grip tightened on Barnes again. "This is the right choice, it is the only choice. For a father. My boy has been kidnapped and the ransom is my soul and the fate of the world, and I will pay it. I will pay it. Goddamn the Master, and goddamn you."

Even Barnes, whose loyalty fell on the side of the vampires, wondered to himself how wise it would be to enter into any sort of agreement with the Master, a being marshaled by no morality or code. A virus, and a ravenous one at that.

But of course Barnes said nothing of the kind to Eph. The man holding a sword near Barnes's throat was a creature worn down almost to the nub, like a pencil eraser with just enough pink rubber left to make one final correction.

"You will do this," said Eph, not asking.

Barnes nodded. "You can count on me." He attempted a smile but his mouth and gums were swollen to the point of disfiguration.

Eph stared at him another long moment, a look of pure disgust coming into his gaunt face. *This is the kind of man you are now making deals with.* Then he threw Barnes's head back, turning with his sword and starting for the door.

Barnes gripped his spared neck but could not hold his bleeding tongue. "And I do understand, Ephraim," he said, "perhaps better than you." Eph stopped, turning beneath the handsome molding framing the doorway. "Everybody has their price. You believe your plight is more noble than mine because your price is the welfare of your son. But to the Master, Zack is nothing more than a coin in its pocket. I am sorry it has taken you so long to see this. That you should have borne all this suffering so unnecessarily."

Eph stood snarling at the floor, his sword hanging heavily in his hand. "And I am only sorry that you haven't suffered more . . ."

Service Garage, Columbia University

WHEN THE SUN backlit the ashen filter of the sky—what passed for daylight now—the city became eerily quiet. Vampire activity ceased, and the streets and buildings lit up with the ever-changing light of television sets. Reruns and rain; that was the norm. Acid, black rain dripped from the tortured sky in fat, oily drops. The ecological cycle was "rinse and repeat," but dirty water never cleaned anything. It would take decades, if it ever self-cleansed at all. For now, the gloaming of the city was like a sunrise that would not turn over.

Gus waited outside the open door of the facility-services garage. Creem was an ally of convenience, and he had always been a squirrely motherfucker. It sounded like he was coming alone, which didn't make much sense, so Gus didn't trust it. Gus had taken a few extra precautions himself. Among them was the shiny Glock tucked into the small of his back, a handgun he had seized from a former drug den in the chaos of the first days. Another was setting the meet here and giving Creem no indication that Gus's underground lair was nearby.

Creem drove up in a yellow Hummer. Bright color aside, this was just the sort of clumsy move Gus expected from him: driving a notorious gas guzzler in a time of very little available fuel. But Gus shrugged it off, because that was who Creem was. And predictability in one's rival was a good thing.

Creem needed the big vehicle to fit his body in behind the steering wheel. Even given all their deprivations, he had managed to keep much of his size—only now there was not an ounce of loose fat on him. Somehow he was eating. He was sustaining. It told Gus that the Sapphires' raids on the vampire establishment were succeeding.

Except he had no other Sapphires with him now. None Gus could see, anyway.

Creem rolled his Hummer into the garage, out of the rain. He killed the engine and worked his way out from the driver's seat. He had a stick of jerky in his mouth, gnawing on it like a thick, meaty pick. His silver grille shone when he smiled. "Hey, Mex."

"You made it in all right."

Creem waved at the air with his short arms. "Your island here is going to shit."

Gus agreed. "Fucking landlord's a real prick."

"Real bloodsucker, huh?"

Niceties aside, they exchanged a simple handshake grip, no gang stuff—while never losing eye contact. Gus said, "Running solo?"

"This trip," said Creem, hiking up his pants. "Gotta keep an eye on things in Jersey. I don't suppose you're alone."

"Never," said Gus.

Creem looked around, nodding, not seeing anyone. "Hiding, eh? I'm cool," he said.

"And I'm careful."

That drew a smile from Creem. Then he bit off the end of the jerky. "Want some of this?"

"I'm good for now." Best to let Creem think Gus was eating well and regularly.

Creem pulled out the jerky. "Doggie treat. We found a warehouse with a whole pet-supply shipment that never went out. I don't know what's in this thing, but it's food, right? Will give me a lustrous pelt, clean my teeth and all that." Creem barked a few times, then snickered. "Cat food cans keep for a good long time. Portable meal. Taste like fucking pâté."

"Food is food," said Gus.

"And breathing is breathing. Look at us here. Two bangers from the projects. Still hustling. Still representing. And everybody else, the ones who thought this city was theirs, the tender souls—they didn't have no real fucking pride, no stake, no claim; where are they now? The walking dead."

"The undead."

"Like I always say, 'Creem rises to the top.' " He laughed again, maybe too hard. "You like the ride?"

"How you fueling it?"

"Got some pumps still flowing in Jersey. Check out the grille? Just like my teeth. Silver."

Gus looked. The front grille of the car was indeed plated in silver. "Now, that I like," said Gus.

"Silver rims are next on my wish list," said Creem. "So, you wanna get your backups out here now, so I don't feel like I'm gonna be ripped off? I'm here in good faith."

Gus whistled and Nora came out from behind a tool cart holding a Steyr semiauto. She lowered the weapon, stopping a safe thirty feet away.

Joaquin appeared from behind a door, his pistol at his side. He could not disguise his limp; his knee was still giving him grief.

Creem opened his stubby arms wide, welcoming them to the meet. "You wanna get to it? I gotta get back over that fucking bridge before the creeps come out."

"Show and tell," said Gus.

Creem went around and opened the rear door. Four open cardboard moving cartons fresh out of a U-Haul store, crammed full of silver. Gus slid one out for inspection, the box heavy with candlesticks, utensils, decorative urns, coins, and even a few dinged-up, mint-stamped silver bars.

Creem said, "All pure, Mex. No sterling shit. No copper base. There's a test kit in there somewhere I'll throw in for free."

"How'd you score all this?"

"Picking up scrap for months, like a junk man, saving it. We got all the metal we need. I know you want this vamp-slaying shit. Me, I like guns." He looked at Nora's piece. "Big guns."

Gus picked through the silver pieces. They'd have to melt them down, forge them, do their best. None of them were smiths. But the swords they had weren't going to last forever.

"I can take all this off your hands," said Gus. "You want firepower?"

"Is that all you sellin'?"

Creem was looking not only at Nora's weapon but at Nora.

Gus said, "I got some batteries, shit like that. But that's it."

Creem didn't take his eyes off Nora. "She got her head smooth like them camp workers."

Nora said, "Why are you talking about me like I'm not here?"

Creem smiled silver. "Can I see the piece?"

Nora brought it forward, handed it to him. He accepted with an interested smile, then turned his attention to the Steyr. He released the bolt and the magazine, checking the load, then fed it back into the buttstock. He sighted a ceiling lamp and pretended to blow it away.

"More like this?" he asked.

"Like it," confirmed Gus. "Not identical. I'll need at least a day though. I got 'em stashed around town."

"And ammo. Plenty of it." He worked the safety off and on. "I'll take this one as a down payment."

Nora said, "Silver is so much more efficient."

Creem smiled at her—eager, condescending. "I didn't get here by being efficient, baldy. I like to make some fucking noise when I waste these bloodsuckers. That's the fun of it."

He reached for her shoulder and Nora batted his hand away, which only made him laugh.

She looked at Gus. "Get this dog-food-eating slob out of here."

Gus said, "Not yet." He turned to Creem. "What about that detonator?"

Creem opened his front door and laid the Steyr down across the front seat, then shut it again. "What about it?"

"Stop dicking around. Can you do it for me?"

Creem made like he was deciding. "Maybe. I have a lead—but I need to know more about this shit you're trying to blow. You know I live just across the river there."

"You don't need to know anything. Just name your price."

"Military-grade detonator?" said Creem. "There's a place in northern Jersey I got my eye on. Military installation. I'm not saying much more than that right now. But you gotta come clean."

Gus looked at Nora, not for her okay but to frown at being put in this position. "Pretty simple," he said. "It's a nuke."

Creem smiled wide. "Where'd you get it?"

"Corner store. Book of coupons."

Creem checked on Nora. "How big?"

"Big enough to do a half-mile of destruction. Shock wave, bent steel—you name it."

Creem was enjoying this. "But you wound up with the floor model. Sold as-is."

"Yes. We need a detonator."

"'Cause I don't know how stupid you think I am, but I am not in the habit of arming my next-door neighbor with a live nuclear bomb without laying down some fucking ground rules."

"Really," said Gus. "Such as?"

"Just that I don't want you fucking up my prize."

"What's that?"

"I do for you, you do for me. So first, I need assurances that this thing is going off at least a few miles away from me. Not in Jersey or Manhattan, bottom line."

"You'll be warned beforehand."

"Not good enough. 'Cause I think I know what the hell you're looking to use this bad boy on. Only one thing worth blowing up in this world. And when the Master goes, that's gonna free up some serious real estate. Which is my price."

"Real estate?" said Gus.

"This city. I own Manhattan outright, after all is said and done. Take it or leave it, Mex."

Gus shook hands with Creem. "Can I interest you in a bridge?"

New York Public Library
Main Branch

ANOTHER ROTATION OF Earth, and they were back together again, the five humans, Fet, Nora, Gus, Joaquin, and Eph, with Mr. Quinlan having traveled ahead under cover of darkness. They came out of Grand Central Station and followed Forty-second Street to Fifth Avenue. There was no rain but an exceptional wind, strong enough to dislodge trash accumulated in doorways. Fast food wrappers, plastic bags, and other pieces of legacy refuse blew down the street like spirits dancing through a graveyard.

They walked up the front steps of the main branch of the New York Public Library, between the twin stone lions, Patience and Fortitude. The beaux arts landmark stood like a great mausoleum. They moved through the portico into the entrance, crossing Astor Hall. The massive reading room had suffered only minor damage: looters, in the brief period of anarchy after the Fall, didn't care much for books. One of the grand chandeliers had come down onto a reading table below, but the ceiling was so high that it may have just been a random structural failing. Some books remained on the tables, some backpacks and their picked-over contents strewn about the tile floor. Chairs were overturned, and a few of the lamp heads were broken off. The silent emptiness of the immense, public room was chilling.

The arched windows high on either side admitted as much light as was available. The ammoniac smell of vampire waste, so omnipresent Eph barely noticed it anymore, registered with him here. It said something that the accumulated knowledge and art of a civilization could be shat upon so carelessly by a marauding force of nature.

"We have to go down?" asked Gus. "What about one of these books here?" The shelves on either side, on two levels along walls running the length of the room below and above the railed walkways, were filled with colored spines.

Fet said, "We need an ornate, old book to double for the *Lumen*. We gotta sell this thing, remember. I've been in here numerous times. Rats and mice are drawn to decaying paper. The ancient texts they keep down below."

They took to the stairs, turning on flashlights and readying night-vision devices. The main branch had been constructed on the site of the Croton Reservoir, a man-made lake that provided water for the island, made obsolete by the beginning of the twentieth century. There were seven full floors beneath street level, and a recent renovation beneath the adjacent Bryant Park on the rear, west side of the library had added more miles of book stacks.

Fet led the way into the darkness. The figure awaiting them on the landing at the third floor was Mr. Quinlan. Gus's flashlight briefly illuminated the Born's face, an almost phosphorescent white, his eyes like red baubles. He and Gus had an exchange.

Gus drew his sword. "Bloodsuckers in the stacks," he said. "We got some clearing to do."

Nora said, "If they pick up on Eph, they'll bounce it to the Master, and we'll be trapped underground."

Mr. Quinlan's mouthless voice entered their heads.

Dr. Goodweather and I will wait inside. I can baffle any attempts at psychic intrusion.

"Good," said Nora, readying her Luma lamp.

Gus was already moving down the stairs to the next floor, sword in hand, Joaquin limping down behind him. "Let's have some fun."

Nora and Fet paired off, following them, while Mr. Quinlan pushed through the nearest door, entering the third underground floor. Eph reluctantly followed him. Inside were wide storage cabinets of aged periodicals and stacked bins of obsolete audio recordings. Mr. Quinlan opened the door to a listening booth, and Eph was obliged to follow him inside.

Mr. Quinlan closed the soundproof door. Eph pulled off his night-vision scope, leaning against a near counter, standing together with the Born in darkness and in silence. Eph worried that the Born could read him and so turned up the white noise in his head by actively imagining and then naming the items surrounding him.

Eph did not want the hunter to detect his potential deceit. Eph was walking a fine line here, playing the same game with both sides. Telling each he was working to subvert the other. In the end, Eph's only loyalty was to Zack. He suffered equally at the thought of potentially turning on his friends—or spending eternity in a world of horror.

I had a family once.

The Born's voice shook a nervous Eph, but he recovered quickly.

The Master turned them all, leaving it to me to destroy them. Something else we share in common.

Eph nodded. "But there was a reason it was

after you. A link. The Master and I have no past. No commonality. I fell into its path purely by accident of my profession as an epidemiologist."

There is a reason. We just don't know what it is.

Eph had devoted hours to this very thought. "My fear is that it has something to do with my son, Zack."

The Born was quiet for a moment.

You must be aware of a similarity between myself and your son. I was turned in the womb of my mother. And through that, the Master became my surrogate father, supplanting my own human forebear. By corrupting the mind of your son in his formative years, the Master is seeking to supplant you, your influence upon your son's maturation.

"You mean, this is a pattern with the Master." Eph should have been discouraged, but instead he found reason to cheer. "Then there's hope," he said. "You turned against the Master. You rejected it. And it had much greater influence over you." Eph stood off the counter, lifted by this theory. "Maybe Zack will too. If I can get to him in time, the way the Ancients got to you. Maybe it's not too late. He is a good kid—I know it . . ."

So long as he remains unturned biologically, there is a chance.

"I have to get him away from the Master. Or, more accurately, get the Master away from him. Can we really destroy it? I mean, if God failed to do it so long ago."

God succeeded. Ozryel was destroyed. It was the blood that rose.

"So, in a sense, we have to fix God's mistake."

God makes no mistakes. In the end, all the rivers go to the sea . . .

"No mistakes. You think that fiery mark in the sky appeared on purpose. Sent for me?"

For me, as well. So that I might know to protect you. To safeguard you from corruption. The elements are falling into place. The ashes are gathered. Fet has the weapon. Fire rained from the sky. Signs and portents—the very language of God. They all will rise and fall with the strength of our alliance.

Again, a pause that Eph could not decipher. Was the Born already inside his head? Had he softened Eph's mind with conversation so that he could read Eph's true intentions?

Mr. Fet and Ms. Martinez have cleared the sixth floor. Mr. Elizalde and Mr. Soto are still engaged on floor five.

Eph said, "I want to go to six."

They went down the stairwell, passing one conspicuous puddle of white vampire blood. Passing the door to the fifth floor, Eph could hear Gus cursing loudly, almost joyously.

The sixth floor began with a map room. Through a heavy glass door, Eph passed into a long room that had once been carefully climate controlled. Panels featuring thermostats and humidity barometers dotted the walls, and the ceiling was spaced with vents, their ribbons hanging limp.

The stacks were long here. Mr. Quinlan fell back, and Eph knew he was somewhere deep beneath Bryant Park now. He proceeded quietly, listening for Fet and Nora, not wanting to surprise them or be surprised by them. He heard voices a few stacks over and moved through a break in the shelves.

They were using a flashlight. That allowed Eph to switch off his night-vision scope. He got close enough to see them through one stack of books. They were standing at a glass table with their backs to him. Above the table, inside a cabinet, were what looked to be the library's most precious acquisitions.

Fet forced the locks and laid the other ancient texts out in front of him. He focused on one book: a Gutenberg Bible. It had the most potential as a fake. Silvering the page edges would not be difficult, and he could lightly paste in some illuminated pages from the other tomes. Defacing literary treasures was a small price to pay for overthrowing the Master and his clan.

"This," said Fet. "The Gutenberg Bible. There were fewer than fifty in existence . . . Now? This may be the last one." He examined it further, turning it around. "This is an incomplete copy, printed on paper, not vellum, and the binding is not original."

Nora looked at him. "You've learned a lot about ancient texts."

Involuntarily, Fet blushed at the compliment. He turned around and reached for an information card in a hard plastic sleeve and showed her he had been reading this information. She slapped him lightly on the arm.

"I'm taking it with us now, along with a handful of others to dummy up."

Fet pulled down a few other illuminated texts, stacking them gently into a backpack.

"Wait!" Nora said. "You're bleeding . . ."

It was true. Fet was bleeding profusely. Nora opened up his shirt and popped open a small bottle of peroxide taken from the kit.

She poured it on the bloodstained fabric. The blood bubbled up and fizzed upon contact. That would destroy the scent for the *strigoi*.

"You must rest," Nora said. "I order it as your physician."

"Oh, my physician," said Fet. "Is that what you are?"

"I am," said Nora with a smile. "I need to get you some antibiotics. Eph and I can find them. You go back with Quinlan . . ."

Delicately, she cleaned Fet's wound and poured peroxide on it again. The liquid ran down the hairs on his massive chest. "You want to make me a blond, eh?" Vasiliy joked. And as terrible as his joke was, Nora laughed at it, rewarding the intent.

Vasiliy pulled off her cap. "Hey, give me that!" she said, and fought Vasiliy's good arm for possession of the cap. Vasiliy gave her the cap but trapped her in an embrace.

"You're still bleeding."

He ran his hand over her bare scalp. "I'm so glad I have you back . . ."

And then, for the first time, Fet told her, in his own way, how he felt about her. "I don't know where I'd be right now without you."

In other circumstances, the burly exterminator's confession would have been ambiguous and insufficient. Nora would have waited for a bit more. But now—here and now—this was enough. She kissed him softly on the lips and felt his massive arms surround her back, engulfing her, pulling her to his chest. And they both felt fear evaporate and time freeze. They were *there, now.* In fact it felt like they'd always been there. No memory of pain or loss.

As they embraced, the beam from the flashlight in Nora's hand glided by the stacks, briefly illuminating Eph hiding there, before he faded back into the book stacks.

Belvedere Castle, Central Park

THIS TIME, DR. Everett Barnes was able to wait until he was out of the helicopter before vomiting. When he was through disgorging his breakfast, he swiped at his mouth and chin with a handkerchief and looked around rather sheepishly. But the vampires showed no reaction to his becoming violently sick. Their expressions, or lack thereof, remained fixed and uncaring. Barnes could have laid a giant egg there in the muddy walkway near the Shakespeare Garden on the Seventy-ninth Street Transverse or had a third arm burst forth from his chest and not suffered any embarrassment in these drones' eyes. His appearance was terrible, his face bloated and purple, his lips engorged with coagulated blood, and his injured hand bandaged and immobilized. But they paid no attention to any of this.

Barnes caught his breath and straightened a few yards free of the whirling helicopter rotors, ready to move along. The chopper lifted off, whipping rain at his back, and once it was away he opened his broad, black umbrella. His sexless undead guards took as little notice of the rain as they had his nausea, moving along at his side like pale, plastic automatons.

The bare heads of dead trees parted, and Belvedere Castle came into view, set high atop Vista Rock, framed against the contaminated sky.

Below, in a thick ring around the base of the stone, stood a legion of vampires. Their stillness was unnerving, their statuelike presence resembling some bizarre and stupefyingly ambitious art installation. And then, as Barnes and his two guards approached the outer edge of the vampire ring, the creatures parted—unbreathing, expressionless—for them, allowing their approach. Barnes stopped about ten rows in, approximately halfway through, looking at this respectful ring of vampires. He trembled a little, the umbrella vibrating such that dirty rain shook off the tips of the ribs. Here he experienced most deeply a sense of the uncanny: being in the middle of all these human predators, who by all rights should have drunk him or torn him to shreds—but instead stood idly as he passed, if not with respect then with enforced indifference. It was as though he had entered the zoo and gone walking past the lions, tigers, and bears without any reaction or interest. This was completely against their nature. Such was the depth of their enslavement to the Master.

Barnes encountered the former Kelly Goodweather at the door to the castle. She stood outside the door, her eyes meeting his, unlike the rest of the drones. He slowed, almost tempted to say something, like "Hello," a courtesy left over from the old world. Instead, he simply passed, and her eyes followed him inside.

The clan lord appeared in his dark cloak, blood worms rippling beneath the skin covering his face as he regarded Barnes.

Goodweather has accepted.

"Yes," Barnes said, thinking, *If you knew that, then why did I have to get in a helicopter to come to this drafty castle to see you?*

Barnes tried to explain the double-cross but became tangled up in the details himself. The Master did not appear particularly interested.

"He's double-crossing his partners," said Barnes, summing up. "He seemed sincere. I don't know that I would trust him, though."

I trust his pitiable need for his son.

"Yes. I see your point. And he trusts your need for the book."

Once I have Goodweather, I have his partners. Once I have the book, I have all the answers.

"What I don't understand is how he was able to overwhelm security at my house. Why others of your clan weren't notified."

It is the Born. He is created by me but not of my blood.

"So he's not on the same wavelength?"

I do not have control over him as I do my others.

"And he's with Goodweather now? Like a double agent? A defector?" The Master did not answer. "Such a being could be very dangerous."

For you? Very. For myself? Not dangerous. Only elusive. The Born has allied himself with the gang member whom the Ancients recruited for day hunting and the rest of the scum that runs with him. I know where to find some information about them . . .

"If Goodweather surrenders himself to you . . . then you would have all the information to find him. The Born."

Yes. Two fathers reuniting with two sons. There's always symmetry in God's plans. If he gives himself to me . . .

A ruckus behind Barnes then made him turn, startled. A teenager, with ragged hair falling over his eyes, stumbling down the spiral staircase. A human, holding one hand to his throat. The boy shook back some of his hair, just enough so that Barnes recognized Ephraim Goodweather in the boy's face. Those same eyes, that same very serious expression—though now showing fear.

Zachary Goodweather. He was in obvious respiratory distress, wheezing and turning grayish blue.

Barnes stood, starting toward him instinctively. Later it would occur to Barnes that it had been a great while since he had acted on medical instinct. He intercepted the boy, holding him by his shoulder. "I am a doctor," said Barnes.

The boy pushed Barnes away, pinwheeling his arm, going straight to the Master. Barnes rocked back a few steps, more shocked than anything.

The floppy-haired boy fell to his knees before the Master, who looked down at his suffering face. The Master let the boy struggle a few moments longer, then raised its arm, the loose sleeve of its cloak sliding back. His thumb and elongated middle finger snapped together in a blur, pricking the skin. The Master held its thumb over the boy's face, a single droplet of blood poised on the tip. Slowly, the bead elongated, dripping free, landing in the back of Zack's open mouth.

Barnes himself swallowed dryly, sickened. He had already thrown up once that morning.

The boy closed his mouth as though having just ingested an eyedropper's worth of medicine. He grimaced—either at the taste or at the pain of the swallow—and within a few moments his hand came away from his throat. His head hung low as he regained normal respiration, his airway opening, his lungs clearing miraculously. Almost instantly, his pallor returned to normal—the new normal, that is, meaning sallow and sun-hungry.

The boy blinked and looked around, seeing the room for the first time since entering in respiratory distress. His mother—or what remained of her—had entered from the doorway, perhaps summoned by her Dear One's distress. Yet her blank face showed neither concern nor relief. Barnes wondered how often this healing ritual was performed. Once every week? Once every day?

The boy looked at Barnes as though for the first time, the white-goateed man he had shoved away just moments before.

"Why is there another human here?" asked Zack Goodweather.

The boy's supercilious manner surprised Barnes, who remembered Goodweather's son as a thoughtful, curious, well-mannered child. Barnes ran his fingers through his own hair, summoning some dignity.

"Zachary, do you remember me?"

The boy's lips curled as though he resented being asked to study Barnes's face. "Vaguely," he said, his tone harsh, his manner haughty.

Barnes remained patient, upbeat. "I was your father's boss. In the old world."

Again, Barnes saw the father in the son—but less so now. Just as the Eph who visited him had changed, so had the boy. His young eyes were distant, distrusting. He had the attitude of a boy-prince.

Zachary Goodweather said, "My father is dead."

Barnes started to speak, then wisely held back his words. He glanced at the Master, and there was no change of expression in the creature's rippling face—but Barnes knew somehow not to contradict. For an instant, as he perceived the big picture and saw everyone's play and position in this particular drama, he felt bad for Eph. His own son . . . But, Barnes being Barnes, the feeling didn't last long and he began to think of a way to profit from this.

Low Library, Columbia University

*C*ONSIDER THIS ABOUT *the* Lumen.

Mr. Quinlan's eyes were unusually vibrant when he said this.

There are two words consigned to the page indicating the Master's Black Site: "obscura" *and* "aeterna." *"Dark"* and *"eternal." No exact coordinates.*

"Every site had them," said Fet. "Except that one."

He was actively working on the Bible, trying to shape it as close to the *Lumen* as possible. He had amassed a pile of books that he examined and cannibalized for pieces or engravings.

Why? And why just those two words?

"Do you think that is the key?"

I believe it is. I always thought the key to finding the site was in the information in the book—but, it turns out, the key is in the information missing from it. The Master was the last one to be born. The youngest one of them all. It took it hundreds of years to reconnect with the Old World and even longer to acquire the influence to destroy the Ancients' origin sites. But now—now it has come back to the New World, back to Manhattan. Why?

"Because it wanted to protect its own origin site."

The fiery mark in the sky confirmed as much. But where is it?

In spite of the thrilling information, Fet seemed distant, distracted.

What is it?

"Sorry. I'm thinking about Eph," said Fet. "He's out. With Nora."

Out where?

"Getting some medicine. For me."

Dr. Goodweather must be protected. He is vulnerable.

Fet was caught short. "I'm sure they'll be fine," he said, but now it was his turn to worry.

Macy's Herald Square

EPH AND NORA exited the subway at Thirty-fourth Street and Pennsylvania Station. It was there at the train station, nearly two years before, that Eph had left Nora, Zack, and Nora's mother, in a last-ditch attempt to get them safely out of the city before New York fell to the vampire plague. A horde of creatures had derailed the train inside the North River Tunnel, foiling their escape, and Kelly had made off with Zack, taking him to the Master.

They were casing a small closed pharmacy occupying the corner of the Macy's store. Nora was watching commuters pass them, downtrodden humans on their way to and from work, or else on their way to the ration station at the Empire State Building to exchange work vouchers for clothing or food.

"Now what?" said Eph.

Nora looked diagonally across Seventh Avenue, seeing Macy's one block away, its front entrance boarded. "We'll go through the store and into the pharmacy. Follow me."

The rotating doors had long ago been locked, the broken glass boarded tight. Shopping, either as a necessity or a leisure-time pursuit, no longer existed. Everything was ration cards and vouchers.

Eph pried a piece of plywood off the Thirty-fourth Street entrance. Inside, the "World's Largest Department Store" was a mess. Racks overturned, clothing torn. It looked less like looting and more like the scene of a fight, or a series of fights. A vampire and human rampage.

They accessed the pharmacy through the store counter. The shelves were almost bare. Nora picked up a few items, including a mild antibiotic and a few syringes. Eph pocketed a bottle of Vicodin when Nora wasn't looking and jammed it into a small pouch.

In a matter of five minutes they had what they came for. Nora looked at Eph. "I need some warm clothes and a pair of sturdy shoes. These camp slippers are worn down."

Eph thought about cracking a joke about women and shopping but kept quiet and nodded. Farther inside, it wasn't so bad. They walked up the famous wooden escalators—the first such set of moving stairs ever installed inside a building.

Their flashlights played over the vacant display floor, unchanged since the end of shopping as the world knew it. The mannequins startled Eph, their bald heads and fixed expressions giving them—in the first moment of illumination—a superficial resemblance to the *strigoi*.

"Same haircut," said Nora with a faint smile. "It's all the rage . . ."

They moved through the floor, casing the place, looking for any signs of danger or vulnerability. "I am afraid, Nora," Eph said, much to her surprise. "The plan . . . I am afraid and I don't mind admitting as much."

"The exchange will be difficult," she said, her voice low as she pulled down shoe boxes in a back room, looking for her size. "That's the trick. I think you should tell it we are getting the book for Mr. Quinlan to study. The Master surely knows about the Born. Tell it you plan to grab the book as soon as you can. We'll have a location to set the bomb—and you'll lure it in. He can bring as much reinforcement as he wants then. A bomb is a bomb . . ."

Eph nodded. He watched her face for some sign of treachery. They were alone now; if she was going to reveal herself to him as the turncoat, this was the time.

She eschewed more-fashionable leather boots for something sturdy and without heels. "The fake book just has to look good," Eph said. "It has to look *right*. I think things will move so quickly, we just need to pass that initial glance test."

"Fet is on it," said Nora with absolute certainty. Almost with pride. "You can trust him . . ." And then she realized who she was talking to. "Listen, Eph. About Fet . . ."

"You don't have to say anything. I understand. The world is fucked and we deserve to be only with those who care for us—above and beyond all things. In a strange way . . . if it was going to be anyone I feel good that it was Fet. Because he will give his life before he allows any harm to come to you. Setrakian knew it and chose him above me and you know it too. He can do what I never could—be there for you."

Nora felt conflicting emotions now. This was Eph at his best: generous, smart, and caring. She would've almost preferred him to be an asshole. Now she saw him for who he really was: the man she had once fallen in love with. Her heart still felt the pull.

"What if the Master wants me to bring the book to it?" asked Eph.

"Maybe you'll tell him we are chasing you. That you need the Master to come and get you. Or maybe you insist on him bringing Zack to you."

Eph's face darkened a moment, remembering the Master's abject refusal on that point. "That raises a major issue," he said. "How can I set this thing off and get away?"

"I don't know. Too many variables right now. This whole thing is going to require a lot of luck. And courage. I wouldn't blame you if you are having second thoughts."

She watched him. Looking for a crack in his demeanor . . . or an opening so that she could reveal her complicity? "Second thoughts?" he said, trying to draw her out. "About going through with this?"

He saw the concern in her face as she shook her head. No hint of duplicity. And he was glad. He was relieved. Things had changed so much between them—but she was at heart the same old freedom fighter she always had been. It helped Eph to believe that he was the same too.

"What is that?" she asked.

"What?" he said.

"It looked almost like you were smiling."

Eph shook his head. "Just me realizing that the bottom line is that Zack goes free. Whatever it takes to achieve that, I'll do."

"I think that's amazing, Eph. I really do."

"You don't think the Master will see right through this?" he said. "You think it will believe that I could do this? That I could betray the rest of you?"

"I do," she said. "I think it fits the way the Master thinks. Don't you?"

Eph nodded, glad she wasn't looking at him at that moment. If not Nora, then who was the turncoat? Not Fet, certainly. Could it be Gus? Could all of his bluster toward Eph be a cover? Or Joaquin was another possible suspect. All this twisty thinking was making him even more crazy.

. . . *can never go down / can never go down the drain.*

He heard something out in the main display area. Stirring noises, once assigned to rodents, nowadays meant only one thing.

Nora had heard it too. They switched off their flashlights.

"Wait here," said Eph. Nora understood that, for this subterfuge to succeed, Eph had to go alone. "And be careful."

"Always," she said, drawing silver.

He slid out through the door, careful not to

bump the handle of the sword jutting out of his backpack. He pulled on his night-vision monocular and waited for the image to stabilize in his vision.

Everything looked still. All the mannequins had normally sized hands, no extended talon for a middle finger. Eph circled right, keeping to the edge of the room, until he saw the hanger swinging gently on a circular rack near the down escalator.

Eph drew his sword and went swiftly to the top wooden step. The nonworking escalator ran along a narrow, walled space. He descended as quickly and as quietly as he could, then took in the next level from the landing. Something told him to keep going down, and so he did.

He slowed at the bottom, smelling something. A vampire had been here; he was close behind. Strange for a vampire to be out on its own, not otherwise industriously employed. Unless patrolling this department store was its assigned task. Eph ventured out from the escalator, the floor revealed in green. Nothing moved. He was about to start toward a large display when he heard a light click in the opposite direction.

Again he saw nothing. Ducking low, he wove around the clothing racks in the direction of the noise. The sign above the open doorway gave directions for the restrooms and the administrative offices, as well as an elevator. Eph crept past the offices first, looking in every open door. He could come back and try the closed doors after he had cleared the rest of the area. He went to the restrooms, nudging open the door to the women's room just a few inches to see if it made much noise. It was nearly silent. He entered and scanned the stalls, pushing open each door, sword in hand.

He returned to the hallway and stood listening, feeling as though he had lost whatever thin trail he had been following. He pulled on the men's-room door and slipped inside. He passed the urinals and poked open each stall door with the tip of his sword, and then, disappointed, turned to leave.

In an explosion of paper and trash, the vampire leaped out of the open trash barrel in the corner near the door, landing on the edge of one of the sinks across the room. Eph lurched backward at first, cursing and swiping at the air with his sword to ward off any stinger attacks. He quickly asserted his position, leading with his silver, not wanting to get backed into a stall. He brandished the weapon at the hissing vampire and circled past it, coming close to the barrel it had sprung from, paper rustling at his feet.

It squatted there, gripping the smooth edge of the sink, its knees up around its head, looking at him. Eph finally got a clear glance at it in the green light of his scope. It was a boy. A ten- or twelve-year-old of African-American descent, with what looked like pure glass in his eyes.

A blind boy. One of the feelers.

The feeler's top lip was curled such that, by night vision, it looked like an appraising smile. His fingers and toes gripped the front edge of the sink counter as though he were about to pounce.

Eph kept the tip of his sword pointed at the feeler's midsection.

"Were you sent to find me?" Eph said.

Yes.

Eph sagged a bit in dismay. Not at the response, but at the voice.

It was Kelly's. Speaking the Master's words.

Eph wondered if Kelly was somehow responsible for the feelers. If she was their wrangler, so to speak. Their dispatcher. And if so, if indeed these blind, psychic vampire children had been placed under her unofficial command, how fitting and sadly ironic at the same time. Kelly Goodweather was still a mother hen, even in death.

"What made it so easy this time?"

You wanted to be found.

The feeler pounced, but not at Eph. The boy sprang from the countertop across the restroom to the wall, then dropped down to the tile floor on all fours.

Eph tracked it with his sword tip. The feeler crouched there, looking at him.

Are you going to slay me, Ephraim?

Kelly's taunting voice. Had it been her idea to send a boy Zack's age?

"Why do you torment me like this?"

I could have a hundred thirsty vampires there in moments, surrounding you. Tell me why I should not send them to you now.

"Because the book is not here. And—more important—if you broke our deal, I would slice my own throat before letting you have access to my mind."

You are bluffing.

Eph lunged at the boy. He skittered backward, bumping into a stall door and stopping inside. "How do you like it?" said Eph. "These threats don't instill much faith in me that you will keep your end of the bargain."

Pray that I do.

"Interesting choice of words, 'pray.' " Eph stood in the doorway to the stall now; the corner of the bathroom reeked from neglect. "Ozryel. Yes, I've been reading the book you want so badly. And talking to Mr. Quinlan, the Born."

Then you should know that I am not in fact Ozryel.

"No, you are the worms that crawled out of the murderous angel's veins. After God had him pulled apart like someone quartering a chicken."

We share the same rebellious nature. A lot like your son, I imagine.

Eph shook that off, determined not to be an easy mark for the Master's abuse any longer. "My son is nothing like you."

Don't be so sure. Where is the book?

"It was hidden in the stacks deep beneath the New York Public Library this entire time, in case you were wondering. I am supposed to be buying a little time for them now."

I presume the Born is studying it avidly.

"Correct. That doesn't worry you?"

To the eyes of the unworthy, it would take years to decipher.

"Good. So you're not in any rush. Maybe I should step back, then. Wait for a better offer from you."

And maybe I should draw and quarter your son.

Eph wanted to run his sword through this undead child's throat. Leave the Master wanting for a while longer. But at the same time he did not want to push the creature too far. Not with Zack's life on the line. "You're the one bluffing now. You are worried and are pretending not to be. You want this book and you want it very badly. Why so soon?"

It did not answer.

"There is no other traitor. You are all lies."

The feeler remained crouched, its back against the wall.

"Fine," said Eph. "Play it that way."

My father is dead.

Eph's heart skipped a beat, stopping dead in his chest for a long moment. Such was the shock of hearing, as clear as though he were there in the room with him, his son Zack's voice.

He was shaking. He fought hard to keep a furious scream from rising in his throat.

"You goddamned . . ."

The Master returned to Kelly's voice. *You will bring the book as soon as you can.*

Eph's first fear was that Zack had been turned. But no; the Master was just throwing Zack's voice, pushing it to Eph through this feeler.

Eph said, "Goddamn you."

God tried to. And where is He now?

"Not here," said Eph, his blade lowering a bit. "Not here."

No. Not in a department store men's room in a deserted Macy's. Why don't you release this poor child,

Ephraim? Look into its blind eyes. Wouldn't striking it down give you great satisfaction?

He did look into its eyes. Glassy and unblinking. Eph saw the vampire . . . but also the boy he once was.

I have thousands of sons. All of them absolutely loyal.

"You have only one true offspring. The Born. And all he wants is to destroy you."

The feeler dropped to its knees, raising its chin, baring its neck to Eph, its arms hanging limp at its sides.

Take him, Ephraim, and be done with it.

The feeler's blind eyes stared into nothingness, in the manner of a supplicant awaiting orders from its lord. The Master wanted him to execute the child. Why?

Eph pointed the tip of his sword at the boy's exposed neck. "Here," he said. "Run him into my sword if you wish him released."

You have no desire to slay him?

"I have every desire to slay him. But no good reason to."

When the boy did not move, Eph stepped back, pulling away his sword. Something wasn't right here.

You cannot slay the boy. You hide behind weakness by calling it strength.

Eph said, "Weakness is giving in to temptation. Strength is resisting it." He looked at the feeler, Kelly's voice still hanging in his head. The feeler had no link to Eph, not without Kelly. And her voice was being projected by the Master, in an attempt to distract and weaken him, but the vampire Kelly could be anywhere at that moment. Anywhere.

Eph backed out of the stall and started running, rushing up the escalator to where he had left Nora.

Kelly stayed close to the wall, padding barefoot past the racks of clothes. The woman's scent lingered in the back room behind the shoe display . . . but her bloodbeat thrummed across the display floor. Kelly approached the changing-room doorway. Nora Martinez waited there with a silver sword.

"Hey, bitch," Nora greeted her.

Kelly seethed, her mind going out to the feelers, calling them close. She had no clear angle of attack. The silver weapon glowed hot in her view as the bald female human started toward her.

"You really let yourself go," said Nora, circling around a register. "Cosmetics is on the first floor, by the way. And maybe a turtleneck to cover up that nasty turkey neck."

The girl feeler came bounding from the stairs, stopping near Kelly.

"Mother-daughter shopping day," said Nora. "How sweet. I've got some silver jewelry I'd love to see you two try on."

Nora feigned a jab; Kelly and the girl feeler just stared at her.

"I used to be afraid," said Nora. "In the train tunnel, I was afraid of you. I'm not afraid now."

Nora unclipped the Luma lamp hanging from

her pack, switching on the battery-powered black light. The ultraviolet rays repelled the vampires, the feeler snarling and backing away on all fours. Kelly remained still, only turning as Nora circled away from them, backing away to the stairs. She was using the mirrors to check behind her, which was how she saw the blurred figure darting up from the handrail.

Nora spun and drove her blade deep into the mouth of the boy feeler, the searing silver releasing him almost immediately. She jerked the blade out and spun back, ready for the attack.

Kelly and the girl feeler were gone. Vanished—as though they had never been there in the first place.

"Nora!"

Eph called to her from the floor below. "Coming down!" she yelled back, descending the wooden steps.

He met her there, anxious, having feared the worst. He saw the slick white blood on her blade.

"You okay?" he asked.

She nodded, grabbing a scarf off a nearby rack to clean off her sword. "Ran into Kelly upstairs. She says hi."

Eph stared at the sword. "Did you . . . ?"

"No, unfortunately. Just one of her little foster monsters."

Eph said, "Let's get out of here."

Outside, she half-expected a swarm of vampires to greet them. But no. Regular humans moving between work and home, shoulders hunched against the rain.

"How did it go?" asked Nora.

"It's a bastard," said Eph. "A true bastard."

"But do you think it bought it?"

Eph could not look her in the eye. "Yes," he said. "It bought it."

Eph was vigilant for vampires, scanning the sidewalks as they went.

"Where are we going?" she asked.

"Keep moving," he said. Across Thirty-sixth Street, he pulled over, ducking under the canopy of a closed market. He looked up through the rain, eyeing the rooftops.

There, high across the street, a feeler leaped from the edge of one building to the next. Tracking them.

"They're following us," said Eph. "Come on." They walked on, trying to lose themselves in the masses. "We have to wait them out until the meridiem."

Columbia University

EPH AND NORA returned to the empty university campus soon after first light, confident they were not followed. Eph figured that Mr. Quinlan had to be underground, probably going over the *Lumen*. He was headed that way when Gus intercepted them—or, more accurately, intercepted Nora while Eph was still with her.

"You have the medicine?" he asked.

Nora showed him a bag full of their loot.

"It's Joaquin," said Gus.

Nora stopped short, thinking vampire involvement. "What happened?"

"I need you to see him. It's bad."

They followed him to a classroom where Joaquin was propped up on top of a desk, his pant leg rolled up. His knee was bulbous in two places, considerably swollen. The gangbanger was in great pain. Gus stood on the other side of the desk, waiting for answers.

"How long has it been like this?" Nora asked Joaquin.

Through a sweaty grimace, Joaquin said, "I dunno. A while."

"I'm going to touch it here."

Joaquin braced himself. Nora explored the swollen areas around the knee. She saw a small wound below the patella, less than an inch in length and crooked, its edges yellowed and crusty. "When did you get this cut?"

"Dunno," said Joaquin. "Think I bumped it at the blood camp. Didn't notice it until long after."

Eph jumped in. "You've been going out on your own sometimes. You hit any hospitals or nursing home facilities?"

"Uh . . . probably. Saint Luke's, sure."

Eph looked at Nora, their silence conveying the seriousness of the infection. "Penicillin?" said Nora.

"Maybe," said Eph. "Let's go think this through." To Joaquin, he said, "Lie back. We'll be right back in."

"Hold up, doc. That don't sound good."

Eph said, "It's an infection, obviously. It would

be fairly routine to treat this in a hospital. Problem is, there are no more hospitals. A sick human is simply disposed of. So we need to discuss how to care for it."

Joaquin nodded, unconvinced, and lay back on the desk. Gus, without a word, followed Eph and Nora out into the hallway.

Gus said, looking mostly at Nora, "No bullshit."

Nora shook her head. "Bacterium, multiresistant. He might have cut himself at the camp, but this is something he picked up at a medical facility. The bug can live on instruments, on surfaces, for a long time. Nasty, and trenchant."

Gus said, "Okay. What do you need?"

"What we need is something we can't get anymore. We just went out looking for it—vancomycin."

There had been a run on vancomycin during the last days of the scourge. Befuddled medical experts, professionals who should have known better than to feed a panic, went on television suggesting this "drug of last resort" as a possible treatment for the still-unidentified strain that was spreading through the country with incredible speed.

"And even if we could find some vancomycin," said Nora, "it would take a severe course of antibiotics and other remedies to rid him of this infection. It's not a vampire sting, but, in terms of life expectancy, it might as well be."

Eph said, "Even if we could get some fluids into him intravenously, it just won't do him any good, except prolonging the inevitable."

Gus looked at Eph as though he were going to hit him. "There's gotta be some other way. You guys are fucking doctors . . ."

Nora said, "Medically, we're halfway back to the Dark Ages now. With no new drugs being manufactured, all the diseases we thought we had beat are back, and taking us early. We can maybe scrounge around, find something to make him more comfortable . . ."

She looked at Eph. Gus did too. Eph didn't care anymore; he pulled off his pack—where he had smuggled the Vicodin—and opened the zippered pouch and pulled out a baggie full of tablets. Dozens of tablets and pills in different shapes, colors, and sizes. He selected a pair of low-dosage Lorcets, some Percodans, and four two-milligram Dilaudid tabs.

"Start him with these," he said, pointing to the Lorcets. "Save the Dilaudids for last." The rest of the bag he turned over to Nora. "Take it all. I'm through with them."

Gus looked at the pills in his hands. "These won't cure him?"

"No," said Nora. "Just manage his pain."

"What about, you know, amputation? Cutting off his leg. I could do it myself."

"It's not just the knee, Gus." Nora touched his arm. "I'm sorry. The way things are now, there's just not much we can do."

Gus stared at the drugs in his hand, dazed, as though he held there the broken pieces of Joaquin.

Fet entered, the shoulders of his duster wet

from outside. He slowed a moment, struck by the strange scene of Eph, Gus, and Nora standing together in an emotional moment.

"He's here," said Fet. "Creem's back. At the garage."

Gus closed the pills in his fist. "You go. Deal with that piece of shit. I'll be along."

He went back inside to Joaquin, caressed his sweaty forehead, and helped him swallow the pills. Gus knew that he was saying good-bye to the last person in the world he cared for. The last person he really loved. His brother, his mother, his closest *compas*: all gone now. He had nothing left now.

Back outside, Fet looked at Nora. "Everything all right? You took a long time."

"We were being followed," she said.

Eph watched them embrace. He had to pretend as though he didn't care.

"Mr. Quinlan get anywhere with the *Lumen*?" asked Eph once they parted.

"No," said Fet. "It's not looking good."

The three of them headed across the Greek-amphitheater-like Low Plaza, past the library, and on to the edge of the campus, where the maintenance building stood. Creem's yellow Hummer was parked inside the garage. The blinged-out leader of the Jersey Sapphires had his fat hand on a shopping cart full of semiautomatic weapons that Gus had promised him. The gang leader grinned wide, his silver-plated teeth glowing

Cheshire Cat–like inside his considerable mouth.

"I could do some damage with these pop guns," he said, sighting one out the open garage door. He looked at Fet, Eph, and Nora. "Where's the Mex?"

"He'll be along," said Fet.

Creem, professionally suspicious, mulled this over before deciding it was okay. "You authorized to speak for him? I made that bean eater a fair offer."

Fet said, "We are all well aware."

"And?"

"Whatever it takes," said Fet. "We have to see the detonator first."

"Yeah, sure, of course. We can arrange that."

"Arrange it?" said Nora. She looked at his ugly yellow truck. "I thought you were bringing it."

"Bringing it? I don't even know what the fuck it looks like. What am I, MacGyver? I show you where to go. Military arsenal. If this place don't have it, I don't know that anyplace does."

Nora looked at Fet. It was clear she didn't trust this Creem. "So, what, you're offering us a ride to the store? That's your great contribution?"

Creem smiled at her. "Intelligence and access. That's what I bring to the table."

"If you don't have this thing yet . . . then why are you here now?"

Creem brandished the unloaded weapon. "I came for my guns, and for the Mex's answer. And a little matter of ammunition to load up these babies." He opened his driver's-side door, reaching for something between the front seats: a map of Jersey, with a hand-drawn map paper-clipped to it.

Nora showed the maps to Fet and then Eph. "This is what you're giving us. For the island of Manhattan." She looked at Fet. "The Native Americans got a better deal than we are."

Creem was amused. "That's a map of the Picatinny Armory. You see there, it's in the northern New Jersey skylands, so only about thirty, forty miles west of here. A giant military reserve that the bloodsuckers now control. But I got a way in. Been raiding munitions for months now. Drawn down on most of their ammo—why I need this here." He patted the weapons as he loaded them into the back of his Hummer. "Started out in the Civil War as a place for the army to store gunpowder. It was military research and manufacturing before the vamp takeover."

Fet looked up from the map. "They have detonators?"

Creem said, "If they don't, nobody does. I seen fuses and timers. You gotta know what type you need. Your nuke here? Not that I know what I'm looking for."

Fet didn't answer that. "It's about three feet by five feet. Portable, but not suitcase-small. Heavy. Like a small keg or a trash can."

"You'll find something that works. Or you won't. I don't make any guarantees, except that I can put you there. Then you take your toy far away and see how she goes. I don't offer any money-back guarantees. Duds are your problem, not mine."

Nora said, "You are offering us next to nothing."

"You want to shop around for a few more years? Be my guest."

Nora said, "I'm glad you find this so funny."

"It's all fucking funny to me, lady," said Creem. "This whole world is a laugh factory. I laugh all day and night. What do you want me to do, bust out weeping? This vampire thing is one colossal joke, and the way I see it, you're either in on the joke, or you're out."

"And you're in on it?" said Nora.

"Put it to you this way, bald beauty," said silver-toothed Creem. "I aim to have the last laugh. So you renegades and rebels better make sure you light the fuse on this fucking thing away from my island here. Take a bite out of . . . fucking Connecticut or something. But stay off my turf here. Part of the deal."

Fet was smiling now. "What do you hope to do with this city once you own it?"

"I don't even know. Who can think that far ahead? I never been a landlord before. This place is a fixer-upper but a one of a kind. Maybe turn this fucker into a casino. Or a skate rink—it's all the same to you."

Gus entered then. His hands were deep in his pockets, his face set tight. He was wearing dark glasses but if you looked carefully enough—like Nora did—you could see his eyes were red.

"Here he is," said Creem. "Looks like we have a deal, Mex."

Gus nodded. "We have a deal."

Nora said, "Hold on. He's got nothing except these maps."

Gus nodded, still not really in the room yet. "How soon can we get it?"

Creem said, "How about tomorrow?"

Gus said, "Tomorrow it is. On one condition. You wait here tonight. With us. Lead us to it before first light."

"Keeping an eye on me, Mex?"

"We'll feed you," said Gus.

Creem was won over. "Fair enough. I like my steak well-done, remember." He swung his trunk door shut. "What's your great plan, anyway?"

"You don't really need to know," said Gus.

"You can't ambush this motherfucker." Creem looked at them all. "Hope you know that."

Gus said, "You can if you have something it wants. Something it needs. *That* is why I'm keeping my eye on you . . ."

Extract from the Diary of Ephraim Goodweather

Dear Zack,

This is my second time writing a letter that no father should ever have to write to his son: a suicide note. The first one I crafted before putting you on that train out of New York City, explaining my reasons for staying behind and fighting what I suspected was a losing battle.

Here I remain, still fighting that fight.

You were taken from me in the cruelest manner possible. For nearly two years now, I have pined for you, I have tried to find a way to set you free from the clutches of those who hold you. You think me dead, but no—not yet. I live, and I live for you.

I am writing this to you in the event that you

survive me and that the Master survives me as well. In that case—which is for me the worst-case scenario—I will have committed a grave crime against humanity, or what was left of it. I will have traded the last hope for the freedom of our subordinated race in order that you, son, will live. Not only live, but live as a human being, unturned by the plague of vampirism spread by the Master.

My dearest hope is that you have by now come to the realization that the Master's way is evil in its basest form. There is a very wise saying: "History is written by the victor." Today I write not of history but of hope. We had a life together once, Zack. A beautiful life, and I include your mother in this also. Please remember that life, its sunlight, laughter, and simple joy. That was your youth. You have been made to grow up much too fast, and any confusion on your part as to who truly loves you and wants the best for you is understandable and forgivable. I forgive you everything. Please forgive my treachery on your behalf. My own life is a small price to pay for yours, but the lives of my friends, and the future of humanity—enormous.

Many times I have given up hope in myself, but never in you. I regret only that I will not see the man you will grow to be. Please let my sacrifice guide you onto the path of goodness.

And now I have one other very important thing to say. If, as I say, this plan comes off as I fear it might, then I have been turned. I am a vampire. And you must understand that, due to the bond of love I feel for you, my vampire self will be coming for you. It will never stop. If, by the time you read this, you have already slain me, I thank you. A thousand times, I thank you. Please feel no guilt, no shame, only the satisfaction of a good deed done well. I am at peace.

But if somehow you have not released me yet—please destroy me the next chance you get. This is my last request. You will want to cut down your mother too. We love you.

If you have found this diary where I intend to leave it—on your boyhood bed, in your mother's house on Kelton Street in Woodside, Queens—then you will find, beneath the bed, a bag of weapons forged of silver that I hope will make your way easier in this world. It is all I have to bequeath you.

It is a cruel world, Zachary Goodweather. Do anything you can to make it better.

Your father,
Dr. Ephraim Goodweather

Columbia University

Eph had skipped Gus's promised meal in order to compose his letter to Zack in one of the empty classrooms down the hall from Joaquin. In doing so, Eph despised the Master at that moment more than he had at any other point in this long, terrible ordeal.

Now he looked over what he had just written. He read it through, trying to approach it as Zack would. Eph had never before considered this from Zachary's perspective. What would his son think?

Dad loved me—yes.

Dad was a traitor to his friends and his people—yes.

Eph realized, reading this, how saddled with guilt Zack would be. To have the weight of the lost world upon his shoulders. His father having chosen slavery for all for the freedom of one.

Was that really an act of love? Or was that something else?

It was a cheat. It was the easy way out. Zack would get to live as a human slave—*if* the Master fulfilled its end of the bargain—and the planet would become a vampire's nest for eternity.

Eph had the sensation of awakening, as though from a fever dream. How could he ever have considered this? It was almost as though, having allowed the Master's voice into his head, he had also allowed a bit of corruption or insanity. As if the Master's malignant presence had mentally nested inside Eph's mind and started to metastasize. Thinking of this actually made him fear for Zack more than ever: he feared Zack being alive next to that monster.

Eph heard someone approaching from the hallway and quickly closed his diary and slid it underneath his pack—just as the door opened.

It was Creem, his bulk nearly filling the door frame. Eph had expected Mr. Quinlan, and Creem's presence threw him off. At the same time, Eph was relieved: Mr. Quinlan would have seen right through his distress, Eph felt.

"Hey, doc. Looking for you. Alone time, huh?"

"Getting my head straight."

"I was looking for that Dr. Martinez, but she's busy."

"I don't know where she is."

"Off somewhere with the big dude, the exterminator." Creem walked in and closed the door, extending his arm, his sleeve rolled back to his thick elbow. A square pad bandage was adhered to his forearm. "I got this cut I need you to look at. I saw the Mex's boy there, Joaquin. He's downright fucked. I need this checked out."

"Uh, sure." Eph tried to clear his head. "Let's see."

Creem came forward, Eph digging a flashlight out of his pack, taking the man's wide forearm in hand.

His skin color looked good under the bright beam.

"Peel it back for me," said Eph.

Creem did, his sausage-thick fingers adorned with silver bling. The bandage pulled off wiry black hairs, but the man didn't flinch.

Eph shone his flashlight down over the revealed flesh. No cut or abrasion.

"I don't see anything," said Eph.

Creem said, "That's because there's nothing to see."

He pulled his arm back, standing there, looking at Eph. Waiting for Eph to figure it out.

Creem said, "The Master said I was to reach out to you in private."

Eph nearly jumped backward. The flashlight fell from his hands, rolling to his foot. Eph picked it up, fumbling with it to turn off the beam.

The gang leader smiled silverly.

"It's you?" said Eph.

"And you?" said Creem. "Didn't make no sense." Creem looked back at the closed door before continuing. "Listen, homeboy. You gotta be more present, you know? Gotta speak up more, play the part. You're not working it hard enough."

Eph barely heard him. "How long . . . ?"

"The Master came to me not too long ago. Fucking mowed down the rest of my crew. But I can respect that. This is the Master's block now, you know?" A silver snap of his fingers. "But it spared me. The Master had other plans. Made me an offer—the same one I made you people."

"Turn us in . . . for Manhattan?"

"Well, for a piece. A little black market, some sex trade, gambling. Said it would help keep people distracted and in line."

"So this . . . this detonator . . . it's all a lie."

"Naw, that's real. I was just supposed to infiltrate you people. It was Gus who came to me with the request."

"What about the book?"

"That silver book you're always whispering about? The Master didn't say. That's what you're giving him?"

Eph had to play along here. So he nodded.

"You're the last one I woulda thought. But hey—those others are soon gonna wish they'd made a deal before us."

Creem smiled silverly again. His metallic expression sickened Eph.

Eph said, "You really think it'll honor its deal with you?"

Creem made a face. "Why wouldn't it? You expect it to honor yours?"

"I don't even know about that."

"You think it'll fuck us?" Creem was getting angry. "Why? What are you getting outta this? Better not say this city."

"My boy."

"And?"

"That's it."

"That's all? Your boy. For this fucking sacred book and your friends."

"He's all I want."

Creem stepped back, acting impressed but—Eph could tell—thinking Eph a fool. "You know, I got to thinking, when I found out about you. Why two plans? What's the Master thinking? Is it going to do both deals?"

"Probably neither," said Eph.

Creem didn't like the sound of that. "Anyway, it occurred to me—one of us is the backup plan. 'Cause, you do the deal first, what's he need me for? I get fucked over, and you get the glory."

"The glory of betraying my friends."

Creem nodded. Eph should have paid more attention to Creem's reaction, but he was too agitated now. Too torn. He saw himself reflected in this bloodless mercenary.

"I think the Master was trying to punk me. I think having the second deal is the same as having no deal. That's why I told the others about the armory location. 'Cause they're never gonna make it there. 'Cause Creem's gotta make his move now."

Eph became aware of the gangbanger's closeness then. He checked the man's hands, and they were empty—but balled into fists.

"Wait," said Eph, sensing what Creem was about to do. "Hold on. Hear me out. I . . . I'm not going to do it. It was madness to even consider it. I'm not turning on these people—and you shouldn't either. You know where a detonator is. We get that, hook it up to Fet's bomb, and we go after the Master's Black Site. That way we all get what we want. I get my boy back. You can have your chunk of real estate. And we nail that fucker once and for all."

Creem nodded, appearing to weigh the offer. "Funny," he said. "That's exactly what I would say if the tables were turned and you were about to double-cross me. *Adiós*, doc."

Creem grasped Eph by his front collar, and there was no time to defend himself. The man's fat fist and silvered knuckles came hurtling at the side of Eph's head, and he didn't feel the blow at first, only noticing the sudden twisting of the room, and then chairs scattering beneath the weight of his falling body. His skull smacked the floor and the room went white and then very, very dark.

The Vision

As usual, out of the fire came the figures of light. Eph stood there, immobile—overwhelmed as they approached him. His solar plexus was hit by the energy of one of them as it struck him full-on. Eph resisted, wrestled for what seemed an eternity. The second figure joined the match—but Ephraim Goodweather didn't give up. He fought bravely, desperately, until he saw Zack's face again, amid the glow.

"Dad—" Zack said, and then the flashpoint occurred again.

But this time Eph did not wake up. The image gave way to a new landscape of verdant green grass under a warm yellow sun, rippling in an unobtrusive breeze.

A field. Part of a farm.

Clear, blue sky. Scudding clouds. Lush trees.

Eph raised his hand to block the direct sun from his eyes so he could see better.

A simple farmhouse. Small, constructed of bright red bricks with a roof of black shingles. The house was a good fifty yards away—but he reached it in just three steps.

Smoke curled out of the pipe chimney in perfect, repeating formation. The breeze shifted, leveling out the smoke stream, and the exhaust formed into alphabet letters written as though in a neat hand.

...LEYRZOLEYRZOLEYRZOLEYRZO...

The smoky letters dissipated, becoming a light ash drifting to the grass. He bent over at the waist in a full jackknife and swiped the blades with his fingers, and found his pads sliced open, red blood oozing out.

A lone, four-paned window in the wall. Eph put his face to it, and when he breathed onto the glass, his breath cleared the opaque window.

A woman sat at the old table in the kitchen. Bright yellow hair, writing in a thick book with a quill made from a beautiful, oversized, brilliant silver feather, dipped in an inkwell filled with red blood.

Kelly turned her head, not all the way toward the window, just enough so that Eph knew that she felt him there. The glass fogged again, and when he breathed it clear, Kelly was gone.

Eph circled the farmhouse, looking for another window or a door. But the house was solid brick, and after one full rotation, he could not even find the wall with the original window. The bricks had darkened to black, and as he backed off from the structure, it became a castle. The ash had turned the grass black at his feet, further sharpening the blades so that every step slashed at his bare feet.

A shadow passed across the sun. It was winged, like a great bird of prey, banking fleetly before sailing away, the shadow fading into the darkening grass.

Atop the castle, a factory-sized smokestack chugged black ash into the sky, turning fair day into ominous night. Kelly appeared on one of the ramparts, and Eph yelled up to her.

"She can't hear you," Fet told him.

Fet wore his exterminator's jumpsuit and smoked a corona, but his head was a rat's head, his eyes small and red.

Eph looked up to the castle again, and Kelly's blond hair blew away like smoke. Now she was bald Nora, disappearing inside the upper reaches of the castle.

"We have to split up," said Fet, pulling the cigar from his mouth with a human hand, blowing silver-gray smoke that curled past his fine, black whiskers. "We don't have much time."

Fet the rat ran to the castle and squeezed himself headfirst into a crack in the foundation, somehow wriggling his big body in between two black stones.

Up top, a man now stood in the turret wearing a work shirt bearing the Sears insignia. It was Matt, Kelly's live-in boyfriend, Eph's first replacement as a father figure and the first vampire Eph had slain. As Eph looked at him, Matt suffered a seizure, his hands clawing at his throat. He convulsed, doubling over, hiding his face, contorting . . . until his hands came away from his head. His middle fingers stretched into thick talons, and the creature straightened, now a good six inches taller. The Master.

The black sky opened up then, rain pouring down from above, but the drops, when they landed, instead of the usual slapping patter noise, made a noise that sounded like "Dad."

Eph stumbled away, turning and running. He tried to outpace the rain through the slashing grass, but drops pelted him at every step, shouting in his ears, "Dad! Dad! Dad!"

Until everything cleared. The rain stopped, the sky turning into a shell of crimson. The grass was gone and the dirt ground reflected the redness of the sky just as the ocean does.

In the distance, a figure approached. It appeared not too far away, but closer, Eph was able to better judge its size. It looked like a human male, but at least three times the height of Eph himself. It stopped some distance away, though its dimensions made it seem nearer.

It was indeed a giant, but its proportions were exactly correct. It was dressed, or bathed, in a glowing nimbus of light.

Eph tried to speak. He felt no direct fear of this creature. He only felt overwhelmed.

Something rustled behind the giant's back. At once, two broad silver wings fanned open, their diameter longer even than the giant's height. The gust from this action blew Eph back a step. Arms at its sides, the archangel—the only thing it could be—beat its wings two more times, whipping at the air and taking flight.

The archangel soared, its great wings doing all the work, arms and legs relaxed as it flew toward Eph with preternatural grace and ease. It landed in front of him, dwarfing Eph three times over. A few silver feathers slipped from its plumage, falling quill-first and sticking into the red earth. One floated toward Eph, and he caught it in his hand. The quill became an ivory handle, the feather a silver sword.

The massive archangel bent down toward Eph. Its face was still obscured by the nimbus of light it exuded. The light felt strangely cool, almost misty.

The archangel fixed its gaze on something behind Eph, and Eph—reluctantly—turned.

At a small dinner table poised on the edge of a cliff, Eldritch Palmer, once the head of the Stoneheart Group, sat dressed in his trademark dark suit with a red swastika armband around his right sleeve, using a fork and knife to eat a dead rat laid out on a china plate. A blur approached from the right, a large white wolf, charging toward the table. Palmer never looked up. The white wolf leaped at Palmer's throat, knocking him from the chair, tearing at his neck.

The white wolf stopped and looked up at Eph—and came racing toward him.

Eph did not run or raise his sword. The wolf slowed near him, paws kicking up dirt. Palmer's blood stained its snowy mouth fur.

Eph recognized the wolf's eyes. They belonged to Abraham Setrakian, as did its voice.

"Ahsųdagų-wah."

Eph shook his head with incomprehension, and then a great hand seized him. He felt the beating of the archangel's wings as he was lifted away from the red land, the ground below shrinking and changing. They neared a large body of water, then banked right, flying over a dense archipelago. The archangel dipped lower, diving straight for one of the thousand islands.

They landed on a basin-shaped wasteland of twisted iron and smoking steel. Torn clothes and burned paper were strewn across the charred ruins; the small island was the ground zero of some catastrophe. Eph turned to the archangel, but it was gone—and in its place was a door. A simple door, standing alone in its frame. A sign affixed to it, written in black Magic Marker, illustrated with gravestones and skeletons and crosses, drawn in a young hand, read:

YOU MAY NOT LIVE BEYOND THIS POINT.

Eph knew this door. And the handwriting. He reached for the knob and opened it, stepping through.

Zack's bed. Eph's diary was set upon it, but instead of a tattered cover, the diary was faced in silver, front and back.

Eph sat down upon the bed, feeling the mattress's familiar give, hearing it creak. He opened his diary, and its parchment pages were those of the *Occido Lumen*, handwritten with illuminated illustrations.

More extraordinary than that was the fact that Eph could read and comprehend the Latin words. He perceived the subtle watermarking that revealed a second layer of text behind the first.

He understood it. In that moment he understood all.

"Ahsųdagų-wah."

As though summoned by the utterance of this very word, the Master stepped through the wall-less door. He threw back the hood shadowing his face, and his clothes fell away; the light of the sun charred his skin, turning it crispy black. Worms wriggled beneath the flesh covering his face.

The Master wanted the book. Eph stood, the feather in his hand a fine sword of silver once again. But instead of attacking, he reversed his grip on the sword's handle, holding it pointing down—as the *Lumen* instructed.

As the Master rushed at him, Eph drove the silver blade into the black ground.

The initial shockwave rode out over the earth in a watery ripple. The eruption that followed was of divine strength, a fireball of bright light that obliterated the Master and everything around it—leaving only Eph, staring at his hands, the hands that had done this. Young hands—not his own.

He reached up and felt his face. He was no longer Eph.

He was Zack.

AWAKENING
TO FIRE

Columbia University

Awake, Goodweather.

The Born's voice called Eph back to consciousness. He opened his eyes. He was lying on the floor, the Born standing over him.

What happened?

Leaving the vision for reality was a shock. Moving from sensory overload to sensory deprivation. Being in the dream had felt like being inside one of the *Lumen*'s illuminated pages. It had seemed more than real.

He sat up, now aware of the headache. The side of his face, sore. Above him, Mr. Quinlan's face was its usual starkly pale self.

Eph blinked a few times, trying to shake off the lingering hypnotic effect of the vision, clinging to him like sticky afterbirth. "I saw it," he said.

Saw what?

Eph heard a percussive beating sound then, growing louder, passing overhead, shaking the building. A helicopter.

We are under attack.

Mr. Quinlan helped him to his feet. "Creem," said Eph. "He told the Master where we are." Eph held his head. "The Master knows we have the *Lumen*."

Mr. Quinlan turned and faced the door. He stood still, as though listening.

They have taken Joaquin.

Eph heard footsteps, soft and distant. Bare feet. Vampires.

Mr. Quinlan grabbed Eph's arm and lifted him to his feet. Eph looked into Mr. Quinlan's red eyes, remembering the dream's end—then quickly put it out of his mind, focusing on the threat at hand.

Give me your spare sword.

Eph did, and after collecting his diary and throwing on his pack, he followed Mr. Quinlan into the corridor. They turned right, finding stairs leading down to the basement, where they entered the underground corridors. Vampires were already in the passages. Noises carried as though conducted on a current. Human yells and sword slashing.

Eph pulled out his sword, turning on his flashlight. Mr. Quinlan moved with great speed, Eph trying to keep up. In a flash, Mr. Quinlan zoomed ahead, and when Eph rounded the corner his beam of light found two decapitated vampires.

Behind you.

Another came out of a side room, Eph spinning and running it through the chest with his blade. The silver weakened it, and Eph withdrew the blade and quickly sliced through its neck.

Mr. Quinlan moved ahead, rushing into battles, slaying vampires before the creatures had a chance to attack. In this way they proceeded through the passageways of the subterranean asylum. A stairway marked with Gus's fluorescent paint brought them to a passage that led to another stairway, back up into the basement of a campus building.

They exited the mathematics building near the center of the campus, behind the library. Their presence immediately attracted the attention of the invading vampires, who came running at them from all sides without regard for the silver weapons they faced. Mr. Quinlan, with his blazing speed and natural immunity to the infectious worms contained in their caustic white blood, cut down three times as many *strigoi* as Eph.

An army helicopter approached from the water, swooping overhead, curling hard over the campus buildings. Eph saw the gun mount, though his mind rejected the image at first. He saw the bald vampire head behind the long barrel, then heard the reports, yet still could not process it until he saw the rounds impact the stone walk near his feet—strafing gunfire heading for him and Mr. Quinlan. Eph turned with Mr. Quinlan and ran for cover, getting in under the overhang of the nearest building as the helicopter swung out to come around again.

They ran to the doorway, ducking out of sight for the moment but not entering the building—too easy to become trapped. Eph fumbled out his night scope and held it to his eye just long enough to see dozens of glowing green vampires entering the amphitheater-style quad, like undead gladiators called into battle.

Mr. Quinlan was still next to him, more still than usual. He stared straight ahead as though seeing something somewhere else.

The Master is here.

"What?" Eph looked around. "It must be here for the book."

The Master is here for everything.

"Where is the book?"

Fet knows.

"You don't?"

I last saw it in the library. In his hands as he looked for a facsimile to forge . . .

"Let's go," said Eph.

Mr. Quinlan did not hesitate. The giant, domed library was almost directly ahead of them, at the front of the quad basin. He raced out from the doorway and the overhang, slashing an oncoming vampire as he went. Eph followed fast, seeing the helicopter coming back around, wide to his right. He cut down the steps, then back up, the gun firing semiautomatic now, chips of granite pricking at his shins.

The helicopter slowed, hovering over the quad, affording the shooter more stability. Eph ducked between two thick pillars holding up the front portico of the library, partially shielding him from the gunfire. Ahead of him, a vampire got close to Mr. Quinlan and had, as its reward, its head manually torn off its torso. Mr. Quinlan held the door open for Eph, who ran inside.

He stopped halfway through the rotunda. Eph could feel the Master's presence somewhere within the library. It wasn't a scent or a vibration; it was the way the air moved in the Master's wake, curling around itself, creating odd crosscurrents.

Mr. Quinlan ran past him, into the main reading room.

"Fet!" called Eph, hearing noises like books falling in the distance. "Nora!"

No reply. He rushed after Mr. Quinlan, but with his sword out, moving it here and there, aware of the Master. He had lost Mr. Quinlan for the moment and so pulled out his flashlight, turning it on.

After nearly a year of disuse, the library had become profoundly dusty. Eph saw the dust hanging in the air in the bright cone of his beam. As he trained his light down along the stacks to an open area at the other end, he noticed a disruption in the dust, as from something moving faster than the eye could see. This disruption, this breathlike rearrangement of particles, moved straight toward Eph at incredible speed.

Eph was struck hard from behind and knocked down. He looked up above him just in time to see Mr. Quinlan take a hard swipe at the advancing air. His sword struck nothing, but on his follow-through he positioned his body to deflect the onrushing threat. The impact was tremendous, though Mr. Quinlan had the advantage of balance.

A stack of bookshelves collapsed next to Eph with tremendous force, the steel fixture driven into the carpeted floor. The loss of momentum revealed the Master, rolling off the downed shelves. Eph saw the dark lord's face—a moment, just enough to see the worms scuttling madly beneath the surface of its flesh—staring at it before the creature righted itself.

A classic rope-a-dope. Mr. Quinlan had ducked out, drawing the Master to an unguarded Eph, only to blindside it as it attacked. The Master realized this at the same time Eph did, unused as it was to being duped.

BASTARD.

The Master was angry. It rose up and lashed out at Mr. Quinlan, unable to do any lasting damage because of the sword, but going in low and thrusting the Born into the facing book stack.

Then it started away, a black blur, back through the rotunda room.

Mr. Quinlan righted himself quickly and raised up Eph with his free hand. They went running after the Master, through the rotunda room, looking for Fet.

Eph heard a scream, identified it as belonging to Nora, and raced into a side room. He found her with his flashlight. Other vampires had entered from the opposite end, one of them threatening

Nora from its perch at the top of a row of stacks, another pair pelting Fet with books. Mr. Quinlan launched himself from a chair, driving at the vampire atop the stacks, catching its neck in his free hand while running it through with his sword, and falling with it into the next row of stacks. That freed Nora to go after the book-hurling vampires. Eph could feel the Master but failed to find it with his flashlight. The marauders were purposeful distractions, Eph knew, but also legitimate threats. He raced down a lane parallel to Fet and Nora's and met two more intruders coming through the far door.

Eph brandished his sword, but they did not stop. They ran at him and he ran straight at them. He slayed them easily—too easily. Their purpose was simply to occupy him. Eph encountered another one entering but, before attacking it, first risked a look back around the end of the row at Fet.

Fet was slashing and hacking, shielding his face and eyes from the books being thrown at him.

Eph turned and sidestepped the vampire that was nearly upon him, driving his blade through its throat. Another two appeared at the door. Eph made ready to fight them off when he was struck hard by a blow across his left ear. He turned with his flashlight beam and found another vampire standing astride the stacks, hurling books at him. Eph knew then that he had to get out of there.

As he cut down the oncoming pair of sacrificial *strigoi*, Eph saw Mr. Quinlan streak across the rear of the room. Mr. Quinlan shouldered the book-wielding nuisance off the stacks, launching the vampire across the room—then stopped. He turned in Fet's direction, and, seeing this, so did Eph.

He watched Fet's broad blade slice into another wilding vampire—just as the Master descended from the stacks above him, landing behind Fet. Fet was aware of the Master, somehow, and tried to turn and slash at it. But the Master gripped Fet's backpack, pulling down sharply. The pack slipped back to Fet's elbows, pinning his arms behind him.

Fet could have shaken free, but that would have meant relinquishing his pack. Mr. Quinlan leaped down off the book stack, racing at the Master. The Master used the thick, sharp nail of its talon-like middle finger to sever the padded shoulder straps, cutting the pack away from Fet even as Fet fought for it. Fet turned and lunged at the Master, and at his pack, with no regard for himself. The Master caught him one-handedly and hurled him—as easily as a book—directly at Mr. Quinlan.

Their collision was violent and loud.

Eph saw the Master with the book bag in hand. Nora faced him now, from the end of her row, standing before him, sword out. What Nora could not see—but the Master and Eph could—were two female vampires racing along the tops of the stacks behind her.

Eph yelled to Nora, but she was transfixed. The

Master's murmur. Eph yelled again, even as he moved, running sword-first at the Master.

The Master turned, deftly anticipating Eph's attack—but not Eph's aim. Eph sliced not at the Master's body, but at the severed strap of the pack itself, just below the Master's grip. He wanted the *Lumen*. He clipped the dangling strap and the bag dropped to the library floor. Eph's momentum took him past the dodging Master—and the action was enough to break Nora's trance. She turned and saw the *strigoi* above her, about to strike. Their stingers lashed out, but Nora's silver sword kept them at bay.

The Master looked back at Eph with ferocious disgust. Eph was off balance and vulnerable to attack—but Mr. Quinlan was getting back on his feet. The Master scooped up the bag of books before Eph could and raced to the rear door.

Mr. Quinlan was up. The Born looked back at Eph, just for a moment, then turned and rushed out the door after the Master. He had no choice. They had to have that book.

Gus chopped at the bloodsucker running at him through the basement, hitting it again before it went down. He ran upstairs to the classroom where Joaquin was and found him lying atop the desk with his head on a folded blanket. He should have been deep in a narcotic sleep, but his eyes were open and staring at the ceiling.

Gus knew. There were no obvious symptoms—

it was too early for that—but he could tell that Mr. Quinlan was right. A combination of the bacterial infection, the drugs, and the vampire sting had Joaquin in a stupor.

"Adiós."

Gus did away with him. One swift chop of his sword, and then he stood staring at the unholy mess he had made until the noises from the building stirred him back into action.

The helicopter had returned outside. He heard gunfire and wanted to get out there. But first he ran back into the underground passages. He attacked and slaughtered two unlucky vampires who intervened on his way to his power room. He broke all of his batteries off their chargers, dumping them into a bag with his lamps and his night scopes.

He was alone now—truly alone. And his hideout was blown.

He strapped one Luma lamp to his free hand and readied his sword and set off to fuck up some bloodsuckers.

Eph made his way to a flight of stairs, looking for an exit. He had to get outside.

A door gave way to a loading area and the humid coolness of the night air. Eph switched off his flashlight, trying to orient himself. No vampires, not at the moment. The helicopter was somewhere on the other side of the library, over the quad. Eph started off toward the maintenance garage, where Gus stored his larger weapons. They were vastly outnumbered, and this hand-to-sword combat worked in the Master's favor. They needed more firepower.

As Eph ran from building to building, anticipating attacks from any direction, he became aware of a presence racing along the rooftops of the campus buildings. A creature following him. Eph caught only glimpses of a partial silhouette, but that was all he needed. He was certain he knew who it was.

As he approached the garage, he noticed a light on inside. That meant a lamp, and a lamp meant a human. Eph ran up to the entrance, close enough to see that the garage door was open. He saw the tricked-out silver grille of a vehicle, Creem's yellow Hummer backed inside.

Eph had believed Creem to be long gone. Eph turned the corner and saw Creem's unmistakable barrel-shaped shadow, loading tools and batteries into the rear of the vehicle.

Eph moved quickly but silently, hoping to sneak up on the much larger man. But Creem was on high alert, and something made him spin around, confronting Eph. He grabbed Eph's wrist, immobilizing his sword arm, then flattened Eph against the Hummer.

Creem got right up in Eph's face, so close Eph could smell the dog treats on his breath, could see the crumbs still stuck in his silver teeth. "Did you think I was going to be outplayed by some white-bread fuckup with a library card?"

Creem reared back his massive hand, forming a silver-knuckled fist. As he brought it forward toward Eph's face, a thin figure ran at him from the front of the car, hooking his arm, driving the bigger Creem back toward the rear of the garage.

Eph came off the Hummer coughing for air. Creem was fighting off the intruder in the shadows of the back. Eph found his flashlight, turning it on.

It was a vampire, snarling and scratching at Creem, who was able to hold his own only because of the repellent silver bling on his fingers and the thick silver chains around his neck. The vampire hissed and weaved, slashing with its long talon finger at Creem's thigh, cutting him, the pain such that the top-heavy Creem collapsed under his own weight.

Eph raised his flashlight beam to the vampire's face. It was Kelly. She had saved him from Creem because she wanted Eph for herself. The flashlight reminded her of this, and she snarled into its brightness, leaving the wounded Creem and starting toward Eph.

Eph searched the cement floor of the garage for his sword but could not find it. He reached into his pack for his spare but remembered that Mr. Quinlan had taken it.

He had nothing. He backed up, hoping to nudge his fallen sword with his heel, but to no avail.

Kelly approached, crouched low, a sneer of anticipatory ecstasy crossing her vampire face. At long last, she was about to have her Dear One.

And then the look was gone, replaced by a startled expression of fear as she looked past Eph with narrow eyes.

Mr. Quinlan had arrived. The Born stepped next to Eph, its silver sword in hand, tipped in white blood.

Kelly went into full hissing mode, her body tense, ready to spring and escape. Eph did not know what words or sounds the Born was putting into her head, but they distracted and enraged her. He checked Mr. Quinlan's other hand and did not see Fet's bag. The book was gone.

Eph, by now at the Hummer's front door, saw inside the automatic weapons that Gus had delivered to Creem. While the Born compelled Kelly, Eph went into the truck and grabbed the nearest weapon, wrapping its shoulder sling around his forearm. He stepped out and fired past Mr. Quinlan at Kelly, the machine gun suddenly coming to life in his hands.

He missed her with his first volley. Now she was moving, darting up and over the roof of the Hummer to avoid his fire. Eph went quickly around the rear of the truck, shooting at will, chasing the leaping Kelly back out of the garage, firing at her as she raced up the side of the building to the roof and away.

Eph went immediately back inside, to the rear, where Creem was on his feet, trying to get to the Hummer. Eph walked right up to him with the smoking-hot weapon pointed at the gang leader's considerable chest.

"What the fuck was that?" yelled Creem, looking down at the blood staining his slashed pant leg. "How many of these bloodsuckers you got fighting over you?"

Eph turned to Mr. Quinlan. "What happened?"

The Master. It got away. Far away.

"With the *Lumen.*"

Fet and Nora came running inside, doubling over, out of breath.

"Watch him," Eph told Mr. Quinlan before darting outside to cut down any pursuers. But he saw none.

Back inside, Fet was checking Nora for blood worms. They were still trying to catch their breath, exhausted from fright, the fight, and the escape.

"We gotta get the hell outta here," said Fet between gasps.

"The Master has the *Lumen,*" said Eph.

"Is everyone all right?" said Nora, seeing Creem in back with Mr. Quinlan. "Where's Gus?"

Eph said, "Did you hear me? The Master's got it. It's gone. We're through."

Nora looked at Fet and smiled. Fet made a swirling motion with his finger and she turned around so that Fet could unzip the pack on her back. He pulled out a parcel of old newspaper and unwrapped it.

Inside was the silverless *Lumen.*

"The Master got the Gutenberg Bible I was working on," said Fet, smiling more at his own cleverness than the happy outcome.

Eph had to touch it to convince himself that it was real. He looked to Mr. Quinlan to confirm that it was.

Nora said, "The Master's going to be pissed."

Fet said, "No. It looks really good. I think he will be pleased . . ."

Eph said, "Holy shit." He looked to Mr. Quinlan. "We should leave. Now."

Mr. Quinlan grabbed Creem roughly by the thick back of his neck.

"What's this?" asked Nora, referring to Mr. Quinlan's rough treatment of Creem.

Eph said, "Creem is the one who brought the Master here." He briefly pointed the weapon at the big man. "But he's had a change of heart. Now he's going to help us. He's going to lead us to the armory to get the detonator. But first we need the bomb."

Fet was wrapping up the *Lumen* and returning it to Nora's backpack. "I can lead you there."

Eph climbed into the driver's seat, setting the machine gun on the broad dashboard. "Lead on."

"Wait," said Fet, jumping into the passenger seat. "First we need Gus."

The others jumped in, and Eph started the engine. The headlamps came on, illuminating two vampires coming their way. "Hold on!"

He punched the gas, rolling out toward the surprised *strigoi*. Eph drove right into them, the creatures perishing on impact with the silver grille. He cut right, off the road, over a dirt lawn, bumping up two steps and onto a campus walkway. Fet took the machine gun and rolled down his window, climbing half out. He sprayed down any pairs or groups of *strigoi* advancing on them.

Eph turned the corner around one of the larger university halls, crushing an old bicycle rack. He saw the rear of the library and gunned it, avoiding a dry fountain and crushing two more straggling vampires. He came out around the front of the library and saw the helicopter hovering over the campus quad.

He was so focused on the helicopter that he did not see, until the last moment, the long flight of broad stone steps leading down in front of him. "Hang on!" he yelled, both to Fet, hanging outside the window, and to Nora, who was moving weapons in back.

The Hummer dipped down hard and jounced along the stairs like a yellow turtle bumping down a washboard set at a forty-five-degree angle. They rattled around fiercely inside the vehicle, Eph knocking his head against the roof. They bottomed out with a final jolt and Eph swung left, toward the *Thinker* statue set outside the philosophy building, near where the helicopter had been hovering.

"There!" yelled Fet, spotting Gus and his violet Luma lamp emerging from behind the statue, where he had taken cover from the chopper's gunfire. The helicopter was turning now toward the truck, Fet raising his weapon and trying to fire one-handedly at the flying machine as he held on to the Hummer's roof rack. Eph zoomed toward the statue, running down another vampire as he pulled up to Gus.

Fet's gun choked dry. Shots from the helicopter drove him back inside, the gunfire just missing the truck. Gus came running up and saw Eph behind the wheel, then quickly reached in behind him, imploring Nora, "Give me one of those!"

She did, and Gus brought the machine gun to

his shoulder, kicking off rounds at the helicopter overhead—first one at a time, drawing a bead on his target, then firing rapid bursts.

The return gunfire stopped, and Eph saw the helicopter pull back, turning fast, then lower its nose and start away. But it was too late. Gus had hit the Stoneheart pilot, who slumped over with his hand still on the joystick.

The helicopter listed and plummeted, dropping to the corner of the quad on its side, crushing another vampire beneath it.

"Fuck yeah," said Gus, watching it go down.

The helicopter then burst into flames. Remarkably, a vampire came crawling out of the wreckage, fully engulfed, and started moving toward them.

Gus felled it with a single burst to the head.

"Get in!" yelled Eph over the ringing in his ears.

Gus looked inside the vehicle, ready to defy Eph, not wanting to be told what to do. Gus wanted to stay and slay every single bloodsucker who had dared invade his turf.

But then Gus saw Nora with the muzzle of her gun at Creem's neck. That intrigued him.

"What's this?" said Gus.

Nora kicked open her door. "Just get in!"

Fet directed Eph east across Manhattan, then south to the low nineties and east again to the water's edge. No helicopters, no sign of anyone following them. The bright yellow Hummer was a little too obvious, but they had no time to switch vehicles. Fet showed Eph where to park it, stashed inside an abandoned construction site.

They hurried to the ferry terminal. Fet had always eyed a tugboat docked there, in case of emergency. "And I guess this is it," he said, stepping behind the controls as they boarded the boat, pushing off into the rough East River.

Eph had taken over watching Creem from Nora. Gus said, "Somebody better explain this."

Nora said, "Creem was in league with the Master. He gave away our position. He brought the Master to us."

Gus walked to Creem, holding on to the side of the rocking tug. "Is that true?"

Creem showed his silver teeth. He was more proud than afraid. "I made a deal, Mex. A good one."

"You brought the bloodsuckers into my crib? To Joaquin?" Gus cocked his head, getting up into Creem's face. He looked like he was about to go off. "They hang traitors, you piece of shit. Or put them up in front of a firing squad."

"Well, you should know, *hombre*, that I wasn't the only one."

Creem smiled and turned to Eph. Gus looked his way, as did all the others. "Is there something else we don't know about?" asked Gus.

Eph said, "The Master came to me through your mother. It offered me a deal for my boy. And I was crazy or weak or whatever you want to call me. But I considered it. I . . . I kept my options open. I know now that it was a no-win, but—"

"So your big plan," Gus said. "Your brainstorm to offer the book up to the Master as a trap. That was no trap."

"It was," said Eph. "If it was going to work. I was playing both sides. I was desperate."

"We're all fucking desperate," said Gus. "But none of us would turn on our own."

"I'm being honest here. I knew it was reprehensible. And I still considered it."

At once, Gus charged at Eph with a silver knife in his hand. Mr. Quinlan, in a blaze of movement, got in front of him just in time, holding Gus back with a palm against his chest.

Gus said to Mr. Quinlan, "Let me at him. Let me kill him right now."

Goodweather has something else to say.

Eph balanced himself against the motion of the boat, the lighthouse end of Roosevelt Island coming into view. He said, "I know where the Black Site is."

Gus glared around Mr. Quinlan at him. "Bull*shit,*" he said.

"I saw it," said Eph. "Creem knocked me out, and I had a vision."

"You had a *fucking dream*?" said Gus. "He's finally snapped! This guy is fucking insane!"

Eph had to admit it came out sounding more than a little crazy. He wasn't sure how to convince them. "It was a . . . a revelation."

"A traitor one minute, a fucking prophet the next!" said Gus, trying to get at Eph again.

"Listen," said Eph. "I know how this sounds. But I saw things. An archangel came to me—"

"Oh fucking hell!" Gus said.

"—with great silver wings."

Gus fought to get after him again, Mr. Quinlan intervening—only this time, Gus tried to fight the Born. Mr. Quinlan took the knife from Gus's hand, nearly cracking his bones, then broke the knife in two and threw the pieces overboard.

Gus, gripping his sore hand, stood back from Mr. Quinlan like a kicked dog. "Fuck him, and his junkie bullshit!"

He wrestled with himself, like Jacob . . . like every leader ever to set foot on this earth. It is not faith that distinguishes our real leaders. It is doubt. Their ability to overcome it.

"The archangel . . . it showed me . . . ," said Eph. "It took me there."

"Took you where?" said Nora. "The site? Where is it?"

Eph feared the vision had started to fade from memory, like a dream. But it remained fixed in his consciousness, though Eph did not think it wise to repeat it now in great detail. "It's on an island. One of many."

"An island? Where?"

"Nearby . . . but I need the book to confirm. I can read it now, I'm positive. I can decipher it."

"Right!" said Gus. "Just bring him the book! The same one he wanted to turn over to the Master! Just hand it over to him. Maybe Quinlan's in on it too."

Mr. Quinlan ignored Gus's accusation.

Nora waved at Gus to be quiet. "How do you know you can read it?"

Eph had no way to explain it. "I just know."

"It is an island. You said that." Nora stepped toward him. "But why? Why were you shown this?"

Eph said, "Our destinies—even those of the angels—are given to us in fragments. The *Occido Lumen* had revelations that most of us ignored—given to a prophet, in a vision, and then consigned to a handful of lost clay tablets. It has always been like this: the clues, the pieces, that form God's wisdom come to us through improbable means: visions, dreams, and omens. Seems to me that God sends the message, but leaves it up to us to decipher it."

"You realize that you are asking us to trust a vision you had," said Nora to Eph. "After just admitting to us that you were going to mislead us."

"I can show you," said Eph. "I know you don't think you can trust me, but you can. You must. I don't know why . . . but I think I can save us. I can save us all. Including Zack. By destroying the Master once and for all."

"You're fucking insane," said Gus. "You were just a stupid asshole but now you are also fucking insane! I bet he knocked back some of the pills he gave Joaquin. He's telling us about a fucking Ambien dream! The doc is a drug addict, and he's tripping out. Or else he has the shakes. And we're supposed to do what he says? After a dream about some *angels*?" Gus threw up his hands. "You believe that, then you people are as fucking crazy as he is."

He is telling the truth. Or what he knows to be the truth.

Gus stared at Mr. Quinlan. "Is that the same as being right?"

Fet said, "I think I believe him." Eph was moved by the nobility of Vasiliy. "I say, back at the blood camp, that sign in the sky was meant for him. There is a reason he had this vision."

Now Nora looked at Eph as though she barely knew him. Any lingering familiarity she felt she had with him was gone now; he saw that. He was an object now, like the *Lumen*. "I think we have to listen to him."

Belvedere Castle

ZACK SAT UPON the big rock inside the snow leopard's habitat, underneath the branches of a dead tree. He sensed that something was up. Something weird. The castle always seemed to reflect the mood of the Master, in the same way that the weather instruments responded to changes in temperature and air pressure. Something was coming. Zack didn't know how, but he felt it.

The rifle lay across his lap. He wondered if he would need to use it. He thought of the snow leopard that had once stalked these grounds. He missed his pet, his friend, and yet, in a sense, the leopard was still there with Zack. Inside him.

He saw movement outside the mesh wall. This

zoo hadn't seen another visitor in two years. He used the rifle sight to locate the intruder.

It was Zack's mother, running his way. Zack had watched her enough to know agitation when he saw it. She slowed as she approached the habitat, seeing Zack inside. A trio of feelers came bounding after her on all fours, like puppies trailing their owner at dinnertime.

These blind vampires were her children now. Not Zack. Now, instead of her having been the one who changed—having turned into a vampire and departed the league of the living—Zack felt that it was he who had passed out of normal existence. That he was the one who had died, in relation to his mother, and lived before her now as a memory she could no longer remember, a ghost in her house. Zack was the strange one. The other.

For a moment, while he had her in his sights, he placed his index finger on the trigger, ready to squeeze. But then he relinquished his grip on the rifle.

He went out through the feeding door, exiting the rear of the habitat, going to her. It was subtle, her agitation. The way her arms hung, her fingers splayed. Zack wondered where she was coming from. And where did she go when the Master sent her out? Zack was her only living Dear One—so whom did she seek? And what now was the sudden emergency?

Her eyes were red and glowing. She turned and started away, commanding the feelers with her eyes, and Zack followed, his rifle at his side.

They exited the zoo in time for Zack to see a large group of vampires—a regiment of the legion that ringed the castle of the Master—running through the trees toward the edge of the park.

Something was happening. And the Master had summoned him.

Roosevelt Island

EPH AND NORA waited on the boat, docked on the Queens side of Roosevelt Island, around the northern point of Lighthouse Park. Creem sat watching them from the rear, watching their guns. Across the other side of the East River, Eph saw the lights of a helicopter between buildings, hovering in the vicinity of Central Park.

"What's going to happen?" Nora asked him, the hood of her jacket keeping out the rain. "Do you know?"

"I don't," he said.

"We're going to make it, right?"

Eph said, "I don't know that."

Nora said, "You were supposed to say yes. Fill me with confidence. Make me believe that we can do this."

"I think we can."

Nora was soothed by the calm in his voice. "And what do we do about him?" she asked, referring to Creem.

"Creem will cooperate. He will take us to the arsenal."

Creem huffed at that.

"Because what else does he have?" said Eph.

"What else do we have?" echoed Nora. "Gus's hideout is blown. So is your place at the ME's office. Now Fet's hideaway here, Creem knows about it."

"We're out of options," said Eph. "Though really we've only had two options all along."

"Which were?" said Nora.

"Quit or destroy."

"Or die trying," she added.

Eph watched the helicopter take off again, zooming north over Manhattan. The darkness wouldn't shield them from vampire eyes. The crossing back would be dangerous.

Voices. Gus and Fet. Eph made out Mr. Quinlan with them, cradling something in his arms, like a beer keg wrapped in a tarpaulin.

Gus climbed in first. "They try anything?" he asked Nora.

Nora shook her head. Eph realized then that she had been left there to keep an eye on both of them, as though he and Creem might try to sail away and strand the others on the island. Nora appeared embarrassed that Gus had let Eph learn this.

Mr. Quinlan boarded, the boat dipping down under his weight and the weight of the device. Yet he set it down easily on the deck, a testament to his great strength.

Gus said, "So let's see this bad boy."

"When we get there," said Fet, hurrying to the controls. "I don't want to open up that thing in this rain. Besides, if we're going to get inside this army arsenal, we have to make it there by sunup."

Gus sat on the floor against the side of the boat. The wetness didn't seem to bother him. He positioned himself and his gun so that he could keep an eye on both Creem and Eph.

They made it back across to the pier, Mr. Quinlan carrying the device to Creem's yellow Hummer. The oak urns had been loaded previously.

Fet took the wheel, driving north across the city, heading for the George Washington Bridge. Eph wondered if they would hit any roadblocks but then realized that the Master still did not know their direction or destination. Unless . . .

Eph turned to Creem, wedged tight in the backseat. "Did you tell the Master about the bomb?"

Creem stared at him, weighing the pros and cons of answering truthfully.

He did not.

Creem looked at Mr. Quinlan with great annoyance, confirming Mr. Quinlan's read of him.

No roadblock. They drove off the bridge into New Jersey, following signs for Interstate 80 West. Eph had dented up Creem's silver grille nudging a few cars out of the way, in order to clear their path, but they encountered no major obstructions. While they were stopped at an intersection, trying to figure out which way to turn, Creem tried to grab Nora's weapon and make a break for it. But his bulk prevented him from making any quick movement, and he ate Mr. Quinlan's elbow, denting his silver grille, just like that of his Hummer.

If their vehicle had been made along the way, the Master would have immediately known their location. But the river, and the proscription against crossing moving bodies of water of their own volition, should have slowed the slaves of the Master who pursued them, if not the Master himself. So it was just the Jersey vampires they had to worry about at the moment.

The Hummer was a fuel guzzler, and the gas-gauge needle leaned close to "E." They were also racing time, needing to reach the armory at sunup while the vampires slept. Mr. Quinlan made Creem talk, giving them directions.

They pulled off the highway and zoomed toward Picatinny. All sixty-five hundred acres of the vast army installation were fenced. Creem's way inside involved parking in the woods and trekking a half mile through a swamp.

"No time for that," said Fet, the Hummer running on fumes. "Where's the main entrance?"

"What about daylight?" said Nora.

"It's coming. We can't wait." He rolled down Eph's window and pointed to the machine gun. "Get ready."

He pulled in, heading straight for the gate, whose sign read, PICATINNY ARSENAL THE JOINT CENTER OF EXCELLENCE FOR ARMAMENTS AND MUNITIONS, and passed a building labeled visitor control. Vamps came out of the guard shack, Fet blinding them with his high beams and roof-rack lights before ramming them with the silver grille. They went down like milk-filled scarecrows. Those who avoided the Hummer's swath of destruction danced at the end of Eph's machine gun, which he fired out from a sitting position, balanced out of the passenger window.

They would communicate Eph's location to the Master, but the coming dawn—just starting to lighten the swirling black clouds overhead—gave the rest of them a couple of hours' head start.

That did not account for the human guards, a few of which came out of the visitors center after the Hummer had passed. They were rushing toward their security vehicles as Fet took a corner, wheeling through what looked like a small town. Creem pointed the way toward the research area, where he believed there to be detonators and fuses. "Here," he said as they approached a block of low-lying, unlabeled buildings. The Hummer coughed and lurched, and Fet turned into a side lot, rolling to a stop. They hopped out, Mr. Quinlan hauling huge Creem from the car like a load of laundry, then pushing the Hummer into a carport space half-hidden from the road. He opened the back and lifted out the nuclear device like luggage, while everyone else, except Creem, grabbed guns.

Inside the unlocked door was a research and development warehouse that had evidently not seen any activity in some time. The lights worked, and the place looked picked over, like a store selling off all its wares at a discount, and the display shelves too. All lethal weapons had been taken, but nonlethal devices and parts remained, on draftsman's tables and work desks.

"What are we looking for?" asked Eph.

Mr. Quinlan set down the package. Fet pulled off the tarp. The device looked like a small barrel: a black cylinder with buckled straps around its sides and over its lid. The straps bore Russian lettering. A tuft of wires sprouted out of the top.

Gus said, "That's it?"

Eph examined the tangle of thick, braided wires that ran from beneath the lid. "You're sure about this thing?" he asked Fet.

"No one's going to be absolutely sure until this thing mushrooms up to the sky," said Fet. "It's a one-kiloton yield, small by nuclear-weapons standards but plenty big for our needs. It's a fission bomb, low efficiency. Plutonium pieces are the trigger. This thing will take out anything within a half-mile radius."

"If you can detonate it," said Gus. "How can we match up Russian and American parts?"

"It works by implosion. The plutonium is projected toward the core like bullets. It's all laid in there. What we need is something to start the shock wave."

Nora said, "Something with a delay."

"Exactly," said Fet.

"And you'll have to do it on the fly. We don't have much time." She looked at Gus. "Can you get another vehicle together for us? Maybe two?"

Gus nodded. "You people hot-wire this nuclear bomb, I'll go hot-wire some cars."

Nora said, "That leaves only one more thing."

She walked over to Eph and pulled off her pack. She handed it to him. The *Lumen* was inside.

"Right," said Eph, intimidated now that the time was here. Fet was already digging through discarded devices. Mr. Quinlan stood near Creem. Eph found a door that led to a hallway of offices and picked one that was void of any personal effects. A desk, a chair, a file cabinet, and a blank, wall-sized whiteboard.

He pulled the *Lumen* from Nora's bag and set it upon the nicked desk. Eph took a deep breath and tried to clear his mind, then opened the first pages. The book felt very ordinary in his hands, nothing like the magical object from his dream. He turned the pages slowly, remaining calm when nothing happened at first, no lightning bolts of inspiration or revelation. The silver threading in the illuminated pages looked dull to his eye underneath the fluorescent ceiling fixtures, the text flat and lifeless. He tried the symbols, touching the page with his fingertips.

Still nothing. How could this be? Perhaps he was just too nervous, too amped up. Nora appeared at his door, Mr. Quinlan behind her. He shaded his eyes with his hands to block them out—trying to block everything out, most important, his own doubts. He closed the book and closed his eyes, trying to force himself to relax. Let the others think what they wanted to think. He went inward. He went to thoughts of Zack. Of freeing his son from the clutches of the Master. To ending this darkness on Earth. To the higher angels flying around inside his head.

He opened his eyes and sat up. He opened the book with confidence. He took his time looking at the text. Studying the same illustrations he had looked at one hundred times before. *It wasn't just a dream,* he told himself. He believed this. But, at the same time, nothing was happening. Something was wrong, something was off. The *Lumen* was holding on to all of its secrets.

"Maybe if you try to sleep," suggested Nora. "Enter it through your subconscious."

Eph smiled, appreciating her encouragement, having expected derision. The others wanted him to succeed. They needed him to succeed. He could not let them down.

Eph looked to Mr. Quinlan, hoping the Born had some suggestion or insight.

It will come.

These words made Eph doubt himself more than ever. Mr. Quinlan had no idea, other than faith, faith in Eph, while Eph's own faith was fading. *What have I done?* he thought. *What will we do now?*

"We'll leave you alone," said Nora, backing away, closing the door.

Eph shook off his despair. He sat back in the chair and rested his hands upon the book and closed his eyes, waiting for something to happen.

He drifted, at times, but kept waking up, having no luck directing his dreams. Nothing came to him. He tried reading the text two more times before giving up, slamming the book shut, and dreading the walk back out to the others.

Heads turned, Fet and Nora read his expression and his posture, their expectations dashed. Eph had no words. He knew that they understood his distress and frustration, but that didn't make failure any more acceptable.

Gus came in, shaking rain off his jacket. He passed Creem sitting on the floor near Mr. Quinlan and the nuclear device.

"I got us two rides," said Gus. "A big army Jeep, enclosed, and an Explorer." He looked at Mr. Quinlan. "We can get the silver grille onto the Jeep, if you want to help me. They run, but no guarantees. We'll have to siphon more fuel along the way, or else find a working gas station." He looked to Fet.

Fet held up his device. "All I know is this is a weatherproof fuse that you can set by hand. Either immediate or delay mode. Just turn this switch."

"How long is the delay?" asked Gus.

"Not sure. At this point, we'll have to take what we can get. The wire connections look like they will match up." Fet shrugged, indicating that he had done as much as he could do. "All we need now is a destination."

Eph said, "I must be doing something wrong. Or something we forgot, or . . . something I just don't know."

Fet said, "We've burned up most of the daylight. When night falls they're going to start coming for us. We have to move on from here, regardless."

Eph nodded fast, gripping the book. "I don't know. I don't know what to tell you."

Gus said, "We're done. That's what you're telling us."

Nora said to Eph, "You didn't get anything from the book? Not even—"

Eph shook his head.

"What about the vision? You said it's an island."

"One of dozens of islands. Over twelve in the Bronx alone, eight or so in Manhattan, half a dozen in Staten Island . . . Like at the mouth of a giant lake." Eph searched his tired mind. "That's all I know."

Nora said, "We can maybe find some military maps. Somewhere around here."

Gus laughed. "I'm crazy for going along with this, for trusting a crazy coward traitor. For not killing you and saving me this misery."

Eph noticed Mr. Quinlan doing his usual silent thing. Standing there with arms folded, patiently waiting for something to happen. Eph wanted to go to him, to tell the Born that his faith in Eph was misplaced.

Fet intervened before Eph could. "Look," he said. "After all we've been through—all that we're going through—there's nothing I can tell you that you don't know yourself. I just want you to remember the old man for a second. He died for that thing in your hands, remember. He sacrificed himself so that we would have it. I'm not saying this to put any more pressure on you here. I'm saying it to take the pressure away. The pressure's gone, as far as I can see. We're at the end. We've got no more. You're it. We're with you, thumbs up or thumbs down. I know you're thinking about your boy; I know it eats at you. But just think about the old man for a moment. Reach down deep. And if there is anything there, you'll find it—you'll find it now."

Eph tried to imagine Professor Setrakian there with him right now, wearing his tweed suit, leaning on the oversized wolf's-head walking stick that hid his silver blade. The vampire scholar and killer. Eph opened the book. He recalled the one time Setrakian got to touch and read these pages he had sought for decades, just after the auction. Eph turned to the illustration Setrakian had shown them, a two-page spread showing a complex mandala in silver, black, and red. Over the illustration, on tracing paper, Setrakian had laid the outline of a six-limbed archangel.

The *Occido Lumen* was a book about vampires—not, Eph realized, a book for vampires. Silver-faced and -edged in order to keep it out of the hands of the dread *strigoi*. Painstakingly designed to be vampire-proof.

Eph thought back to his vision . . . finding the book upon the outdoor bed . . .

It had been daylight . . .

Eph walked to the door. He opened it and stepped out into the parking lot, looking up at the swirling dark clouds beginning to efface the pale orb of the sun.

The others followed him outside into the gloaming, except for Mr. Quinlan, Creem, and Gus, who remained at the door.

Eph ignored them, turning his gaze to the book in his hands. Sunlight. Even if vampires could somehow circumvent the silver protections of the *Lumen*, they could never read it by natural light, due to the virus-killing properties of the ultraviolet C range.

He opened the book, tipping its pages toward the fading sun like a face basking in the last of the day's warmth. The text took on new life, jumping off the ancient paper. Eph flipped to the first of the illustrations, the inlaid silver strands sparkling, the image bright with new life.

He quickly searched the text. Words appeared behind words, as though written in invisible ink. Watermarks changed the very nature of the illustrations, and detailed designs emerged behind otherwise bare pages of straightforward text. A new layer of ink reacted to the ultraviolet light . . .

The two-page mandala, viewed in direct sunlight, evinced the archangel image in a delicate hand, appearing quite silver against the aged paper.

The Latin text did not quite translate itself as magically as it had in his dream, but its meaning became clear. Most elucidating was a diagram revealed in the shape of a biohazard symbol, with points inside the flower arranged like points on a map.

On another page, certain letters were highlighted, which, when put together, formed a peculiar yet familiar word:

A H S D A G –W A H.

Eph read quickly, the insights leaping into his

brain through his eyes. The pale sunlight faded quickly at the end, and so did the book's enhancements. So much more to read and to learn. But for now, Eph had seen enough. His hands continued to tremble. The *Lumen* had shown him the way.

Eph walked back inside past Fet and Nora. He felt neither relief nor exhilaration, still vibrating like a tuning fork.

Eph looked at Mr. Quinlan, who saw it in his face.

Sunlight. Of course.

The others knew something had happened. Except for Gus, who remained skeptical.

"Well?" said Nora.

Eph said, "I'm ready now."

"Ready for what?" said Fet. "Ready to go?"

Eph looked at Nora. "I need a map."

She ran off into the offices. They heard desk drawers slamming.

Eph just stood there, like a man recovering from an electric shock. "It was the sunlight," he explained. "Reading the *Lumen* in natural sunlight. It was like the pages opened up for me. I saw it all . . . or would have, if I'd had more time. The original Native American name for this place was 'Burned Earth.' But their word for 'burned' is the same as 'black.' "

Oscura. Dark.

"Chernobyl, the failed attempt—the simulation," said Fet. "It appeased the Ancients because

'Chernobyl' means 'Black Soil.' And I saw a Stoneheart crew excavating sites around a geologically active area of hot springs outside Reykjavik known as Black Pool."

"But there are no coordinates in the book," said Nora.

"Because it was beneath the water," said Eph. "At the time Ozryel's remains were cast away, this site was underwater. The Master didn't emerge until hundreds of years later."

The youngest one. The last.

A triumphant yell, and then Nora came running back with a sheaf of oversized topographical maps of the northeastern United States, with cellophane street atlas overlays.

Eph flipped the pages to New York State. The top part of the map included the southern region of Ontario, Canada.

"Lake Ontario," he said. "To the east here." At the mouth of the Saint Lawrence River, east of Wolfe Island, a cluster of tiny, unnamed islands was grouped together, labeled "Thousand Islands." "It's there. One of those. Just off the New York coast."

"The burial site?" said Fet.

"I don't know what its name is today. The original Native American name for the island was 'Ahs dag -wah.' Roughly translated from the Onondaga language as 'Dark Place' or 'Black Place.' "

Fet slid the road atlas out from beneath Eph's hands, flipping back to New Jersey.

"How do we find the island?" said Nora.

Eph said, "It's shaped roughly like the biohazard symbol, like a three-petaled flower."

Fet quickly plotted their course through New Jersey into Pennsylvania, then north to the top of New York State. He ripped out the pages. "Interstate Eighty West to Interstate Eighty-one North. Gets us right to the Saint Lawrence River."

"How long?" said Nora.

"Roughly three hundred miles. We can do that in five or six hours."

"Maybe straight highway time," said Nora. "Something tells me it won't be as simple as that."

"It's going to figure out which way we're headed and try to cut us off," Fet said.

"We have to get going," said Nora. "We barely have a head start as it is." She looked to the Born. "Can you load the bomb in the—"

When her voice dropped off, the others turned in alarm. Mr. Quinlan stood next to the unwrapped device. But Creem was gone.

Gus ran to the door. "What the . . . ?" He came back to the Born. "You let him get away? I brought him into this thing—I was going to take him out."

We don't need him anymore. And yet he can still be of use to us.

Gus stared. "How? That rat bastard doesn't deserve to live."

Nora said, "What if they catch him? He knows too much."

He knows just enough. Trust me.

"Just enough?"

To draw fear from the Master.

Eph understood now. He saw it as plain as he had the symbolism in the *Lumen*. "The Master will be on his way here; that's guaranteed. We need to challenge it. To scare it. The Master pretends to be above all emotion, but I have seen it angry. It is, going back to biblical times, a vengeful creature. That hasn't changed. When it administers its kingdom dispassionately, then it is in complete control. It is efficient and detached, all-seeing. But when it is challenged directly, it makes mistakes. It acts rashly. Remember, it became possessed of a bloodlust after laying siege to Sodom and Gomorrah. It murdered a fellow archangel in the grip of a homicidal mania. It lost control."

"You *want* the Master to find him?"

"We want the Master to know we have the nuke and the means to detonate it. And that we know the location of the Black Site. We have to get it to overcommit. We have the upper hand now. It's the Master's turn to be desperate."

To be afraid.

Gus stepped up to Eph then. Standing close, trying to read Eph the way Eph had read the book. Taking the measure of the man. Gus held in his hands a small carton of smoke grenades, some of the nonlethal weapons the vampires had left behind.

"So now we have to protect the guy who was going to stab us all in the back," said Gus. "I don't get you. And I don't get this—any of this, but especially you being able to read the book. Why you? Of all of us."

Eph's response was frank and honest. "I don't

know, Gus. But I think that part of this is I'm going to find out."

Gus wasn't expecting such a guileless response. He saw in Eph's eyes the look of a man who was scared, and also accepting. Of a man resigned to his fate, whichever way it went.

Gus wasn't ready to drink the Kool-Aid yet, but he was ready to commit to the final leg of this journey. "I think we're all going to find out," he said.

Fet said, "The Master most of all."

The Dark Place

THE THROAT WAS buried deep in the earth beneath the cold Atlantic sea. The silt around it had turned black upon contact with it and nothing would grow or live near it.

The same was true of every other site where the remains of Ozryel were interred. The angelic flesh remained incorrupt and unchanged, but its blood seeped into the earth and slowly radiated out. The blood had a will of its own, each strand moving blindly, instinctively upward, traversing the soil, hidden from the sun, seeking a host. This is the manner in which the blood worms were born. Within them they contained the remnant of the human blood, tinting their tissue, guiding them toward the scent of their potential host. But also within them they carried the will of their original flesh. The will of the arms, the wings, the throat . . .

Their thin bodies wriggled blindly for the longest distances. Many of the worms died, infertile emissaries baked by the merciless heat of the earth or stopped by a geological obstacle that proved impossible to negotiate. They all strayed from their birth sites, some even transported away along with the earth on unwitting insect or animal vectors. Eventually they found a host—and they dug in the flesh, like a dutiful parasite, burrowing deep. In the beginning, it took the pathogen weeks to supplant, to hijack, the will and the tissue of the infected victim. Even parasites and viruses learn through trial and error—and learn they did. By the fifth human host body, the Ancients began to master the art of survival and supplantation. They extended their domain through infection, and they learned to play by the new earthbound rules of this game.

And they became masters at it.

The youngest one, the last to be born, was the Master, the throat. God's capricious verbs gave movement to the very earth and the sea and made them clash and push upward the land that formed the Master's birth site. It was a peninsula and then, hundreds of years later, an island.

The capillary worms that emanated from the throat were separated from their site of origin and wandered away the farthest, for in this newly formed land, humans had not yet set foot. It was useless and painful to try to nurture or dominate a lower form of life, a wolf or a bear; their control was imperfect and limited, and their synapses were alien and short-lived. Each of these invasions proved fruitless, but the lesson learned by one parasite was instantly learned by the hive mind. Soon their numbers were reduced to only a handful, scattered far away from the birth site: blind, lost, and weak.

Under a cold autumn moon a young Iroquois brave set camp on an earth patch dozens of miles from the birth site of the throat. He was an Onondaga—a keeper of the fire—and as he lay down on the ground, he was overtaken by a single capillary worm, burying itself into his neck.

The pain awakened the man and he instantly reached for the wounded area. The worm was still not entirely burrowed in, so he was able to grab the tail end of it. He pulled with all his might, but the thing wiggled and squirmed against his efforts and finally slipped from his grip, digging into the muscular structure of his neck. The pain was unbearable, like a slow, burning stab, as it wriggled down his throat and chest and finally disappeared under his left arm as the creature blindly discovered his circulation system.

As the parasite overtook the body, a fever started, lasting for almost two weeks and dehydrating its host body. But once the supplantation was complete, the Master sought refuge in the darkened caves and the cold, soothing filth in them. It found that, for reasons beyond its comprehension, the soil in which it overtook its host body provided it with the most comfort, and so it carried around a small clump of earth wherever it went. By now the worms had invaded and taken nourishment from almost every organ in the host's body, multiplying in his bloodstream. His skin grew taut and pale, contrasting sharply with his tribal tattoos and his ravenous eyes, veiled by the nictitating membrane, glowing brightly in the moonlight. A few weeks went by without any nourishment but finally, close to dawn, he fell upon a group of Mohawk hunters.

The Master's control over its vehicle was still tentative, but thirst compensated for fighting precision and ability. The transference was faster the next time—multiple worms going into each victim through the wet stinger. Even when the attacks were clumsy and barely completed, they accomplished their end. Two of the hunters fought bravely, their throw-axes doing damage to the body of the possessed Onondaga warrior. But, in the end, even as that body slowly bled out into the earth, the parasites overtook the bodies of their attackers and soon the pack multiplied. Now the Master was three.

Through the years, the Master learned to use its skills and tactics to suit its needs for secrecy and stealth. The land was inhabited by fierce warriors and the places where it could hide were limited to caves and crevices that were well-known to hunters and trappers. The Master seldom transmitted its will into a new body and only did so if the stature or strength of a new host was overwhelmingly desirable. And through the years it gained in legend and name and the Algonquian Indians called it the wendigo.

It longed to commune with the Ancients, whom it naturally sensed and whose empathic beacon it felt across the sea. But every time it attempted to cross running water its human body would fail and be struck by a seizure, no matter the might of the occupied body. Was this tied to the place of his dismemberment? Trapped within the flowing arms of the river Yarden? Was it a secret alchemy, a deterrent written upon his forehead by the finger of God? This and many other rules it would come to learn during its existence.

It moved west and north looking for a route to the "other land," the continent where the Ancients were thriving. It felt their call—and the urge inside it grew, sustaining the Master over the grueling trek from one edge of the continent to the other.

It reached the forbidding ocean in the frozen lands at the uppermost northwest, where it hunted and fed on the inhabitants of that cold wasteland, the Unangam. They were men of narrow eyes and tanned skin, who wore animal pelts for warmth. The Master, entering the minds of its victims, learned of a crossing to a great land on the other side of the sea, at a place where the shores almost touched, reaching like outstretched hands. It scouted the cold shore, searching for this launching point.

One fateful night, the Master saw a cluster of narrow, primitive fishing ships near a cliff, unloading the fish and seal they had hunted. The Master knew it could cross the ocean aided by them. It had learned to ford smaller bodies of water with human assistance, so why not a larger one? The Master knew how to bend and terrorize the soul of even the hardest man. It knew how to gain and feed upon the fear of its subjects. The Master would kill half the group and announce itself as a deity, a fury of the wood, an elemental force of grander power than his already amazing one. It would suffocate any dissidence and gain every alliance either by pardon or by favor . . . and then it would travel across the waters.

While hidden beneath a heavy coat of pelts, lying upon a small bed of soil, the Master would attempt the crossing that would reunite it with those closest to its nature.

Picatinny Armory

CREEM HID IN another building for a while, scared of that Quinlan dude and what his reach was. Creem's mouth still hurt from the elbow he had taken, and now his silver teeth wouldn't bite right. He was pissed at himself for going back to the maintenance garage at the university for the guns, for being greedy. Always so hungry for more, more, more . . .

After a while, he heard a car go past, but not too fast, and quiet. It sounded like an electrical car, one of those plug-in compacts.

He headed out toward the one place he used to avoid, the front entrance of Picatinny Armory. Darkness had fallen again, and he walked toward a cluster of lights, wet and hungry and holding the cramp in his side. He turned the corner and saw the smashed gate where they had entered and beings clustered near the Visitor Control building. Creem put his hands up and walked until they saw him.

He explained himself to the humans, but they put him in a locked bathroom anyway, when all Creem wanted was something to eat. He kicked at the door a few times, but it was surprisingly solid; he realized the restroom had doubled as a secret holding cell for problem visitors to the armory. So he sat back on the closed toilet seat and he waited.

A tremendous crash, almost like a blast, shook the walls. The building had taken a blow, and Creem's first thought was that those assholes had hit a speed bump on the way out and nuked half of Jersey. Then the door opened and the Master stood there in its cloak. It carried a wolf's-head walking stick in one hand. Two of its little critters, the blind children, scampered around its legs like eager pets.

Where are they?

Creem sat back against the tank of the toilet, oddly relaxed now in the king bloodsucker's presence.

"They're gone. They hit the road. Little while ago."

How long?

"I don't know. Two vehicles. At least two."

Which direction?

"I was locked in a fucking bathroom here, how would I know? That vampire they got on their side, the hunter, Quinlan—he's an asshole. Dented my grille." Creem touched the unaligned silver in his mouth. "So, hey, do me a favor? When you catch them? Give him and the Mexican an extra kick in the head from me."

They have the book?

"They got that book. They have a nuclear bomb too. And they know where they are headed. Some Black Site or something."

The Master stood there, saying nothing. Creem waited. Even the feelers noticed the Master's silence.

"I said they're heading for—"

Did they say where?

The Master's speech pattern was different. The timing of his words was slower.

Creem said, "You know what I could use to jog my memory? Some food. I'm getting weak with fatigue here—"

At once the Master swooped in and gathered Creem in its hands, holding him up off the floor.

Ah yes, said the Master, its stinger slipping from its mouth. *Nourishment. Perhaps a bite would help us both.*

Creem felt the stinger press against his neck.

I asked you where they are going.

"I . . . I don't know. The doc, your other little friend there—he read it in that book. All I know."

There are other ways to ensure your total compliance.

Creem felt a soft, piston-like thump against his neck. Then a pinprick, and a gentle warmth. He shrieked, expecting to be emptied.

But the Master just held his stinger there and squeezed Creem's shoulders together, Creem feeling pressure against his shoulder blades and his clavicle, as though the Master was about to crush him like a tin can.

You know these roads?

"Do I know these roads? Sure, I know these roads."

With an effortless pivot, the Master threw Creem bodily out through the restroom door into the greater Visitor Control building, the big gang leader sprawling on the floor.

Drive.

Creem got up and nodded . . . unaware of the small drop of blood forming on the side of his neck where the stinger had touched him.

Barnes's bodyguards walked into his outer office inside Camp Liberty without knocking. Barnes's assistant's throat-clearing alerted him to stash the detective book he had been reading in a drawer and pretend to be going over the papers on his desk. They entered, their necks darkly patterned with tattoos, and held the door.

Come.

Barnes nodded after a moment, stuffing some papers into his attaché case. "What is this about?"

No answer. He accompanied them down the stairs and across to the guard at the gate, who let them through. There was a light, dark mist, not enough to warrant an umbrella. It did not appear that he was in any kind of trouble, but then again it was impossible to read anything into his stone-faced bodyguards.

His car pulled up, and they rode sitting next to him, Barnes remaining calm, searching his memory for some mistake or unintended slight he might have made. He was reasonably confident there had been none, but he had never been summoned anywhere quite this way before.

They were heading back to his home, which he thought was a good sign. He saw no other vehicles in the driveway. They walked inside and there was no one there waiting for him, most especially the Master. Barnes informed his bodyguards that he was going to visit the bathroom and spent his alone time in there running the water and teaming up with his reflection in the mirror to try to figure out this thing. He was too old for this level of stress.

He went into the kitchen to prepare a snack. He had just pulled open the refrigerator door when he heard the helicopter rotors approaching. His bodyguards appeared at his side.

He walked to the front door and opened it, watching the helicopter rotate overhead and descend. The skids set down gently on the once-white stones of his wide, circular driveway. The pilot was human, a Stoneheart; Barnes saw that instantly from the man's black suit jacket and necktie. There was a passenger, but not cloaked, therefore not the Master. Barnes let out a subtle breath of relief, waiting for the engine to turn off and the rotors to slow, allowing the visitor to disembark. Instead, Barnes's bodyguards each gripped one of his arms and walked him down the front steps and out over the stones toward the waiting chopper. They ducked beneath the screaming rotors and opened the door.

The passenger, sitting with twin seat belts crossed over his chest, was young Zachary Goodweather.

Barnes's bodyguards boosted him inside, as though he might try to escape. He sat in the chair next to Zack, while they took facing seats. Barnes strapped on his safety restraints; his bodyguards did not.

"Hello again," said Barnes.

The boy looked at him but did not answer. More youthful arrogance—and maybe something more.

"What's this about?" asked Barnes. "Where are we going?"

The boy, it seemed to Barnes, had picked up on his fear. Zack looked away with a mixture of dismissal and disgust.

"The Master needs me," said Zack, looking out the window as the chopper started to rise. "I don't know why you're here."

Interstate 80

THEY DROVE ALONG Interstate 80, west through New Jersey. Fet drove with his foot to the floor, high beams all the way. Occasional debris, or an abandoned car or bus, slowed him down. A few times they passed some skinny deer. But no vampires, not on the interstate—at least, none they could see. Eph sat in the backseat of the Jeep, next to Mr. Quinlan, who was attuned to the vampires' mental frequency. The Born was like a vampire radar detector: so long as he remained silent, they were okay.

Gus and Nora followed in the Explorer, a backup vehicle in case one of them broke down, which was a real possibility.

The highways were nearly clear. People had tried to evacuate once the plague reached true panic stages (the default human response to an infectious disease outbreak—escape—despite there being no virus-free zone to escape to), and highways jammed all across the country. However, few had been turned in their cars, at least not on the highway itself. Most were taken when they pulled off the main routes, usually to sleep.

"Scranton," said Fet, passing a sign for Interstate 81 North. "I didn't think it would be this easy."

"Long way to go," said Eph, looking out the window at the darkness rushing past. "How's our fuel?"

"Okay for now. I don't want to stop anywhere near a city."

"No way," agreed Eph.

"I'd like to get over the border into New York State first."

Eph looked out at Scranton as they navigated the increasingly cluttered overpasses to the north. He noticed a section of one block burning in the distance and wondered if there were other rebels such as themselves, smaller-scale fighters in smaller urban centers. Occasional electric lights shining in windows drew his eye and made him wonder at all the desperation going on there in Scranton and in similar small cities all across the country and the world. He wondered also where the nearest blood camp was.

"There must be a list of Stoneheart Corporation meatpacking plants somewhere, a master list that would clue us in to the blood camp locations," said Eph. "Once we get this done, there's going to be a lot of liberating to do."

"And how," said Fet. "If it's like it was with the other Ancients, then the Master's clan will die out with him. Vanish. People in the camps won't know what hit them."

"Trick will be getting the word out. Without mass media, I mean. We'll have all these little duchies and fiefdoms popping up across the country. People trying to take control. I'm not so sure democracy will automatically bloom."

"No," said Fet. "It's going to be tricky. Lots of work. But let's not get ahead of ourselves."

Eph looked at Mr. Quinlan sitting next to him. He noticed the leather sack between his boots. "Do you die with all the others when the Master is destroyed?"

When the Master is obliterated, his bloodline is no more.

Eph nodded, feeling the heat of the half-breed's supercharged metabolism. "Nothing in your nature prevents you from working toward something that will ultimately result in your own demise?"

You've never worked toward something that went against your own self-interest?

Eph said, "No, I don't think I have. Nothing that could kill me, that's for sure."

There is a greater good at stake. And vengeance is a uniquely compelling motivation. Revenge trumps self-preservation.

"What is it you're carrying in that leather pack?"

I am sure you already know.

Eph remembered the Ancients' chamber beneath Central Park, their ashes set inside receptacles of white oak. "Why are you bringing along the Ancients' remains?"

You did not see that in the Lumen*?*

Eph had not. "Are you . . . intending on bringing them back? Resurrecting them somehow?"

No. What is done cannot be undone.

"Why, then?"

Because it is foretold.

Eph puzzled over that one. "Is something going to happen?"

Are you not concerned about the ramifications of success? You said yourself that you are uncertain democracy will spontaneously bloom. Humans have never truly had self-rule. It has been that way for centuries. Do you think you will be able to manage on your own?

Eph had no answer for him. He knew that the Born was right. The Ancients had been pulling strings since near the beginning of human history. What would the world look like without their intervention?

Eph watched out his window as the distant

blaze, which was substantial, faded from view. How to put it all back together again? Recovery seemed like an impossibly daunting task. The world was already irretrievably broken. For a moment he even wondered if it was worth it.

Of course, that was just fatigue talking. But what had once seemed like the end of their troubles—destroying the Master and retaking stewardship of the planet—would in reality be the beginning of a brand-new struggle.

Zachary and the Master

ARE YOU LOYAL? asked the Master. *Are you thankful for all I have provided, for all that I have shown you?*

"I am," answered Zachary Goodweather with not a moment's doubt. The spiderlike shape of Kelly Goodweather watched her son, perched on a ledge nearby.

The end of times is near. Where we define together this new earth. All that you knew—all of those that were close to you—will be gone. Are you to be faithful to me?

"I will be," answered Zack.

I have been betrayed many times in the past. You should know that I am thus familiar with the mechanics of such plotting. Part of my will resides in you. You can hear my voice with distinct clarity, and in return, I am privy to your innermost thoughts.

The Master got up and examined the boy. There was no doubt detectable in him. He was in awe of the Master, and the gratitude he expressed was genuine.

I was betrayed once by those who should have been the closest to me. Those that I shared my very essence with—the Ancients. They had no pride in them—no real hunger. They were content living their lives in the shade. They blamed me for our condition and took shelter in the refuse of mankind. They thought themselves powerful, but they were quite weak. They sought alliance. I seek domination. You understand that, don't you?

"The snow leopard," said Zack.

Precisely. All relationships are based on power. Domination and submission. There is no other way. No equality, no congeniality, no shared domain. There is only one king in a kingdom.

And here, the Master looked at Zack with calculated precision—enacting what the Master believed human kindness should look like—before adding, *One king and one prince. You understand that too, don't you? My son.*

Zack nodded. And with that he accepted both the notion and the title. The Master scanned every gesture, every nuance on the young man's face. It listened carefully to the rhythm of his heart, looked at the pulse in his carotid artery. The boy was moved—excited by this simulated bond.

The caged leopard was an illusion. One that you needed to destroy. Bars and cages are symbols of weakness. Imperfect measures of control. One may choose to believe they are there to subjugate the creature inside—to humiliate it—but in due time one realizes they also are there to keep it away. They become a symbol of your fear. They limit you as much as the beast within. Your cage is just bigger, and the freedom of the leopard lies in those confines.

"But if you destroy it," said Zack, developing the thought himself, "if you destroy it . . . there is no doubt left."

Consumption is the ultimate form of control. Yes. And now we stand together at the brink of control. Absolute domination of this earth. So—I have to make sure that nothing stands between you and me.

"Nothing," said Zack with absolute conviction.

The Master nodded, apparently pensive, but in fact building a pause calculated long before for maximum effect. The revelation he was about to give to Zack needed that careful timing.

What if I said to you that your father was still alive?

And then the Master felt it—a torrent of emotions swirling inside Zack. A turmoil that the Master had thoroughly anticipated but that intoxicated him all the same. It loved the taste of broken hopes.

"My father is dead," said Zack. "He died with Professor Setrakian and—"

He is alive. This has been brought to my attention only recently. As to the question of why he has never attempted to rescue you or contact you, I'm afraid I cannot be of assistance. But he is very much alive and seeks to destroy me.

"I will not let him," said Zack, and he meant it. And, in spite of itself, the Master felt strangely flattered by the purity of sentiment the young man had for him. Natural human empathy—the phenomenon known as "Stockholm syndrome," whereby captives come to identify with and defend their captors—was a simple enough tune for the Master to play. It was a virtuoso of human behavior. But this was something more. This was true allegiance. This, the Master believed, was love.

You are now making a choice, Zachary. Perhaps your first choice as an adult, and what you choose now will define you and define the world around you. You need to be completely sure.

Zack felt a lump in his throat. He felt resentment. All the years of mourning were alchemically transformed into abandonment. Where had his dad been? Why had he left him behind? He looked at Kelly, standing nearby, a horrible squalid specter—a monstrous freak. She, too, had been abandoned. Was it not all Eph's fault? Had he not sacrificed all of them—his mother, Matt, and Zack himself—in pursuit of the Master? There was more loyalty from his twisted scarecrow of a mother than from his human father. Always late, always far away, always unavailable.

"I choose you," said Zack to the Master. "My father is dead. Let him stay that way."

And once again, he meant it.

Interstate 80

NORTH OF SCRANTON, they began to see *strigoi* standing at the side of the highway like sentinels. Passive, camera-like beings appearing out of the darkness, standing just off the road, watching the vehicles zoom past them.

Fet reacted to the first few of them, tempted to slow and slay them, but Eph told him not to bother. "They have already seen us," said Eph.

"Look at this one," said Fet.

Eph first saw the WELCOME TO NEW YORK STATE sign by the side of the highway. Then, eyes glowing like glass, the female vampire standing beneath it, watching them pass. The vampires communicated the vehicles' location to the Master in a sort of internalized, instinctual GPS. The Master knew that they were now making their way north.

"Hand me the maps," said Eph. Fet did, and Eph read it by flashlight. "We're making great time on the highway. But we have to be smart. It's only a matter of time before they throw something at us."

The walkie-talkie in the front seat crackled. "Did you see that one?" asked Nora in the trailing Explorer.

Fet picked up the radio and answered. "The welcoming committee? We saw her."

"We have to go back roads."

"We're with you. Eph's looking at the map now."

Eph said, "Tell her we'll head up to Binghamton for gas. Then stay off the highway after that."

They did just that, pulling sharply off the highway at the first Binghamton exit advertising fuel, following the arrow at the end of the off-ramp to a cluster of gas stations, fast food restaurants, a furniture store, and two or three little strip malls, each anchored by a different coffee shop drive-through. Fet skipped the first gas station, wanting more room in case of emergency. The second, a Mobil, featured three aisles of tanks angled in front of an On the Go convenience mart. The sun had long ago faded all the blue letters on the mobil sign, and now only the red "O" was visible, like a hungry, round mouth.

No electricity, but they had kept Creem's hand pump from the Hummer, knowing that they would have to do some siphoning. The ground caps were all still in place, which was a good indication that fuel remained in the underground tanks. Fet pulled the Jeep next to one and pried up the cap with a tire iron. The gasoline smell was pungent, welcome. Gus pulled in and Fet waved him over to back up near the tank opening. Fet pulled out the pump and narrow tubing, feeding the longer end into the ground tank and the shorter end into the Jeep.

His wound had started to hurt again and it bled intermittently, but Fet hid both facts from the group. He told himself he was doing this in order to see it all through—to stick to the end. But he knew that, for the better part, he wanted to be there between Eph and Nora.

Mr. Quinlan stood at the roadside, looking up and down the dark lane. Eph wore his weapon pack over one shoulder. Gus carried a Steyr submachine gun loaded half with silver and half with lead. Nora went around the side of the building, relieving herself and quickly returning to the cars.

Fet was pumping hard, but it was slow work, the fuel only now starting to spray into the Jeep's tank. It sounded like cow's milk hitting a tin can. He had to pump faster to achieve a steady flow.

"Don't go too deep," said Eph. "Water settles at the bottom, remember?"

Fet nodded impatiently. "I know."

Eph asked if he wanted to trade off, but Fet refused, his big arms and shoulders doing the work. Gus left them, walking out into the road near Mr. Quinlan. Eph thought about stretching his legs more but found that he did not want to be too far away from the *Lumen*.

Nora said, "Did you work on the trigger fuse?"

Fet shook his head as he worked.

Eph said, "You know how mechanical I am."

Nora nodded. "Not at all."

Eph said, "I'm driving the next leg. Fet can work on the detonator."

"I don't like taking so much time," said Nora.

"We need to wait for the next meridiem anyway. With the sun up, we can work freely."

Nora said, "A whole day? That's too much time. Too much risk."

"I know," said Eph. "But we need daylight to do this thing right. Got to hold off the vamps until then."

"But once we get to the water, they can't touch us."

"Getting on the water is another task altogether."

Nora looked to the dark sky. A cool breeze came along and she shrugged her shoulders against it. "Daylight seems like a long time away. I hope we don't lose our head start here." She turned her gaze to the deadness of the street. "Christ, I feel like there are one hundred eyes staring at me."

Gus was jogging back toward them from the sidewalk. "You're not far off," he said.

"Huh?" said Nora.

Gus opened the hatch on the Explorer, pulling out two road flares. He ran back to the street, far enough away from the gas fumes, and sparked them to life. One he tossed end over end into the parking lot of the Wendy's across the road. The spitting red flame lit the forms of three *strigoi* standing at the building's corner.

The other he hurled toward some abandoned cars in an old rental car parking lot. That flare bounced off a vampire's chest before hitting the asphalt. The vampire never flinched.

"Shit," said Gus. He pointed at Mr. Quinlan. "Why didn't he say anything?"

They have been here the entire time.

"Jesus," said Gus. He went running toward the rental car company and opened up on the vampire there. The machine gun reports echoed long after he was done, and the vampire lay on the ground, not dead but down for good and full of bleeding white holes.

Nora said, "We should get out of here."

"Won't get far without gas," said Eph. "Fet?"

Fet was pumping, the fuel flowing more freely now. Getting there.

Gus fired his Steyr across at the other flare, trying to scatter the vampires in the Wendy's lot, but they didn't scare. Eph drew his sword, seeing movement behind the cars in the parking lot on the other side. Figures running.

Gus yelled out, "Cars!"

Eph heard the engines approaching. No headlights, but vehicles coming out of the darkness, underneath the highway overpass, slowing to a stop.

"Fet, you want me to—?"

"Just keep them back!" Fet pumped and pumped, trying not to breathe the toxic fumes.

Nora reached inside both cars, turning on each set of headlights, illuminating the immediate area east and west.

To the east, opposite the highway, vampires crowded the edge of the light, their red eyes reflecting like glass baubles.

To the west, coming from the highway, two vans, figures emptying out of them. Local vampires called into duty.

"Fet?" said Eph.

"Here, switch tanks," said Fet, pumping hard, not stopping. Eph pulled the tubing from the Jeep's almost-full tank and quickly transferred it to the Explorer, gasoline spraying out onto the hardtop.

Footsteps now, and it took Eph a moment to locate them. Overhead, on top of the canopy roof, right above them. The vampires were encircling them and closing in.

Gus opened up his gun on the trucks, winging a vampire or two but not doing any real damage.

"Move away from the tank!" yelled Fet. "I don't want any sparks nearby!"

Mr. Quinlan returned from the roadside, near Eph at the vehicles. The Born felt it was his responsibility to protect him.

"Here they come!" said Nora.

The vampires began to swarm. A coordinated effort, first focusing on Gus. Four vampires, two running at him from either side. Gus fired on one pair, shredding them, then wheeled and put down the other two, but only just in time.

While he was occupied, a handful of dark figures seized the opportunity to break from the adjoining lots, running toward the Mobil.

Gus turned and sprayed them, hobbling a few, but had to turn back around as more advanced on him.

Mr. Quinlan darted forward with amazing agility, meeting three advancing fellow *strigoi* and forcefully driving his open hands into their throats, snapping their necks.

Bang! A small vampire, a child, dropped down onto the roof of the Jeep from the carport roof. Nora swiped at it, and the little vampire hissed and darted backward, the Jeep rocking gently. Eph rushed around past the headlights to the other side of the Jeep, looking to slay the nasty little thing. It wasn't there.

"Not here!" said Eph.

"Not here either!" called Nora.

Eph said, "Underneath!"

Nora got down and swung her sword underneath the vehicle's carriage, the blade's reach long enough to drive the child back out toward Eph's side. He cut at its lower right leg, severing the Achilles tendon. But instead of retreating again, the maimed vampire came right out from beneath the Jeep and sprang up at him,

Eph's sword meeting it halfway, cutting down the blood-rabid *strigoi* in midair. He felt the effort more than ever. He felt his muscles twitch and spasm. A flash of pain ran from his elbow to his lower back. His arm curled in a brutal cramp. He knew what it was: he was malnourished, perhaps even to the point of starvation. He ate very little and very badly—no minerals, no electrolytes, his nerve endings terminally raw. He was coming to an end as a fighter. He fell down, releasing his sword, feeling a million years old.

A wet crunching sound startled Eph from behind. Mr. Quinlan was behind him, bright in the headlights, the head of another child vampire in one hand, the body in his other. The vampire had gotten the drop on Eph, but Mr. Quinlan saved him. The Born threw the dripping body parts to the blacktop as he turned, anticipating the next attack.

Gus's gun rattled out in the street as more vampires converged on them from the edges of darkness. Eph cut down two more adult *strigoi* running up from behind the gas station store. He was worried about Nora being on her own, on the other side of the cars.

"Fet! Come on!" he yelled.

"Almost!" Fet yelled back.

Mr. Quinlan lashed out, dropping more sacrificial *strigoi*, his hands dripping white. They just kept coming.

"They're trying to hold us here," said Eph. "Slow us down!"

The Master is en route. And others. I can sense it.

Eph stabbed the closest *strigoi* by the throat, then kicked it in the chest, retrieved his blade, and ran around to the other side of the Jeep. "Gus!" he called.

Gus was already retreating, his smoking gun silent. "I'm out."

Eph chopped at a pair of vampires coming up on Nora, then whipped the fuel line out of the Explorer's tank. Fet saw this and finally gave up pumping. He grabbed Eph's spare sword out of his pack and took care of another animal-like vampire coming over the Explorer's hood.

Gus jumped into the front seat of the Explorer, grabbing another weapon. "Go! Get out of here!"

There was no time to throw the gas-soaked pump into the truck. They abandoned it there, gas still drooling out of the tube, slicking the hardtop.

"Don't shoot this close!" said Fet. "You'll blow us up!"

Eph went for the Jeep's door. He watched through the windows as Mr. Quinlan grabbed a female vampire by her legs and whipped her head against a steel column. Fet was in the backseat behind Eph, fighting off vamps trying to get in the door. Eph jumped into the driver's seat, slamming the door shut and turning the key.

The engine started up. Eph saw that Nora was inside the Explorer. Mr. Quinlan was the last, climbing into the backseat of the Jeep with *strigoi* running up to his window. Eph threw the truck into drive and curled out into the street, mowing down two vampires with the Jeep's silver grille.

He saw Nora zoom the Explorer out to the edge of the road, then stop short. Gus jumped out with his machine gun and bent low, firing laterally across the hardtop at the leading edge of the fuel spill. It ignited and he jumped into the Explorer, and both trucks sped away as the flame slid toward the uncapped ground tank, igniting the fumes above for one brief, beautiful moment of winged flame—then the ground tank erupted, an angry orange-black blast, making the ground shudder, splitting the canopy, and frying the *strigoi* still there.

"Jesus," said Fet, watching out the back window, past the tarp-covered nuclear bomb. "And that's nothing compared to what we've got here."

Eph gunned it past the vehicles in the road, some of the vampires rushing to get behind the wheel. He wasn't worried about outrunning them. Only the Master.

Late-arriving vampires darted out into the street, practically throwing themselves into the path of the Jeep in an attempt to slow them down. Eph tore through them, seeing hideous faces for an instant in the headlights just at impact. The caustic white blood ate at the Jeep's rubber wiper blades after a few back-and-forth swipes. A gang had gathered on the entrance ramp leading back onto Interstate 81, but Eph went right by that ramp, heading down the dark town road.

He followed the main road, handing the map back to Fet, watching for the Explorer's headlights in his rearview mirror. He didn't see them.

He felt for the walkie-talkie, finding it on the seat near his hip. "Nora? You get out? You two okay?"

Her voice came back a moment later, adrenalized. "We're good! We're out!"

"I don't see you."

"We're . . . I don't know. Probably behind you."

"Just keep heading north. If we get separated, meet up at Fishers Landing as soon as you can get there. You got that? Fishers Landing."

"Fishers Landing," she said. "Okay." Her voice crackled.

"Run with your headlights off when you can—but only when you can. Nora?"

"We're going to . . . up . . . onward."

"Nora, I'm losing you."

". . . Eph . . ."

Eph felt Fet leaning up behind him. "Radio range is only about one mile."

Eph checked his mirrors. "They must have headed down another road. So long as they stay off the highway . . ."

Fet took the radio, trying to raise her, but got nothing. "Shit," he said.

"She got the rendezvous point," said Eph. "She's with Gus. She'll be all right."

Fet handed back the radio. "They have enough fuel, anyway. Now all we have to do is stay alive until sunrise."

At the roadside, beneath a blank marquee sign for an old abandoned drive-in movie theater, an expressionless *strigoi* followed the Jeep with his eyes as it passed him by.

* * *

The Master reached out with its mind. Although it seemed counterintuitive, engaging many different perspectives at once served to focus the Master's thoughts and soothe its temper.

Through the eyes of one of its minions, the Master watched the green vehicle driven by Dr. Ephraim Goodweather barrel through an unlit intersection in rural upstate New York, the oversized Jeep following the central yellow line. Moving ever north.

It viewed the Explorer driven by Dr. Nora Martinez driving past a church in a small town square. The criminal Augustin Elizalde leaned out the front window, and there was a muzzle flash and the Master's view disappeared. They were also moving north, along the other side of the highway they had started out on—the interstate on which the Master was now traveling at a high rate of speed.

It saw the boy, Zachary Goodweather, seated in the helicopter crossing the state through the air, traveling northwest on a sharp diagonal. The boy looked out the window of the flying machine, ignoring the airsick Dr. Everett Barnes seated next to him, the older man's face a bluish shade of gray. The boy, and perhaps Barnes, would be instrumental to the Master in distracting or otherwise persuading Goodweather.

The Master also saw through Kelly Goodweather's perception. Traveling inside a moving vehicle dulled her homing impulse somewhat, but still the Master felt her closeness to Dr. Goodweather, her former human mate. Her sensitivity gave the Master another perspective with which to triangulate his focus on Dr. Goodweather.

Turn off here.

The town car swerved and zoomed down the exit ramp, the gang leader Creem driving with a heavy foot.

"Shit," said Creem upon seeing the still-burning service station just up the road. The smell of burned fuel entered the automobile's ventilation system.

Left.

Creem followed directions, turning away from the blast site, wasting no time. They passed the drive-in theater marquee and the vampire standing watch there. The Master dipped again into its vision and saw itself inside the black town car, hurtling down the roadway.

They were gaining on Goodweather.

Eph roared along country roads, winding their way north. He kept changing routes to keep his pursuers guessing. Vampire sentinels stood watch at every turn. Eph could tell if he had been on the same road for too long when they put obstacles in his way, trying to slow him down or make him crash: other cars, a wheelbarrow, planters from a garden store. Driving upwards of fifty miles per hour on a pitch-black road, these things came up fast in his headlights and were dangerous to maneuver around.

A few times the vampires tried to ram them

with a car or follow them. That was Fet's cue to rise up out of the sunroof with the machine gun in hand.

Eph avoided the city of Syracuse altogether, traveling east around the outskirts. The Master knew where they were—but it still did not know where they were going. That was the only thing saving them right now. Otherwise it would mass its slaves at the shore of the Saint Lawrence River, keeping Eph and the others from getting through.

If possible, Eph would have just kept driving until daylight. But gasoline was an issue, and stopping to refuel was simply too dangerous. They were going to have to risk waiting for daylight at the river, potentially as sitting ducks.

On the plus side, the farther north they drove, the fewer roadside *strigoi* they saw. The lower rural population was in their favor.

Nora was at the wheel. Reading maps was not one of Gus's strengths. Nora was confident they were moving north in general but knew that they had occasionally gotten sidetracked a little too far east or west. They were past Syracuse, but suddenly Watertown—the last city of any size before the Canadian border—seemed so far away.

The radio at her hip had crackled a few times, but every time she tried to raise Eph, she received only silence in return. After a while she stopped trying. She did not want to chance running down the batteries.

Fishers Landing. That was what Eph had said,

where they were to meet. Nora had lost track of how many hours it had been since sundown, how many more it would be until sunrise—all she knew was that it was too many. She wanted daylight far too badly to dare to trust her own gut estimation.

Just get there, she thought. *Get there and figure it out.*

"Here they come, doc," said Gus.

Nora looked all around the street in front of her. She saw nothing, driving so intently through the darkness. Then she saw it: a hint of light through the treetops.

Moving light. A helicopter.

"They're looking for us," said Gus. "Haven't spotted us yet, I don't think."

Nora kept one eye on the light and the other on the road. They passed a sign for the highway and realized they had drifted back near the interstate. Not good.

The helicopter circled toward them. "I'm cutting the headlights," she said, which also meant slowing way down.

They drifted down the dark road, watching the helicopter come around, approaching near. The light grew brighter as it began to descend, maybe a few hundred yards north of them.

"Hold up, hold up," said Gus. "It's landing."

She saw the light setting down. "That must be the highway."

Gus said, "I don't think they saw us at all."

She continued to roll down the road, judging its margins by the black treetop branches framed against the less-black sky. Trying to decide what to do.

"Should we take off?" she said. "Risk it?"

Gus was trying to see through the windshield up to the highway. "You know what?" he said. "I don't think they were looking for us after all."

Nora kept her eyes on the road. "What is it, then?"

"You got me. Question is—do we dare to find out?"

Nora had spent enough time with Gus to know that this was not actually a question. "No," she said quickly. "We need to go. To keep going."

"It could be something."

"Like what?"

"I don't know. Why we have to look. I haven't seen any roadside bloodsuckers for a few miles anyway. I think we're good for a quick look."

"A *quick* look," said Nora, as though she could hold him to that.

"Come on," he said. "You're curious too. Besides—they were using their light, right? That means humans."

She pulled over to the left side of the road and turned off the engine. They got out of the car, forgetting that the interior lights came on once the doors were opened. They closed them quickly without slamming them and stood and listened.

The rotors were still spinning but slowing down. The engine had just been turned off. Gus held his machine gun away from himself as he scrambled up the weedy, rocky embankment, with Nora just behind and to the left of him.

They slowed at the top, their faces rising beneath the guardrail. The chopper was another one hundred yards or so down the highway. There were no cars in sight. The rotors stopped rotating, though the helicopter light remained illuminated, shining off to the opposite side of the road. Nora made out four silhouettes, one of them shorter than the others. And she could not be sure, but she believed that the pilot—probably a human, judging by the light—was still inside the cockpit, waiting. For what? Taking off again soon?

They ducked back down. "A rendezvous?" said Nora.

"Something like that. You don't think it's the Master, do you?"

"Can't tell," she said.

"One of them was small. Looked like a kid."

"Yeah," said Nora, nodding . . . and then she stopped nodding. Her head shot up again, and this time she looked over the top of the guardrail. Gus pulled her back down by her belt, but not before she had convinced herself of the identity of the ragged-haired boy. "Oh my God."

"What?" said Gus. "What the hell's gotten into you?"

She drew her sword. "We have to get over there."

"Well, sure, now you're talking. But what's the—"

"Shoot the adults but not the kid. Just don't let them get away."

Nora was up and over the guardrail before Gus

could get to his feet. She was running straight at them, Gus having to hustle to keep up. She watched the larger two figures turn her way before she had made any real noise. The vampires saw her heat impression, sensing the silver in her sword. They stopped and turned back to the humans. One grabbed the boy and tried to lift him inside the helicopter. They were going to take off again. The engine turned over, the rotors starting their hydraulic whine.

Gus opened up his weapon, picking at the long tail of the helicopter at first, then stitching up the side toward the passenger compartment. That was enough to drive the vampire carrying the boy away from the chopper. Nora was more than halfway to them now. Gus fanned out wide to her left, picking at the cockpit glass. The glass did not shatter, the rounds punching clean through until a spray of red went out over the opposite end.

The pilot's body slumped forward. The rotors continued to speed up but the chopper did not move.

One vampire left the man he was guarding and ran at Nora. She saw the dark, decorative ink on its neck and immediately placed the vamp as one of the prison bodyguards—one of Barnes's bodyguards. The thought of Barnes erased all fear, and Nora came at the vampire with her sword high and her voice at full yell. The big vampire went low at the last moment, surprising her, but she sidestepped him like a matador, bringing down her sword on his back. He skidded across the blacktop on his front side, burning off flesh, then hopped back up to his feet. Pale skin hung from his thighs, chest, and one cheek. That didn't slow him down. The silver wound to his back did.

Gus's gun rattled and the big vampire twitched. The shots stunned him but did not put him down. Nora did not give the powerful *strigoi* time to mount another attack. She treated his neck tattoos like targets and took off his head.

She turned back toward the helicopter, squinting into its rotor wash. The other tattooed vampire was away from the humans, circling Gus. It understood and respected the power of silver—but not the power of a machine gun. Gus walked up on the hissing *strigoi*, right up inside its stinging radius, and fired a cluster of head shots. The vamp went down backward and Gus advanced and shot up its neck, releasing the creature.

The man was down on one knee, bracing himself on the open door of the helicopter. The boy watched both vampires go down. He turned and ran toward the roadside, in the direction the helicopter light was shining. Nora saw something in his hands, which he held in front of him as he ran.

Nora yelled, "Gus, get him!" because Gus was closest. Gus took off after the kid. The skinny kid was fast enough but unsteady. He jumped over the guardrail and landed all right, but in the shadowy ground beyond he misjudged a step or two and got tangled up in his own feet.

* * *

Nora was standing near Barnes beneath the whirling rotor umbrella of the helicopter. He was still airsick and on his knee. Yet when he looked up and recognized Nora's face, he paled even more.

Nora raised her sword and was ready to strike when she heard four sharp cracks, dulled beneath the sound of the helicopter. It was a small rifle, the boy firing at them in a panic. Nora wasn't hit but the bullets exploded awfully near. She moved away from Barnes and entered the underbrush. She saw Gus lunge for the boy and tackle him before he could fire again. He picked the kid up by his shirt, turning him toward the light, Gus making sure he wasn't dealing with a vampire. Gus pulled the empty rifle out of his hand and threw it into the trees. The kid bucked, so Gus gave him a good shake, just violent enough to let him know what could happen to him if he tried to fight. Still, the kid squinted in the light, trying to pull away, genuinely afraid of Gus.

"Easy, kid. Jesus."

He dragged the squirming boy back over the guardrail.

Nora said, "You okay, Gus?"

Gus wrestled with the kid. "He's a lousy shot, so yeah."

Nora looked back at the chopper. Barnes had vanished. She squinted past the helicopter light, searching for him, but to no avail. Nora cursed softly.

Gus took another look at the kid's face there and noticed something about him, his eyes, the structure of his face. He looked familiar. Too familiar.

Gus looked at Nora. "Oh, come on," said Gus.

The kid kicked at Gus with the heel of his sneaker. Gus kicked him back, only harder.

"Christ—just like your father," Gus said.

That slowed the kid down. He looked at Gus, though still trying to pull away. "What do you know?" he said.

When Nora looked at Zack, she both recognized him at once and not at all: the boy's eyes were nothing like she had remembered. His features had matured as any boy's would have over a two-year period—but his eyes lacked the light they had once had. If the curiosity was still there, it was darker now, it was deeper. It was as though his personality had retreated into his mind, wanting to read but not to be read. Or maybe he was just in shock. He was only thirteen, after all.

He is hollow. He is not there.

"Zachary," she said, not knowing what to do.

The boy looked at her for some moments before recognition crept into his eyes. "Nora," he said, pronouncing the word slowly, as though having nearly forgotten it.

Despite the fact that there were fewer drones available to monitor the various potential automobile routes in northern New York State, the Master's path grew ever more certain. The Master had viewed Dr. Martinez's ambush through the eyes of Dr. Barnes's security detail, until their violent release. Currently, the Master saw the helicopter in the highway, rotors still spinning, viewed through Kelly Goodweather's eyes.

The Master watched as Kelly directed her driver down a steep embankment to an auxiliary road, driving fast, following the Explorer's path. Kelly's bond with Zachary was much more intense than her bond with her ex-mate Dr. Ephraim Goodweather. Her longing was much more pronounced—and, in this moment, productive.

And now the Master had an even better read on the infidels' progress. They had taken the bait the Master knew would prove irresistible. The Master watched through Zachary's eyes, sitting in the backseat of the automobile driven by Augustin Elizalde. The Master was all but with them there in the vehicle as they headed to rendezvous with Dr. Goodweather, who had possession of the *Lumen* and knowledge of the location of the Black Site.

"I am following them," said Barnes, his voice crackling on a radio. "I will keep you informed. You have me on the GPS."

And indeed, a dot was visible on the GPS. An imperfect, pale, mechanical imitation of the Master's bond, but one he could share with the traitor Barnes.

"I have the gun with me," said Barnes. "I am ready for your command."

The Master smiled. So obsequious.

They were close, perhaps mere miles away

from their destination. Their northern trajectory put them on a path toward Lake Ontario or the Saint Lawrence River. And if a water crossing was in order, no matter. The Master had Creem to ferry him across, if needed, as the gang leader was still nominally human but wholly under his command.

The Master directed the helicopters north at full speed.

Creem's mouth hurt. His gums burned where his dented silver teeth were attached. At first he thought this was more lingering effects resulting from the elbow he had taken from Mr. Quinlan. But now his fingers were growing sore, enough so that he plucked the bling off his knuckles, giving his digits a rest, the silver jewelry piling up in the cup holder.

He didn't feel right. He felt woozy and warm. At first he feared some sort of bacterial infection like the one that had claimed Gus's man. But the more he looked into his rearview mirror at the Master's dark, worm-writhing face, the more Creem grew anxious, wondering if the Master had infected him. For an instant, he felt something move through his forearm and into his biceps. Something more than a tingle. Something en route to his heart.

Eph's Jeep reached Fishers Landing first. The northernmost road ran along the edge of the

Saint Lawrence. Mr. Quinlan couldn't pick up on any vampires in the immediate area. They saw a CAMP RIVERSIDE sign pointing toward an area where the road left the water's edge. They turned down the dirt road, riding out to a large spit of land jutting into the river. There were cabins and a restaurant with an adjacent sweets shop, and a sandy beach boxed in by a dock long and wide enough to be just barely visible over the water.

Eph pulled up sharply in the lot at the end of the road, leaving his headlamps on, and pointed at the water. He wanted to get out on that dock. They needed a boat.

As soon as he shut his door, a powerful light filled his vision, effectively blinding him. By thrusting up his arm, he could just make out multiple sources, one from near the restaurant, the other near a towel shack. He panicked a moment but then realized that these were artificial light sources—something vampires had no need or use for.

A voice called out, "Stop right there! Don't move!"

A real voice, not a vampire voice projected into his head.

"Okay, okay!" said Eph, trying to shield his eyes. "I'm a human!"

"We see that now," said the female voice.

A male voice from the other side said, "This one's armed!"

Eph looked over at Fet on the other side of the Jeep. Fet said, "Are you armed?"

"You better believe it!" called the male voice.

"Can we both put them down and talk?" said Fet.

"No," said the female voice. "We're glad you aren't stingers, but that doesn't mean you aren't raiders. Or Stonehearts in disguise."

"We aren't either," said Eph, holding off the lights with his open hands. "We're here on a . . . a sort of mission. But there isn't much time."

"There's one more in the backseat!" yelled the male voice. "Show yourself!"

Oh, shit, thought Eph. Where to begin? "Look," he said. "We came here all the way from New York City."

"I'm sure they'll be happy to see you return."

"You . . . you sound like fighters. Against the vampires. We're fighters too. Part of a resistance."

"We're full up here, friend."

Eph said, "We need to get out to one of the islands."

"Feel free. Just do it from some other point along the Saint Lawrence. We don't want any trouble, but we're ready enough for it."

"If I could have just ten minutes to explain—"

"You got ten seconds to leave. I can see your eyes, and your friend's. They're right enough in the light. But if your other friend isn't getting out of the car, we're going to start shooting."

"First of all, we have something fragile and explosive in the car, so for your sake, don't shoot. Second, you're not going to like what you see in our other friend here."

Fet chimed in. "He reads vamp. His pupils will glass up in the light. Because he's part stinger."

The male voice said, "No such thing."

"One such thing," said Eph. "He's on our side, and I can explain—or try to—if you'll give me a chance."

Eph sensed the light source moving. Advancing on him. He stiffened, expecting an attack.

The male voice from the other light said, "Careful, Ann!"

The woman behind the light stopped about ten yards away from Eph, near enough that he could feel heat coming off the lamp. He made out rubber boots and an elbow behind the beam.

"William!" the female voice called.

William, the bearer of the other light, came running toward Fet. "What is it?"

"Take a good look at his face," she said.

For a moment, Eph had both beams directly on him.

"What?" said William. "He ain't no vamp."

"No, dummy. From the news reports. The wanted man. Are you Goodweather?"

"Yes. Ephraim is my name."

"Goodweather, the fugitive doctor. Who killed Eldritch Palmer."

"Actually," Eph said, "I was falsely accused. I didn't kill the old bastard. I did try, though."

"They wanted you real bad, didn't they? Those motherfuckers."

Eph nodded. "They still do."

William said, "I don't know, Ann."

Ann said, "You've got ten minutes, asshole. But your so-called friend stays in the car, and if he tries to get out, you're all fish food."

* * *

Fet stood before the back of the Jeep, showing them the device and the timer he had attached by flashlight.

"Shee-it. A goddamn nuclear bomb," said Ann, revealed to be a woman in her fifties with a long, fraying braid of gray hair, dressed in waders under a fisherman's slicker.

"You thought it would be bigger," said Fet.

"I don't know what I thought." She looked again at Eph and Fet. William—a man in his forties, wearing a wool sweater shaggy with pulls and droopy blue jeans—remained off to the side, both hands on his rifle. The lamps lay at his feet, one of them still turned on. The indirect light cast Mr. Quinlan, now standing outside the vehicle, in an intimidating cloak of shadows. "Except that your situation here is too bizarre to be untrue."

Eph said, "We don't want anything from you, except a map of these islands and a means to get out there."

"You're going to detonate this little fucker."

Eph said, "We are indeed. You'll want to relocate away from here, whether the island is more than a half mile offshore or not."

"We don't live here," said William.

At first, Ann shot him a look that said he had told too much. But then she softened, allowing that she could be open with Eph and Fet since they had been open with her.

"We live out in the islands," she said. "Where the damn stingers can't go. There are old forts from the Revolutionary War out there. We're in them."

"How many?"

"All told there's forty-two of us. Was fifty-six; we've lost that many. We're in three living groups, 'cause even after the world's ended some assholes still can't get along. We're mostly neighbors who didn't know one another before this damn thing. We keep coming back to the mainland to scavenge for arms, tools, and food, kind of like Robinson Crusoe if you consider the mainland the shipwreck."

Eph said, "You have boats."

"We do have fucking boats. Three motorboats and a whole bunch of li'l skiffs."

"Good," said Eph. "Very good. I hope you can see fit to loan us one. I'm sorry we're bringing this trouble your way." He checked with the Born, who was standing very still. "Anything yet?"

Nothing imminent.

But Eph could tell by the way he answered that they were running out of time. He said to Ann, "You know these islands?"

She nodded. "William knows them best. Like the back of his hand."

Eph said to William, "Can we go inside the restaurant and you sketch me out directions? I know what I'm looking for. It's an island with very little growth on it, rocky, shaped like a trefoil, which is like a series of three overlapping rings. Like a biohazard symbol, if you can picture that."

Ann and William looked at each other in a

way that showed they both knew exactly which island Eph was referring to. Eph felt a spike of adrenaline.

A radio crackle surprised them, making jumpy William step back. The walkie-talkie in the front seat of the Jeep. "Friends of ours," said Fet, moving to the door, reaching in for the radio. "Nora?"

"Oh, thank God," she said, her voice fuzzy over the airwaves. "We're in Fishers Landing finally. Where are you?"

"Follow the signs for the public beach. You'll see a sign for Camp Riverside. Follow the dirt road to the water. Hurry up, but come quietly. We've met some others who can help us get out onto the water."

"Some others?" she said.

"Just trust me and get out here, now."

"Okay, I see a sign for the beach," she said. "We'll be right there."

Fet set down the radio. "They're close."

"Good," said Eph, turning again to Mr. Quinlan. The Born was watching the sky, as though for a sign. This worried Eph. "Anything we need to know?"

All quiet.

"How many hours do we have until the meridiem?"

Too many, I am afraid.

"Something is troubling you," said Eph. "What is it?"

I do not enjoy traveling over water.

"I realize that. And?"

We should have seen the Master by now. I don't like the fact that we have not . . .

Ann and William wanted to talk, but Eph just wanted them to sketch out the route to the island. So he left them drawing on the back of a paper place mat and returned to Fet, standing before the bomb set upon the candy shop ice cream counter adjacent to the restaurant. Through the glass doors, Eph saw Mr. Quinlan waiting for vampires in front of the beach.

Eph said, "How long will we have?"

Fet said, "I don't know. I hope long enough." He showed him the switch with the safety on. "Turn this way for the delay." It was set to a clock icon raised on the small panel. "Don't turn it this way." Toward the X. "Then run like hell."

Eph felt another cramp crawling up his arm. He clenched his fist and hid the pain best as he could.

"I don't like the idea of leaving it there. A lot can go wrong in a few minutes."

"We don't have an alternative. Not if we want to survive."

They both looked up at the approaching headlights. Fet ran out to Nora's car, and Eph remained behind, returning to monitor William's work. Ann was making suggestions and William was annoyed. "It is four islands out and one over."

Ann said, "What about Little Thumb?"

"You can't give these islands pet names and expect everyone else to memorize them."

Ann looked at Eph and explained, "The third island looks like it has a little thumb."

Eph looked at the sketch. The route appeared clear enough; that was all that mattered.

Eph said, "Can you take the others down the river to your island ahead of us? We won't stay, we won't be using up your resources. Just a place to hide and wait until this is all over."

Ann said, "Sure. Especially if you think you can do what you say you can do."

Eph nodded. "Life on Earth is going to change again."

"Back to normal."

"I wouldn't say that," said Eph. "We'll have a long way to go to get back to anything resembling normal. But we won't have these bloodsuckers running us anymore."

Ann looked like a woman who had learned not to get her hopes up too high. "I am sorry I called you an asshole, buddy," she said. "What you are is really a tough motherfucker."

Eph couldn't help but smile. These days he would take any compliment, no matter how backhanded it was.

"Can you tell us about the city?" said Ann. "We heard that all of midtown burned down."

"No, it's—"

The glass doors opened in the candy shop and Eph turned. Gus entered, holding a machine gun in one hand. Then he saw, through the glass, Nora approaching the door. Instead of Fet, a tall boy of about thirteen walked at her side. They entered and Eph could neither move nor speak . . .

but his dry eyes instantly stung with tears and his throat closed with emotion.

Zack looked around apprehensively, his eyes going past Eph to the old ice cream signs on the wall . . . then slowly coming back to his father's face.

Eph walked to him. The boy's mouth opened but he did not speak. Eph got down on one knee before him, this boy who used to be at about Eph's eye level when he did that. Now Eph looked up a few inches at him. The mess of hair falling down over his face partially hid his eyes.

Zack said quietly to his father, "What are you doing here?"

He was so much taller now. His hair was long and ragged, swept back from his ears, exactly the way a boy that age would choose to grow his hair without parental intervention. He looked reasonably clean. He appeared well fed.

Eph grabbed him and hugged him hard. In doing so, he was making the boy real. Zack felt strange in his arms, smelled different, was different—older. *Weak.* It occurred to Eph how gaunt he must have looked to Zack in return.

The boy did not hug him back, standing stiffly, enduring the embrace.

He pushed him backward to look at him again. He wanted to know everything, how Zack had gotten here—but realized nothing else mattered right now.

He was here. He was still human. He was free.

"Oh, Zack," said Eph, remembering the day

he had lost him nearly two years before. He had tears in his eyes. "I'm so sorry. So, so sorry."

But Zack was looking at him strangely. "For what?"

He started to say, "For allowing your mother to take you away—" But he stopped. "Zachary," said Eph, overwhelmed by joy. "Look at you. So tall! You're a man . . ."

The boy's mouth remained open, but he was too stunned to speak. He stared at his father—the man who had haunted his dreams like an all-powerful ghost. The father who had abandoned him, deserted him, the one he remembered as being tall, so powerful, so wise, was a feeble, dry, insignificant thing. Unkempt, trembling, and weak.

Zack felt a surge of disgust.

Are you loyal?

"I never stopped looking," said Eph. "I never gave up. I know they told you I was dead—I've been fighting this whole time. For two years, I've been trying to get you back . . ."

Zack looked around the room. Mr. Quinlan had entered the shop. Zack looked longest at the Born.

"Mother is coming for me," said Zack. "She's going to be angry."

Eph nodded firmly. "I know she will. But . . . it's almost over."

"I know that," said Zack.

Are you thankful for all I have provided, for all that I have shown you?

"Come here . . . ," said Eph, squeezing Zack's

shoulders and walking him to the bomb. Fet moved to intercept them, but Eph barely noticed. "This is a nuclear device. We're going to use it to blow up an island. To wipe out the Master and all of its kind."

Zack stared at the device. "Why?" he asked in spite of himself.

The end of times is near.

Fet looked at Nora, a chill running down his spine. But Eph didn't seem to notice, rapt in the role of the prodigal father.

"To make things the way they used to be," said Eph. "Before the *strigoi*. Before the darkness."

Zack looked strangely at Eph. The boy was blinking noticeably, purposefully, like a nervous, self-consoling tic. "I want to go home."

Eph nodded quickly. "And I want to take you there. All your stuff is in your bedroom just like you left it. Everything. We'll go as soon as all this is over."

Zack shook his head, no longer looking at Eph. He was looking at Mr. Quinlan. "Home is the castle. In Central Park."

Eph's hopeful expression faltered. "No, you're never going back there again. I know it's going to take a little time, but you're going to be fine."

The boy is turned.

Eph's head whipped around to Mr. Quinlan. The Born stood looking at Zack.

Eph stared at his son. He had all his hair; his complexion was good. His eyes weren't black moons on a sea of red. His throat was not distended. "No. You're wrong. He's human."

Physically, yes. But look into his eyes. He brought someone here with him.

Eph gripped the boy by the chin. He pushed the hair off his eyes. They were a little dim, maybe. A little withdrawn. Zack stared defiantly at first, then tried to look away, as any young teenager would.

"No," said Eph. "He's fine. He will be fine. He resents me . . . it's only normal. He's angry at me, and . . . we just need to put him on a boat. Get him on the river." Eph looked at Nora and Fet. "The sooner the better."

They are here.

"What?" said Nora.

Mr. Quinlan pulled his hood down tighter over his head.

Take to the river. I will hold off as many as I can.

The Born went out through the door. Eph grabbed Zack, started him toward the door, then stopped. To Fet, he said, "We'll move him and the bomb at the same time."

Fet didn't like it but said nothing. "He is my son, Vasiliy," said Eph, choking, begging. "My son . . . all I have. But I will carry my mission through. I will not fail us."

For the first time in ages, Fet saw in Eph the old resolve—the leadership that he used to begrudgingly admire. This was the man Nora had once loved, and Fet had once followed.

"You stay here then," said Fet, grabbing his pack and moving out after Gus and Nora.

Ann and William rushed over to him with the map. Eph said, "Go to the boats. Wait for us."

"We won't have enough room for everyone, if you're going to the island."

"We'll work it out," said Eph. "Now go. Before they try to scuttle them."

Eph locked the door behind them, then turned back to Zack. He looked at his son's face, seeking reassurance. "It's okay, Z. We're going to be okay. It's going to be over soon."

Zack blinked rapidly as he watched his father fold the map and stuff it into his coat pocket.

The *strigoi* came out of the darkness. Mr. Quinlan saw their heat impressions rushing through the trees and waited to intercept them. Dozens of vampires, with more following behind—perhaps hundreds. Gus came up firing down the dirt road at an unlit vehicle. Sparks popped off the hood and the windshield crackled, but the car kept coming. Gus stood in front of it until he was certain he had put a good kill pattern in the windshield, then jumped out of the way at what he thought was the last moment.

But the car turned his way as he went diving into the woods. A thick trunk stopped the vehicle with a ringing crash, though not before the front grille struck Gus's legs and sent him flying into the trees. His left arm cracked like a tree branch, and when he got back to his feet he saw it hanging crookedly at his side—broken at the elbow, and maybe the shoulder too.

Gus swore through clenched teeth, the pain severe. Still, his combat instincts kicked in, and he made himself run to the car, expecting vamps to come spilling out like circus clowns.

Gus reached in with his good hand—the one holding his Steyr—and pulled back the driver's head from the steering wheel. It was Creem, his head now lying back in the seat as though he were napping, except that he had taken two of Gus's rounds in the forehead, one in the chest.

"Reverse Mozambique, motherfucker," said Gus, and let the head go, its nose crunching softly against the steering wheel crossbar.

Gus saw no other occupants—though the rear door was strangely open.

The Master . . .

Mr. Quinlan had moved on in the blink of an eye, hunting his prey. Gus leaned a moment against the vehicle, beginning to gauge the gravity of his arm injury. It was then that he noticed a rivulet of blood oozing from Creem's neck . . .

Not a bullet wound.

Creem's eyes snapped open. He burst from the car, hurling himself toward Gus. The impact of Creem's massive body knocked the air from Gus's lungs, like a bull striking a matador, sending him sailing with almost as much force as the car had. Gus held on to his gun, but Creem's hand closed around his entire forearm with incredible strength, crushing his tendons, forcing his fingers open. Creem's knee was against Gus's damaged left arm, grinding the broken bone like a mortar.

Gus screamed, both in rage and pain.

Creem's eyes were wide open, looking crazed

and slightly misaligned. His bling smile began to smoke and steam, his vampiric gums burning away from contact with the silver implants. The flesh burned away from his knuckles for the same reason. But Creem held on, puppeteered by the will of the Master. As Creem's jaw opened and unhinged with a loud crack, Gus understood that the Master meant to take Gus and through him learn how to trump their plan. The grinding of his left arm drove Gus to howling distraction, but he could see Creem's stinger budding in his mouth—oddly fascinating and slow—the reddened flesh parting, unfolding, revealing new layers as it awakened to its purpose.

Creem was being forced into overdrive transformation by the Master's will. The stinger became engorged amid the clouds of silver vapor, getting ready to strike. Drool and residual blood spilled onto Gus's chest as the demented being that once had been Creem reared its vampiric head.

In a final effort, Gus managed to twist his gun hand enough to aim loosely at Creem's head. He fired once, twice, three times and, at such close range, each round ripped away huge amounts of flesh and bone from Creem's face and neck.

Creem's stinger darted wildly into the air, seeking contact with Gus. Gus kept firing, one round striking the stinger. *Strigoi* blood and worms flew everywhere, as Gus finally succeeded in shattering Creem's vertebrae and severing his spinal cord.

Creem tipped over, slumping hard to the ground, twitching and steaming.

Gus rolled away from the energized blood worms. He felt an immediate sting in his leg, and quickly pulled up his left pant leg. He saw a worm sinking into his flesh. Instinctively, he reached for a sharp piece of the damaged automobile grille and dug into his leg. He sliced it open enough so that he could see the wriggling worm, rooting deeper and deeper. Gus grabbed the thing and yanked it out of his wound. The worm's barbs grabbed hold, and it was excruciating—but he did it, dragging out the thin worm and pounding it into the ground, killing it.

Gus got to his feet, chest heaving, leg bleeding. He didn't mind seeing his own blood, so long as it remained red. Mr. Quinlan returned and took in the entire scene, especially Creem's steaming corpse.

Gus grinned. "See, *compa*? You can't leave me alone for one fucking minute."

The Born felt other interlopers advancing along the windy shoreline and pointed Fet in that direction. The first of the raiders advanced on the Born. They came hard, this first sacrificial wave, and Mr. Quinlan matched their viciousness. As he fought, he tracked three feelers to his right, clustered around a female vampire. One of the feelers broke off and engaged him, romping toward the Born on all fours. Mr. Quinlan knocked a two-legged vampire aside to deal with the nimble blind one. He swatted it away, the feeler tumbling backward before springing up again on all fours like an animal pushed off a potential meal. Two other vampires came at him, and Mr. Quinlan moved fast to avoid them, keeping an eye on the feeler.

A body came flying, launching off one of the storefront tables, landing on Mr. Quinlan's back and shoulders with a high-pitched squeal. It was Kelly Goodweather, her right hand lashing out, raking the Born's face. He howled and punched backward, and she slashed at him again, but he blocked it, grasping her wrist.

A burst from Gus's machine gun sent her leaping off Mr. Quinlan's shoulders. Mr. Quinlan anticipated another attack from the feeler, then saw it lying in the dirt, full of holes.

Mr. Quinlan touched his face. His hand came away sticky and white. He turned to go after Kelly, but she was nowhere to be seen.

Glass shattered somewhere in the restaurant. Eph readied his silver sword. He moved Zack to the corner of the candy counter, keeping him out of harm's way and yet basically trapped and unable to run. The bomb remained on the wall end of the counter, over Gus's pack and the Born's black leather satchel.

A nasty little feeler galloped in from the restaurant, followed by another on its heels. Eph held out his silver blade, letting the blind creatures sense it. A form appeared in the dim doorway behind them, barely a silhouette, dark as a panther.

Kelly.

She looked horribly decayed, her features barely recognizable even to her former husband. The royal red wattle of her neck swayed limply, under dead eyes black and red.

She was there for Zack. Eph knew what he had to do. There was only one way to break the spell. Committing to this made Eph's sword tremble in his hands—but the vibration originated from the sword itself, not his nerves. As he held the blade before him, it seemed to be glowing faintly.

She walked toward him, flanked by the agitated feelers. Eph showed her his blade. He said, "This is the end, Kelly . . . and I am so sorry . . . so goddamn sorry . . ."

She had no eyes for Eph, only for Zack standing behind him. Her face was unable to register any emotion, but Eph understood the compulsion to have and to protect. He understood it keenly. His back spasmed and the pain became almost unbearable. But somehow he conquered it and held on.

Kelly focused on Eph. She made a motion with her hand, a flick forward, and the feelers rushed him like attack dogs. They came in a crisscross motion, and Eph had a split second to choose between them. He struck at one and missed but managed to kick the other one to the side. The one he missed came right back at him, and Eph caught her with his sword, but off balance and only with the flat of the blade against her head. She went rolling back, dazed and slow to rise.

Kelly leaped onto a table and sprang off it, attempting to jump past Eph to Zack. Eph moved right into her path, however, and they collided, Kelly spinning off to the side and Eph almost falling backward.

Eph saw the other feeler sizing him up from the side and readied his blade. Then Zack burst past him. Eph just barely caught the boy by the collar of his parka, yanking him back. Zack slipped out of the jacket but stayed put, standing just in front of his father.

"Stop it!" Zack said. He held one hand out to his mother and the other to Eph. "Don't!"

"Zack!" yelled Eph. The boy was near enough to both of them that Eph feared he and Kelly would both grab a hand, resulting in a tug-of-war.

"Stop it!" yelled Zack. "Please! Please—don't hurt her! She's all I have . . . !"

And in saying so, it hit Eph. It was he, the absent father, who was the anomaly. He had always been the anomaly. Kelly's posture relaxed a moment, her arms dropping down at her bare sides.

Zack said to her, "I'll go with you. I want to go back."

But then another force came into Kelly's eyes, a monstrous, alien will. She sprang all at once, violently shoving Zack aside. Her jaw dropped and her stinger lashed out at Eph, who barely moved in time, watching the muscular appendage snap out into the space where his neck had just been. He swiped at her stinger, but he was off balance and missed.

The feelers pounced on Zack, holding him down. The boy was yelling. Kelly's stinger retracted, the end tip lolling out of her mouth like a thin, bifurcated tongue. She threw herself at Eph, ducking her head and plowing into his midsection, driving him to the floor. He slid backward, coming to rest hard against the bottom of the counter.

He quickly struggled up to his knees, back in full spasm, his ribs immediately jabbing his chest, a few of them broken and driving into his lungs. This shortened his swing as he brought the sword across, trying to keep her back. Kelly kicked his arm, her bare foot catching him beneath the elbow, his fists slamming against the lower part of the counter. The sword broke free from his grip and clanged to the floor.

Eph looked up. There was a bright red glare in her eyes as Kelly rushed at him for the kill.

Eph reached down without looking and somehow the handle of the sword found his fingers. He got the blade up just as her jaw fell and she thrust forward.

The blade ran straight back through her throat. It came out the back end of her neck, cleaving the root mechanism of her stinger. Eph stared in horror as her stinger went limp, her gaze unbelieving. Her open mouth filled with wormy white blood, her body sagging against the silver sword.

For a moment—probably imagined by Eph, but he accepted it anyway—he saw the formerly human Kelly behind her eyes, looking at him with an expression of peace.

Then the creature returned and sagged in release.

Eph remained holding her up until her white blood ran almost down to his sword handle. Then, overcoming his shock, he pivoted and removed the blade, and Kelly's body lay upon the floor.

Zack was screaming now. He rose up in a fit of strength and rage, throwing off the feelers. The blind vampire children went wild themselves and ran at Eph. He swung his slickened blade diagonally upward, easily slaying the first one. That made the second jump back. Eph watched as it retreated, loping out of the room with its head turned almost fully over its shoulder, watching Eph until it was gone.

Eph lowered his sword. Zack stood over the remains of his vampire mother, crying and gasping. Zack looked at his father with a look of anguished disgust.

"You killed her," said Zack.

"I killed the vampire that had taken her away from us. Away from you."

"I hate you! I fucking hate you!"

In his fury, Zack found a long-handled flashlight on the countertop and grabbed it, going after his father. Eph blocked the strike to his head, but the boy's forward momentum carried him into Eph and he fell on top of him, pressing against Eph's broken ribs. The boy was surprisingly strong, and Eph was in agony. Zack hammered away at Eph, Eph blocking the blows with his forearm. The boy lost the flashlight but kept fighting, his fists striking Eph's chest, hands reaching inside Eph's coat. Finally Eph dropped his sword in order to grip the boy's wrists and hold him off.

Eph saw, crumpled in the boy's left fist, a piece of paper. Zack saw that Eph had noticed and fought his father's attempts to pry open his fingers.

Eph pulled out the crumpled paper map. Zack had tried to take it from him. He stared into his son's eyes and saw the presence. He saw the Master seeing through Zack.

"No," said Eph. "No—please. No!"

Eph pushed the boy away. He was sickened. He looked at the map, then slipped it back into his pocket. Zack stood, backpedaling. Eph saw that the boy was about to take a run at the nuke. At the detonator.

The Born was there, Mr. Quinlan intercepting the boy and swallowing him up in a bear hug, spinning him away. The Born had a diagonal scrape across his face, from his left eye to his right cheek. Eph got to his feet, the ripping pain in his chest nothing compared to the loss of Zack.

Eph picked up his sword and went to Zack, still held by the Born. Zack was grimacing and nodding his head rhythmically. Eph held the silver blade near his son, watching for a response.

The silver did not repel him. The Master was in his mind but not his body.

"This isn't you," said Eph, speaking to Zack and also convincing himself. "You're going to be okay. I have to get you out of here."

We must hurry.

Eph grabbed Zack from him. "Let's go to the boats."

The Born lifted his leather pack to his shoulder, then gripped the straps of the bomb, pulling it off the counter. Eph grabbed the pack at his feet and pushed Zack toward the door.

Dr. Everett Barnes hid behind the trash shed located twenty feet from the restaurant, on the edge of the dirt parking lot. He sucked air through his broken teeth and felt the pleasurable sting of pain that produced.

If there truly was a nuclear bomb in play—which, judging by Ephraim's apparent obsession with vengeance, there was—then Barnes needed to get as far away from this place as possible, but not before he shot that bitch. He had a gun. A nine-millimeter, with a full clip. He was supposed to use it against Ephraim, but the way he saw it, Nora would be a bonus. The cherry on top.

He tried to catch his breath in order to slow his heart rate. Placing his fingers to his chest, he felt a strange arrhythmia. He barely knew where he was, obeying blindly the GPS that connected him to the Master and that read the positioning of Zack with a unit hidden in the teenager's shoe. In spite of the Master's assurances, Barnes was nervous; with these vampires wilding all around the property, there was no guarantee they would be able to know a friend from an enemy. Just in case, Barnes was determined to get to some sort of vehicle if he had any chance to escape before this camp went up in a mushroom cloud.

He spotted Nora about a hundred feet away. He aimed at her as best he could and opened fire. Five rounds cracked out of the gun in rapid succession, and at least one of them connected with Nora, who fell down behind a line of trees . . . leaving a faint mist of blood floating in the air.

"I got you—you fucking cunt!" said Barnes triumphantly.

He pushed off from the gate and ran across the open lot toward the outlying trees. If he could follow the dirt road back out to the main street, he could find a car or some other means of transportation.

He reached the first line of trees, stopping there, shuddering as he discovered a puddle of blood on the ground . . . but no Nora.

"Oh, shit!" he said, and instinctively turned and rushed into the woods, tucking the gun in his pants. It burned him. *"Shit,"* he squealed. He never knew guns got this hot. He bent both arms protectively before his face, the branches ripping at his uniform and stripping medals off his chest. He paused in a clearing and hid in the underbrush, panting, the hot muzzle burning his leg.

"Looking for me?"

Barnes turned until he saw Nora Martinez just three trees away. Her forehead bore a gash, a bleeding, open wound the size of a finger. But she was unharmed otherwise.

He tried to run, but she grabbed the back of his jacket collar, pulling him back.

"We never had that last date you wanted," she said, hauling him through the trees to the dirt drive.

"Please, Nora—"

She pulled him into the clear and looked him over. Barnes's heart was racing, his breath short.

She said, "You don't run this particular camp, do you?"

He pulled the gun out but it tangled on his Sansabelt pants. Nora quickly took it away and cocked it in a single expert move. She pressed it against his face.

He held up his hands. "Please."

"Ah. Here they come."

Out of the trees came the vampires, ready to converge, hesitant only because of the silver sword in Nora's hand. They circled the two humans, looking for an opening.

"I am Dr. Everett Barnes," Barnes announced.

"Don't think they care for titles right now," she said, holding them at bay. She frisked Barnes and found the GPS receiver. She stomped on it. "And I would say you've just about outlived your usefulness right now."

"What are you going to do?" he asked.

"I'm going to release a bunch of these bloodsuckers, of course," she said. "The question is, what are you going to do?"

"I . . . I have no weapon anymore."

"That's too bad. Because, like you, they don't care much for a fair fight."

"You . . . you wouldn't," he said.

"I am," she said. "I've got bigger problems than you."

"Give me a weapon . . . please . . . and I will do whatever you want. Whatever you need, I will give you . . ."

"You want a weapon?" asked Nora.

Barnes whimpered something like "Yes."

"Then," Nora said, "have one . . ."

Out of her pocket, she produced the butter-knife shank she had painfully crafted and buried it firmly in Barnes's shoulder, jamming it between the humerus and the collarbone.

Barnes squealed and, more important, bled.

With a battle cry, she raced out at the largest vampire, cutting him down, then spinning, drawing more to her.

The rest paused just a moment to confirm that the other human held no silver and that the scent of blood came from him. Then they ran at him like pound dogs thrown a slab of meat.

Eph dragged Zack with him, following the Born to the shoreline where the dock began. He watched Mr. Quinlan hesitate a moment, the keg-shaped bomb in his arms, before crossing from the sand onto the wood planking of the long dock.

Nora came running to meet them. Fet was alarmed at her wound, rushing to her. "Who did this to you?" he roared.

"Barnes," she said. "But don't worry. We won't be seeing him again." She then looked at

Mr. Quinlan. "You have to go! You know you can't wait for daylight."

The Master expects that. So I will stay. This is perhaps the last time we will see the sun.

"We're going now," said Eph, Zack pulling at his arm.

"I'm ready," said Fet, starting toward the dock.

Eph raised his sword, holding the point near Fet's throat. Fet looked at him, anger rising.

"Just me," Eph said.

"What the . . . ?" Fet used his own sword to bat Eph's away. "What the hell do you think you're doing?"

Eph shook his head. "You stay with Nora."

Nora looked from Fet to Eph.

"No," said Fet. "You need me to do this."

"She needs you," said Eph, the words stinging as he spoke them. "I have Mr. Quinlan." He looked back at the dock, needing to go. "Get to a skiff and sail downriver. I've gotta give Zack to Ann and William, to get him out of here. I'll tell them to be looking for you."

Nora said, "Let Mr. Quinlan set the detonator. You just drop him off."

"I have to make sure it's set. Then I'll be along."

Nora hugged him hard, then stepped back. She lifted Zack's chin to look at his face, to try to give him some confidence or consolation. The boy blinked and looked away.

"You're going to be okay," she told him.

But the boy's attention was elsewhere. He was looking skyward, and after a moment Eph heard it too.

Black helicopters. Approaching from the south. Coming in low.

Gus came hobbling down from the beach. Eph saw immediately that his left arm was badly broken—his left hand swelling with blood—though that condition did not in any way cool the gangbanger's anger toward him. "Choppers!" yelled Gus. "What the hell are you waiting for?"

Eph quickly slipped off his pack. "Take it," he said to Fet. The *Lumen* was inside.

"Fuck the manual, man," Gus said. "This is practice!"

Gus dropped his gun, shaking off his own pack with a painful grunt—first his good arm, and then Nora helped him lift it off his broken one—then rummaged inside for two purple-colored canisters from his pack. He pulled the pins with his teeth, rolling the smoke grenades to the right and to the left.

Violet smoke billowed, lifted by the shore wind, shielding the beach and dock from view and providing some intermediate cover from the approaching helicopters. "Get outta here!" yelled Gus. "You and your boy. Take care of the Master. I'll cover your ass—but you remember, Goodweather, you and me, we got business to settle after." Gus gently, though with great pain, pushed the jacket sleeve up from the swollen wrist of his bad arm, showing Eph the scarred word *"MADRE,"* left there from all of Gus's bloodletting.

"Eph," said Nora. "Don't forget—the Master is still out here somewhere."

* * *

At the far corner of the dock, some thirty yards from shore, Ann and William waited inside two ten-foot aluminum rowboats with outboard motors. Eph ran Zack to the first boat. When the boy would not board willingly, Eph lifted him up bodily and placed him in there. He looked at his son. "We're going to get through this, okay, Z?"

Zack had no response. He watched the Born loading the bomb onto the other boat, between the rear and middle bench seats, and gently but firmly lift William out, depositing him back on the dock.

Eph remembered the Master was in Zack's head, seeing this too. Seeing Eph right now.

"It's just about over," Eph said.

The violet smoke cover billowed up off the beach, blowing across to the trees, revealing more advancing vampires. "The Master needs a human to take him across water," said Fet, stepping up with Nora and Gus. "I don't think there's anybody left here but us three. We just have to make sure nobody else gets to the skiffs."

The violet smoke parted strangely, as though folding in on itself. As though something had passed through it at incredible speed.

"Wait—did you see that?" yelled Fet.

Nora heard the thrumming presence of the Master. Impossibly, the wall of smoke changed course completely, curling back from the trees and rolling against the river breeze toward the shore—consuming them. Nora and Fet were immediately separated, vampires rushing at them silently out of the smoke, their bare feet soft on the damp sand.

Helicopter rotors chopped at the air overhead. Cracks and thumps made the sand jump at their shoes, rifle fire from above. Snipers shooting blindly into the smoke cover. A vampire took one to the top of its head just as Nora was about to cut it down. The rotors whipped smoke back at her, and she did a full three-sixty with her sword straight out, blindly coughing, choking. Suddenly she was unsure which side was shore and which was water. She saw a swirling in the smoke, like a dust devil, and heard the thrumming loudly again.

The Master. She kept swinging, fighting the smoke and everything in it.

Gus, keeping his bad arm behind him, rushed blindly sideways through the choking violet cloud, keeping to the shore. The sailboats were tied to a dock unconnected to land, anchored some forty or fifty feet out in the water.

Gus's left side was throbbing, his arm swollen. He felt feverish as he broke from the edge of the violet cloud, before the river-facing windows of the restaurant, expecting a column of hungry vampires. But he was alone on the beach.

Not so in the air. He saw the black helicopters, six of them directly overhead, with another six or so coming up behind. They hovered low, swarming like giant mechanized bees, whipping sand into Gus's face. One of them moved out over the river, scattering the surface water, whipping moisture with the force of shards of glass.

Gus heard the rifle cracks and knew they were shooting at the skiffs. Trying to scuttle them. Thumps at his feet told him they were shooting at him too, but he was more concerned about the choppers starting off over the lake—searching for Goodweather, for the nuke.

"Que chingados esperas?" he cursed in Spanish. "What are you waiting for?"

Gus fired at those choppers, trying to bring them down. A scorching stab in his calf dropped him to one knee, and he knew he had been shot. He kept firing at the helicopters heading out over the river, seeing sparks fly off the tail.

Another rifle round pierced his side with the force of an arrow. "Do it, Eph! Do it!" he yelled, falling to his elbow and still firing.

One helicopter wobbled, and a human figure fell from it into the water. The chopper failed to right itself, its rear tail spinning frontward until it collided with another chopper, and both aircraft rolled and crashed down into the river.

Gus was out of ammo. He lay back on the beach, just a few yards from the water, watching the death birds hover over him. In an instant, his body was covered with laser sights projecting out of the colored fog.

"Goodweather gets fucking angels," said Gus,

laughing, sucking air. "I get laser sights." He saw the snipers leaning out of their open cabin doors, sighting him. "Light me up, motherfuckers!"

The sand danced all around him as he was shot through many times. Dozens of bullets rattled his body, severing it, grinding it . . . and Gus's last thought was, *You better not mess up this one too, doc.*

Where are you taking me?"

Zack stood in the middle of the boat, rocking in the wake. Their puttering motor had faded into the darkness and the purple fog, leaving only the usual humming sensation in Zack's head. It mixed with the low throb of the helicopters approaching.

The woman named Ann pushed off from the dock cleat, while William pulled and pulled the rip cord of the coughing outboard motor, streams of violet smoke trailing past them. "To our island downriver." She looked to William. "Hurry."

Zack said, "What do you have there?"

"We have shelter. Warm beds."

"And?"

"We have chickens. A garden. Chores. It's an old fort from the American Revolution. There are children your age. Don't worry, you'll be safe there."

The Master's voice said, *You were safe here.*

Zack nodded, blinking. He lived like a prince, in a real castle in the center of a giant city. He owned a zoo. Everything he wanted.

Until your father tried to take you away.

Something told Zack to stay focused on the dock. The motor turned over, sputtering to life, and William turned in the rear seat and worked the tiller, steering them into the current. The helicopters were visible now, their lights and laser sights brightening the purple smoke on the beach. Zack counted off seven sets of seven blinks as the dock began to recede from view.

A blur of purple smoke burst from the long edge of the dock, flying through the air toward them. Out of it appeared the Master, its cloak flying behind it like wings, arms outstretched, the wolf-headed walking stick in one hand.

Its two bare feet landed in the aluminum boat with a bang. Ann, kneeling at the front point, barely had time to turn. "Fuck me . . ." She saw the Master before her—recognizing the pallid flesh of Gabriel Bolivar. This was the guy her niece was always yapping about. She wore him on T-shirts, hung his posters on her walls. And now, all that Ann could think of was, *I never liked his fucking music . . .*

The Master set down his staff, then reached for her and, in a ripping motion, tore her in half at the waist the way strongmen do very thick phone books—then hurled both halves into the river.

William was transfixed by the sight of the Master, who lifted him by his armpit and flat-handed his face with such tremendous force that William's neck snapped and his head flopped back off his shoulders like a removed coat hood. It dumped him into the river water as well, then retrieved its walking stick and looked down at the boy.

Take me there, my son.

Zack moved to the tiller and changed course, the Master standing astride the middle bench, its cloak swirling in the wind, as they followed the first boat's disappearing wake.

The smoke began to thin out, and Nora's calls to Fet were answered. They found each other and then found their way back to the restaurant, outrunning the rounds from the helicopter snipers overhead.

Inside, they found the rest of Gus's weapons. Fet grabbed Nora's hand and they ran to the riverside windows, opening one onto the deck. Nora had picked up the *Lumen* and had it with her.

They saw the boats bobbing offshore. "Where's Gus?" asked Nora.

"We'll have to swim for it," said Fet. His injured arm was now covered in blood, the wound reopened. "But first—"

Fet fired at the chopper spotlights, shattering the first one he aimed at.

"They can't shoot what they can't see!" he yelled.

Nora did the same, the weapon chugging in her grip. She got one too. The remaining lights swept the shoreline for the source of the automatic gunfire.

That was when Nora saw Gus's body laid out in the sand, river water lapping at his side.

Her shock and sorrow only paralyzed her a moment. Immediately, Gus's fighting spirit came over her, as well as Fet. *Don't mourn—fight.* They moved out aggressively onto the beach, firing away at the Master's helicopters.

The farther they got away from shore, the harder the boat rocked. The Born held tight to the nuke's belt straps while Eph steered, trying to keep them from pitching over into the river. Thick, green-black water sloshed over the sides, spraying the bomb's casing and the oak urns, a thin puddle forming underneath. It was spraying rain again, and they were sailing into the wind.

Mr. Quinlan lifted the urns off the wet floor of the boat, moved them away from the water. Eph did not know what it meant, but the act of bringing the remains of the Ancients to the origin site of the last of their number reminded Eph that it was all about to end. The shock of seeing Zack that way had thrown him off.

He motored past the second island, a long, rocky beach backed by bare, dying trees. Eph checked the map, the paper in his hand growing damp, the ink starting to run and spread.

Eph yelled over the motor and the wind, the pain in his ribs constricting his voice. "How, without turning him, did the Master create this . . . symbiotic relationship with my boy?"

I don't know. The key is that he is away from the Master now.

"The Master's influence will disappear once we do away with it, like all of its vampires?"

Everything that the Master was will cease.

Eph was cheered. He felt real hope. He believed that they could be father and son again. "It'll be a little like cult deprogramming, I suppose. No such thing as therapy anymore. I just want to get him back to his old bedroom. Start there."

Survival is the only therapy. I did not want to tell you before, for fear of your losing focus. But I believe the Master was grooming your son for its future self.

Eph swallowed. "I feared it myself. I couldn't think of any other reason to keep him and not turn him. But—why? Why Zack?"

It may have little to do with your son.

"You mean, it's because of me?"

I can't know. All I know is that the Master is a perverse being. It loves to take root in pain. To subvert and corrupt. Perhaps in you it saw a challenge. You were the first one to board the aircraft on which it traveled to New York. You aligned yourself with Abraham Setrakian, its sworn enemy. Achieving the subjugation of an entire race of beings is a feat, but an impersonal one. The Master is one that needs to inflict pain personally. It needs to feel another's suffering. It needs to experience it firsthand. "Sadism" is your closest modern term for it. And here it has been its undoing.

Exhausted, Eph watched the third dark island pass. After the fourth island, he banked the boat. Difficult to tell the shape of the landmass from the river—and in the darkness impossible to see all six outcroppings without circling it first—but somehow Eph knew that the map was true and this was the Black Site. The bare, black trees on this uninhabited island resembled many-fingered giants burned stiff, arms raised to the heavens in mid-cry.

Eph spotted an inlet and turned toward it, cutting the engine, nosing right onto land. The Born grabbed the nuke and stood, stepping onto the rocky shore.

Nora was right. Leave me here to finish it. Go back to your boy.

Eph looked at the hooded vampire, his face slashed, ready to end his existence. Suicide was an unnatural act for mortal humans to commit—but for an immortal? Mr. Quinlan's martyrdom was a many times more transgressive, unnatural, violent act.

"I don't know what to say," said Eph.

The Born nodded. *Then it is time to go.*

With that, the Born started up the rocky rise with the keg-sized bomb in his arms and the remains of the Ancients in his pack. Eph's only hesitation was a memory of his vision and its haunting images. The Born had not been foreseen as the redeemer. But Eph had not had enough time with the *Occido Lumen*, and perhaps the prophetic reading was different.

Eph dipped the propeller back into the water and gripped the zip cord. He was about to pull when he heard a motor, the sound carrying to him on the swirling wind.

Another boat, approaching. But there had been only one other motorized boat.

Zack's boat.

Eph looked back for the Born, but he had already disappeared over the rise. Eph's heart pounded as he stared into the dark mist over the river, straining to see the approaching craft. It sounded like it was coming in fast.

Eph stood and jumped out of the boat onto the rocks, one arm across his broken ribs, the twin handles of his swords wobbling over his shoulders. He charged up the rocky rise as fast as he could, the ground smoking with mist rising into the spitting rain as though the land were heating up in anticipation of the atomic cremation to come.

Eph topped the rise, unable to spot Mr. Quinlan among the trees. He rushed into the dead woods, calling to him, "Quinlan!" as loudly as his chest would allow, then emerged on the other side into a marshy clearing.

The mist was high. The Born had set the weapon down in the approximate center of the trefoil-shaped island, in the middle of a ring of inlaid stones resembling rocky black blisters. He was moving around the device and setting up the white oak receptacles containing the Ancients' ashes.

Mr. Quinlan heard Eph calling him and turned his way—and just then picked up the Master's approach.

"It's here!" yelled Eph. "It's—"

A blast of wind stirred up the mist. Mr. Quinlan just had time to brace himself before impact, grabbing on to the Master as it streaked in from out of nowhere. The momentum of the body strike carried them many yards away, rolling unseen into the mist. Eph saw something twist and fall through the air—and believed it was Setrakian's old wolf-handled walking stick.

Eph forgot about his chest pain, running for the bomb, pulling out his sword. Then the mist swirled up around it, obscuring the device.

"Dad!"

Eph turned, feeling Zack's voice right behind him. He whipped back around fast, knowing he had been suckered. His ribs ached. He went into the haze, looking for the bomb. Feeling the ground for the inlaid stones, trying to find his way.

Then before him, rising out of the mist: the Master.

Eph stumbled backward, shocked at the sight of it. Two slashes crossed the monster's face in a rough X, the result of the Master's collision and ensuing fight with the Born.

Fool.

Eph still could not right himself or find words. His head roared as though he had just heard an explosion. He saw ripples beneath the Master's flesh, a blood worm exiting one open scratch mark and crawling over its open eye to reenter the next. The Master did not flinch. It raised its arms from its sides and took in the smoky island of its origin, then looked triumphantly at the dark heavens above.

Eph summoned all his strength and ran at the Master, sword first, aiming for its throat.

The Master backhanded him squarely across the face with enough force to send Eph airborne, cartwheeling, landing on the stone ground some yards away.

Ahsųdagų-wah. Black ground.

Eph first thought that the Master had snapped a vertebra in his neck. The breath was knocked out of him when he hit the ground, and he feared a punctured lung. His other sword had fallen out of his pack, landing somewhere on the ground between them.

Onondaga language. The invading Europeans did not care to translate the name correctly, or at all. You see, Goodweather? Cultures die. Life is not circular but ruthlessly straight.

Eph fought to stand, his fractured ribs stabbing him. "Quinlan!" he called out, his voice mostly just breath.

You should have followed through with our deal, Goodweather. I would never have honored my end of the bargain, of course. But you could have at least spared yourself this humiliation. This pain. Surrender is always easier.

Eph was bursting with every emotion. He stood as tall as he could with the pain in his chest pulling at him. He saw, through the mist, just a few arm lengths away, the outline of the nuclear bomb.

Eph said, "Then let me offer you one last chance to surrender."

He limped to the device, feeling for the detonator. He thought it a stroke of great luck that the Master had thrown him so close to the device . . . and it was this very thought that made him look back at the creature.

Eph saw another form emerge from the ground mist. Zack, approaching the Master's side, no doubt summoned telepathically. Zack looked almost like a man to Eph, like the loved child you one day can no longer recognize. Zack stood with the Master, and suddenly Eph didn't care anymore—and, at the same time, he cared more than ever.

It is over, Goodweather. Now the book will be closed forever.

The Master had been counting on this. The Master believed that Eph would not harm his son—that he could not blow up the Master if it meant sacrificing Zack too.

Sons are meant to rebel against their fathers. The Master lifted its hands toward the sky again. *It has always been that way.*

Eph stared at Zack, standing with this monster. With tears in his eyes, Eph smiled at his boy. "I forgive you, Zack, I do . . . ," he said. "And I hope to hell that you forgive me."

Eph turned the screw switch from time delay to manual. He worked as fast as he could, and yet still the Master burst ahead, covering the distance between them. Eph released the detonator just in time, or else the blow from the Master would have torn the wires from the device, rendering it inoperable.

Eph landed in a heap. He shook off the impact, trying to stand. He saw the Master coming for him, its eyes flaring red inside the crooked X.

Behind it, the Born came flying. Mr. Quinlan had Eph's second sword. It impaled the beast before it could turn, the Master arching with pain.

The Born pulled back the blade, and the Master turned, facing him. Mr. Quinlan's face was broken, his left cheek collapsed, his jaw unhinged, iridescent blood coating his neck. But still he swiped at the Master, slicing at the creature's hands and arms.

The Master's psychic fury sent the mist fleeing as, undeterred by the pain, it stalked its own wounded creation, backing the Born away from the bomb. Father and son entangled in the fiercest battle.

Eph saw Zack standing alone behind Mr. Quinlan, watching raptly, something like fire in his eyes. Then Zack turned, as though his attention had been called to something. The Master was directing him. Zack reached down and picked up something long.

Setrakian's walking stick. The boy knew that a good twist of the handle shed the bottom wooden sheath, baring the silver blade.

Zack held the sword with both hands. He looked at Mr. Quinlan from behind.

Eph was already running toward him. He got in front of Zack, between him and the Born, one arm over his searing chest, the other holding a sword.

Zack stared at his father before him. He did not lower his blade.

Eph lowered his. He wanted Zack to take a chop at him. It would have made what he had to do that much easier.

The boy trembled. Maybe he was fighting himself inside, resisting what the Master was telling him to do.

Eph reached for his wrists and pulled Setrakian's sword out of his hands. "Okay," said Eph. "It's okay."

Mr. Quinlan overpowered the Master. Eph could not hear what their minds were saying to one another; he only knew that the roar in his own head was deafening. Mr. Quinlan grabbed the neck of the Master and sank his fingers into it, piercing its flesh, trying to shatter it.

Father.

And then the Master shot out its stinger—and like a piston, it embedded itself in the Born's neck. Such was its force that it shattered the vertebrae. Blood worms invaded Mr. Quinlan's immaculate body, coursing under his pale skin for the very first—and very last—time.

Eph saw the lights and heard the helicopter rotors approaching the island. They had found them. The spotlights searched the blighted land. It was now or never.

Eph ran as fast as his punctured lungs would

allow, the barrel-shaped device shaking in his view. He was just a few yards out when a howl came up and a blow caught him on the back of the head.

Both swords slipped from his hands. Eph felt something gripping the side of his chest, the pain excruciating. He clawed at the soft dirt, seeing Setrakian's sword blade glowing silver-white. He'd just grasped the wolf's-head handle when the Master hoisted him into the air, spinning him.

The Master's arms, face, and neck were cut and bleeding white. The creature could of course heal itself but had had no chance to yet. Eph slashed at the Master's neck with the old man's silver, but the creature caught Eph's sword arm, stopping the blow. The pain in Eph's chest was too great, and the Master's strength was tremendous. It forced Eph's hand back, pointing Setrakian's sword at Eph's own throat.

A helicopter spotlight hit them. In the haze, Eph looked down into the Master's glowing, scratched-open face. He saw the blood worms rippling beneath its skin, invigorated by the nearness of human blood and the anticipation of the kill. The thrumming roared in Eph's head, achieving a voice, its tenor rising to almost a nearly angelic level.

I have a new body ready and waiting. The next time anyone looks at your son's face—they will be looking at me.

The worms bubbled beneath the flesh of its face, as though in ecstasy.

Good-bye, Goodweather.

But Eph eased his resistance against the Master's grip just before the Master could finish him off. Eph pricked his own throat, opening a vein. He saw his own red blood spurt out, spraying right into the Master's face—making the blood worms crazy.

They sprang from the Master's open wounds. They crawled up from the slices in its arms and the hole in its chest, trying to get at the blood.

The Master groaned and shook, hurling Eph away as it brought its own hands to its face.

Eph landed hard. He twisted, needing all his strength to turn back.

Within the column of helicopter light, the Master stumbled backward, trying to stop its own parasitic worms from feasting on the human blood coating its face, obstructing its vision.

Eph watched all of this through a daze, everything slowed down. Then a thump in the ground at his side brought him back to speed.

The snipers. Another spotlight lit him up, red laser sights dancing on his chest and head . . . and the nuke, just a few feet away.

Eph dragged himself through the dirt, scratching toward the device as rounds pelted the ground around him. He reached it, pulling himself up on it in order to reach the detonator.

He got it in his hand and found the button, then risked one look back at Zack.

The boy stood near where the Born lay. A few of the blood parasites had reached him, and Eph saw Zack struggling to brush them off . . . then watched as they burrowed in under his forearm and neck.

Mr. Quinlan's body arose, a new look in his eyes—a new will. That of the Master, who understood the dark side of human nature completely, but not love.

"This is love," said Eph. *"God, it hurts—but this is love . . ."*

And he, who had been late to most everything in his life, was on time for this, the most important appointment he ever had. He pushed the switch.

And nothing happened. For one agonizing moment, the island was an oasis of stillness to Eph, though the helicopters were hovering overhead.

Eph saw Mr. Quinlan coming at him, one final lunge of the Master's will.

Then two punches to his chest. Eph was down on the ground, looking at his wounds. Seeing the bloody holes there, just to the right of his heart. His blood seeping into the ground.

Eph looked past Mr. Quinlan at Zack, his face glowing in the helicopter light. His will still present, still not overcome. He saw Zack's eyes—*his son,* even now, *his son*—he still had the most beautiful eyes . . .

Eph smiled.

And then the miracle happened.

It was the gentlest of things: no earthquake, no hurricane, no parting of the seas. The sky cleared for a moment and a brilliant column of pure, sterilizing light a million times more powerful than any helicopter spotlight poured down. The dark cloud cover opened and cleansing light emerged.

The Born, now infected by the Master's blood, hissed and writhed in the brilliant light. Smoke and vapor surged from its body as the Born screamed like a lobster being boiled.

None of this shook Eph's gaze from the eyes of his son. And as Zack saw his father smile at him there—in the powerful light of glorious day—he recognized him for all that he was, recognized him as—

"Dad—" Zack said softly.

And then the nuclear device detonated. Everything around the flashpoint evaporated—bodies, sand, vegetation, helicopters—all gone.

Purged.

From a beach well down the river, close to Lake Ontario, Nora watched this only for a moment. Then Fet pulled her around a rocky outcropping, both of them dropping into a ball on the sand.

The shock wave made the old abandoned fort near them shudder, shaking dust and stone fragments from the walls. Nora was certain the entire structure would collapse into the river. Her ears popped and the water around them heaved in a great gush—and even with her eyes tightly closed and her arms over her head, she still saw bright light.

Rain blew sideways, the ground emitted a

howl of pain . . . and then the light faded, the stone fort settled without collapsing, and everything became quiet and still.

Later, she would realize that she and Fet had been rendered temporarily deaf by the blast, but for the moment the silence was profound and spiritual. Fet uncurled himself from shielding Nora, and together they ventured back out around the rock barrier as the water receded from the beach.

What she saw—the larger miracle in the sky—she did not fully understand until later.

Gabriel, the first archangel—an entity of light so bright that it made the sun and the atomic glow pale—came spiraling down around the shaft of light on glowing silver wings.

Michael, the murdered one, tucked his wings and bolted straight down, leveling out about a mile above the island, gliding down the rest of the way.

Then, rising as though out of the earth itself, came Ozryel, together again, resurrected from the collective ashes. Rock and dirt fell from its great wings as it ascended. A spirit again, flesh no more.

Nora witnessed all these portents in the absolute silence of momentary deafness. And that, perhaps, made it sink even deeper into her psyche. She could not hear the raging rumble that her feet felt, she could not hear the crackling of the blinding light that warmed her face and her soul. A true Old Testament moment witnessed by someone dressed not in linen robes but off-the-shelf Gap. This moment rattled her senses and her faith for the rest of her life. Without even noticing it, Nora cried freely.

Gabriel and Michael joined Ozryel and together they soared into the light. The hole in the clouds brightened brilliantly as the three archangels reached it—and then with one last flare of divine illumination, the opening swallowed them up and then closed.

Nora and Fet looked around. The river was still raging, and their skiff had been swept away. Fet checked Nora, making sure she was okay.

We're alive, he mouthed—no words audible.

Did you see that? asked Nora.

Fet shook his head, not as in, *No,* but as in, *I don't believe it.*

The couple looked at the sky, waiting for something else to happen.

Meanwhile, all around them, large sections of sandy beach had turned to opalescent glass.

The fort residents came out, a few dozen men and women in tatters, some carrying children. Nora and Fet had warned them to take cover, and now the islanders looked to them for an explanation.

Nora had to yell in order to be heard. "Ann and William?" she said. "They had a boy with them, a thirteen-year-old boy!"

The adults shook their heads.

Nora said, "They left before us!"

One man said, "Maybe on another island?"

Nora nodded—though she didn't believe it. She and Fet had made it to their fort island in a sailboat. Ann and William should have landed long ago.

Fet rested his hand on Nora's shoulder. "What about Eph?"

There was no way to confirm it, but she knew he was never coming back.

EPILOGUE

The origin blast obliterated the Master's strain. Every remaining vampire vaporized at the moment of immolation. Vanished.

They confirmed this over the next few days. First by venturing back to the mainland once the waters receded. Then by checking impassioned dispatches over the liberated Internet. Rather than celebrating, people stumbled around in a post-traumatic haze. The atmosphere was still contaminated and the hours of daylight were few. Superstition remained and darkness was, if anything, feared even more than before. Reports of vampires still in existence flared up again and again, every single one eventually attributed to hysteria.

Things did not "go back to normal." Indeed,

the islanders remained in their settlements for months, working to reclaim their mainland properties but reluctant to commit to the old ways just yet. Everything everybody had thought they knew about nature and history and biology had been proved wrong, or at least incomplete. And then for two years, they had come to accept a new reality and a new regime. Old faiths had been shattered; others had been reaffirmed. But everything was open to question. Uncertainty was the new plague.

Nora counted herself among those who needed time to make sure that this way of life was going to stick. That there weren't any other nasty surprises waiting for them just around the corner.

Fet said one day, broaching the subject gently, "What are we going to do? We have to return to New York sometime."

"Do we?" asked Nora. "I don't know if it's there for me anymore." She took his hand. "Do you?"

Fet squeezed her hand and looked out over the river. He would let her take as much time as she needed.

As it turned out, Nora and Fet never went back. They took advantage of the Federal Property Reclamation Act proposed by the interim government and moved into a farmhouse in northern Vermont, safely outside the void zone caused by the detonation of the nuclear device in the Saint

Lawrence River. They never married—neither of them felt the need—but they had two children of their own, a boy named Ephraim and a girl named Mariela, after Nora's mother. Fet posted the annotated contents of the *Occido Lumen* on the reinvigorated Internet and attempted to retain his anonymity. But when its veracity was eventually questioned, he embarked upon "the Setrakian Project," curating and posting the entirety of the old professor's writings and source materials on the Internet, free for all. Fet's lifelong project became the tracing of the Ancients' influence over the course of human history. He wanted to know the mistakes we had collectively made and devoted himself to avoiding their being repeated ever again.

For a time there was unrest and talk of criminal trials to identify and punish those guilty of human rights abuses under the shade of the holocaust. Guards and sympathizers were occasionally spotted and lynched, and revenge murders were widely suspected, but, in the end, more tolerant voices rose to answer to the question of who did this to us. We all did. And—little by little—with all our rancor and ghosts bearing the weight of our past, people learned to coexist once again.

In due time, others claimed to have taken down the *strigoi*. A biologist claimed to have released a vaccine into the water system, a few gang members exhibited assorted trophies claiming to have killed the Master, and, in the strangest twist, a large group of skeptics began to deny that the plague itself ever occurred. They attributed it all to a huge new-world-order plot, calling the entire event a manufactured coup. Disappointed, but never bitter, Fet slowly restarted his exterminating business. The rats had returned, thriving once again, another challenge to be met. He was not one to believe in perfection or happy endings: this was the world they had saved, rats and all. But to a handful of believers, Vasiliy Fet became a cult hero, and though he was uncomfortable with fame of any kind, he settled for this, and counted his blessings.

Nora, every night she put her baby boy, Ephraim, down to sleep, rubbed his hair and thought of his namesake, and his namesake's son, and wondered what the end had been like for them. For the first few years of his life, she often speculated about what her life—with Eph—might have resembled had the strain never occurred. Sometimes she cried, and on those occasions, Fet knew better than to ask. This was a part of Nora that he did not share—that he would never share—and he gave her the room to grieve alone. But as the boy grew older and came into his own, becoming so much like his father and nothing at all like his namesake, the reality of the days washed away the possibilities of the past, and time moved on. For Nora, death was no longer one of her fears, because she had vanquished its more malignant alternative.

She carried with her always the mark on her forehead: the scar from Barnes's gunshot. She regarded this scar as a symbol of how close she had come to a fate worse than death, though, in her later years, it became instead for her a symbol of luck. For now, as Nora gazed into the face of her baby—unmarked and full of peace—a great serenity overcame her, and out of nowhere, she remembered her mother's words:

Looking back on one's life, you see that love was the answer to everything.

How right she was.

The authors wish to acknowledge Dr. Seth Richardson at the University of Chicago for his assistance with Mesopotamian and biblical lore.